# The Crush of Wine and War

## MOLLY FUMIA

Black Rose Writing | Texas

ISBN: 978-1-68513-459-4
PUBLISHED BY BLACK ROSE WRITING
www.blackrosewriting.com

Printed in the United States of America
Suggested Retail Price (SRP) $24.95

*The Crush of Wine and War* is printed in Garamond Premier Pro

*As a planet-friendly publisher, Black Rose Writing does its best to eliminate unnecessary waste to reduce paper usage and energy costs, while never compromising the reading experience. As a result, the final word count vs. page count may not meet common expectations.

Cover Art by Nancy Holleran

# Praise for
# *The Crush of Wine and War*

"In *The Crush of Wine and War*, Molly Fumia has written an extraordinary story of two families taking on the Nazi Empire. Years of intensive research also led her to issue a literary challenge to a nation, Austria, and a religious institution, the Catholic Church, to continue to tell the truth about their participation in one of the greatest evils of all time. Her characters are at once good-hearted and flawed, hesitant and zealous. I found it an irresistible read."
**–Bishop Thomas Gumbleton, Archdiocese of Detroit**

## Praise for Molly Fumia

*Safe Passage*:
"is there a remedy to grief? Molly Fumia's moving words... are both inspired and inspiring."
**–Elie Wiesel**

"Here is a book of exquisite honesty and profound depth... Along the way grief becomes a dance in the dark and suffering turns to love."
**–Sue Monk Kidd, author of *The Book of Longings***

*Honor Thy Children*:
"This is a story that will break your heart and make it whole again. It will bring you into realms of humanness and compassion you didn't know you had. It might even set you free to love in ways you've never loved before."
**–Helen Prejean, author of *Dead Man Walking***

*For my friends, Maria and Tom*

# Author's Note

*The Crush of Wine and War* began with my unexpected, often humbling, and deeply appreciated  relationship with Elie Wiesel, perhaps the most celebrated Holocaust author of all time and winner of the Nobel Peace Prize. Our friendship sent me careening into years of holocaust study.

So in 1984, when I met Franziska Jägerstätter, the widow of Franz Jägerstätter, an Austrian peasant farmer who was beheaded in 1943 for refusing to be inducted into the army of the Third Reich, I was primed to be intrigued. The Austrian resistance had been meager at best.

This was an unusual Austrian couple  They were from different towns, a rare occurence in rural Austria, where a young woman typically married the farmer next door.  He took her on a honeymoon to Rome, which was totally unheard of. The most fascinating facet of their relationship was that they were deeply, passionately, in love.

In 1940, Franz was required to report to boot camp in Enns.  During the next three years, the couple exchanged letters that while filled with love and longing, suggested the slow build-up of tension between two people of different minds.  Franz was increasingly sure that in good conscience, he could not fight for Hitler. Franziska pushed back with complaints about the hard physical labor required of her on their farm, the tribulations of three small children, and suggestions of other forms of military service, such as serving on the local police or volunteering to be a medic.

He was called to active duty in February, 1943. He again reported to Enns, but declared his refusal to enlist and was sent to Brandenburg Prison in Berlin.  On August 8, Franziska visited him, continuing to beg him to find a way out.  But it was too late, and he was executed the next day.

The woman I met was warm, friendly, and engaging. But several of her grandchildren remember her as being distant and often angry.  We had become good friends by the time the Catholic Church elevated Franz to martyr status and Franziska to faithful wife, supportive at all costs. I wondered about that.  However a courageous, faith-filled human being Franz had been, she lost the love of her life in a situation she might have felt, deep-down, could have been prevented with some compromise on his part. Why would someone so deeply in love acquiesce to her husband's deliberate destruction of their family?

That conflict inspired me, and in 1990, I asked her if I could write her story. She said, "only after I'm dead." A decade later, I asked how she would feel if I wrote a novel, loosely inspired by her life. We sat around her kitchen table, me with a phone book, her with a pencil, deciding on her "new name." She chose Hannah.

In the end, I "borrowed" only a few facts from their lives:

1. My couple, Hannah and Sebastien Brandl, also come from two different towns.
2. The Brandls meet in a bar; Franziska met Franz in a Gasthaus where she was a waitress and spent time in the garden setting up bowling pins that he and his friends knocked down.
3. Sexual passion is also part of Hannah and Sebastien's love story.
4. Sebastien, like Franz, votes NO in the referendum that demanded all Austrians confirm their allegiance to Hitler and the Nazi Regime.

When Franziska died in 2013, I decided to keep my promise to her. When Elie died in 2016, grief cut through me. And yet, I marveled at my fortune, to have known and loved these two survivors of unspeakable evil. I can only hope to honor Elie's memory in those parts of my novel that describe the persecution of his people. As for Franziska and Franz Jägerstätter, this is not their story, but they live in my words.

# The
# Crush
## of
# Wine and War

# The Cast

## *MOOSFELD 1934-1948*

Bernard Maislinger, farmer
Sophie Maislinger, his wife
Their daughters: Margarete, cloistered nun
Sieglinde "Siegi"
Hannah


Faber Ratzener, *Oberführer* in Third Reich
His brothers: *Rolf Lonauer, head doctor, Hartheim Euthanasia center
Viktor Lonauer, restaurant owner, *Der Wachauerhof*
Otto Lonauer, works at *Der Wachauerhof*, married to Siegi Maislinger


Gertraud-barmaid at *Der Wachauerhof*
Finn Binder, son of farmer next door to Maislingers

## *VIENNA/ KAHLENBERGERDORF 1935-1948*

Maximillian Mayr, winemaker, owner of *Schloß Winzertal*
Lili Mayr, his wife
Their sons: Michel, university student, war resister
Stefan
Helga Mayr, Max' mother


Rafe Klein, Viennese war resister
Sigrid Jungmeier, his girlfriend, Viennese war resister
Remi Schnaitl, friend of Michel


Rabbi Elie Schett, old friend of Mayrs
Tovah Schett, his wife
Rena Mendelsson, Jewish refugee
Isaac, Muriel, Libby and Emil Bergmann, Jewish refugees


*Pfarrer Roman Scholz, monk at Klosterneuberg Abbey, war resister
*Viktor Reitmann, his partner in resistance
*Fritz Lehmann, actor, war resister

*Otto Hartmann, actor, Nazi spy
Johannes Veit, monk, war resister

*Ludwig and Josephine Hawelke–founding owners of Café Hawelke
*Hauptscharführer* Klaus Kolbe

### *ALKOVEN, 1942*
*Leopold Hilgarth, war resister
*Franz Sitter, employee of Hartheim Euthanasia Center
Helene Sitter, his sister

### *BERLIN 1935*
Fritz Tollner–one of Heinrich Himmler's secretaries


*Historical characters, fictionalized for the purpose of the story
**The towns of St. Jakob and Moosfeld are fictional. All other locations are real.

# A Guide to Some of the German Pronunciations:

| | |
|---|---|
| *St. Jakob* | Sankt Yah Kob |
| *Gasthaus Zum Grünen Baum* | Gast house Zoom Groo nen bomb |
| *Schloß Winzertal* | SchlOsch vin zer tall |
| *Moosfeld* | Moose felt |
| *Wachauerhof* | Vak hour hOf |
| *Weingut* | Vine goot |
| *Hawelke* | Hah vell kah |
| *Sebastien* | Se bas tee en |
| *Gabriele* | Gob brEE el |
| *Georg* | GAY org |
| *Elke* | EL kee |
| *Siegi* | SIG EE |
| *Faber* | FAH ber |
| *Michel* | MEE kell |
| *Sivan* | SEE von |
| *Moshe* | MO SHEE |
| *Pfarrer* | Far |
| *Oberführer* | Ober few er |
| *Hochleutnant* | Hok loyt naunt |

# PROLOGUE

*"We must always take sides."*
*–Elie Wiesel*

*St Jakob, Austria, Friday, October 13, 1989*

Defying all logic, the older gentleman pulls a green feathered hat over his eyes and makes yet another covert walk up the road toward the center of the tiny village. Shielded by a patch of pine trees, he watches a flock of young people greet the woman who emerges from the back of *Gasthaus Zum Grünen Baum,* one of the most famous inns in Austria.

Hannah Brandl. The widow of Sebastien Brandl, a recently crowned hero. Two chatty couples surround the petite woman, and she shakes each extended hand. Her head turns toward him, and without thinking, he lifts the brim of his hat. The crown of dark auburn curls he remembers has turned creamy silver. Those blue eyes seem bigger from behind the round, rimless spectacles perched on her nose.

An attractive, grinning woman appears at her side. Gabriele, Hannah's daughter, tucks her mother's arm under her own. She resembles her father; her light brown hair, held back from her oval face by a tortoiseshell clip, is thick and luscious.

They start down the path to St. Jakob's miniature church. On this morning, the attendees were limited to devout matrons and a few reluctant men. Nothing like years ago, when a priest held his congregation hostage by any number of deific threats.

Since his arrival, the gentleman has been using long abandoned tricks to remain unseen. He observed that *Pfarrer* Primo Baumgartner, pastor of the churches in both St. Jakob and the nearby village of Moosfeld, declared the yearly Crush party, which celebrated the end of the grape harvest, would also be a tribute to Hannah Brandl on her seventy-third birthday.

Tributes. That Hannah and Sebastien shared the same birthday enhanced the Brandl mystique.

He also heard the priest suggest to a group of villagers that Sebastien might even be a Righteous Gentile, which immediately disgusted him. He knew Sebastien Brandl, and a Righteous Gentile he was not.

He returns to his hotel. He had no choice but to stay at the wholly inferior inn down the street from *Grünen Baum*. Taking a room there would have dangled him at the edge of being recognized. He wearily mounts the stairs to his room, pushes through the door, and senses immediately he is not alone.

"So," he scowls at his visitor, glancing at the open window and the eaves beyond. "You're here for a report?"

The creature nestles deeper into the folds of the eiderdown and pokes one paw up in a long stretch.

"The report is she forgets me." The cat, snowy white, extremely well-fed, shows minimal interest in this intrusion and resumes his nap.

He strokes the silky white head. "So, you're the famous Ludwig. "I knew an ancestor of yours, Chopin, as I recall." Ludwig opens one eye, mildly curious about his lineage. "I don't think we've been properly introduced. My name is Sivan."

He considers telling the cat the rest of it. Sivan is one of several names. At least three identities over the course of a lifetime. But instead, he again wrestles with his sudden decision to return to St. Jakob. But there was no way he could have missed the article in the *New York Times* about the discovery of an unheralded war resister, an innkeeper named Sebastien Brandl. Hah. One would think Brandl had thrown himself in front of a tank. No mention of his one notable deed.

Leaning into the mirror above his sink, Sivan runs a hand from the back of his head over his brow and down his face. Sprigs of brown hair, streaked with gray, stick out forlornly in all directions. Why would she recognize him? Hannah Brandl lived a long life after he staggered away, a man driven by the need to again become a changeling, not even recognizing himself.

Sivan watches the cat, one leg up in the air, having his bath. "Ah, Ludwig," he says. "I am not only an old man, but an old idiot.'

•    •    •    •    •

Sivan jerks awake. After a restless night, he has slept until noon. Ludwig appears from under his bed and pads toward his hat, still sitting on the floor where Sivan flung it, and gingerly sets one paw on the green felt.

"Go no further, Herr Ludwig," Sivan commands. The cat settles in on top, his long tail winding around the brim. He rubs an enormous pink ear on the felt, tastes the tip of the feather, and purrs.

"Fine. You can be part of my disguise. No one will notice an old man wearing a cat on his head."

Sivan plods downstairs and slips onto a stool at the end of the bar. He signals the bartender and interprets the young man's half smirk as a plea for patience. A group of young people waving near empty beer glasses at a table, and shouting, "To the new Austria!"

Eventually, Sivan's gaze falls on a couple sitting at a table nearby, frowning at the commotion. He turns away, his heart racing. "That cat should have warned me," he growls into his glass.

Some recollections are cruelly resilient. Veronika Reiter, the former bakery madam, had played a part in driving away a young Jew, deadened with grief, who, in this very town, briefly imagined a new life.

He takes another look. Veronika is well into her seventies, heavier than he remembers, dressed in a stylish blue suit. Her red fingernails drum on the table. Sivan hears her brash whisper, "Those delinquents belong at *Grünen Baum.*"

"They're deluded," the man across from Veronika growls. "They would have their parents and grandparents take the blame for the war alongside Germany."

Veronika frowns. "Never mind how we suffered, Viktor."

Sivan's head jerks up. Viktor Lonauer. The husband of Hannah's sister, Siegi? No, that was Otto Lonauer. This Viktor is Otto's brother, the one the Nazis had on a leash.

Now on his third beer, Sivan stares openly. *Mein Gott. Grünen Baum* and the bakery, *Bäckerei Crème.* Is it possible Hannah and Veronika are still next-door neighbors?

Veronika's agitation has risen dramatically. "*Pfarrer* Baumgartner has ruined the Crush party." Her voice is now loud enough to reach the far corners of the restaurant. "He's forcing us to celebrate the birthday of a menace who tried to kill us all, and the whore who sent my brother away to be gassed!"

Sivan is out of his seat. "No," he cries. He throws money onto the bar and bolts off his stool, wanting only to escape. On the way up the stairs, he slips, curses when pain rifles through his shin, and limps into his room. Breathing hard, he sinks onto the bed.

The truth, he reminds himself, is that Sebastien Brandl abandoned his wife and child and left them to the wolves.

He would have stayed.

•     •     •     •     •

*Pfarrer* Primo Baumgartner stands at the back door of *Grünen Baum* that opens into the Brandl family kitchen, affectionately called the *kochecke*, little kitchen, yet small only when compared to the immense restaurant kitchen. Even though it is late, the door is usually unlocked. Not used to being denied entry, the priest raps urgently enough to rattle the window he is peering through.

Eventually, he sees Gabriele coming toward him. "Primo," she says as she opens the door and ushers him in. "Is something wrong?"

"The door is locked."

"We're not trying to keep you out," she smiles. Primo pushes his short, solid frame onto the cushioned banquette that surrounds half of the massive kitchen table. If it was anyone else's house, he would take the chair reserved for the head of the household.

"Is your mother here, or is she sleeping in her little house?" Hannah divided her time between her own cozy cabin next to the inn and her suite at *Grünen Baum*.

"She's here. She's had a few more people coming to her door lately," Gabi explains. "Sometimes they just walk in." She gives him a plate and fork. "Have a piece of pie. Apricot."

"They want to meet the widow, "Primo says dismissively, struggling to move a slice to his plate without losing the filling, until Gabi does it for him. "That's why I'm here," he continues. "This weekend," he shovels pie into his mouth, "there might be more visitors than usual."

"What did you do, Primo?"

"I sent out invitations to some priest friends. One or two journalists."

"Are you deliberately trying to incite my mother to violence?"

On Easter Sunday the previous April, in the lingering shadow of the floodlit Austrian president Kurt Waldheim, whose Nazi collaboration had recently been exposed, a sermon delivered in Vienna's St. Stephen's Cathedral praised a rural innkeeper who joined the underground resistance. The story, apparently, had made its way out to the world.

"There's quite a lot of interest in Sebastien Brandl."

Gabi narrows her eyes. "One man's story can't change history."

The rest of the pie ends up on Primo's plate, delivered with a cup of dark coffee. "And, as I expected, they want to know the details only Hannah has. Why not share?" A glob of apricot perches on his chin. Behind him, the door into the kitchen is slowly opening.

"Because," comes the voice from the doorway, "The details are gray." Hannah Brandl, looking grim, walks to the table and sits in her chair.

Gabi clears the *Pfarrer*'s plate and cup. "Mutti, I can't believe you're still up."

Primo jumps to his feet. "You must be tired. Why don't we talk about this tomorrow?" He leans down and makes a sign of the cross on Hannah's forehead. "May God be with you as you sleep."

Hannah reaches up and makes the same gesture on his forehead. "And with you, Primo." A moment crawls by. Then the priest nods, turns, and lets himself out.

Gabi grins. "So, you're finally going to call him by his first name?"

"It just came out."

"Don't let Primo's quest for attention get to you, Mutti. Wait until you're ready."

Hannah frowns. "What is it I'm supposed to know?"

"A story that might redeem them."

"It won't redeem me."

Gabi covers her mother's hand with her own. "When are you going to let go of whatever part of your past makes you so irritable?"

"I honestly don't know. Did Primo eat all the pie?"

Gabi sighs and rummages around the pantry. She comes back with half of a chocolate tart. Hannah raises an eyebrow, but bites into it.

"Would it hurt to tell these people about how you and Papa met and fell in love, and the happy times at *Grünen Baum?*"

"But then what would I say?"

"That your husband cared about what was happening in Austria, and tried to make it right."

Hannah wets her finger and stabs at the remaining morsels of tart. "Sebastien has died so many times."

Gabi gently kneads her mother's shoulders. "I think it's time for bed."

Hannah follows her daughter up the stairs to the inn's family wing. She collapses onto the bed she once shared with Sebastien. Having slept in her clothes before, she simply pulls up a quilt. It comforts her, knowing she can leave quickly, escape the tediousness of the night, when the specter of regret sneaks in and keeps her awake.

# Part 1

*"The Book of Righteousness is a metaphor of our struggle for excellence... and for standing erect in a profusion of schemers."*
**–Rabbi Maurice Lamm**

# 1

*Moosfeld, Austria, October 14, 1934*

The night Hannah Maislinger told her parents she no longer wanted to be a nun, they had been sitting companionably at the kitchen table. Her belated eighteenth birthday celebration was over, and her sister, Siegi, who married Otto Lonauer even though Papa suggested he might be abnormal, decided to stay the night and took her children upstairs.

Hannah helped her mother wrap the leftover cheese and meat and store it in the cooler. Her father was drinking wine and eating his third piece of walnut cake while his wife of almost thirty years clucked disapprovingly.

"Bernard," was all she said to him.

"Sophie," he smiled. He offered her the final crumbs clinging to his fork. "For you, *Liebling.*"

Hannah grimaced. She was about to ruin a lovely moment. Her decision to enter the convent, which in hindsight was more of a whim, and actually the second time she veered in that vocational direction, had twice seemed the natural thing to do. In school, she memorized the catechism easily and recited her prayers with fervor. Compared to other children, *Pfarrer* Becker, their old parish priest, never worried little Hannah Maislinger would wander off the holy road.

Childhood far behind her, she returned home one cold January day from her visit with the Mother Abbess that sealed her destiny. Bernard started the fire, and while Sophie squeezed the word *Schwester* in front of Hannah's name in the family bible, she had taken several very long sips of wine. Her family patted her head, which happened often because everything about Hannah was small, and she basked in their approval.

The Mother Abbess had explained that besides prayer, Hannah's day would be spent in God's work, like gardening, sewing, or working in the kitchen. Sophie was nodding happily, as if to say, how nice, Hannah, what a wonderful time you'll have. The problem was that Hannah wasn't particularly adept at any of those things. But then the Mother Abbess mentioned the choir, which even postulants were welcome to join.

Hannah was relieved; she may not be capable of embroidering tulips on a pillowcase, but everyone told her she had a beautiful voice. She imagined herself in a wimple. Even then, something wasn't right.

Seven months later, any attraction to the Abbey had soured. Knowing she would set off an alarm, she poured two more large glasses from the bottle of Riesling they had been sharing and shoved one at her mother. "Prost," she exclaimed, raising her glass.

Warily, her parents raised their arms. "Prost," they mumbled, as their daughter announced her rejection of God's plan for her.

"I don't want to be a nun anymore."

Hannah first studied her mother, looking for signs of a breakdown. But Sophie, whose standing in the community had blossomed when their oldest daughter, Greta, moved up the hill to the Abbey, and who for months had been telling everyone in Moosfeld, *Gott sei dank*, her youngest had also been called, seemed more perplexed than heartbroken. For Sophie Maislinger, one always took the path that had been cleared.

"But Hannah," she said, "the Mother Abbess said you were a perfect candidate."

"I know, and I'm sorry."

Her mother's normally fine posture withered into her chair, the hem of her long faded blue skirt covering her scuffed boots. Her father, who had stood up but not yet spoken, peered at his daughter through his spectacles, his blue eyes, usually enormous through his thick lenses, narrowed to tiny slits. "Are you saying you won't go?"

Hannah's eyes darted around the room like moths flitting against a lantern. "I'm confused."

"What is it that has suddenly muddled your brain?"

Hannah could see her reflection in the window behind them, her uncommon smattering of freckles, her incessantly tangled curly hair falling out of its clip atop her head. Greta and Siegi were blond like their mother, but Hannah's hair was an un-Austrian deep auburn, and thicker, like her Papa insisted his used to be, a small consolation.

She plunged in. "Many people live holy lives. Even if one is, for instance," Hannah paused, as if searching a long list, "an innkeeper."

Bernard's eyes widened. "Viktor Lonauer leads a holy life?" The morally dubious owner of *Der Wachauerhof*, the largest tavern in Moosfeld, had been Hannah's employer for the last three months.

"Actually, I am speaking of another innkeeper. In St. Jakob, at *Gasthaus Zum Grünen Baum,* Herr Brandl told his workers to give food to anyone who is hungry, even if they can't pay. Wouldn't you agree, Papa, feeding the hungry is very...biblical?"

He folded his arms across his chest. "Andreas Brandl is a good Christian man."

"Yes, well, Papa, Herr Brandl has a son."

"He has two sons."

"Sebastien. His son, Sebastien," Hannah stammered.

"And it is this Herr Brandl who is giving away food?"

"Food that might end up being thrown away!"

"Hmm. And how did you hear of these biblical activities?"

"Sebastien, um, Herr Brandl, was in *Der Wachauerhof.*"

Bernard nodded, not in approval, but in the way he did when he was listening to what he called the 'underside' of words. "It seems you and Herr Brandl had quite a conversation." His hands swung behind his back. "So, Hannah, let us review. Only a year ago, you declared you would never marry because you could not bear to leave your mother and me and our wonderful farm. We knew that wouldn't last. Then you said God wanted you to leave the farm and go to the Abbey. Until you stopped paying attention to God and set your sights on Finn Binder."

How did he know about that? "That was Siegi's idea."

"And does Sieglinde also tell you when to go to the toilet?"

Siegi had been Hannah's protector from the time she could walk, a position that allowed the slightly older sister to boss her around, but also kept Hannah safe from outside forces, like the children who teased her for being short.

Siegi had confronted her about her wavering vocation. "Before you throw your life away like Greta, you need at least one experience with a boy. Once you get sucked into that place, they'll never let you out."

Curiosity sparked, Hannah looked around for a suitable candidate. Moosfeld was no different than any other Austrian farming town: if a young woman wanted a boyfriend, the farmer next door had eligible sons. Thus, Hannah decided on Finn Binder.

Her slightest glance encouraged him to rush to her side, where he stood too close and laughed at his own jokes. Then one day, as she mindlessly fed the family chickens, he snuck up behind her, and before she could gather her wits, he was pulling her into the darkest corner of their barn. Without preamble, he kissed her. Hannah let it go on for a few seconds, as kissing was an important part of Siegi's plan. She felt nothing, except worry they were standing in cow dung, and broke away. He leaned in again, pushing harder against her clenched teeth. She sent him stumbling backwards into the hay, ran from the barn, and was back on track for the Abbey by supper.

Bernard's baritone sunk deeper. "And then, you renounced men and retrieved your vocation, which you insisted was 'solid as a rock.'" He jabbed a finger in his daughter's face, and his breath, which was coming out in ragged puffs, smothered her nose. "Am I right?"

"Finn Binder was only an experiment, Papa."

Resorting to violence was not really his way, so he waited for a moment, obviously intent on clinging to some measure of calm.

"Next," he resumed, "you begged me to allow you, as a favor to your pregnant sister, to take over Siegi's job at *Der Wachauerhof*. And I thought that might be unusual for a girl on her way to the convent, and possibly invite the scrutiny of our neighbors. But since my daughter had once again pledged herself to the Lord, I reluctantly agreed."

"I really did want to help Siegi."

"And today that daughter brings into my house talk of one Herr Brandl of *Gasthaus Zum Grünen Baum*. She does not speak, however, of the respected Andreas, but of his wayward son Sebastien."

Sophie finally spoke. "I've never heard of him."

'That," Bernard snapped, "is because your daughter has taken up with a *Jakober*!"

Sebastien Brandl was from the village of St. Jakob, three kilometers up the road from Moosfeld. The simmering rivalry between the two towns bubbled up now and then, but at this moment the Alps may well have uprooted, flown through the air, and replanted between them.

A squeak came from Sophie. "Why would you give up your place among the saints for a man we don't know who isn't even from our town?"

Bernard paced the kitchen. Red blotches had crept up his short neck. He arrived in front of his daughter, one calloused hand on his hip, the other waving in her face. "Do you think I have not heard of him?"

Sophie fiddled with the edge of the tablecloth. "Who will tell the Mother Abbess?"

"I will tell her myself," Hannah assured her, wondering what her father had heard.

Her mother straightened a little. However, for her father, the admired Bernard Maislinger, an honest, hardworking farmer who had once been mayor of Moosfeld, only hot rocks awaited him on the streets of their town. Everyone would ask him about that Brandl fellow, a man with more rumors hanging on him than socks on a clothesline.

"But who will tell Greta?" Sophie fretted further. "She is expecting you at the Abbey right after Christmas."

Hannah sighed. Her mother was picturing her poor sister, cloistered eight years already, waiting by the gate in the swirling snow.

"Sophie!" her father exploded. "No one is talking to Greta."

"That is also my responsibility," Hannah said, ignoring him and patting her mother's arm.

"But it is against the rules for you to speak to a cloistered nun," Sophie said.

"I'll ask the Mother Abbess to make an exception!"

Bernard cleared his voice loudly enough to alert the Binder farm, swept both of them into his gaze, and began his own list of messy facts. "This boy," he said stonily, "is the youngest son of Andreas Brandl and his wife Amalie. May she rest in peace."

They crossed themselves.

"His family has lived in St. Jakob for centuries. When the older son moved to Vienna, the poor man naturally expected his younger son to be with him in the restaurant, but then he also disappeared into Vienna. Do you know what goes on in Vienna?"

As a matter of fact Hannah did. "Horseracing."

Bernard threw up his arms.

"Sebastien has a racehorse, but he, I mean the horse, doesn't race anymore. He rescued Apfel from the meat wagon. He's lovely, and very Austrian! He likes *edelweiß*."

Sophie said, "There's a fine for eating our national flower."

Her husband sat back down and dropped his head into his hands.

"What about Wenzel or Dieter?" her mother continued, referring to Finn Binder's older brothers. Hannah's next step should be to give the leftovers a try.

"I'm sorry, Mutti, but I don't care for any of the Binder boys in that way."

"Oh, dear." Blinking back tears, Sophie fumbled in her sweater pocket for a handkerchief until her daughter pulled her own from her sleeve and pressed it into her hand. Hannah yearned to flee the kitchen and retreat into one of her secret places, behind the apple jelly lined up on shelves in the cellar, or in the dusty, forgotten cabinet next to the pantry. Or run to her room upstairs, pull away the wood slats that covered the old opening into the barn and fling herself onto the sweet-scented fresh straw awaiting the cows.

Instead, she sat down and feared for her father. The red had spread all over his face and beneath his hair, which had thinned considerably during his time as mayor.

After several moments of stony silence, Bernard raised his head and gazed at his daughter with such sadness she was tempted to tell him the whole matter was a terrible joke.

"What has happened to my little Hannah?"

Please don't cry. His tears would finish her.

"Maybe you're just anxious," Sophie said. "Greta could hardly walk up the steps, remember? But then the Mother Abbess took her inside and everything was fine."

How Hannah wished she could go back in time. But since she had obviously ruined all of their lives, she went ahead and shouted at her mother. "How would you know that? Maybe Greta cries every night. Maybe she wants to be rescued!"

Never would she have imagined behaving in such a way toward these two kind people, who had shown her more affection and given her more freedom than either of their other daughters. But Hannah could not back down.

"I'm not sick, Mutti," she said quietly.

"No," Bernard said, "but you are crazy. Go to bed. We are all going to bed." He grasped Sophie's arm and pulled her across the kitchen to the bottom of the steps leading upstairs.

"Please," Hannah said to their backs, "I can't go to the Abbey."

They stopped on the second step.

"I won't change my mind. Not this time."

They stood where they were.

"He asked to talk to you, Papa."

They took another step toward their bed and the comfort of thick, worn quilts and lovingly embroidered pillowcases. One, two more steps.

"You tell that boy to come," her father ordered. "Tomorrow."

Their backs, their legs, and finally their stocking feet disappeared from view.

# 2

*Moosfeld, three months earlier*

Hannah felt only an act of God had persuaded her father to allow her to replace Siegi at *Der Wachauerhof* until she went to the Abbey. She had begged him, reminding him of the extra money she would bring to their family, or donate to the Church, which made him relent. She was going to be such a good nun.

The Maislingers' first daughter, Margarete, who was born in 1908. Then Sophie became convinced God had forgotten them. Seven years later, God remembered them again and Sieglinde was born. Hannah arrived the next year in October, 1916. Overwhelmed by females, Bernard prayed God skip them and remember someone else.

In 1932,with Greta already tucked away in the cloistered Abbey in Durnstein, the nearest town right on the river, Siegi married the youngest Lonauer son, Otto. A sweet man, he adored his bride and allowed her to have her way. She was pregnant immediately and nine months later had a son, whom they named Ernst, after Bernard's father.

Hannah liked Otto, even though he was not quite the son their Papa envisioned. He wore thick glasses, and according to Siegi, was forever groping his way around the furniture to find them. Otto had a way of drifting out of a conversation, and then returning with something absolutely unrelated which had been brewing in his mind. Like the time he asked Sophie her shoe size.

"No one cares!" Siegi exclaimed. Hannah told her sister to leave the poor man alone. He was not peculiar. He simply had a busy brain.

Otto Lonauer was wholly overshadowed by his older brothers. Faber Ratzener, who kept his father's last name, was the oldest and would later become part of the Austrian SS. His mother remarried and had three more sons before her second husband passed suddenly. Rudolf Lonauer was a Reich doctor in Linz. Viktor Lonauer took his father's place as proprietor of *Der Wachauerhof.* Otto Lonauer worked for Viktor.

When Otto's new wife arrived, Viktor directed her into the kitchen and told her to be quiet and do what she was told, none of which was natural for Siegi. After several outbursts, she was relegated to serving and clearing. In an advanced state of pregnancy, she couldn't seem to help bump into men heading for the bar.

Viktor cornered Otto in the back of the kitchen. "She's losing me customers!"

Regrettably, Otto apologized for his wife, and Siegi promptly banned him from their bedroom above the restaurant. "I'll ask my brother if there is something else you can do, liebchen," he called to her from outside the door.

"I could sit on the customers," Siegi shouted. All of this took a toll on her strong spirit. Now, eight months into her second pregnancy, Hannah did her best to soothe her, but it was like directing a bull to move out of the road. Siegi complained bitterly about Otto's ready submission to Viktor's rants. Hannah suggested that rather than blame her husband, she should point her dagger at Viktor, for whom bullying was an art.

Because of this strife, a job opened up for Hannah.

•   •   •   •   •

To quell her nervousness on the way to her first day of work, Hannah kept her head up and considered the scenery. The flowers of summer surrounded her, unorganized fields of blossoms at play. She congratulated them all for being unfooled by the sneaky sun of early spring. She warned the buds forming on their magnolia tree to wait for the sun to be more reliable, or end up flattened under a late snow.

Later, her greatest concern was not to be magnolia trees, but a man in Berlin who imagined himself to be the sun, spewing blinding light full of promises of prosperity and retribution. But on that day, in *Der Wachauerhof,* and any of a thousand pastoral taverns, the patrons, for whom crisis and celebration were defined by the whims of weather and insects, reassured each other that the recent rabble-rousing in Germany was of no Austrian concern.

The day Hannah arrived, Frau Lonauer grabbed Hannah's arm and yanked her around to face the bar.

"You see that?" she hissed, glaring at her son, Viktor. "He hired a tart to wait tables in my restaurant." At that moment, Viktor Lonauer was leaning against the bar. Her hips thrust forward, the tart's foot was nudging his.

"Oh dear," Hannah said. She had been in the building for two minutes and already faced working beside a loose woman.

"She should be in Vienna," Frau Lonauer sputtered." They have lots of jobs for whores."

In the villages of Lower Austria, questionable people were always directed to Vienna.

Hannah did her job in a quiet and orderly way. The interests of the tart, whose name was Gertraud, were not hers. What Hannah knew about men she learned from her sisters and their friends, her two disgusting minutes with Finn Binder in the barn, and more recently, by observing the group who drank beer and shouted at each other in Viktor's *biergarten.*

On that first day, Gertraud gave her a dirndl to wear that was way too big. She pointed to one of the *biergarten's* tables, where a pile of playing cards sat next to a vase of wilting flowers.

"I suppose cards are against nun laws."

"I'm not a nun yet."

"You play *schnapsen*?"

"Everyone plays *schnapsen,*"

One day when Hannah was observing Gertrude on the prowl, Viktor's older brother Faber came in, sat down at the bar, and unfolded the newspaper someone had left on the stool next to him. Gertraud blew past her customers and greeted him with a saccharine smile.

"*Guten tag,* Herr Ratzener," she cooed. "Or can I call you Faber?"

He ignored her, so she peeked over his newspaper. "What's the news?" she asked, as if the world around her mattered.

Faber eyed her. "Chancellor Dollfuss is still making a fool of himself. He's clinging to his imaginary control."

"Dollfuss is stupid," Gertraud nodded vigorously.

"Austrians better get used to the idea that change is coming to Austria."

"Oh, I agree."

Hannah snickered. Gertrude probably thought they were getting a new flag.

Viktor flew across the room and stepped in front of Gertraud, "Go make salad." She winked at Faber and flounced away, stopping to order Hannah to clean under the bar.

Hannah tried to keep her broom from brushing against their feet and listened. Faber had recently married a woman in Vienna, and was advising his brother to do the same.

"When I get home, there she is, waiting for me to inspect the house. Sometimes I point out spots she forgot to dust. I don't want her becoming complacent."

"I have our mother for all that," Viktor said.

"I assume you don't have our mother in your bed. Besides, you're the *bürgermeister*. Better to have a woman to serve you."

"But what would I do with a wife," Viktor said, nodding toward Gertraud's backside as she sashayed across the room, "when I can have that one for free?"

Only a few months, Hannah told herself. The Abbey had never seemed more inviting.

# 3

In the *biergarten*, Hannah's job was to clean up after the young men. She deliberately avoided memorizing their names, but she couldn't help but enjoy watching them play *Schnapsen*. "Please, Hannah," one of them would plead, "We need an unbiased person to deal!" One day, after a minor protest, she sat down. She dealt the cards but never played, spoke when spoken to, and learned how to cheat.

On one particular Sunday, Gertraud announced she was changing her name.

"Can you do that?" Hannah wondered.

"Of course. From now on, call me Aurelia."

"Oh, like St. Aurelia?" Hannah was a saint scholar.

"Not that St. Aurelia, you dummy! The princess Aurelia."

"Actually, St. Aurelia was a princess before she became a hermit and spent her life as a cloistered nun in Salzburg."

"You're the one who's going to the convent," Gertraud said as she strutted away. "Maybe you'll meet up with *your* Aurelia."

"They've both been dead for a thousand years," Hannah called after her.

Siegi delivered two healthy girls during the second week of July. They named them Juliane and Anke, after Siegi and Otto's grandmothers. Whenever Hannah went upstairs to visit the twins, she was dismayed to find her sister in tears. "There's two of them!" she wailed.

Hannah tried to relieve her, cuddling one twin while Siegi fed the other. As they switched, Siegi looked down at her bare breasts, a ripe melon and a deflated balloon, and bawled.

Siegi's "breakdown" was by then well known throughout the town, as she had made no attempt to keep her misery to herself. Everywhere Otto went, neighbors and even passing acquaintances offered him their sympathies. The twins were three weeks old when Sophie, knowing her daughter was beyond reason, brought them to the Maislinger farm. Hannah missed them, but Siegi's temporary relocation was a relief to most of Moosfeld.

Halfway through the summer, Viktor decided to add music. He lined up a fiddler and an accordion player, sure this would produce a larger crowd.

"I'm calling it *Biermusik*. Isn't that perfect? And I expect the two of you to be on duty until the last customer leaves," he commanded Hannah and Gertraud.

"He's adding entertainment?" Bernard said when Hannah relayed Viktor's plan.

"He wants me to stay late, Papa."

Bernard, in a jovial mood after Sophie's peach cobbler, snorted, "Of course he does. What do you think, Sophie? We might enjoy coming down to listen occasionally, have a beer together, share some pretzels."

Sophie nodded happily. "I love all our traditional folk songs."

Viktor advertised, and the crowd grew in anticipation. Hannah circled the room for empty beer glasses and steins, lugged them to the bar, and delivered them back, foam slopping over the sides. But the show did not materialize until the day Viktor conferred with his brother Faber for several hours during the afternoon. When he left, Viktor darted to the table where Hannah was clearing and Otto was sitting, Ernst on his lap, playing with cardboard coasters.

"We need a cabaret feel," he said, "like the bars Faber goes to in Vienna." Viktor ordered his brother to find him a singer, preferably a woman, to headline the show.

"Hannah has quite a pleasing voice," Otto said.

A plate slipped out of Hannah's hand and swirled around the table to a stop. Ernst started dropping the coasters, one by one, onto the floor.

Viktor ignored the commotion. "I don't want hymns, you idiot."

Several days went by and Otto produced no prospects. The next Friday night, desperate, Viktor summoned Hannah to the makeshift stage he had set up in the biergarten, where his musicians were waiting.

"This is Tomas, from St. Jakob. And Jorg, from Dürnstein."

"Viktor tells me you sing," Tomas said to Hannah.

"Only at Church!" she cried. "And in our house, sometimes."

"It might be better to ease into the floor show with something familiar," Viktor said, "but with a touch of bawdiness."

Tomas put down his fiddle and gave Hannah a friendly smile. "What's your name?"

"Hannah Maislinger. But I don't entertain."

"I understand your hesitancy. Crowds in beer halls can get wild."

Even in her state of shock, Hannah appreciated the sentiment. Tomas had reduced *Der Wachauerhof* to a room with a wet floor and the stench of stale ale.

Jorg played a few perky notes on his accordion and Hannah panicked. "I can't do this!" What would people say? What would her parents say?

"It's settled then," Viktor declared as he slid away.

Hannah bit back tears. "Sometimes," she wavered, "My family sings 'Peter's Pub.'"

Tomas was incredulous. "You yodel?"

She nodded. The musicians shared a look.

"Wait until Lonauer hears this," Jorg grinned.

The tables in the *biergarten* were bursting. Tomas clapped his hands and shouted for quiet. "For our opening show, Hannah Maislinger has agreed to sing for us." He and Jorg played the introduction, and shaking uncontrollably, she warbled the first few lines.

*And so I went to Peter's Pub*
*And there I drank some wine.*

Most of the audience were still chatting or demanding more beer. When she began to yodel, a few heads popped up.

*Holadi, holera, diria, holera,*
*Cuckoo, cuckoo,*
*Holadi, holera, diria, holera,*
*Cuckoo, cuckoo,*
*Holadi, holera, diria, ho!*

Behind the new bar in the *biergarten*, Gertraud smirked. Whatever she said to the men in front of her had them toppling off their stools. Then, from somewhere across the garden, a voice bellowed, "Stop being rude and shut up!"

Hannah looked up to see Siegi holding Ernst, who stood on a table next to her, clapping his little hands. The crowd, afraid Siegi might come unhinged, quieted considerably. She started to sing along with Hannah, waving her arms for the customers to join in.

*Buy for me my green jacket*
*Buy for me my pretty hat*
*Buy for me my nice Alpine dress*
*Because I must report for duty.*

Suddenly, everyone was keen to yodel. Customers poured out of the restaurant, and with wild enthusiasm, launched into the second chorus while Hannah yodeled louder. A third time, she added a few dance steps. Her audience pounded the tables and stomped their feet. At the end, the yodeling collapsed into thunderous applause punctuated with drunken cheers.

"Do you know this one?" Tomas' fingers danced across the strings of his fiddle. It was an Austrian drinking song.

"*Trink, trink, Brüderlein, trink,*" she began.

The patrons roared their approval and again joined in, their glasses aloft. Gertraud came out from behind the bar, seized a beer from a careening customer and stormed the stage.

"Play it like you have balls," she commanded Tomas and Jorg. Gertraud grabbed Hannah's arm. Her crooked teeth splayed out like fangs. "Take a seat, nun-girl."

Hannah waved at the two musicians and left the stage. They began again, louder and faster. Gertraud pulled her skirt up above her knees, thrust her chest forward, and leaned down to make her ample cleavage star of the show.

Hannah met up with Siegi in the back. "I'm so glad you're here!"

Siegi grinned. "I think your career as a showgirl is over." Viktor was smiling at Gertraud's provocative performance. Word would spread, and next week would be even more profitable.

Hannah scooped up little Ernst in her arms. A loose woman had rescued her.

•    •    •    •    •

One Sunday in early August, someone new, wearing baggy cotton pants and black suspenders over a starched gray shirt, sat amid the young men in the *biergarten*. They slapped his back as if he had just returned from war.

Hannah studied him from a table nearby. She first noticed the tiny indentations on his long nose that looked like moguls on a ski hill. Yet he was not unattractive. He had startling green eyes and a thick, tousled head of blond hair.

In the evening, he and his friends settled into two long tables inside.

"Who's the new one?" Hannah asked Gertraud, as casually as she could.

"Sebastien Brandl. He's from St. Jakob," Gertraud said slyly, and Hannah knew instantly a gulf had spread between her and this intriguing young man. She was not from St. Jakob, which would put her in line behind all the girls that were. If, of course, she had any interest in being in line.

"I think Sebastien's a bit wild for you, Hannah," she taunted. "See the one in the red hat?" She pointed to a boy with terrible skin and pants that should have been passed on to a younger brother. The poor fellow was the only one standing, leaning awkwardly into the conversation. "He might be interested."

"I'm not," Hannah declared.

"Did you know Sebastien has a racehorse? And a motorcycle. And," Gertraud whispered menacingly, "a rich lady in Vienna."

"Does he have a wife in Vienna?" Hannah shot back.

"Brazen words," Gertraud scoffed as she headed out the door, "from a girl with one leg on the lap of God."

Was this the moment her road to the Abbey sunk into potholes? Hannah craned her neck to see if the newcomer was still there. His seat was empty.

# 4

At the kitchen sink, Hannah poured too much soap into the running water, feeling inappropriately disappointed that a boy of whom she knew only questionable things had gone home. Watching dirty dishes float down into the bubbles, a knock on the half-open window above the sink startled her. She dropped a platter, and suds splashed down the front of her apron. She looked up. And he was there.

"May I come in?"

"To the kitchen?" Could she sound more idiotic?

"I could help."

Hannah lowered her eyes and went back to struggling with the slippery platter. "Customers are not allowed in the kitchen."

"I imagine those big plates are very heavy for such a petite young lady."

Smooth as silk, Siegi would have said.

"No," she said firmly. "I carry a pile of these around all the time."

"I'll dry them."

Now, that was something.

"I wash, too," he said, hoisting himself over the window box and leaning in to snatch the towel tucked into her apron. "I mean, if you want to dry. You choose."

Hannah glanced nervously through the open door into the dining room. No Gertraud, no Viktor. She hoped this was one of those times they disappeared.

"I guess you can stay. But only for two minutes," she added.

He dashed around the corner and entered the kitchen from the *biergarten*. Surveying the stacks of dishes and glasses she had already washed, he commented, "We've made too much work for you."

"They pay me," Hannah said.

"Good. Look at all of this," he said, waving his arms. A glass toppled off the counter, but he leaned down and caught it before it hit the ground. Helpless, she surrendered the dripping platter.

"When I lived in Vienna, I kept my place tidy. Dinner cooked and dishes cleaned. Laundry done. Floor swept." He grinned. "Socks darned."

That, Hannah would never believe. No man cooks and cleans, much less takes up a needle.

"Tomas the Fiddler works with me in St. Jakob. He's been crowing about your stunning voice, so I had to make a visit to your mediocre restaurant here in Moosfeld."

"It's not my restaurant."

"Thank God."

"And I'm no longer the entertainment."

"That's terrible news," he cried, as though the earth had stopped spinning. He continued with the platter, drying one spot at a time. "I haven't introduced myself." He stuck out a hand. "Sebastien Brandl."

"Hannah Maislinger." They shook, suds and all. She wondered what his companions would say, seeing him with her, holding a dishtowel. In silence, she washed and he dried for a few moments. Now and then, she stole a glance at him.

"You're looking at me," he said.

"I am not."

"Oh, well, I was looking at you."

"You should go back to your friends," she said. The dish water was dirty and cold. She would have to change it for the rest of the plates and a counter full of beer glasses.

"They're quite drunk," he said, adding another platter to the pile. "And they're not my friends."

"You're not from Moosfeld," Hannah said.

Oh, Lord. The words had involuntarily dropped from her mouth. She wished she could follow the swirling brown water down the drain. He set down the towel. The last drops of dishwater gurgled away. If she simply ignored him, he might retreat to his table, where she would hear laughter as he recounted his conversation with this strange girl. Hannah's shame ripened on her face. He had a racehorse, and a motorcycle-she did not know which was more foreboding-and most likely, a rich, sophisticated girlfriend in Vienna.

He moved nearer and leaned into her ear. "Moosfeld," he said, "is a beautiful town."

•　　•　　•　　•　　•

Hannah's brief singing career at an end, her parents expected her to be home at 9 o'clock. But Sebastian rarely appeared before then on the few nights each week he came to find her. She constructed a list of excuses, each of them somewhat true, to deliver to her father when she arrived home at least an hour late to find him waiting up for her.

Hannah learned Sebastien's family owned the beautiful *Gasthaus Zum Grünen Baum* in St. Jakob. She remembered little of her previous visit to the inn, at age eight, interested only in the banquet of desserts offered to her family. Sebastien spoke fondly of his brother in Vienna, Hubert, who worked at *Café Hawelke,* which was close to *Der Graben*, Sebastien's favorite square. They discovered their shared birthday.

"Serendipity," Sebastien said sagely.

Hannah told him about their farm, her family, Siegi's unpredictability, and her intention to join Greta at the Abbey. At any mention of her impending departure, Sebastien changed the subject to unrelated queries.

"So, what is your favorite color?" he asked the first time she brought it up. The next time, he wanted to know if their cows had names. Then it was her feeling about lentils.

Hannah told him to ask again about her favorite color.

"Hannah," he said, "what is your favorite color?"

"Virgin Mary Blue." She got a face full of suds.

•    •    •    •    •

One evening, Hannah emerged from the kitchen to find Sebastien sitting at a table with two unfamiliar men. He stood up when she came to take their order.

"Hannah, these are my oldest friends." He pointed to a tall, pleasant-looking young man with a slightly receding hairline. "Say hello to Georg Wangermann. We made a lot of mischief in his family's vineyards, and now he is the master winemaker at the unsurpassable *Weingut Maria Theresia.*"

Rows of Wangermann grapes framed the road next to both their towns. Over a hundred vineyards crowded into the Wachau Valley, but her father maintained *Maria Theresia* was the best. Looking embarrassed, Georg unfolded himself from his chair and shook her hand. Hannah felt like a pony being greeted by a giraffe—long legs, long neck, even the huge, dark brown, gentle eyes.

"And this is Gerhard," indicating a serious looking man wearing tortoiseshell glasses and, curiously, a sweater. "He got started working for Georg, but recently he abandoned him to sell wine in Krems. He thinks he's above picking and stomping."

"Actually, we now have a machine for grape-squashing," Georg explained.

"Soon, Gerhard will be the *bürgermeister*," Sebastien said, "and he's still a newlywed." It was unusual for both villages to have a young mayor. Sebastien's father Andreas, as well as their town butcher, had already served St. Jakob in years prior, and been approached about taking the job again. But neither had any interest in conversing with Viktor over mayoral issues concerning both towns, or the even more unattractive prospect of dining with his scheming brother Faber.

She took their order and smiled all the way back to the bar. Sebastien wanted her to meet his friends.

When she returned with their plates, he moved over and patted the bench for Hannah to join them. Gertraud walked by, scowled, and mercifully kept going. "Don't worry about her," Sebastien said. "She's about as deep as a puddle."

As if Hannah had been there the whole time, the three men resumed their conversation. "Hitler's a clown. Can't everyone see that?" Sebastien said, slurping his noodle soup.

"That's why Chancellor Dollfuss banned National Socialism in Austria," Georg said.

"And now, Dollfuss is dead." Their embattled Chancellor had been assassinated only days before.

Georg sat back. "Hitler doesn't simply see himself as Germany's Chancellor. He fancies himself the next Messiah. People respond to his diatribes, especially when he demands the rest of Europe be punished for all that has befallen Germany after the debacle of a horrible war."

"A German-made, Austrian provoked-war, he fails to mention," Sebastien said. "He's always ranting about 'the stench of Versailles.'"

Gerhard chewed noisily on his pork loin in mushroom sauce. "But the Treaty ruined both Germany and Austria. People are poor and hungry. Can you blame them?"

"Hitler wants to make everyone into a lemming," Sebastien said. They stared at him.

"What?" he demanded. "Those little fish that follow each other over the brink."

"He might actually have some good ideas," Gerhard said casually, forking a large piece into his mouth.

Georg sighed, took a long draught of beer, and stared down into his glass. "How can ideas be good without any opposition newspapers, the Reichstag overtaken by the NS after some mysterious fire, the blameless hunted down, and even the oldest families in Berlin looking over their shoulders?" His words rustled through the room like birds in the brush, and a handful of customers went on alert.

"But the Germans voted him in," Gerhard countered, "and affirmed his referendum about leaving the League of Nations. Where's the opposition?"

"Hiding," Sebastien said.

At the end of their table, a woman tittered. "I hardly think it's funny," Sebastien snapped.

Hannah felt compelled to defend her, but Viktor was watching. She scrambled to her feet and declared, "More beer!"

Georg smiled at Viktor. "A good employee."

At the bar, Hannah lined up the empty glasses. The foam rose evenly, snow over amber.

Occasionally bringing his friends, Sebastien argued politics in *Der Wachauerhof.* The verbal skirmishes became more heated every week. Viktor Lonauer's presence, and worse, the addition of his brother Faber, stained a conversation like red wine on a white tablecloth, spreading until those around them couldn't help but stare at the huge spot.

"You could get into trouble, Brandl," Viktor said one day after they almost ran over Hannah, balancing several plates, approaching Sebastien's table. Inviting themselves to sit down, he added, "powerful people are listening. You don't want to find yourself on the wrong side."

Georg held his hand up before Sebastien could reply. "We are all on the side of Austria."

Faber laughed. "Alarming naivete, Wangermann. It's obvious to me none of you understand Adolph Hitler is offering affluence," he paused, "and retribution. Those who turn their backs will be discarded with the trash."

Sebastien glared at the man he had played *fußbal* alongside in his youth. Neither town had enough for a side, and in a rare show of comradery, Moosfeld and St. Jakob fielded a team.

"I much prefer *Grünen Baum*," Georg remarked to Sebastien when they were gone, "but we hate to leave you to the sharks."

Gerhard sat back and crossed his arms. "They do keep up with the news."

"And the propaganda," Sebastien said.

"Not all of it, my friend. National Socialism is worth our attention."

Later, Sebastien came to the kitchen window to say goodnight to Hannah.

"Why do you come here?" She wondered. "The Lonauer brothers love to torture you. Except Otto, of course."

"It's not that bad," Sebastien said. And surely you know why I come here."

Hannah felt her face grow hot.

"Frau Lonauer's buttered noodles, of course."

She slammed the window shut, but could still hear his laughter echoing into the night.

# 5

Apparently, Sebastien was comfortable in any kitchen. Besides his handiness with the dishes, he was proficient at wiping off the counters, packing up food, and untying Hannah's apron behind her back. When she questioned how he could be away from his own inn, he always had a ready answer. "A slow day," he would say. Or, "I have to check out the competition."

When the cook was taking a break, Sebastien sometimes seasoned a pot of sauce.

"How nice of you to improve *Wachauerhof's* reputation," she teased him.

"This food needs me."

One afternoon, after she finished polishing the silver, as she did every Sunday, they sat on the kitchen steps eating the sweet corn Sebastien had "borrowed" on his way to the restaurant. "Do you like my friends?" He asked her, tossing the naked cob over the fence.

"Uh, yes, Sebastien. They're lovely."

"Lovely!" He hooted. "That's not a word I would have chosen."

"You know what I mean. Nice. Friendly. Are they all married?"

"Gerhard married Elke Reiter, a friend of mine from *Bacherei Crème*, the bakery next door to us. She can't wait to meet you."

Sebastien was talking to his friends about her, charging ahead as if they were like any other couple, from the same town, and without the problem of her approaching confinement. Hannah no longer fantasized about life in the Abbey. Instead, she imagined ascending its massive steps, pulling the bell chord, and being swallowed up like Jonah.

•    •    •    •    •

It was as if being with Sebastien meant nothing bad could ever happen again. And for a few weeks, nothing did.

One Wednesday morning, Hannah sang as she walked to work and arrived in the kitchen just as Sebastien sailed through the garden door. He put hands beneath her arms and lifted her onto the worktable next to two dead chickens.

"Hannah," he said. "Will you come to Church with me in St. Jakob?"

Her blissful state evaporated. "That is not a good idea."

His face fell. "Would it be easier for me to come to Mass in Moosfeld?"

"No!"

Papa and Mutti would think her irrational, bringing this man, whom they did not know and was way out of bounds, to sit with them in their usual pew. She told herself to banish him from the kitchen before it was too late. The thought made her miserable.

Sebastien moved the chickens and sat where they had been on the table.

"Your pants are going to smell," she said tightly.

"I'm a patient man. We won't sit together in your drafty Church or my cramped little chapel until I have your full permission."

Before she could argue, he lifted his fingers to her right eye and then the left, tenderly closing each lid. "Come with me, I brought a friend." He walked her forward. The warm breeze ruffled her skirt as they strolled through the *biergarten*. "Now," he whispered.

She opened her eyes and squealed. Behind a tree in the far corner of the garden, a huge white horse was calmly munching on Viktor's *edelweiß*.

"His name is Apfel."

"You do have a racehorse!" She broke free and ran through the tables. She stroked Apfel's soft mane, and the animal lowered his head so she could stare up into cavernous black eyes.

Sebastien clicked his tongue. "C'mon, beautiful boy," he said. Apfel followed them back to the kitchen.

"Much better than a motorcycle," Hannah declared.

"I have one of those, too, but it's sleeping in a garage in Vienna. I need new tires, and a few other things, but I'm too poor right now."

"What a surprise."

Sebastien's head dipped. "You're correct. I have not been as diligent as I could be at *Grünen Baum*. For the simple reason," he said, reaching over and pulling her into his arms, "that this is the kitchen I want to be in."

Hannah suddenly felt short of breath. And then he was kissing her, right in front of God and Apfel and probably Gertraud. Her lips went rigid. Why hadn't she practiced with Siegi and her friends?

He leaned back. "I surprised you. Shall we try that again?"

She pushed him away, ashamed of both the kiss and how terrible she had been at it.

"Please," he said. "I can do better."

What? Her eyes went to his lips.

Sebastien closed in again, and this time she softened. When he moved his lips, she moved hers.

He dragged his mouth away. "Hannah," he breathed against her. " I think you should come to work at *Grünen Baum*. This place is beginning to stink of National Socialists."

She stared at him.

"And I think I should meet your parents."

The trance she had sunk into fizzled. "No!"

"Why not?" he demanded.

"Because I'm going to be a nun. In three months!"

"If that is still true," he sighed, "then I've lost my touch." He caressed one of her taut knuckles. "'I'm going to be a nun' is not the usual response I get after I kiss a girl."

How many minutes had they been carrying on? Hannah glanced into the *biergarten*, and through the door to the restaurant. The last afternoon customers were sitting back drowsily, emptying their glasses. She lowered her voice. "You've always known."

"I assumed I could change your mind. Now I'm going to make it my life's work."

"You are making me crazy."

"Is that a yes?"

"No. Yes to what?"

"To talking to your parents?"

She didn't want to protest anymore. But she would have to engage in one more skirmish before surrendering. "Sebastien, do you have another woman, or a wife, or a child, somewhere else?"

Sebastien threw his arms around her. "Of course not," he cried, just as Gertraud barged into the kitchen.

"Hannah," she said in a singsong voice, "your parents are here!"

Sebastien smiled eagerly. "This is good!"

She wanted to shake him. "This is very bad."

Gertraud was not about to skip this opportunity to make mayhem. "Go on in," she said, giving Sebastien a shove. "I'm sure they'd love to meet you."

He reached for Hannah's hand. She snatched it back. She wanted nothing to do with him, or Gertraud, or even the people in the next room, waiting for their own special waitress.

"It's all right, Hannah," Sebastien said quietly. "I'll be outside if you need me."

"I won't," she snapped.

He gave Apfel a pat as he slipped out of the kitchen. Gertraud humming some drinking song and trailing behind him.

Bernard and Sophie Maislinger, sitting at a table with Siegi, Otto, and their children, waited expectantly, and gave her a little cheer as she approached. Hannah stood at the opposite side of the table from her father and tried to act normal.

Siegi elbowed her. "What day is it, Hannah?"

*Mutter Gottes.* "Happy Birthday, Mutti." Silence prevailed while her father inclined his head toward his wife and raised his eyebrows. Hannah hurried around the table and kissed her cheeks.

"Are you all right?" Siegi asked, eyeing her suspiciously.

"Fine. Good. Busy."

"Leave Hannah alone," Sophie scolded. "This is the first time we've all been here together. She wants to do her best for us."

"Yes! Let's start with something to drink. Beer? Wine, Mutti?"

She poured four beers and a glass of mediocre *Grüner Veltliner* Viktor touted as "a class above Wangermann's." She surreptitiously checked the room for any sign of Gertraud or Sebastien, delivered the drinks, and took their orders to the cook.

When she returned, Viktor was hovering over her family. "You can sit with them for a while if you want to," he said smoothly.

Hannah climbed in next to Siegi, who immediately pinched her younger sister, which meant they would talk later.

The meal was pleasant enough. One of the Maislinger horses had recently given birth to a handsome colt, which led Otto into a lecture on saddles. Sophie laughed at everything. Bernard nodded his head and ate heartily, while Siegi declared the rum cake awful, but she ate two pieces. The youngest Maislinger had little to say, and the meal ended without any visitors from the garden. Viktor returned to ask her father if he had joined the Party yet.

Bernard ignored him and held up their glasses. "My wife and I are still thirsty." Viktor frowned, and Hannah almost laughed.

Finally, Bernard and Sophie, each carrying a twin, headed for the door. While Hannah cleared away their plates, Siegi, her stomach hardly deflated despite the recent emergence of two babies, perched precariously on a wobbly barstool.

"Not so fast," she said, grabbing Hannah's arm as she rushed by.

Hannah peered into the restaurant's corners. "Where's Otto?"

"He's right there," Siegi said, nodding toward the other end of the bar. "With *Pfarrer* Schönfeld." The disarming young pastor picked that moment to look up and break into a perky smile.

"Hello Hannah," he said.

She mumbled a greeting, yanked Siegi off her bar stool, and steered her toward the bottom of the stairs. "Go. I'll be up in a minute." She raced back into the restaurant and almost collided with Viktor. "I was coming to find you."

"You almost flattened me."

"I'm sorry, but I need a few moments with my sister."

"You've already frittered away the afternoon."

Hannah didn't move.

"Only if you can guarantee she won't bring those squalling creatures down here. Gertraud will be happy to finish up." His sarcasm not lost on her, Hannah took the stairs two at a time.

"Come on in, you little liar." Siegi was sitting in her rocking chair, eating a bar of chocolate. "So, Mutti told everyone you've been working late, being extremely helpful."

"Gertraud is too busy lining up dates," Hannah retorted.

"Not too busy to inform me you were talking to Sebastien Brandl in the kitchen and didn't care that we'd arrived."

"Oh my God. Did Mutti and Papa hear that?"

"Just me."

"It was nothing."

"Then why was your face on fire and it took ten minutes for an intelligent word to come out of your mouth?"

"Gertraud made me feel guilty for making you wait." Hannah stammered.

"You're becoming quite the storyteller."

Hannah plopped down on the unmade bed. "Believe what you want."

Siegi gasped. "Oh my God, are you, I mean, have you, been with him?"

Comprehension crashed over Hannah like a dead tree. "Of course not," she cried.

"Maybe I should go to the Abbey right now."

"You're not Greta," her sister said in a deceptively gentle tone.

Hannah had recently spent a lot of time thinking about that. "There's nothing wrong, except that I'm tired."

"All that working late!".

Hannah stormed out of the room. As soon as she appeared at the bottom of the stairs, Sebastien was at her side.

"Hannah," he began. "I'm sorry."

"Sorry for what? Where's Gertraud?"

"Don't worry. I threatened to tell everyone she had an unmentionable disease."

Hannah had no energy to laugh. No need to make things better between them. She cleared a nearby table. He picked up some plates and, like a puppy close on her heels, followed her into the kitchen. "Hannah," he said urgently, pulling her around to face him.

"I can't worry about you," she moaned, "hide from my parents. Construct lies. You always know what to say. I go blank and can barely stay upright."

"What can I do to convince you of what our lives could be together? Are you going to be happy closed up in concrete, away from everything and everyone you love? Aren't you going to miss...living?" He enclosed her in his arms. "It's fine to want more, sweet Hannah."

Her wall of resistance collapsed. She knew he was right. She wanted more than a contemplative life, which Sebastien had convinced her was no life at all. And this wonderful man would take her far from the Abbey, safe from Viktor and Gertraud and National Socialism.

She wiped her nose on the fabric of his shirt. "I'm sorry," she murmured.

"I've got another shirt. Everything will be fine after I talk to your father."

This man believed he could get anything he wanted simply by asking. Before that moment, she wouldn't have given Sebastien Brandl much of a chance against Bernard Maislinger. But Sebastien made light of the impossible.

Three days passed, and she had not approached her father. She told Sebastien she wasn't ready.

"Why not? It can't be Siegi and the babies. Your parents already rescued them from Viktor."

In the uncloistered world of the present, her star was about to fall with a mighty thud. She would relay Sebastien's request. Not because she was blessed with courage, but because he gave her a little garnet hanging on a gold necklace for her birthday. She must confront her parents or wear high collars for the rest of her life.

# 6

*Moosfeld, October 15, 1934*

No one spoke during breakfast. Hannah waited for her father to say he had changed his mind and the Mother Abbess would be there any minute to talk some sense into her. All she wanted was to escape down the road before her father jumped on his horse and unfurled his rope.

That day, a huge, overdone wedding party had even Gertraud hurrying to deliver platters of lukewarm food. Sebastien found Hannah talking to the junior bridesmaids, who were the only ones still sober. "Hello," he said, sidling up to her shoulder.

"Eight o'clock tonight."

"How did they take the news?"

"Not well. Papa has heard rumors, and Mutti suggested several other men who would be more appropriate."

Sebastien looked away, deflated.

That evening, following a tense supper Hannah could barely get down, Bernard set up a courtroom in a small room next to the front door regularly avoided in favor of the kitchen. One chair, the hardest in the house, faced three others, a table between them.

To her dismay, when the knock came, her father was first to the door. She heard Sebastien say courteously, *"Guten Abend, Herr* Maislinger."

When Hannah failed to speak, Bernard introduced Sophie. He sat Sebastien down in the single chair and motioned his wife and daughter to the others. He remained standing, curling his lower lip up over his teeth like he did when counting the money paid to him for a wagonload of hay.

Hannah was sure her father would go right to the rumored indiscretions in Vienna. She imagined him repelling Sebastien's attempted explanations, and shouting at him for stealing her from the church and turning her into some lovesick, misdirected female.

Bernard's first question surprised them all.

"Do you have any money, Herr Brandl?" Hovering over the accused, Bernard seemed taller than he had been only minutes before.

"Not much, Herr Maislinger."

Bernard rubbed his nose. "When I met Sophie, I didn't have much either. But I worked hard," he said, ceremoniously sweeping his arms around the room, "and Sophie and my three daughters were always warm and well fed." His lips twitched in a private smile aimed at his wife. "Once in a while they could even go out and buy a new hat."

"I do not need a new hat, Papa," Hannah said. "I need Sebastien."

"Hannah, Herr Brandl and I will do all the talking." He turned back to Sebastien and threw his first dart. "What gives you the right to lure my daughter away from her God-given vocation? It must be easy for an experienced fellow like you, to prey on an innocent girl."

Sebastien was ready. "Herr Maislinger," he said, with the same earnest look he used to enchant Hannah every day, "I'm sorry if you are disappointed Hannah's plans have changed. I would take the blame, but that would suggest Hannah doesn't know her own mind."

"I do, Papa," Hannah blurted out.

"Quiet!"

"I'm taking more responsibility at *Grünen Baum*," Sebastien said. "My father is getting a little older, and a little more tired," he smiled. "Believe me, he is happy to become the overseer. Whenever I'm cooking, he leans over me and says, "I just have one little tip.""

Bernard turned a murderous eye toward Sebastien, who was quick to add, "Which I am of course grateful to receive, because one should always keep learning."

"Huh," Bernard said. "I realize, Herr Brandl, rumors around here might as well be a game of post office played by gossips. But there's always a flicker of truth in the words that survive. So," her father continued, peering into Sebastien's eyes. "Do you have a lover in Vienna, and God forbid, an abandoned child?"

"Bernard!" Sophie pleaded.

"Let's get right to the point, Sophie. Your daughter is obviously in some make-believe land and unable to think clearly. You must resist joining her until we know exactly how this man behaved in Vienna while his father single-handedly held together the largest inn on the Danube."

Sebastien waited for a moment before he said, "Actually, Herr Maislinger, *Grünen Baum* is not the largest. But I hope it is the best."

"For which you should be thanking your ancestors."

"Certainly, sir. As for Vienna, I can assure you there is no girlfriend, wife, or child of mine in Vienna. I left St. Jakob after my mother died. My father gave me his blessing, and I was too selfish to understand he was grieving as deeply as I was."

Sebastien peeked at Hannah and cleared his throat.

"I arrived there with little money and an old motorcycle I had worked on behind our ice house. It broke down just inside the city limits, and I walked it to the nearest garage. I couldn't afford to fix it, but they gave me a job making less serious repairs on another motorcycle in their shop."

"Go on," Bernard said, his hand clutching his chin.

"At first I was in a daze. I lived in a cramped room in a decrepit building I would be ashamed to show your daughter. I missed my mother, and felt guilty about my father. My brother Hubert had been living in Vienna for some time, but I was afraid to visit him. If Papa told Hubert what I had done, he might abandon his own life to help with the inn."

"I didn't hear your brother had returned to St. Jakob," Bernard said.

"No, because my father didn't tell him. He had given us both what he felt we needed—the possibility of a different life."

Sophie had quietly moved her chair a little farther away from the proceedings, as if to prepare for what else might be coming.

"At the end of my second year in Vienna, I met a woman whose automobile had stalled on a nearby street. We pushed it to the garage, and while I was diagnosing her problem, she told me she had been on her way to the Vienna Derby, near the Ferris wheel on the grounds of *Der Prater*."

"What is a Vienna Derby?" Sophie asked from her corner.

"It's a horserace," Hannah piped up.

Bernard again turned on his daughter. "Did I ask you to speak?"

Sebastien took a breath. "A few days later, she came by the garage and asked me if I would like to go with her to the track."

"And who, exactly, was this woman?" Bernard demanded.

"Her name is Mitzi Poppmeier, sir."

"What kind of name is Mitzi Poppmeier?" Sophie wanted to know.

Her husband nodded once, as if to say, good question. "Tell us more about this Fraulein Poppmeier."

Sebastien winced. "*Frau* Poppmeier."

Bernard took a step back and almost tripped over the empty chair.

"But when I met her, she was no longer married."

"A widow, I hope," Bernard said.

"Bernard!" Sophie cried again.

"Oh, Sophie, that's not what I meant. Of course it's too bad if her husband died."

"Truthfully, sir, she's divorced."

Hannah put her head down. They didn't know anyone who was divorced.

"After the races Mitzi took me to the stables to show me her horse, who had won his race. People surrounded the horse, rubbing them down, feeding them treats. At the end of the row, one horse stood all alone. Mitzi said when an owner has given up on his horse, maybe he wasn't winning, he would leave him in his paddock at the end of the race day, a sign he was available. Sometimes another owner bought the horse for a pitiful price. But, if after a day or two no one bothered with him, the animal was doomed. This one looked so sad and lonely, I could hardly bear it."

"Oh, no," Sophie said, raising her hand to her mouth.

"Sebastien saved his life!" Hannah exclaimed.

"Ridiculous!" Bernard barked. "It sounds as if you were barely eating. How could you afford a horse?"

"Right, Herr Brandl. And even if I had the money, what was I going to do with him? I couldn't very well fit him into my flat, or park him behind the garage. But Mitzi offered to buy him and add him to her stable, as long as I assumed caring for him."

"You must have been very grateful."

Sebastien swallowed. "For a while, I kept company with Mitzi. She is a fine woman with a good heart. Our conversations were stimulating. She made me forget my woes. I felt invigorated-a feeling I feared I'd lost forever."

Papa pointed a finger at Sebastien. "How old are you?"

"Twenty-four."

"And how old was this generous, friendly woman?" He looked as if he was about to win a lucrative bet.

"When I met her, she was thirty-four, Herr Maislinger."

"Did you hear that, Sophie? Thirty-four."

Hannah wondered why Sebastien seemed to be deliberately confirming her father's suspicions. Bernard was good at setting verbal traps, but maybe Sebastien was better.

"After a few mindless months," he continued, "I realized my gratitude for her help with Apfel was being misinterpreted. What I felt for Mitzi was not love. It was time to go home and face my responsibilities."

Sebastien waited. Hannah waited. Tension, like what one feels while trying to navigate a barbed wire fence, threatened to bloody the room.

Bernard brought his trembling finger to within an inch of Sebastien's face. "Are you finished?"

Hannah crumbled. She feared his stack of sins was about to rise.

"You have probably heard about my night in jail. When I first arrived, I went to a rather sordid establishment not far from the garage. Several very drunk men got in a fight, and when the police showed up, even the bystanders were tossed into a green wagon and hauled away."

This was news to Hannah. What else had he failed to tell her?

"Do you have more questions, Herr Maislinger?"

Bernard's arm dropped to his side. He walked back and forth across the room while they waited for the verdict.

He went to his wife, helped her up, and pushed her chair back to its starting place. "Come sit with us, Sophie. You too, Brandl," he said with a wave of his hand. Sebastien slid closer and sat with one hand in his lap and the other grazing the table, as if measuring the grain of the wood.

"You have taken the adage *jung und dumm* to the farthest reaches of the universe."

Hannah could not believe what she was hearing. Had her father made a little joke?

"That, sir, is entirely fair."

"What about the horse?"

"I bought him from Frau Poppmeier with the money I'd saved to get the parts I needed for my motorcycle. It took a couple of days, but I rode her all the way home."

"*Dumm*," Bernard repeated. The red blotches on his neck, which had returned during Sebastien's recitation of his time with Mitzi Poppmeier, had receded. Hannah felt the air shift. A pronouncement was coming.

"You are not from Moosfeld. You abandoned your father at his time of need. You consorted with a divorced woman in Vienna. You own a racehorse and a motorcycle. You have not yet proved yourself as an innkeeper, having recently decided to work for a living."

"Yes, sir."

Bernard looked at his wife, whose smile was hopeful, the pieces of her world settling back into place. From the front of the house came an impatient bray.

"Apfel is outside, Frau Brandl," Sebastien said, "if you would like to see him." They all moved to the window and eyed the white horse, tied to a tree. A wise move, Hannah thought.

Sebastien spoke. "One more thing, Herr Brandl. I think Hannah should come to work at *Grünen Baum.*"

Bernard continued to stare out the window. "I agree."

Hannah did not yet understand the coalition that was being formed, thinking only that permission had been granted to be with Sebastien and nothing of Viktor's increasingly hostile clientele.

"All right," he said. "Let us go see this Apfel."

Hannah hoped Sebastien would reach for her hand. But he simply opened the front door and ushered them all outside. Maybe later, she thought, her hunger for him pulsating like the wheels of a locomotive.

# 7

By the end of the next day, all the excitement and two nights of questionable sleep, in addition to having to do Gertraud's chores after her fight with Viktor roared into a full-blown tantrum, Hannah was exhausted and a headache was threatening. Sebastien came late in the afternoon, whispered in passing his father would welcome her at *Grünen Baum*, and disappeared into the garden.

Night arrived. She took off her apron and picked her handbag off its peg in the grimy washroom used by the employees. She was surprised to see Sebastien still in the *biergarten*, sitting at a table with *Pfarrer* Nikolas Schönfeld, the new priest in both Moosfeld and St. Jakob.

"There you are," Sebastien cried. "Come over here. Niko and I have been waiting for you."

Had he already revealed their secret? And since when did Sebastien call a priest by his given name? He wore the same long-sleeved white shirt Sebastien often did. His smooth face was kindly, his green eyes warm, and his manner, she had already concluded, unusually approachable. He patted the place next to him. "Please, join us."

Sebastien went inside to get her a glass of wine.

"I didn't know you two were such close friends," she said when he returned.

Sebastien grinned. "Niko's also a good friend of my brother Hubert."

"*Café Hawelke* is one of my favorite spots." the priest said. He lowered his voice. "I hope you don't mind a little political talk. I was just telling Sebastien about a bishop who suggested Hitler's rants against the Jews are evil. He wrote a Pastoral Letter condemning National Socialism."

Hannah wondered if she was supposed to say something.

"Wait," Sebastien said gravely, "there's more."

Nico leaned forward. "But then, in the same missive, he says it is the duty of all Catholics to adopt a "moral form of anti-Semitism."

Sebastien scowled. "We can hate the Jews, as long as we hate them nicely."

"When I was twelve," Hannah said, "a new family moved to Moosfeld with their two children. Papa became friends with their father, *Doktor* Jerecki, and I took piano lessons from his wife. When I asked Papa why we never saw them at Mass, he explained they were Jewish and worshipped at a synagogue in Dürnstein."

"I know them," Sebastien said. "They've come to *Grünen Baum*. My mother loved the whole family."

"Well," Niko sighed. "I'm afraid the situation is much worse than the equivocation of a member of the hierarchy. You must have heard that after Hitler took control, he introduced the Nuremberg Laws, a set of anti-Semitic decrees, at a Party Rally. If you have four German grandparents, you're German. Three or four Jewish grandparents, you're Jewish. One or two, you're a *mischling*.

"Mixed blood," Sebastien said. "The Church should have refuted those laws immediately. Where was the damn Pope?"

"Sebastien!" Hannah admonished him.

The young priest reached for Hannah's hand. "I didn't mean to put a damper on your news."

Hannah tried to ignore the oddness of his touch. "I'm fine, *Pfarrer* Schönfeld."

"Please, It's Niko."

She pondered this troubling conversation while she looked into his kind eyes. "We aren't innocent anymore, are we?"

"Ah, Hannah. Don't be afraid to allow your conscience to awaken."

He stood and addressed Sebastien. "You might want to write down your feelings. That's what I do. It helps me go down the most reasonable path." He smiled, and disappeared out the back of the *biergarten.*

"What did he mean by that?" Hannah asked.

Sebastien laughed. "That I should let my disgust with what's happening in Germany flow through a pen before it comes out of my mouth."

Hannah sagged. "I want to go home, Sebastien."

"Have you told Viktor you're leaving?"

"It's only been one day."

"Why wait?"

"Why hurry? I guess I thought it might be our secret for a while, but you've already told your friend the *pfarrer.*" Her head pounded mercilessly.

Sebastien cradled her face with his hands. "You're tired. Go home and sleep." He kissed the top of her head, and with a cherry wave, left her alone.

It was as if Sebastien had already moved on from her father's blessing to more important things. He loved her, yet she might never be his whole life, as surely he would be hers.

•　　•　　•　　•　　•

After sleeping soundly for eight hours, she couldn't wait one more minute to tell Viktor she was leaving, and better yet, would work for the Brandls.

Her employer was not pleased. "Do you think I haven't seen you flirting with that firebrand Sebastien Brandl in the kitchen? I have the ear of the only people that count in the Wachauer Valley, and I'll make sure not even the nunnery will take you!"

She lifted her chin. "Andreas Brandl is going to pay me twice as much as you do."

She swore she could see steam coming out of his ears.

It quickly became apparent finding her replacement would be at Viktor's leisure. Three days later Bernard arrived at the restaurant before noon and informed him Hannah would be leaving. "I'll be over later to pick up what you owe her. "Come Hannah, we're late for *mittagessen,*" He marched out the door and said over his shoulder, "in St. Jakob."

•   •   •   •   •

Sebastien was there to greet them at the front door, intricately carved with a forest, the Danube running through it. When he took her hand Hannah blushed, knowing her father would not approve premature liberties.

"Welcome, Herr Maislinger," Sebastien said. "Would you like to eat outside? The weather is perfect."

"Anywhere is fine, Herr Brandl," Bernard said, putting himself between them.

Hannah could hardly take it all in. The hallway had large windows on both sides. On the left, an immense kitchen, where workers were scrubbing the surfaces and exchanging friendly banter. To the right, the spacious main restaurant, its walls and ceiling composed of a variety of woods, with tables and booths complimented by colorfully and comfortably cushioned banquettes and chairs.

"The wood…" she began, trailing off.

"Isn't it gorgeous?" Sebastien exclaimed. "Newcomers take turns guessing the different species. You hear them asking, 'Is it cedar?' 'Does this pine come from the Tyrol?' The entire staff plays the game."

Another bar ran the length of the entire wall opposite them, splendidly carved with grapevines. In a daze, Hannah walked toward a glass fronted pavilion overlooking the *biergarten*. Its huge framed windows were wide open, the room warm and breezy. It also had its own bar backed by Tyrolean-themed tiles. The tables were of a light-colored wood, each one with a white candle cradled in its miniature bronze holder.

"A *wintergarten*," she breathed. Coming to her side, Sebastien explained that underneath the floor were pipes to heat the room on the coldest days.

Outside, flower boxes and a polished stone patio were only a prelude to the delights a few steps beyond. Conversation, loud and lusty, rose from white-clothed tables set on a plush green grass carpet. Of course, Hannah thought, *Grünen Baum*. Trees of green. Pines, but also fruit trees, apple and apricot, provided abundant shade. Flowers splashed the scene with color.

Sebastien pulled her around to an enormous vegetable garden, still bursting with various colors and shapes. A red henhouse sat in back, and several formidable looking hens were minding a clutch of chicks pecking dinner off the ground.

Back on the patio, four places were set at a table covered with a spotless white tablecloth. Hannah studied the plates and utensils, wine glasses and coffee cups as if previously she had only eaten with her fingers and drunk from a trough. In the middle of the table sat a bronze-encased vase, bursting with daisies.

"I did that myself," Sebastien beamed.

Apparently, flowers stuck in water were a significant accomplishment.

Hannah watched a posse of squealing children playing tag. At the end of the *biergarten,* a mantle of marigolds hung over a low fence. Beyond it all, on the other side of the Danube, endless geometric rows of vineyard terraces between the steep wooded hills of the Wachau Valley created the look of an elaborately sewn quilt.

Four foaming beer glasses arrived almost immediately. "My father is hoping to join us," Sebastien explained. A white kitten scampered by, then came back around to rub against Hannah's legs. "Who's this?" she asked.

"Chopin. He likes you." Sebastien said.

It was not just the beer that was making Hannah giddy. A good amount of exuberance enlivened most Austrian *biergartens*, but for Hannah, this one was unparalleled magic, invented in a dream.

"Bernard!" came a shout from behind them. A medium height white haired man in traditional Austrian vest and trousers tapped her father's shoulder.

"Andreas!" They grasped each other's arms in greeting.

"Hannah," Sebastien said, "this is my father."

Andreas Brandl gave Hannah a little bow and slipped into the empty chair. "So, you're the reason my son keeps disappearing. I'm truly delighted to meet you, and I welcome you to *Grünen Baum*, where we hope you will find the work pleasant and the company tolerable."

"I think I'll manage," Hannah laughed. "Hopefully Sebastien didn't pester you too much to make a place for me."

"He threatened to move back to Vienna if I didn't hire you. I told him he could go, but then he made me my favorite Linzer Torte, so I kept him. You're the bonus."

"Thank you, Herr Brandl."

"Call me Andreas, or Andi."

A few moments later, a robust, middle-aged woman with a dirty apron and flour in her hair approached their table. "You'll love Mathilde Marti," Sebastien said, saturating a fresh roll with butter and handing it to Hannah. "She organizes the housekeeping, but she's also an excellent chef."

"Tilda wanted to be the one who prepared your first meal here," Andreas said, giving her an affectionate wink. "So Sebastien and I made the beds this morning while she locked herself in my kitchen."

"And I'll probably have to remake them, Hannah," Mathilde said. She flicked the top of Sebastien's head. "Are you going to sit there, all puppy-eyed, or are you going to serve that special bottle of wine you hid this morning?"

Sebastien retrieved the bottle from behind the bar and began to pour. "*Weingut Maria Theresia*, Georg's winery, is just through those trees," he told Hannah, nodding toward the right side of the *biergarten*. "Lucky, don't you think? Superior wine. And convenient."

"Are you in the kitchen or behind the bar these days?" Bernard chided his old friend.

"My son is good with people," he said. "Our bar is always full."

Bernard laughed and raised his glass. "To the bar," he said.

The Maislingers gushed their way through roast pheasant with three different *Knödel*, dumplings with mushrooms, ground pork, and onions, accompanied by white asparagus. What followed was impossibly delicious ice cream with apricot sauce and poppy seeds, a *Wachauer* Valley specialty. Sophie also made apricot sauce, but as their eyes met over their spoons, father and daughter were thinking the same thing: This sauce might be better, and they would never tell.

When Sebastien put his wineglass on his head, Hannah's eyes widened.

"At *Grünen Baum*, if you want more wine, you put your glass on your head," Andreas explained. He sent the bartender a cheery wave, who hurried over with another bottle.

Bernard addressed the table. "I don't want to drive into a tree on the way home, so I'll simply say thank you, Andreas, for your gracious hospitality and this meal, for which I have no words." He looked down at Sebastien, who was gazing dreamily at Hannah. Mathilde reappeared, and the table raised glasses and cheered.

She regarded Andreas fondly. "I have been fortunate to be allowed into the *Grünen Baum* kitchen, where I could spy on the best chef in Austria."

Andreas laughed. "Tilda has obviously been partaking of the cherry *schnaps*."

Bernard stood.

"I can bring Hannah home," Sebastien said quickly.

"It's a five-minute drive in my truck."

"Fifteen minutes on Apfel, sir."

Andreas Brandl clapped his hand on the table. "Be strong, Bernard. Don't let my sly son have the last word."

Standing there in his coat and hat, Bernard stared intently at Sebastien, as if boring a hole into the core of this man's wizardry. His eyes moved to his spellbound daughter. He shook his head. But then, a decision made, he simply said "*Schuße,*" and was gone.

# 8

A short, pleasant looking man, wearing a beard and a traditional Bavarian hat, came up to their table. "Ah, Tobi," Andreas said, "come meet Sebastien's charming friend."

"Hannah," Mathilde said, "this is my husband, Tobias."

Andreas explained that Tobias Marti was St. Jakob's artist in residence, a sculptor who created, among other things, ironwork memorials for church cemeteries as far away as Melk. "He made all the candle holders in the inn, and each one is different."

Hannah had taken notice. On their table, the stems of two small roses supported buds and a little red candle. On the buffet that held extra plates and silverware, a cage made of delicate metal lattice, a tiny bird on top, housed a soft blue candle. Hanging from the trees outside were bronze lanterns where, at night, candlelight would peek through a labyrinth of stars, hearts, and flowers.

"Take one home for your parents," Tobias said. He walked over to a nearby table and picked up a candle encompassed by woven metal bells. "This is one of my favorites," he said, placing it in her hand.

Helpless to refuse, Hannah put her hand over his. "Thank you. We will treasure it."

"We're worried Tobi will become so famous we will lose him and the indispensable Mathilde to an art colony in Vienna," Andreas said.

"My Tilda will never leave you," Tobias said, "and I will never leave her."

"Oh poof," Mathilde said, but she smiled and kissed his cheek.

This was nothing like Hannah's introduction to Frau Lonauer or the awful Gertraud on her first day at *Der Wachauerhof*. These people were beloved, members of the family.

"So," Mathilde said, "I'm taking Hannah for a tour."

"Don't get lost, *liebchen*," Sebastien teased.

He needn't worry. She would never wander far.

•　　•　　•　　•　　•

Mathilde led Hannah into the spacious restaurant kitchen to show her the six-burner stove and the hanging pots, pointing out which one was for stew, gravy, soup, or soufflé. Tomas the Fiddler stopped what he was doing to welcome her with a hug.

"You escaped!" he cried. "We saved a place for you in the kitchen."

"I'm not much of a cook," Hannah confessed.

"Why learn to cook?" Mathilde tittered. "You grew up the youngest of three sisters and Sebastien kidnapped you on your way to the Abbey." Obviously, Sebastien prepared Mathilde, his father, and God knows who else, for the gaping holes in her domestic experience.

"I can wash dishes."

Mathilde was unfazed. "I'm sure you'll be an accomplished cook someday. But as far as the dishes go, you might have to wrestle Daniel for a towel."

Next to the sink was a young, light-haired man with an engaging grin on his wide-open face, perhaps twenty years old, wearing two aprons, one tied across his chest and the other around his hips.

"Hannah," Mathilde said, her eyes shining, "This is Daniel Reiter. His family owns *Bäckerei Crème*, the bakery next door, and in the mornings he has to help with the fresh bread. But we are quite lucky to have Daniel as our kitchen captain later for *mittagessen*."

He nodded. "You want to see?" He picked up a long wooden spoon from the counter and motioned her towards a bank of cabinets that came close to taking up the entire back wall of the kitchen. He chose one in the middle and reached for a set of knobs.

"Are you ready?"

Hannah nodded.

Daniel threw open the doors, banging them against the neighboring cabinets.

"Surprise!" he shouted, reaching out for her hand and tugging her closer. She beheld a vault of perfectly stacked dinner plates.

"Daniel," Mathilde scolded, "try not to break anything."

He opened the next set of doors more carefully. Perfectly balanced jars on top of jars, equal spaces between the rows, were as precisely presented as the plates.

"What's your favorite?" he asked Hannah. "She can take her favorite, right, Tilda?"

'You're in charge, Daniel."

Tentatively, Hannah selected a jar of apricot jam.

"*Marille,* that's my favorite too!" He raised the spoon and, like a schoolteacher at the blackboard, pointed to the highest row. "See, these are *apfel*, and these are *birne,* and these are *brombeere.*"

Hannah blinked. "They're in alphabetical order?"

Mathilde pulled a piece of paper from the side of one cabinet, and Hannah saw the alphabet in large letters.

Daniel grabbed the sheet from her hand and crumpled it. "I don't need that."

Andreas came into the kitchen and inclined his head toward a metal contraption at the end of one of the preparation tables. "Have they boasted about our new toy?"

"What is it?" Hannah asked.

"It's Luigi, our coffee machine," he said proudly. "The Italians wanted to serve each customer their own coffee on the spot. But the beans were too coarse and the temperature of the boiler was too high. It came out scalded and ugly."

"Ugly coffee!" Daniel squealed.

"Finally, a man named Luigi Bezzera created a high-pressure machine to make a finer grind. Now each customer enjoys a freshly made cup of expresso."

"I like mine with cream," Daniel said.

"A cappuccino!" Hannah said. Such a kitchen.

She followed Mathilde up the stairs to the first-floor landing, a sitting room with comfortable sofas and a thick rug. They walked down the hall and into a room adorned with a brass 14.

Mathilde explained there were three floors of rooms in the longer left wing. "In the shorter right wing, the two floors above the restaurant and kitchens are reserved for the family." She gave Hannah a poke. "I suspect you'll be living there one day."

Hannah blanched, not at all ready for that.

"Anyway, Andreas' grandfather was one of nine children. The top floor of the long wing was divided into tiny little rooms where he lived with his siblings alongside the servants. Those rooms are bigger now. They are less expensive, but even the shared bathrooms are really very nice."

Hannah's family didn't have indoor plumbing at their farm, and in Moosfeld, only the owners of *Der Wachauerhof, Gasthaus Renner,* and a few homes of the well-to-do could afford to install it.

Hannah imagined guests drowning in coziness; the wallpaper of tiny red roses, the lovely, carved oak armoire, a vase of fresh flowers on the writing table. She patted what had to be the plumpest comforter in Austria, where little Chopin was taking a nap. With all these luxuries, the warmest quilt on your bed, a toilet in your room, and the superb food downstairs, Hannah couldn't imagine how once the guests checked in, the Brandls were able to get them out.

Mathilde removed Chopin from the bed, and he darted under it. Together, they stripped and remade it with clean, soft linens. Bed making, Hannah thought, this she could do.

"Frau Marti," Hannah said.

"Why don't we skip ahead to Tilda and Hannah."

Hannah smiled. "I'd love to. But I'm curious about Daniel's pantry. How does he know that *pfirsisch* comes before *pflaume*?"

"We assume he simply goes through the alphabet again with the second letter, and so on. No one knows for sure. It's his system, and pity the person who mixes them up. That's almost the only time you will see him really flustered."

"He has a contagious smile."

"Every part of him is contagious." They walked into room 15, where Mathilde fluffed pillows and inspected flower pots. "Daniel is the youngest of four Reiter children that grew up above the bakery. Closest to him is Elke, the girl who married Gerhard Eigner a few months ago. Gerhard wants to be the next mayor of St. Jakob, which doesn't mean much. Several hundred people and the chickens."

"And at least one big white horse," Hannah said.

"You're 18, right? Daniel is your age. Elke is a year older. Willi Reiter is two years older than Elke. He's the quiet one. Wears *lederhosen* while he works in the bakery. The oldest is Veronika. Their parents were Heinrich and Lotte Reiter, may God rest their souls. They were kind to a fault, gave away more bread than they sold."

So, Hannah thought, Sebastien learned generosity from the coalition between his father and the bakers next door.

"Poor Lotte died when Veronika was thirteen. Heinrich had to rely on her to watch over her siblings when he was working in the bakery. But four years later, Heinrich died. Veronika found him, cold and stiff—you could hear her shrieking all over town. But between you and me, Hannah, it wasn't grief that laid her flat. It was the prospect of running the bakery."

"She was so young."

"When I think of what those children lost when Lotte died, and then Heinrich. Maybe it was too much to ask of a seventeen-year-old, but Veronika had Willi and Elke. She ordered them to come straight home from school to work in the bakery so that she could be free to run around town in a new dress and flirt with the boys. When Veronika informed Willi he didn't need to go to school, Andi had to set her straight."

"What about Daniel?"

Mathilde frowned. "Can you imagine that sweet boy being kept in a closet when Sebastien and Georg came into the bakery?"

"That's terrible," Hannah said.

"Eventually, Andreas taught him to handle the dishes and gave him a job. Later, the perfect rows of plates and jam jars—that's all Daniel's doing."

"So he has a place here, where he knows he's needed."

"Yes. But Veronika dismisses Daniel's amazing organizational skill, and says Andreas feels sorry for him."

Nowhere is perfect, Hannah reminded herself. Just as *Der Wachauerhof* had Viktor Lonauer, *Grünen Baum* had Veronika next door.

Moving to the family wing, Mathilde showed her the three spacious apartments, even warmer and cozier than the guest rooms. A delightful sunporch with a long window seat lined with plush pillows and shelves full of unorganized books and toys awaited grandchildren. A rocking horse swayed next to the open window. A child's sink held sponges and a full can of paintbrushes.

She followed Mathilde down the hall. "Andreas lives in one apartment, and Sebastien lives at the end. The third one is for Hubert, but sadly, he's rarely here."

"Sebastien misses him," Hannah said.

"We all do."

Hours later, twilight had descended, and Hannah was glad to find a moment to sit down. Her last lesson had been about the magnificent wood, added gradually by a succession of ancestors. The oldest wood had been milled long ago from other structures in surrounding towns, floated down the Danube, and lugged uphill on wagons and shoulders. Mathilde told her that the cypress, which looked like gold and olive-green honeycombs, was dragged out of the river after aging underwater for a century.

Hannah shook her head. She would never learn all of this. She sat basking in the latent warmth of the *wintergarten*, wondering what she had done to deserve this change in fortune.

# 9

Hannah didn't know Sebastien was in the room until the lights went off. She sensed him walking toward her. He pulled her in and feasted on her lips, urging her mouth to open so he could touch his tongue to hers. In the seductive darkness, she lost herself in him.

He was the one to pull back. "Hannah," he said ruggedly. "We have to go."

She pulled herself together. "I'll get my coat."

He took her hand and walked her across the restaurant. Andreas called from the *kochecke*. "Sebastien! We're waiting for you."

Sebastien tugged her down the hall. Hannah's eyes went wide. Not only her father, but her mother was there, surrounded by Mathilde, Tobias, Gerhard and a woman Hannah assumed was his wife, Elke. She looked back at Sebastien. "Surprise," he said softly.

She glanced down at the smudges on her dress and the rings under her arms. She wasn't dressed for a party. Coming in from the back door, Daniel and his brother Willi carried two bread baskets stuffed with fresh rolls, an enormous rye loaf and thick pretzels, still warm. Daniel hugged her. Willi said hello and sat down on the banquette, where he would smile and only occasionally converse for the rest of the night.

They greeted Hannah like she was finally back where she belonged. A table twice as long as the one in their kitchen was surrounded by banquettes with padded pillows and bronze button tacks and a random collection of wood chairs. Elke slid in and pulled Hannah down beside her.

Andreas and Mathilde set out platters of cold meats and cheeses. Georg Wangermann introduced himself to Bernard and Sophie. He brought with him what would be Hannah's first taste of red wine, three bottles of a special blend of *Blaufränkisch* and Cabernet Sauvignon. Andreas bragged Georg was one of a limited number of vintners in Austria successfully creating blends of red grapes. "He won't tell how he does it."

All Hannah knew was the wine went over her taste buds and down her throat so smoothly she emptied two glasses before the first toast. Sebastien did most of the salutes; to Hannah, to her father, to his father, to everyone else, and finally, to Apfel. Into her third glass, Hannah giddily declared she, too, would make a toast.

She wobbled to her feet. "To...pretzels."

A cheer went up. "Pretzels!"

"And cheese! And butter!" Daniel added.

"To cheese and butter!" The table shook with pounding fists and an explosion of laughter.

"We have guests upstairs," Andreas chided, but his cheeks, too, had turned a merry red.

In time, the elders at the party succumbed to yawning. "Carry on," Andreas exclaimed as he waved from the stairs. After embracing both Sebastien and Hannah, Mathilde and Tobias said their goodbyes.

Sebastien gave Bernard a little bow. "I know it's getting late, Herr Maislinger, but I would be honored to bring Hannah home."

Bernard sighed. "Only days ago, I'm struggling to convince Hannah that you are some ruffian she only thinks she loves, and a moment later you are charming my wife and we are looking at a horse." He kissed Hannah and took Sophie's hand to leave.

Sebastien walked a reluctant Daniel home to the bakery. When he returned, he settled down with Gerhard and Georg for a discussion of food and wine, not unusual topics, and left Elke and Hannah to learn about each other. Though married to Gerhard now, Elke still worked at *Bäckerei Crème* with her brother Willi, and her sister, Veronika, but she was rarely around. Gerhard was nineteen when he went to work selling Wangermann wine. As

Sebastien told her when they met, he had left Georg to become an independent wine dealer.

"Gerhard could sell a bottle of wine to Apfel, Elke laughed." She leaned into Hannah. "Daniel likes you. He told me, 'Hannah's beautiful, but I'm taller.'"

"I'm used to that. But Daniel is the beautiful one."

"My brother is proof of angels." They drank to Daniel. "I couldn't wait for us to meet, Hannah. I've heard nice things about you."

"Uh-oh."

Elke's laugh, Hannah noticed, lit up her entire face, her light brown waves swishing across her shoulders.

"Anyway, when they were younger, Sebastien, Gerhard, and Georg made serious mischief. Not everyone in the village appreciated their capers, especially *Herr* Haas, the postmaster.

Daniel had already reported to Hannah that he read all the village mail.

"He lives above the mail room with his two cats and a suspicious stamp collection. Years ago, he built a wall around the post office. People had to ring a bell to be allowed in. Sebi and Gerhard painted it purple in the middle of the night. Haas was so angry he took an ax to it. The town secretly applauded them."

"What about Georg?" Hannah laughed.

"He was their silent partner."

Hannah looked around the room and sighed wistfully. "I could do this every night."

"You will. Almost every evening Andreas and Sebastien sit right here while people start arriving. Georg brings the wine. I've been here with the four of us, but you'd be surprised how many times there's a dozen of us around this booth."

"Do you have a favorite story?" Hannah asked.

"Oh, yes. Sebastien told me they needed my help with a doomed litter of puppies in a farmer's barn. Rumor had it he was planning to put them in a grain sack with some heavy rocks and throw them into the pond."

"No!"

"Georg made a plan to abduct them late at night. The farmer was here at the bar most evenings. Thank goodness, because we made quite a commotion. The barn door squeaked horribly when we rolled it open, and the mother, whose name was Flocki, barked at us while we corralled the puppies.

"What did you do with them?"

"Sebastien stashed them in a corner of the bakery cellar and put me in charge. I was proud to have been given such an important job, until I figured out stealing five puppies was nothing compared to taking care of them. I was up all night feeding them with an eyedropper and cleaning up puppy dung."

"Oh, dear," Hannah said, "what did you say to the boys?"

"I told them to go back and get the mother."

"What about the farmer?"

"He came into the bakery complaining his dog was missing, never suspecting at that moment Flocki was enjoying *Grünen Baum* leftovers with her offspring. After five weeks the puppies were weaned and given away, and Sebastien put Flocki back." The next day the farmer decreed his dog had miraculously returned."

Georg retired for the night, and while the women chatted, Sebastien and Gerhard did the dishes. Hannah kept an eye on them, marveling.

"I know," Elke said softly. "Many times, it's the two of them chatting with dishtowels in their hands."

Hannah shook her head. "Things are making a lot more sense."

# 10

Veronika Reiter slithered into Hannah's life while Mathilde was teaching her to make *Grünen Baum*'s special potato salad.

"*Güten Morgen*, Veronika," Mathilde said, vigorously chopping parsley. "This is Hannah Maislinger." She winked at her. "Our new cook."

Hannah winced and looked around for Daniel, who a moment ago had been fussing with his jams.

"This is Veronika Reiter from *Bäckerei Crème*," Mathilde continued pleasantly. "You've already met her younger brothers and sister."

Veronika frowned, obviously displeased to have missed something. "Whatever did you do to lose your job at *Der Wachauerhof*? Viktor told me it was best you moved on."

"You must have misunderstood," Mathilde said while Hannah was trying to coax a sound from her throat. "She left him to work for us, and we're lucky to have her."

"I'm pleased to finally meet you," Hannah said shakily.

Sebastien walked in and dropped an enormous box of cabbage on the counter. "Good morning, Veronika," he said. "Did you meet Hannah? I stole her from Viktor Ratzener."

"I heard he was about to fire her," Veronika countered, and moved to stand in front of Sebastien, gazing up into his eyes. "Could I speak to you about something, privately?"

"Of course," Sebastien said. "Would you like some coffee?"

"That would be nice." Veronika brought a box from behind her back. "Your favorite lemon crème tart."

"I can't wait," Sebastien said, ushering her out of the kitchen.

"Could she be more obvious?" Mathilde muttered.

Hannah didn't know what to make of Veronika. She was pretty, with a high forehead, deep-set eyes and high cheekbones. She held herself erect, like a statue come to life, regally attired for the middle of the day in a velvet green dress with a lace collar. This woman had made a deliberate demonstration of intimacy with the man for whom Hannah recently abandoned a predictable life.

"What was that all about?" Mathilde demanded when Sebastien returned to the kitchen after being in Veronika's company for almost an hour. He walked over and wrapped an arm around Hannah's shoulder.

"Nothing," he said, looking down into her eyes. "Absolutely nothing."

By November, Veronika had exposed several other sour sides. She was often disagreeable toward anyone she considered beneath her, whether it be the young woman serving her dinner or the farmer delivering her butter and eggs. Elke said Veronika loved Daniel, although she struggled to show it. Hannah had witnessed moments of concern for her younger brother that seemed sincere, albeit overbearing. Her tone turned nasty when he showed the least amount bit of resistance.

Lately, Daniel had become more vocal about wanting to stay later at *Grünen Baum*. "I have work in the kitchen," he told Veronika when she came to retrieve him.

"Daniel dear, I'm sure you're in the way."

"I'm not in the way," he pouted. "I'm the captain."

"Don't be silly," Veronika said, taking him by the arm. Her brother shrugged her off. Veronika glanced at Andreas, Mathilde, Hannah and two cooks witnessing Daniel's rebellion. "I'm sorry for this disruption."

"I beg your pardon, Veronika," Andreas replied. "Your concern for him is commendable, but rest assured, he performs a valuable service for our restaurant."

Veronika hastily rearranged herself. "Is my brother being paid?"

"We've tried to pay him," Mathilde offered. "But he won't take the money. We've found his wages left all over the Inn."

"As his legal guardian, I will collect his wages and make sure his money is safe."

With that, Daniel perked up. "That's a good idea, Andi. You can pay Veronika because I don't need any money."

"Well then," Veronika said, "that's taken care of." Their exit from the kitchen was peaceful enough, but once outside the door, they could hear her berating Daniel.

"But he doesn't want to be Herr Brandl," they heard him say before their voices grew faint. "He wants to be Andi."

After a few weeks, Hannah was sufficiently exposed to the wiles of Veronika to ask Sebastien about her.

"Her parents, Lotte and Heinrich, were good friends to Papa and Mutti. They gave Hubert and I sweets when Mutti wasn't looking. When they found a rare evening to come to *Grünen Baum*, they never saw a bill. As children, we were always running back and forth between the inn and the bakery.

It was difficult for Hannah to imagine Veronika as a lighthearted child.

"Heinrich found Daniel pulling at his mother, lying dead on the floor, begging her to get up. For a long time, Daniel continued to wait for Lotte to wake him up in the morning. Every day, Heinrich had to coax him down to breakfast."

"How sad," Hannah said.

"When Heinrich died, everyone offered to help Veronika, and she didn't turn them down. Anything to get out of the bakery and have a moment where she could still be a pretty, flirty girl."

"Did it work?"

Sebastien gave her a quick kiss. "Never on me. But I suppose she turned other heads. She made it sound like working in the bakery was drudgery. We felt sorry for her. But she was already teaching Willi and Elke all the recipes, and how to take orders and make sales. Within two years she gave over the running of a bakery to a fourteen-year-old and his ten-year-old sister. She ignored the fact that even with Daniel's limitations, he was growing and revealing talents no one knew he had. Did you know he's a wizard with numbers?"

"Hmm. Not yet."

"Anyway, Veronika wanted credit for caring for her brother, but she also wanted to be seen as a martyr for doing it. She doesn't want him to be different. To this day she thinks she can badger him into being, as she puts it, 'less odd.'"

"But he's interesting, and so lovable."

"Wait," Sebastien said. "I'm lovable, too."

•    •    •    •    •

Hannah had thought she would help with the housecleaning, but Sebastien had other plans. He had her taking orders, serving and cleaning tables. The diners began to greet her by name, and he told her she was attracting new customers.

"I'm feeling guilty," she said as a busy Sunday afternoon finally wound down, "Isn't it my turn to work upstairs?"

"She's training two more maids to do it all. We want Tilda in the kitchen, and you belong here, with me."

She pondered this: A stranger from Moosfeld. Snatched from the convent door. The new girl who skipped cleaning bathrooms and went straight to serving. Sebastien's choice for a girlfriend, despite the plans of the cadre of indignant mothers of village daughters. She had probably displeased a lot more people than Veronika.

It felt like everyone in town stopped into *Grünen Baum* at least once a day, if only to say hello to Andreas, Sebastien, or Mathilde, or any of the staff. A friend of a bartender got a little cognac after his meal. The girl who helped with the ironing was thrilled to invite her mother in for coffee and fresh spice cake. If Andreas and Sebastien missed their employees' guests, they assured them, "Next time, we'll all sit down for a glass of wine together."

One day, Tomas the Fiddler, in charge of soup and stews, stopped stirring to dance Hannah around as she went by juggling her orders.

"How tall are you, anyway?" he asked, smiling.

Her brow knitted.

"Just curious. There's nothing wrong with short."

"I'm at least 1.6 meters."

"That's 5 feet, one inch," Daniel said. "In America."

Hannah rifled through her stack again. "I'm pretty sure we need nine bowls of goulash."

Tomas sighed. "Somebody sees the special coming to the next table and they have to have it."

Hannah could hardly believe each menu item was available all day and into the night. Different from *Der Wachauerhof*, where *weiner schnitzel*, or *kaiserschmarren*, a fluffy dessert omelet, could not be served before *mittagessen*. At *Grünen Baum*, there were plenty of regulars who wanted a cutlet or a big pancake for breakfast.

Periodically Viktor ventured over to St. Jakob, usually when his brother Faber was in town, to have a meal, often with Gerhard Eigner, which tested the Brandl commitment to equitable hospitality.

Eavesdropping, Hannah heard Faber boasting about his unprecedented rise in the Party. He was already a *stabsscharführer*, a senior officer in the Austrian SS in Vienna. He and his brother criticized the new Austrian chancellor, Kurt von Schuschnigg, for urging Mussolini to support an independent Austria.

Sebastien materialized at their table. "Mussolini hasn't noticed that Hitler has designs on Italy," he said gravely.

"Seb," Gerhard said, holding up a roll. "More butter?"

Faber pressed Gerhard to join the Party. "As the mayor of St. Jakob, it's expected. And get your friend Sebastien to join too. It would be good for business."

Sebastien dumped a silver serving plate of butter in front of Gerhard. "I suggest," he said to his old friend, "we make our own party."

"Still thirsty?" Hannah croaked.

Faber stood and turned his hostile gaze on her. "We're finished here."

As Hannah stacked their plates and glasses on a tray, Viktor lay a hand on hers and brought his mouth to her ear, so close, she shuttered to think he might lick it. "You should have stayed," he whispered. "Better food," he jerked his head towards Sebastien. "Less delusion."

Disconcerted, Hannah followed Sebastien into the little office he shared with his father. A cozy room between the restaurant kitchen and the *kochecke,* it had a small, messy booth they used for their desk and shelves sagging with cookbooks and ledgers.

He started kissing her immediately, and she forgot all about Viktor, or anything else. Sebastien and this extraordinary place threatened to lull her into permanent bliss.

He did what he could to court Hannah properly. One morning Hannah awoke to her mother's cry of delight, having found an enormous bouquet of roses on their doorstep. "They're exquisite," Sophie gushed, laying them in her daughter's arms as she arrived at the bottom of the stairs.

"They're excessive," Bernard growled from the breakfast table.

Hannah wasn't sure the heavily laden stems were properly purchased from the flower truck. She set out on foot to share them, passing by beekeepers tending tiny hives that looked like they belonged in a children's garden. Siegi received them with two wailing infants in her arms. The mother Abbess, who had accepted her defection graciously, assured her Greta would be first to enjoy the stunning bouquet.

Her father had one request. "No *stubbing!*"

*Stubbing* involved a young man on a ladder in the middle of the night to knock at the window of the woman he is courting. If she opens the window, it is a sign she accepts his attention. Siegi's suitors all had terrible voices, and twice, yielding their biggest pot and a stick from the wood box by the fireplace, Bernard ran outside in his nightclothes and scared them away.

·　　·　　·　　·　　·

Sebastien was in a hurry. In early November, Hannah was walking down the hall into the restaurant, balancing four plates for the first time. Concentrating, she didn't see him until he blocked her way.

"Sebastien!" she cried. "You're going to be wearing pork gravy!"

He took two of the plates. "Hannah Maislinger," he said quietly, "Will you marry me?"

What?

"You don't look too steady." He rearranged her plates deftly on one arm and leaned in. "My dearest love, will you be my wife?"

Hannah finally spoke. "Did you ask Papa?"

One by one he returned the plates to her arms, assuring her patiently Bernard Maislinger had, indeed, given him his blessing.

In a daze, she continued down the hall.

"Hannah?" Sebastien called after her.

"Yes," she said, not looking back. He let out a wild whoop.

Elke and Siegi wanted details. "I admit I was stunned," Hannah told them.

"Why?" Siegi asked, plopped in a chair in the *kochecke* while Daniel chased a squealing Ernst, and Anke and Juliane competed for her tired breasts.

Elke laughed. "The entire Wachau Valley knows Sebastien Brandl is determined to marry Hannah Maislinger."

"He asked me in a hallway."

"True. Even though he's so in love with you he can't make change, I suppose you could have expected a more romantic setting. Have you decided on a wedding date?"

"It's only been twenty minutes."

Sebastien planned a meeting with *Pfarrer* Niko for the next day. He suggested they marry on May 4, the feast of St. Niko, patron saint of Upper Austria and chimney sweeps.

Sebastien frowned and snuck a peek at Niko's prayer book. "How about St. Clemens Maria Hofbauer, the patron saint of Vienna? March 15."

Let's see," Niko said, flipping through the pages, Sebastien peering over his shoulder.

"What's that one," Sebastien said, pointing.

"February 15. St. Liutberger, a woman of great intellect, who refused to be impeded by what some called 'the imbecility of her sex.'"

Hannah laughed. "That might be perfect."

"Keep going," Sebastien said.

"January 28? St Joseph Freinademetz, a fine missionary in China. No? Ah, here's one I like. This would be the perfect day for your wedding. January 15. St. Romedius, the patron saint of bears!"

Sebastien nodded happily. "That would be enough time, wouldn't it Hannah?" he asked, as if it suddenly occurred to him to him a wedding needed some amount of preparation.

"Not really."

Niko clapped his hands and reached for a bottle on the sideboard. "Shall we toast the day?" he said after pouring three glasses of brandy.

Sebastien took Hannah's hand and said, "Go ahead, *schatz*, you make the toast."

She smiled and raised her glass. "To the feast of St. Stephen. Unfortunately, he was stoned to death. But he was a fervent Christian."

"Yes, he was indeed," Niko said with a wink.

Sebastien mouthed his question. "When?"

"December 26," the priest said gaily.

The brandy went down like sweet cream.

# 11

Sophie was beside herself. "Seven weeks. And who gets married the day after Christmas?"

Their wedding would be unusual, and not only because they were both from out of town. As a compromise, they would marry in the church in Moosfeld and hold the wedding celebration at *Grünen Baum*. Hannah and Sebastien hoped this would make everyone happy, but it provoked endless discussion in both towns during the entire month of December. The Moosfelders couldn't understand why the daughter of Bernard Maislinger, who had once been the *Bürgermeister,* decided *Der Wachauerhof* or *Gasthaus Brenner* weren't good enough for the wedding dinner. Hannah suspected most of them wouldn't turn down the better food at *Grünen Baum.*

As more information leaked from the Maislinger farm, the couple's transgressions mounted. Both sets of guests complained that because freezing temperatures were predicted, they would have to drive between the two towns. Why hadn't they waited until the spring, when everyone would enjoy a pleasant stroll to St. Jakob?

All the grumbling was upsetting for Sophie, but Bernard said people were incredibly silly and didn't have enough to talk about. But would people still come? Hannah imagined her mother's worried face as she studied the church pews for those who weren't there.

Sebastien kept inviting everyone he ran into, no matter how remotely he knew them. When the guest list had doubled in size, Hannah told him for the fourth time to stop. "If the Church fills up, the latecomers can't stand outside in the cold, Sebastien. And at *Grünen Baum*, the crowd won't be spilling into the garden."

But Sebastien had only one genuine concern. He wanted Hubert to be beside him when he married. His brother wrote he would arrive from Vienna early on Christmas Eve. Hannah would be home with her family, and would have to wait until she walked into the Church for her first glimpse of Hubert Brandl.

"You'll get to know him on our wedding trip, liebchen," Sebastien assured her. They were going to Vienna, and Hubert's *Café Hawelke* was on the itinerary.

Hannah wore her happiness like a cozy sweater. Christmas eve finally arrived. But when Bernard solemnly declared this was Hannah's last night as her father's daughter, her mood unraveled. Then, everyone came at once. Jumping in and out of their grandparents' laps, the children opened their gifts. Hannah and Siegi finished preparing a *gulhupf,* the original version of a raisin and almond-filled cake that, according to Sophie, Marie Antoinette stole from Austria to take to France. Wedding custom demanded the priest receive a cake as a gift from the bridesmaids, but Niko suggested they share it with him the night before. Yet another custom re-arranged momentarily silenced Hannah's parents.

"Why not?" Niko laughed while he shook the snow off his coat. "We've invited two towns to cooperate and like it, Hannah has a married bridesmaid, and you'll help me devour this divine *Gulhupf* on Christmas night. All is as it should be."

•　　•　　•　　•　　•

The children had fallen asleep on Bernard and Sophie's bed. The men remained at the table with a bottle of *schnaps* while Siegi and her mother followed Hannah to her room upstairs.

Even before the door was closed, Siegi became the voice of experience. "How much do you know, little sister?"

"Only what I've picked up from you, Sieglinde," Hannah retorted, pulling clothes from her small armoire and tossing them randomly toward an open satchel. In twenty-four hours, she would be alone in a hotel with a man.

"The first thing is, it hurts."

Ignoring her daughters, Sophie took up the job of organizing the jumble on the bed. For the next twenty minutes, they assembled Hannah's trousseau: three dresses, one new and the others perfectly presentable, a sweater, a new white woolen nightgown, her nicest underclothes, heavy stockings because it would be cold in Vienna, and a new pair of warm boots.

Suddenly, Sophie spoke. "I just laid there the first time. I thought if I didn't move, I couldn't do anything wrong."

"Oh yes," Siegi said. "You're lucky Sebastien has experience. Otto fumbled around like a blind man playing darts."

Hannah snapped the satchel shut and dumped it on the floor. "Thank you. I feel fully prepared. Let's go down and have some of Papa's cherry *schnaps*."

She was first into the kitchen. The decidedly male conversation came to an abrupt halt when she helped herself to the bottle.

"Prost," she said, taking a long swallow.

Not needing much encouragement after several bottles of wine and half of *the schnaps*, they shouted their response just as the women joined them. "Prost!"

"Oh!" Sophie said, putting her hand over her heart.

"Oh yes," Siegi laughed, and continued to fill Hannah's glass, until her nervousness blurred and vanished.

•　　•　　•　　•　　•

The next morning, the snow melted as the temperature climbed. Continuing to ignore tradition, it had been decided Bernard, Sophie and Siegi would bring Hannah to the Registry Office in Dürnstein for the secular ceremony and then deliver her to the church in Moosfeld, where she would change into her dress in the baptistry. But catastrophe struck. The Office was closed. Bernard got out of the car to read the hastily scrawled note tacked to the door. They would re-open at two o'clock. No explanation was offered.

"We had an appointment," Hannah moaned when Bernard told her the news. "They can't just leave, can they?"

Sebastien's truck pulled up. The groom sat between Georg, who was driving, and Niko, who invited himself to come along even though he should be in the church preparing for the ceremony. He rolled down the window as Bernard approached.

From the back-seat Hannah saw the door fly open, the priest tumble out, and Sebastien take off toward the registry door. He pulled off the sign, threw it on the ground, and stomped on it with his foot.

In the front seat, Sophie said, "Oh, my."

Bernard, with Niko's help, grabbed the gesturing, cursing Sebastien, and steered him away from his bride. A long conversation ensued. Finally, Niko got Sebastien back into the truck. Georg started the engine and roared away while Bernard walked back to them.

"Papa's smiling," Siegi reported, patting Hannah's hand.

"Why?" she sniffled. "The most important day of my life is never going to happen." Sophie and Siegi turned away. "This isn't funny!"

"I know, dear," Sophie said, reaching back to console her youngest daughter. "But I will never forget Sebastien stomping his foot."

"He massacred that piece of paper," Siegi said.

Bernard got in the car and clapped his gloved hands together. "Don't cry, *Schätchen*. It's good news. *Pfarrer* Schönfeld decided it would be all right to have the church ceremony first, then the wedding dinner, and then Hubert and Siegi can bring you here for the civil ceremony and be your witnesses. He will direct them to stay open."

Sophie was instantly alarmed. "Has that ever been done?"

"Calm down, Sophie. First of all, *Pfarrer* Schönfeld said that just because the order of the day had been rearranged, it doesn't mean the marriage would be any less proper. He also said we might choose not to mention the new procedure."

The bride gasped. "Someone is sure to find out!"

"If it's Veronika," Siegi said, "Everyone will know before we arrive at the church."

"You're not helping, Siegalinde," Bernard said sternly.

Sophie grabbed some fabric from her dress and twisted it into a clump. "Sebastien is missing his wedding breakfast."

"He'll be there to walk with his friends to the Church."

"He's probably too upset to eat anyway, Siegi said.

"Enough!" Hannah cried. "Papa, turn the car on. We need to get to Moosfeld. Mutti, stop that, you're ruining your dress." Sophie made a frantic attempt to smooth out the wrinkles.

Sebastien had suggested Bernard walk his daughter down the aisle, an American custom he had seen in a movie. Bernard, who had given up on convention early on, was delighted, and Niko assured Sophie that Hannah on her father's arm would not invalidate the marriage.

Siegi started down the aisle, and in the back of the Church, Hannah glued herself to her father. He gently loosened her grip as they took their first steps toward the altar. Daniel leaned out of his row and waved wildly until Veronika, looking annoyed at yet another unorthodox decision made by the attention-hungry couple, pulled him back. On the other side, Finn Binder stood smirking.

What finally cleared her mind was the sight of Mathilde and Tobias, holding hands and staring into each other's eyes. Sebastien, who had worn his wedding coat over a white shirt to the Registry Office, had added a shimmering vest with green taffeta panels embroidered with a gold-threaded jacquard stag and circlets of fauna. Like the sun meeting a blanket of dew, the space between them evaporated. Happy tears trickled down both their cheeks, and Bernard was hardly any better. Hannah gave her handkerchief to her father and Siegi pressed the wrinkles out of hers before handing it to Hannah, who passed it to Sebastien. A wave of warm laughter rippled across the rows of guests.

A tall version of Andreas smiled down at Hannah. Hubert, Sebastien's beloved brother, with a striking handlebar mustache. His eyes danced, warm and accepting. They repeated their vows, blessed her wedding ring, and were proclaimed a married couple. The Nuptial Mass continued. As they knelt together, closer than was customary, Sebastien brazenly took his new bride's hand.

"People are watching," she whispered, but he didn't let go. The feel of his hand mesmerized her, especially when she gently squeezed, and he squeezed back. Their fingers entwined and moved against each other, as if in intimate conversation. Beneath her dress, intense sensations rose. Sebastien was staring straight ahead. They released each other only when Niko approached them with communion.

•     •     •     •     •

*Grünen Baum* was gloriously decorated. On every table, at Sebastien's bequest, bowls of forbidden *edelweiß* lay like creampuffs on green embroidered runners over dazzling white table cloths. *Burgermeister* Gerhard had assured Sophie there would be no arrests during the wedding.

After the bridal waltz, played by a single violin, Sebastien and Hannah sat down on gold chairs, their backs to the brilliant winter sun streaming through the *wintergarten*. Hannah's nieces and nephew took up residence under their table. Musicians from both villages and led by Tomas, brought out their accordions, two cellos, a bass and more violins, and a similarly integrated choir of children sang folk songs to the bride and groom.

Spoons tapping on glasses sprinkled through the crowd, and they kissed, several times. Their guests toasted them lustily. Sebastien whispered, "Can we leave now?"

"I don't think so." Hannah had to smile at Sebastien's eagerness to abandon the party, make the stop in Dürnstein, and begin their wedding trip to Vienna. Despite her simmering anxiety, the idea of being finally and legally alone thrilled her.

The dancing was spirited and merry. Having thrown off his wedding coat, Sebastien swung his wife around the dance floor until they were both panting. Slowing down to waltz, Sebastien pointed out Veronika, standing next to Georg and Hubert, who were deep in conversation. "She wants one of them to ask her to dance," Sebastien said. "Hopefully they'll catch on."

"Still here?" Gerhard teased Sebastien when he and Elke danced by.

Eventually, Georg allowed Veronika to pull him onto the dance floor. She laughed at something Georg said, which startled Hannah, to see for the first time the smiling, unburdened girl well hidden under the resentful, lonely woman. Meanwhile, Bernard danced with Sophie, whose worries had been replaced by wedding euphoria.

Emerging from the crowd came Gerhard, along with Viktor Lonauer, who was there because Bernard had felt obligated to include him with the other guests from Moosfeld. Both mayors walked up to them.

"So, Brandl," Viktor said, "you've got yourself a wife. She's rather unique, don't you think?"

"She's a rare jewel."

"I mean the way she looks."

"Extraordinarily beautiful," Sebastien said evenly.

Viktor bent down to Hannah. "My brother Faber has been talking about you. Your hair is somewhat red and curly. Your skin isn't like most Aryans." He looked sideways at Sebastien. "Are you sure you didn't get a Jewish bride?"

Sebastien jumped up and poked his finger into Viktor's chest. "Did Hitler teach you to hate? Get out of my wedding."

Viktor laughed. "A little tip, Brandl. You should have invited Faber. You wouldn't want someone in his position feeling left out."

"Auburn is not red," Hannah said as she took her scowling new husband's arm. "Do you think I look Jewish?"

"The way you look is one of the things that made me leap into Lonauer's kitchen. You're a sparkling treasure, Hannah. He's the school bully."

Back on the dance floor, he twirled her madly while a large circle of clapping guests gleefully cheered them on. As the song ended, Sebastien dipped her down for a sound kiss, lifted her into his arms and carried her off. For many days to come, the event would be the talk of two towns.

# 12

With the wedding certificate finally secured, Hubert and Siegi dropped the newlyweds off in Krems to board the train to Vienna. Arriving at the *Hüteledorf* Station, they took the Vienna City Railway into the city center. From there, satchels in hand, they strolled down *Marc-Aurel Straße,* a wide street lined with raised cobblestone sidewalks, toward the Danube. They passed a group of women in stylish two-piece wool suits, their hair styled in bobs.

"Maybe I should cut my hair," Hannah commented.

"That's a good idea," Sebastien said. "You complain about how much time it takes to untangle."

Hannah hesitated. "You want me to cut my hair?"

"I want whatever you want."

They passed a chimney sweep. "Touch him, Hannah, its good luck." The man, covered with dirty black streaks and ashes that floated off of him as he walked, waited until she touched his coat, and they all grinned at each other.

Quickly coming into view was the magnificent *Hotel Metropole*, which had opened in April 1873 in time for the World Exposition. While Hannah admired the immense portico and marble columns, Sebastien tugged her up the steps. They walked through heavy, blue-carved doors into the hotel lobby court, easily the most opulent room Hannah had ever seen.

"Sebastien," she whispered. "What are we doing here?"

"We're getting a key."

"We can't afford this, can we?"

"I sold my motorcycle. Wait until you see the dining room."

So this was not the first time her new husband had been in this hotel.

"Reservation for Brandl," Sebastien said, pulling off his cap and smiling broadly at the clerk. A porter picked up their bags, gave them a little bow and said, "Right this way, Herr Brandl, Frau Brandl."

"Such sweet words," Sebastien whispered.

Hannah had never been in an elevator, and her stomach lurched as they ascended to the third floor. The porter set down their luggage in their room. Hannah gawked and had to stop herself from jumping up and down. "Is there anything else I can do for you?" he asked, impervious to her delight.

Sebastien reached in his pocket for a few coins and showed the porter to the door.

Hannah twirled over to plop down on the bed, then speedily abandoned it for the plush red divan next to a gold coffee table with a glass top etched in flowers. Sebastien came to her, pulled her up into an embrace, tipped her chin and kissed her deeply.

He pulled back. "Hmm," he said, "why don't we change our clothes and go down to dinner? Are you hungry?"

She wasn't at all hungry, but she would force something down, if only to flee this room and its bed.

Sebastien took off his wedding coat and laid it on the back of the chair. He started to take off his trousers, but the look on Hannah's face stopped him. "Would you feel more comfortable changing your clothes in the bathroom?"

Hannah threw open her satchel, grabbed the dress on top and hurried across the room. At the door, she came to an abrupt halt. The bathroom was tiled in purple, with a lavender sink, toilet and tub, and a bidet, which Siegi had assured her would be handy. Huge white towels as thick as pillows sat folded on a rolling cart.

"Come see this, Sebastien," she said without thinking. He appeared, shirtless. "Touch this towel. How do they make them so soft?"

"Magic. Do you need help getting out of that dress?"

"Oh," she said, suddenly realizing she did.

"Turn around." He began to undo twenty-four tiny pearl buttons. Hannah stood silently as Sebastien slowly made his way down her back, his fingers working each button through its heavily threaded loop. The last button was well below her waistline and when he was done, she was trembling.

Sebastien gave her neck a nuzzle. "Don't take too long."

The dining room glowed. Between the chandeliers, the glasses, the silverware, the candles, and the mirrors, dazzling light reflected back and forth across the room in soft lines and patterns. Fussing white-gloved servers darted about and Hannah wondered aloud if each table had its own. The orchestra was dressed in white, playing a Mozart waltz.

""Would you like me to order?" Sebastien asked his befuddled bride.

The first course was a plate of Liptauer cheese with fresh rolls and *Powidl*, a sweet jam made from plums. Next came roast duck and braised rabbit. Hannah was so mesmerized, Sebastien had to remind his bride to eat.

The perfect finale was *apfelstrudel*, and they ate it slowly with the last of their wine. They danced only one dance, and when it ended, Sebastien took his wife's hand and walked her to the elevator.

Time to be a wife.

•　　•　　•　　•　　•

Hannah changed into her nightgown in the bathroom. Sebastien waited by the door for her to emerge, gathered her into a sensual embrace and poked his tongue into her mouth. She stiffened.

He immediately drew back. "I'm sorry. That was a terrible way to begin our first night together."

"It's fine."

"No, it's not. Can we start again?" He took her hand and led her to the bed, where he pulled her into his lap. His eyes traveled down her body. "Beautiful," he whispered hoarsely.

His kisses were gentle, moving across her face like firelight on a wall. His hand cupped the back of her head and his fingers played with her hair. After a few delicious moments, he lifted her to her feet and pulled down the plush down comforter. He took his time drawing away her nightgown. Hannah shivered.

"Are you cold?"

She shook her head.

Slowly, delicately, he pulled off her undergarments, and when he had finished, looked into her eyes. She returned his gaze while he lowered her onto the bed and lay down beside her.

He made circles around her breasts with his fingers. When a cry of pleasure escaped her, he smiled encouragingly. His mouth hovered over her nipple and again his eyes met hers with a silent question.

Hardly believing what he was about to do, Hannah nodded. As he feasted, her body throbbed.

"Are you all right? Am I hurting you?"

"No, I've just never felt," she gulped in air, "this way."

He smiled. "Give me one minute." He removed his clothes, seemingly in one motion, and they were naked, together. She didn't feel embarrassed, as Siegi warned her she would. Instead, she felt their union eternally sealed. No one else would ever again be part of this moment, nor lie next to this man.

He sank down on top of her and Hannah eagerly met his tongue with hers. He ran his hands down her sides, reached under her to knead her bottom, then caressed his way back to her breasts. Hannah could only tighten her hold on him, aching with desire. Eventually, Sebastien came up on his knees and placed his hands on the inside of her legs. She opened. Tenderly, his hand brushed over the wetness between them. She writhed beneath his fingers. He entered her gently, pushed through in a quick motion, and waited.

She closed her eyes, absorbing the sting. They lay unmoving until Hannah began to feel the swell of pleasure returning. "Sebastien," she breathed into his chest. Rhythmically, he probed more deeply. Waves of passion overtook her as they rocked and she heard herself cry out. They rose together, shuttered, and sank into the bed, still entwined. Sharing a blissful, dreamless sleep, sometime during the night they separated.

They woke before dawn, "Mmm," Sebastien said, wasting no time for a kiss. Hannah pulled him to her, and it was enchantingly unhurried, and pain free.

•    •    •    •    •

Hannah opened her eyes. Nine o'clock and still in the arms of her new husband. She smiled at the decadence of it all. About lovemaking, her sisters had left out so much. She giggled at the preposterous difference between a convent cell and their wedding bed.

"And what is so funny this morning," Sebastien said, planting kisses all over her face.

"I'm really glad I didn't go to the Abbey."

"As am I," Sebastien roared, and rolled her around the bed. "Let's get dressed. We've got a big day ahead of us."

The big day began with *Hotel Metropole's* lavish breakfast buffet. They filled their plates with eggs, smoked bacon and cut sausages and ate as if it had been days. As soon as they sat back, an efficient young woman whisked their plates away, and they filled new plates with Muesli, tomatoes as sweet as those from the Maislinger farm, olives and pickled herring.

"Indulgent," Hannah said guiltily.

He squeezed a cherry crepe onto his crowded plate. "Delectable."

A server came by. "*Kapuziner?*"

His mouth full, Sebastien nodded.

Hannah was deep in thought. "Did you know cappuccino got its name from the Capuchin monks?"

"Tell me. I can't wait."

"St. Francis inspired the wearing of robes. Later the different orders chose their color and shape. The Capuchins chose reddish brown. Whoever thought to put the cream on top of the coffee called it a *kapuziner*.

He turned to the couple at the next table. "And this remarkable woman is mine." The man winked at Sebastien. The woman waved at Hannah.

The weather in Vienna was warm enough for people to be out walking. Exultant children darted around them as they ambled along in no particular direction. They walked by chestnut vendors with strips of cardboard on their shoes to keep them warm. Women wearing babushkas selling flowers out of enormous round baskets. Families in traditional Austrian style suits and dresses, covered by heavy knit sweaters and green jackets. Dormant arbors, glistening with snowflakes and icicles. On the Danube, men rowing long canoes, oblivious to the scattering of ice chunks across the water. Next to a long line of streetcars, plodding slowly on the cobblestones, a horse-drawn milk truck.

They boarded a streetcar. A large group of stocky, unsmiling women holding their bags from the *Naschmarkt*, lined up on the bench across from them.

"Are they the *Straßenbahn Frauen*?" Hannah whispered. She had heard of these stern matrons, perpetually angry at the world.

"Yes," Sebastien said. "We seem to have a whole flock of them along for our ride."

They ended up in the old Greek Quarter, and Sebastien led her into *Der Griechenbeisl*, an old and inviting *brasserie*.

"I can't believe I'm hungry," Hannah laughed.

"We expended a lot of energy last night."

Marriage was nothing like she imagined.

Inside, they wound through nooks with low ceilings and warm yellow light and arrived at an odd shaped room with writing all over the walls. "Welcome to *Griechenbeisl*," a young man said, breathless with enthusiasm, "the oldest restaurant in Vienna, first mentioned in the registry in 1447." He handed them menus. "Beer?"

Sebastien nodded and he hurried off. "There's some dispute about that," Sebastien whispered, leaning over the table, "Another restaurant, *Gösser Bierklinik,* makes the same claim. 1406. *Griechenbeisl* argues *Gösser Bierklinik* wasn't a restaurant until 1683."

The beer arrived and they ordered. "Famous people ate here," Hannah remarked. "It's on the menu. Beethoven, Shubert, Wagner, Strauss, Brahms," she recited. "Look Sebastien," she pointed behind him. "There are autographs on the wall. "Who's Mark Twain?"

"He's American. I read *Huckleberry Finn.*, He was a rogue, like me," he grinned.

A trouble-maker. Hannah felt a sliver of worry, which she instantly dismissed.

They dined on roast pork and sauerkraut, and groaned when offered dessert.

"I can't," Hannah said.

"Good. Save room for coffee and cake." Sebastien paused and brought out the pocket watch she had given him as a wedding present. "In two and a half hours."

Back at the *Metropole*, they lay side by side on top of their silky down comforter for a nap. Hannah stared at the ornate ceiling while minutes ticked by. She didn't want to sleep; she wanted her husband. Beside her, she heard a soft snore.

What had gotten into her? Hannah hoped she wasn't becoming a loose woman.

It was dark when they arrived at the *Sacher Hotel*, famous for its *sacher torte*, brimming with Opera-goers wearing lavish evening clothes. Later, they would later walk down the street to enjoy *La Boehme* being performed in Vienna's *Staatsoper*, the famed opera house and symphony hall.

Waiting to be seated, Hannah watched, fascinated, as a woman in a coat made of several minks circling her neck greeted a man in tails, white tie and top hat.

"Look, Sebastien," she whispered. "I feel sorry for those little minks."

"It's all right. They're going to the Opera."

The harried host approached them. "All of our tables are filled."

"We only want coffee and *sacher torte*," Sebastien told him.

"Then would you mind sitting over here?" He led them toward the back of the room where one of the blue velvet couches was empty.

"This is perfect," Sebastien said. They sat down, and he promptly pulled his wife toward him. "It wouldn't be right to take up the whole couch."

"Incorrigible," Hannah sighed, marveling at how sapphire blue couches blended smoothly into a room with forest green walls.

He nuzzled her neck. "You know what I love about being married to you?"

She smiled. "Tell me."

"For a long time, I've been one. Just one. Now I'm two."

"Two," she repeated, melting inside.

The noise rose dramatically They ate slowly, taking in the production unfolding before them.. They were scraping the crumbs off their plates when at precisely the same time, most of the patrons left for the Opera House. "There must be a secret signal, " Sebastien said, and ordered wine.

Warm and heady, they ventured into the cold night. Now and then the odd snowflake settled on their coats. At the *Chriskindlmarkt* in front of City Hall, they bought little gifts for Siegi's children and drank hot wine punch, eventually stumbling happily back to the hotel.

Sebastien started kissing her in the elevator.

"What are we doing?" she mumbled.

"Isn't this what elevators are for?"

Sebastien started shedding his clothes before the door was fully closed. Hannah stood transfixed, watching her husband of two days leave a trail of garments as he crossed to the bed. He turned and grinned at her, wearing only his stockings.

"What's wrong," he said. "Am I going too fast?"

She began to unbutton her dress.

Sebastien pulled off his socks and tossed them over his head. "I think you need some help."

Her dress, and then her undergarments, landed on the ground. Hannah purred with delicious anticipation of what this night, and all their nights, would be like.

# 13

*Vienna, Austria, December 28, 1934*

They slept in. Hannah was again in awe when she peered at the clock next to the bed. Sebastien opened one eye and groaned.

At noon, they were finally out of the hotel and wandering down the *Mariahilfer Straße*, clogged with exuberant shoppers. Beggars, young and old, slept in doorways. One woman in a ragged, dirty dress and no coat sat with her head down on the side of the uneven cobblestone street. The trembling child huddled in her lap held a cracked bowl. Pedestrians skirted around them.

Sebastien crouched next to the woman. "A schilling for each of you," he said, offering two coins to the child, who burrowed her head into her mother's bosom. Hannah winced, so palpable was the woman's embarrassment.

They were almost at *Café Hawelke* to meet Hubert when three young men stumbled out of a seamy-looking bar and blocked their path.

The biggest one, bearded and dressed in a jacket with animal horn buttons, confronted Sebastien. "*Heil* Hitler," he said, flapping his arm. He lurched toward Hannah. "We'll take some of this."

Sebastien lurched into him, nose-to-nose. "Not if you value your face." Hannah watched her new husband's mouth clench shut and his body square off, barely in control.

"Heil Hitler," the bearded sod repeated.

"No," Sebastien said. "Damn him to hell."

*Muschi*!" the animal-horn man growled.

After a tense stare down, Sebastien allowed himself to be away. "Bastard. He called me a pussy. I could have broken every bone in his face."

"He might have been talking about me."

He stopped and stared at her. She shrugged.

While they walked, Hannah fretted. Who is this man I married? Beneath his lust for life, something else smoldered.

· · · · ·

*Café Hawelke* was the lovechild of Leopold and Josephine Hawelke. It had become a meeting place for writers, artists, and musicians, as well as a few political oddballs, as Leopold liked to call the Nazi enthusiasts. A rosy-red-cheeked woman who seemed to know who they were seated Hannah and Sebastien, declared she was quite fond of Sebastien's big brother, and would they like a newspaper? She gave them a wooden pole with the daily paper attached that took up most of the table. An enormous hat tree loomed over Hannah, its branches laden with coats and scarves. Customers sauntered in and sat wherever they found an open chair.

Hannah didn't see anyone eating anything but dark rye bread, butter and Swiss cheese. The bar, however, was well-stocked. Customers and servers juggled each other to reach for drinks. An old radio played a scratchy polka. A nearby sign on the wall read: *Dogs stay on the floor without exception*! Hubert greeted them warmly.

"This must be the only place where Viennese share tables," Sebastien remarked.

"It's different," Hubert agreed. His lanky frame settled into a chair. The air was thick with the smell of strong coffee and cigarettes. Hannah marveled at the lace curtains, still white despite their daily saturation of smoke. On the far side of the room, people were mere silhouettes through the haze.

"People can become specters here, hiding in the gray mist," Hubert commented.

"Sing to her, brother," Sebastien prompted.

"Ah yes." Hubert cleared his throat and began lustily, '*There is a naked man sitting in the Hawelke...*"

Hannah clapped delightedly and waited for more.

He twirled his mustache. "That's the only line I know. But I think it's the most important one."

The woman, who turned out to be Josephine Hawelke, brought beer, the bread, butter and cheese, and bowls of steaming lentil soup. While they ate, Hubert told funny stories about Sebastien as a child. "He was always running to Mutti with a new scratch or scrape, and twice, a broken arm."

"I was curious," Sebastien explained, "I liked to explore."

"You were foolhardy and pesky," Hubert countered. He waved at a man dressed in a suit with a red bowtie and introduced them to Leopold Hawelke, who winked at Hubert and said, "Shall I bring it now?"

Sebastien's brother had stashed an exquisite bottle of red wine, *Winzertal Zwiegelt*, in the kitchen pantry. He said he had received it from the renowned Viennese wine master Maximillian Mayr, who frequented *Café Hawelke.* They had become friends.

Leopold opened it. The newlyweds took their first sips, and stared into their glasses as if they had tasted gold.

"I think this is the smoothest wine I've ever tasted," Sebastien exclaimed. "Georg has been growing red grapes for a while, but it was the white grape that made him rich."

"The best red wine in Austria," Leopold declared. "Herr Mayr is a genius."

"I've never met him," Sebastien said. Between his father and Georg Wangermann, he had been introduced to many premier winemakers.

"Would you like to?" Hubert asked, eyes twinkling. Across the room, a fit-looking man with light brown hair, chiseled features, and signs of having spent a great deal of time in the sun, sat in a booth. He was dressed in a white shirt and green tie, a charcoal-colored wool jacket, and heavy grey trousers. He smiled at them from above his newspaper. Hubert stood up and opened his arms. "Come meet my family!"

The man picked up his chair and carried it to their table.

"Max," Hubert beamed, "this is my vagabond, mediocre-cook brother Sebastien and his much more acceptable new wife, Hannah."

"Thrilled to meet you," he said, shaking both of their hands and squeezing in between Hannah and Hubert.

"I feel the same, Herr Mayr," Sebastien said. "We live next to *Winegut Maria Theresia*, but its owner says you are Austria's wine king."

"My dear friend Georg Wangermann," he said, "has no business being humble."

"When you're together, do you argue not about the best wine, but the second-best wine?"

He laughed. "I don't see George enough. Can we be Max and Sebastien, please? As a child, I visited *Gasthaus Zum Grünen Baum* with my family. You, too, have nothing to be humble about."

Josephine reappeared bearing a pan of savory-smelling rolls. "I saved you my *Buchteln,*" she told Hubert, giving his arm a squeeze. Every child in Austria loved these sweet yeast rolls filled with jam. Still warm, she pulled them apart, set them on plates and topped them with vanilla sauce. She leaned toward Hannah. "I have my own secret recipe."

"They certainly smell good," Hannah said, glancing around, wondering if anyone resented their special treatment.

From the café's mudroom, a man and woman with dirt-streaked faces and worn, dangerously thin coats peered in, a baby fussing in her arms. Just as quickly, they retreated into the cold.

"I'll be back," Hubert said, and went after them. After a brief conversation, the family followed Hubert around the side of the café.

When he returned, Max asked, "Where did you put them?"

"In a nice warm corner, eating Goulash."

"Does this happen a lot?" Sebastien asked.

"More and more often. I try to make them comfortable. And out of Leo's way," he added under his breath. "He fears we'll soon be feeding half the city from our back door."

"Poverty has risen significantly in Vienna," Max frowned, and glanced at Hubert.

"You can trust them," he said. "Especially Hannah."

"Thank you," she said, giving her husband a sweet smile.

Max lowered his voice but kept a pleasant look on his face. "The number of beggars is going up as more people join the Party. They actually believe the National Socialist propaganda about the exciting new German economy that Hitler could bring to Austria."

"How does that make more people poor?" Hannah asked.

"That's a good question, one that should be in the mind of every otherwise decent man and woman in Vienna. The problem is the NS preach prosperity based on separating the unworthy from the worthy. Talk of Aryan purity used to come up here and there, but most Viennese dismissed it as irrelevant. Now, I can hardly go anywhere without hearing Jews being blamed for someone's store losing money or their property's sinking value because they live next door. The newest poor are Jews."

"National Socialism is poisoning us!" Sebastien said bitterly. "What I don't understand is why more Austrians don't feel the venom entering their veins."

"Keep your voice down," Hubert warned. "I know our café looks harmless, but you never know who's sitting at the next table, taking all of this in."

Hannah clasped her hands in her lap.

'I'm sorry," Sebastien whispered, "but sometimes I feel so angry I want to go out in the street and scream at my neighbors to wake up."

Max nodded. "I understand your frustration. But I'm sorry for introducing ugliness into this wonderful gathering. We can talk about something else." He turned to Hannah, "Did you visit the *Staatsoper*?"

"We saw the people all dressed up, waiting to go inside," she said, relaxing somewhat.

"And you didn't follow them?"

"We've been busy. Eating, mostly."

"Have you heard a recording of the Viennese Symphony?"

"On the phonograph. To hear them in person would be thrilling."

Max sat back and sighed. "More and more I feel the need for Viennese music and the Opera to feed my soul, and be reminded of the beauty of Austria."

"That's a thought," Sebastien mused. "All those who have joined the Party might regain their sanity if they listened to Austrian music instead of German pomposity."

They turned to easier conversation, about the gigantic Prader Ferris wheel, which needed a facelift, horse racing, and, of course, wine.

Hubert stood up. "Don't go away."

Max regarded Sebastien. "You must miss your brother."

"I fear Hubert will make Vienna his permanent home."

"But don't you think he'd be less comfortable in a little town where everyone knows everyone else's business?"

Hubert rejoined them, dressed in black pants, white shirt, waistcoat and tie.

"You look like a movie star," Hannah said.

He swirled around. "Am I dapper? I've always wanted to be dapper."

"Hubert," she paused, but only momentarily, "did my husband ever bring another woman here?"

Hubert looked at Sebastien, who looked at the floor. Max tried not to laugh.

"Let me say this. A few girls got in the door but I invited only one to stay."

Sebastien gave his brother the eye. "Totally forgotten."

"Give me a moment," Max said and trotted out the door.

"I like him," Sebastien said to Hubert. "I'm going to stop worrying about you being lonely."

"He didn't talk about his family," Hannah commented.

"He never does," Hubert said. Max returned with two bottles of wine and snow sprinkled on his head and shoulders. "I'm not sure why I went outside without my coat," he laughed. "This time with you has been a wonderful distraction." He presented the wine. "A wedding gift. St. Laurent. I hope you like it."

"Thank you," Sebastien said. "I'm sure we'll enjoy every drop."

Max again gathered the couple's hands into his. "Stay well, and safe." He hooked his arm with Hubert's. "And you. Don't spill anything."

Sebastien hugged his brother at the door. "Max seems to think Vienna suits you."

"I'm happy enough," Hubert agreed. "You never know. Life is fleeting and unpredictable. But for now, I'm content."

Sebastien and Hannah walked quickly through a solid curtain of snowflakes. They were almost back to the Metropole when she said, "Sebastien, does it make you sad that Hubert would rather be in Vienna than St. Jakob?"

"It's as if something holds him here."

"Yes," Hannah agreed. "What Max said…it almost sounded like St. Jakob could somehow do him harm." She suddenly realized that even Sebastien knew little about Hubert's Viennese life. They had squandered an opportunity to learn more.

Later, when they went to bed, she snuggled next to her husband and studied his unsmiling face. "What are you thinking?" she asked.

"Oh Hannah, thoughts unfit for a honeymoon. I'm tired, though, aren't you?"

He was soon asleep. It took Hannah much longer. An hour later, just as she began to doze, Sebastien sighed, mumbled her name, and tightened his arm around her. Fully awake, she turned her head. His eyes were an inch from her own.

"What are you doing?" she whispered.

"I'm looking at the most exquisite woman in the world." He kissed her mouth softly, and then abruptly rolled away from her and out of bed. "Come with me."

Hannah followed him across the room to the long, plush divan." He drew open the heavy blue drapes and sat beside her. Outside, the snow had stopped. They looked back down the street toward the canal. Lights sparkled across the water, where two boats passed each other, gently rocking back and forth, nodding a greeting.

Sebastien took her in his arms and kissed her, his ardor intensifying as he leaned her back.

"Sebastien," Hannah murmured. "People can see us."

"No one cares."

They made love leisurely at first, allowing the fire to rise. They drew out each pulse of pleasure, and their shared climax lasted a sublimely long time. Sebastien finally carried her back to bed. His mouth moved sensually, lingering on her neck, and finally encircling her breast, toying with her nipple, sucking tenderly, until he let it go to begin on the other. Hannah stirred against him, aroused once more. Sebastien finally pulled back, raised himself up on his elbows, and waited for his bride to open her eyes.

"What?" she whispered, stroking his face.

"I want more of you," he said, his voice course. She felt the flutter of his tongue across her skin, moving down her body. She tensed, and he stopped short of his destination.

Was this permitted? Desire beat back reason. "Yes," she breathed.

He nuzzled into her soft mound of curly auburn hair. When his tongue met her most delicate spot, she cried out. She squirmed against him, lost in a frenzy of joy and aching, until she pulled him up and into her in one smooth motion of brilliant release.

Hours later, nestled together, arms and legs still perfectly mingled, Hannah came awake to a moment of resolution. Even if what had happened between them was wrong, she would never take it into the confessional. Satisfied with herself, she returned to sleep.

The next morning, the scent of melancholy filled their room as they packed. Before the wedding, Hannah fantasized about what it would be like at *Grünen Baum*, when Fraulein Maislinger reappeared as Frau Brandl. She would soon find out.

# Part 2

*"A tragic section of life, acted to perfection,*
*Drew rave reviews and a standing ovation."*
**–Mary Lou Kownacki, OSB**

# 14

***Kahlenbergerdorf, January, 1935***

Maximillian Mayr sat at his desk, smiling at Hubert's bottle of Georg Wangermann's wine. His friend knew how to needle him.

Reluctantly, he turned back to his stacks of inventories and shipping schedules. Like most wineries, *Schloß Winzertal* had been in his family for many generations. The tiny town of Kahlenbergerdorf was nestled in a narrow valley on the west side of the Danube, where viticulture could be traced back 2500 years. Above the village, Maximillian Mayr's immense property stretched over rolling hills to forested ridges connecting to the Vienna Woods. Blessed with rich soil, it was perfect for many varietals.

He let the phone ring several times before he sat back and answered. He knew who it was. "What have you got for me, Fritz?"

Max met Fritz Tollner at a meeting of winemakers in Berlin years before. He was surprised, and disturbed, when Tollner told him he had been hired to work in Hitler's Chancellery offices in Berlin.

"Wait," Tollner said. "Somebody walked in. I'll tell you later."

"Tell me now," Max insisted.

"You have no idea the danger you put me in."

Max sighed. Their phone conversations had fallen into a frustrating pattern. Tollner called, and then panicked, leaving Max to coerce a word or two out of him.

"All right, call me back."

"Okay, okay. The Olympic Games. Hitler is calling it 'his stage.'"

"It's a pity they're in Berlin. He'll get a lot of attention."

"But listen to this. The plan is to take down the anti-Semite signs and clean up the detention centers, and then open them up for people to view happy, well-fed prisoners."

"Are you saying Jews will be temporarily tolerated?"

"It will still be an Aryan team, Max. No Jewish blood allowed. And they will examine each athlete's family to see if they have shown opposition to the Third Reich, or if they have non-Aryan friends."

Max almost laughed. "Does he realize other countries will bring non-Aryans?"

"He says they won't be allowed to win."

"He's not in control, my friend."

"You don't get it, Max. Ever since his SS wiped out the SA leaders, and any opposition he could find and drag out into the streets, Berliners suspect their own family members."

The SA, *Sturmabteilung*, the storm detachment, were thugs with brown uniforms who made up the original paramilitary of the National Socialist Party. Without them and their talent for unpredictable violence, Hitler might never have pillaged his way to power. But once he was chancellor, the *Schutzstaffel*, or SS, emerged as his favored corps of walking lethal weapons.

Tollner's next words were barely above a whisper. "There were hundreds of official murders all over Berlin. We walked around asking each other, 'are you still among the living?'"

"So what color are the SS uniforms?" Max asked.

Tollner missed the sarcasm. "Black. Hugo Boss designed them. Himmler makes each SS officer pledge unconditional allegiance."

"Himmler is that powerful?"

"He's Hitler's private secretary. He controls access."

"But you are Himmler's private secretary, Fritz. How much information slides over your desk?"

"What are you asking?"

"Austria. What is his plan?"

"Hell, I can't do this. Don't call me again"

"You called me."

"*Gott verdammt*, Max... If anyone learned I'm telling party secrets to a non-sympathetic Austrian..."

"Calm down. We're old friends. And now I'm your confessor."

# 15

*St. Jakob, 1936*

Over a year had passed, and Hannah was not yet pregnant. As it happened, neither was her new best friend, Gerhard's wife, Elke.

Then, in early spring, just as the blossoms were popping and the utter greenness of everything covered the land with anticipation of a wealth of crops, Hannah's time to bleed went by. Her breasts hurt. She had always skipped the perfunctory afternoon nap, but now she craved a few minutes on the couch as the restaurant emptied after *mittagessen*.

"Let's not tell anyone yet," she suggested to Sebastien.

"I was going to put a sign over the bar."

"I want to speak to Elke first."

"Ah, I hadn't thought of that."

If Elke was upset, she hid it well. Hannah hugged her. "When I tell my sister, Siegi will start sewing despite herself, and Papa will fight with Sebastien about who's going to construct the cradle."

The midwife, Frau Steinbrenner, confirmed Hannah was "quite pregnant" and due in December. The news the Brandls were expecting flew through the town with tornado-like fury.

The rise of temperatures in May promised that the summer would be hotter than usual. Sebastien and Andreas brought the winter's load of ice up from the cellar and installed it in the iceboxes and fruit cupboard. Sebastien returned from a shopping trip to Krems with two ceiling fans featuring brass-finished motors, wooden blades and fixtures of frosted glass. He and Tomas mounted them in the restaurant and kitchen.

The staff was delighted. "Flies don't like our fan," Daniel observed as they studied the blur of the blades. Sebastien also bought a table fan for the *kochecke* and made Hannah sit in front of it.

Andreas suggested Sebastien take half of Sunday and every Monday off. By the end of June, when Hannah's appetite made a hearty return, they spent Sunday evenings with Georg and *Pfarrer* Niko at *Winegut Maria Theresia*. His villa, though traditionally Austrian, was uniquely open-aired, with an enormous veranda spanning the entire front of the thick wooden-planked structure. They sat outside and savored the hypnotic view of endless rows of grapes and the Danube beyond. At dusk, Georg shepherded them inside to listen to the radio.

Hitler had taken over German Radio. Every broadcast was a marching band of carefully constructed propaganda. Afterwards, they stewed together. Sebastien protested the surge of pro-Third Reich voices at the inn. Georg, in his frequent dealings with the wine community in Vienna, and Niko, in his correspondence with fellow clerics, agreed many ordinary Austrians were falling under Hitler's spell. It was clear most Austrians hadn't noticed Germany re-inventing itself into a predatory threat.

Meanwhile, the glow of sunset over the vines was magnificent. After several radio nights, Hannah begged off, saying she enjoyed staying outside in the cooler air.

"I've been missing you," Sebastien remarked one evening during their ten-minute walk home.

"Why would you want our baby to hear that voice?"

Sebastien stopped and caught her arm.

She spit out her feelings. "Sometimes I wish I didn't know what's happening, but you and your friends and that radio have made sure I do."

"I assumed you wanted to be with us, keeping up to date."

"Hitler. It's always about Hitler. *Pfarrer* Niko says he's sweeping people up like dead flies."

"The bloody *Fuhrer* doesn't care about St. Jakob, *liebchen*." He pressed his face to hers. "We're safe."

They went straight to bed. Sebastien's passion for her inflamed her senses and dulled her mind. It wasn't until morning, after he had gone downstairs to open the restaurant, that her thoughts drifted to the previous night. She believed Sebastien would protect them. But considering the mounting enthusiasm for Hitler, what did it mean that others knew he vehemently disagreed?

In the weeks that followed, Sebastien, Georg and Niko made lighter conversation around Hannah, which tempered her worry. Their daily routine was solid, and their friendships surely unbreakable.

Sebastien suggested they go to a movie in Krems. The American film, *King Kong,* had finally come to Austria, and he thought it might be a welcome diversion for his wife. By the next day, a group had formed. Sebastien and Hannah rode with Gerhard and Elke. Georg took Niko, Daniel, and as they were leaving, Veronika.

"I was informed about the outing only this evening," she huffed. "Luckily, I had no other engagements." She re-assigned the men to the back seat and climbed in next to Georg.

On the way, an uncomfortable conversation in Gerhard's car developed around Hitler's plans to build a stadium for 400,000 spectators for the Summer Olympics. Sebastien thought it was ridiculous, and Hannah wondered if it was even possible. Gerhard argued that Germany was becoming more tolerant, because anti-Jewish propaganda had been removed.

"But what will happen when the world goes home?" Elke asked.

Afterwards, they exited the movie house in great spirits, except for Daniel, who was in tears over the terrible death of King Kong. "He just wanted the beautiful lady."

'It's pretend, Daniel," Sebastien said.

"They shot bullets at him and he fell off the building!"

Veronika, holding on to Georg's arm as if she needed help walking, dismissed Daniel's distress. "He can't understand any of it," she said. "We shouldn't have brought him."

Hannah grimaced. No, we shouldn't have brought you.

Returning to *Grünen Baum*, they found the bar in an uproar and Andreas sprinting back and forth behind it. "How was the movie?" He called out.

"Wonderful," Sebastien said.

Herr Haas, the short, skinny postmaster with a forehead and teeth too big for his face, rolled off his stool and walked toward them. Elke had told Hannah that despite barely over thirty, he was already a curmudgeon. "Happy to hear you're all coming around."

"We went to see *King Kong*," Georg said. "It's hardly a political statement."

Haas, whose first name, coincidentally, was Adolf, gave them a haughty smirk. "King Kong is *Der Fuhrer's* favorite film."

The smiles left their faces. Finally, Daniel piped up. "It would have been better if Hitler had been on the building and the planes had shot him and made him fall off."

Veronika grabbed her brother by the arm. "Don't say things like that," she hissed, pulling him toward the door, muttering to Herr Haas, "He's not right, you know." Elke hurried after her sister, fire in her eyes. Gerhard shrugged and followed them out.

Sebastien and Georg raised their glasses.

"To Daniel."

•　　•　　•　　•　　•

On Christmas day, the baby was a week late, and Hannah was miserable. Andreas and Sebastien offered to host her entire family at *Grünen Baum*. The commotion of Christmas dinner and more gifts to open sufficiently distracted the mother-to-be. It was almost midnight when they fell into bed.

"Thank you for sorting out the day. I didn't want to miss Christmas, but the thought of having to visit my parents' toilet so often, I mean, it's outside. I'm spoiled."

Sebastien chuckled. "A disaster avoided."

Only an hour later, Hannah felt the need to get up. After one step, a gush of water ran down her legs and spread across the floor.

"Sebastien!" she shouted.

He bolted out of bed. "What?"

"I'm all wet," Hannah said.

"Did you, uh, not make it to the toilet, *liebchen?*"

"I've already been to the toilet!"

Without a word Sebastien flew down the stairs, on his way to the post office and the town's only phone.

"Shouldn't you get dressed?" Hannah asked the empty room, and then fetched an armload of towels for herself and the floor.

When Frau Steinbrenner arrived, she told Sebastien to go away while she settled Hannah in to wait for her labor to start. Still breathing hard, he announced, "we're getting a telephone."

Night turned into day. Andreas closed the restaurant, so Mathilde delivered breakfast to the guest bedrooms. Sophie arrived and offered to help the midwife, which soothed Hannah considerably. Sebastien was again shooed out, her mother explaining to him that pacing up and down and scowling did not make the baby come faster.

Eleven hours after the flood on the floor, Hannah delivered a little girl. The new father waited patiently outside their bedroom while Frau Steinbrenner made Hannah clean and comfortable in a fresh nightgown, her new daughter in her arms. Sebastien tiptoed to her side. "My two beauties," Sebastien declared.

Hannah moved over to make room for her husband. "Happy Anniversary."

"Oh," Sebastien said, having forgotten Christmas Day was long over. He slid onto the bed and put his arms around both of them. They stared at their daughter's peaceful pink face, rosebud lips, and tiny tuffs of light hair.

"What shall we name her?" Hannah whispered.

"You convinced me it was going to be a boy."

"You convinced you."

"How about Gabriele?"

"Couldn't we go with Maria, or Louisa? Something a little more normal?"

Chopin slipped in, jumped on the bed, and was introduced to the baby, followed by Bernard and Sophie. "We couldn't wait any longer!" They said together.

"Is she ready for viewing?" Bernard asked anxiously. Sebastien placed the infant into Sophie's arms. Another knock, and Niko's voice came from behind the door. "Is it too soon?" He peeked in.

Sophie held her up. "Here she is."

"Splendid," he exclaimed. "What's her name?" Sebastien and Hannah exchanged what Niko interpreted as a lukewarm look. "Oh. Is there a difference of opinion?"

"I don't know," Hannah reached for her husband's hand. "Maybe not."

Sebastien sighed happily. "Her name is Gabriele."

Hannah's parents were only momentarily stunned. "A grand name," Bernard said.

While Sebastien took a short break to re-open the restaurant, Elke sat at her friend's side, watching the new mother's first attempts to nurse her newborn. "She's getting it," she said encouragingly

Hannah gave her a sad smile. I'm so happy, but I wish...."

"You can be happy for me, too."

"Really? Hannah cried, making her daughter start. Both women leaned over her, cooing and caressing her tiny cheeks. Gabriele opened her mouth and again found her mother's breast. Her eyes fluttered closed.

Two weeks later, Gabriele Brandl was baptized in the little church in St. Jakob. Hubert came for the day, and joined Siegi as proud godparents. Afterwards, everyone stood outside and gossiped about the baby's name.

# 16

*Kahlenbergerdorf, February, 1937*

Outside Max's office door, sixteen-year-old Stefan Mayr heard a chair scrape across the floor. He backed down the hall, but not quickly enough.

"Stefan. Have you been eavesdropping again?"

"I was just about to knock!"

Max ushered his son back into his home office at *Schloß Winzertal*. He had another office in the winery itself, and one in Vienna. But this was where he liked to retreat, thanks to the creative touches of his wife, Lili; a comfortable couch with deep green pillows, matching chairs and a low table in front of the fireplace. Above the mantle she hung a large painting of two young boys at play in a field of flowers.

Max had been shocked when she unveiled it years before. The likenesses were astounding. The older boy, Michel, would grow up to be was the shorter of the two, solid in stature and with wavy dark brown hair. His younger brother, Stefan, was tall with lighter hair. Michel had inherited the features of his mother's family, and Stefan, his father's.

In the twenty-one years they had been married, Lili had brightened each one of their seventeen rooms. Their home was an imposing, yet exquisite, alpine chateau made of the finest woods and supported by an unyielding stone foundation. Six steps proceeded the front door to the living and dining areas, a music room, Lili's library and Max's office. There were also six steps up to the back door into the kitchen, clearly the favored entrance.

Settled onto the couch, Max put his arm around his son. "What's the matter, schatz?"

"He came looking for you again. I told him you were in Vienna on business."

"I assume we are talking about Klaus Kolbe?"

"The one who acts like he's your friend."

"Not quite." Max sighed. "I knew him as a capable police officer, but he was ambitious, joined the Party, and before long he was Deputy Chief."

"Why doesn't he wear a uniform?"

"Because," Max said, unsure of how much to tell his son, "He has a new job. He's part of the Austrian SS. Technically, it's a protection squadron."

"I don't want them protecting us."

"Names are sometimes meant to confuse, Stefan, and it's becoming dangerous to oppose him out loud." Max gently kneaded his son's head with his fist. "We think before we speak."

"Kolbe is our enemy, Papa, like Hitler."

"Are you listening, Stefan? For now, we must pretend."

"Like a spy," Stefan brightened. "So we can learn things from the enemy." Stefan's favorite books were *The Prisoner of Zenda, The Scarlett Pimpernel*, and every spy novel by the English writer, Edgar Wallace.

Max considered his son. "You listen well on the sly. You can melt into draperies and closet corners. You breathe very quietly. But promise me you'll run to the winery next time Kolbe comes and let me handle him."

Stefan scowled. Apparently, his father was aware of his furtive talents.

"What are you two up to?" Lili Mayr, with her pretty face and subdued smile, clad in one of her pastel dirndls and white blouses she wore to her bookstore, stood in the doorway.

# 17

*St Jakob, July, 1937*

In July, Siegi insisted that the twins' birthday party be at *Grünen Baum*. There would be no talk of National Socialism. Anke and Juliane sat on the lawn in the *biergarten* surrounded by a mound of gifts, which Gabi helped them open in less than five minutes.

The party was quieting down and little Benno Eigner, only a week old, needed to be fed. The men took the children, Elke carried Benno upstairs, and Mathilde joined Hannah and Siegi in the *kochecke*.

"Did you see Veronika shove Gerhard aside so she could sit next to Georg?" Siegi began. "She's finally realized Sebastien is permanently taken, and moved on to his best friend."

Hannah was aghast. "Veronika and Georg?"

"She's right," Mathilde agreed. "While you were busy being pregnant, Veronika started appearing whenever Georg came to see Sebastien."

Siegi snorted. "She hides out in the forest until he walks by."

Hannah stared at both of them. "But he's so...nice."

"Exactly, "Siegi said. "What's that obnoxious cow doing with such a prince of a man?"

"It's strange," Mathilde mused.

Sebastien entered the kitchen. All conversation ceased. "What's going on? Silence between you three is not normal. Especially you, Siegi." He reached for his daughter.

"Have you noticed anything odd between Veronika and Georg?" Hannah asked him.

"Just that she has this uncanny way of knowing when he's here."

"I knew it!" Siegi said. "She hiding in the trees."

"Siegi suggested Veronika is after him," Hannah explained.

Sebastien laughed. "I don't think so." The baby burped, and milk ran out the corners of her mouth. Tenderly, he brushed her lips with his finger. "Georg isn't interested in Veronika."

"We choose you to ask him," Mathilde said. Hannah and Siegi nodded eagerly.

"He'll say I'm a fool."

"Let's go investigate what she's doing," Mathilde said.

Siegi let out a whoop. "You're right, Tilda. We need to check on poor Georg."

"We'll rescue him," Hannah agreed.

"We might have to use force."

Mathilde's eyes narrowed. "That won't be a problem." They headed for the door.

"I never allow fisticuffs in the dining room," Sebastien explained to his daughter.

•　　•　　•　　•　　•

Late one evening, while Daniel reorganized the family pantry, Sebastien, Hannah and Georg discussed romantic movies.

"American films are the best for kissing," Sebastien concluded.

The pantry forgotten, Daniel rushed to join them at the table.

"I loved *An American in Paris*, " Hannah giggled. "But we need more research."

Daniel puckered his lips and leaned toward Hannah.

"She's taken," Sebastien scolded. Just then, Veronika burst into the *kochecke*, her face red with her usual fluster. "Daniel! What are you doing here?"

"Kissing."

"We're talking about kissing," Hannah clarified. "In movies."

Veronika shifted gears. "Maybe we could all go to that new American movie, *Top Hat*."

She sidled up to Georg. "Fred Astaire and Ginger Rodgers, and plenty of kissing."

"That might be nice," he said.

She winked at Georg. "Maybe just the two of us?"

After she left, Sebastien grabbed another bottle of wine. "What's going on, Georg? But please wait until I open this to tell me."

Georg emptied his glass in one gulp. "She's not so bad," he said quietly. "I think it would be good for me to get married, and I don't think she'll bother me too much. Planning parties for *Maria Theresia* will keep her busy."

"I can't believe what I'm hearing. Marriage? You could have any woman. Why her?"

"She's lonely. I guess I am too."

"That's not a reason to get married." Hannah said sternly.

"Do I need to remind you how rich you are?" Sebastien barked.

"If she only wants me for my money," Georg said crossly," I won't have to pay attention to her at all."

"Why would you want to marry someone you don't want to spend time with?"

"It's better this way. People will stop pestering me, and Veronika will liven up the winery."

Sebastien shot his last arrow. "She's using you to get out of the bakery for good."

Georg stood. "Be on my side, please." He left them to nurse their disapproval.

Sebastien and Hannah lay staring at the ceiling. "I don't get it," Hannah said.

"Neither do I. Georg is the most reasonable man I know. I don't know what to do. I don't think she will ruin him, but she can do a lot of damage."

"She'll hurt his business?"

"Worse. She'll wound his soul."

# 18

*Kahlenbergerdorf, August, 1937*

Max and Lili Mayr ran through a light snowfall across the expansive courtyard between their chateau and the winery. They entered a large wood-paneled room. Behind the bar, multiple rows of wine glasses twinkled under strings of tiny lights. Heavy beams supported a peaked ceiling painted in pastels and depicting idyllic mountain scenes. Ten long wood tables were festively set with blue checked tablecloths and white napkins in anticipation of a party the following night. In the adjoining kitchen, they had installed refrigeration units for those intriguing reds.

Very few people were aware of the vast subterranean structure beneath them. Kahlenbergerdorf had been mined for magnesite and iron ore, and Max's ancestors, using pick-axes, shovels and wicker baskets for the excavated material, turned the old tunnels into wide passageways lined with wine racks that had become, through the centuries, a maze of slumbering bottles. Off the passageways they created rooms, some large enough for equipment. Wide stone steps accessed the two levels below the winery. As with other winemakers, they called them wine caves.

A seldom-used tunnel connected the family chateau's personal wine cellar to the caves. In addition, as his father had shown him and Max showed his sons, another, cruder tunnel, made up of an ascending set of ladders perched on rock ledges, extended from the winery up to an opening on the hill. It was an engineering marvel—escape for miners and winemakers alike.

Without mention to his parents, Michel camouflaged the iron grill at the top.

Max and Lili climbed down to the lower cave. He lit a kerosene lamp and poured the wine. They sat on a soft couch between centuries-old barrels and winemaking equipment. He pulled a heavy fur blanket around them and leaned over to kiss his wife.

"Hmm," she murmured, kissing him back.

Max had met Lili while visiting his mother, Helga, who lived in a small, impeccably kept house in Vienna next door to a bookstore called *Der Buchwald*. It was appropriate, as Anno Kerber, the soft-spoken, hunchbacked proprietor, had created a friendly forest of books.

Helga insisted her son help her pick out something new to read, but upon their arrival, she marched him over to the counter where a slender, dark-haired woman was making a sale. "This is Lili," Helga said proudly, as if personally responsible for this beguiling creature.

Outside, Max pounced on his mother. "Who is she?"

Helga laughed and related everything she knew. Lili Huber was Austrian, but had grown up in Poland. When her husband died, she and her eight-month-old son, Michel, returned to Vienna.

"How long has she been working here?"

"Only a few months. Anno offered her a job and a place to stay in the store's garret on the first day she appeared, looking very sad." Helga, upon hearing the wail of a baby, offered to babysit.

"After all those years in Poland, language was a problem, so when she finishes at the store and comes for Michel, we work on her German. I told her about you."

"What did you say?" Max mused.

"That you were not married."

"Mutti!"

"I also said you are handsome, successful, and only fifteen years older than her."

The next evening when Lili arrived, Max emerged from his mother's kitchen. As Helga put morsels of cake on Michel's tongue, the two lost themselves in amiable conversation. She told him she enjoyed wine. He told her about his favored Rieslings and Gruner Veltliners. That night he brought something special, and Lili savored her first red wine.

From then on, she visited *Schloß Winzertal* often. One evening, she sat Max down and stood solemnly before him.

"My name isn't Lili Huber."

"All right," he said slowly.

"It's Ester Marek Fieg. I'm a Polish Jew. I grew up in Kielce. Last November, there was a pogrom in our town. The Jewish community was having a meeting in the theatre. They felt it was safe to say anything, even complain about some of their neighbors harassing them, but there were Polish spies inside, and just outside the doors, an angry mob."

Max took her hands.

"They dragged everyone out. Four people were beaten to death. My parents, Jo'el and Chajka Marek, and my husband, Moshe Fieg, were three of them. I was holding my baby boy, watching my entire world on the ground, bleeding into the dirt." Her voice faltered. "They had smashed in their beautiful faces with clubs."

Max clutched her to him.

"The owner of the theatre told me our house was on fire and I should run. So, I did."

He wiped away her tears, and then his own. "All the way to Vienna, my love?" I can't imagine how you survived, with a little baby."

"Sometimes a farmer gave us a ride. We hid in forests and barns. I didn't have enough milk. I pulled drops out of the teats," she said with the hint of a smile, "of several very annoyed cows."

Eventually, he would learn the details of what had been her happy life in Kielce. But Max quickly recognized the tragedy and her escape had shrouded her entire being with a permanent, profound fear. She often reiterated that she wanted to keep her name, and that of little Moshe, her son, whom she had renamed Michel, and their Jewish identity, private. Unfailingly, Max gave her his solemn promise.

One evening, lifelong friends of Max and his family surprised them. "Lili," Max called from the door. "Come meet the best people in the world."

A bushy-haired man with round spectacles and sparkling blue eyes stepped forward. "I'm Elie Schett. And this is my wife, Tovah."

Max put his arm around Lili's shoulder. "I'm not a very good Catholic, but at least I have my own Rabbi."

Lili's eyes delved into Elie's. "Can I have him too?"

"You've found a treasure," Elie told Max later, when Lili had allowed Max to share her story with him and the warm, lovely Tovah. Fully aware harassment of Viennese Jews was increasing, Elie assured Lili her need for privacy was not extreme, but vigilant.

Three months later, they married in an ancient chapel in Kahlenbergerdorf. Max had suggested a civil ceremony, but Lili insisted on a Catholic wedding, to further the ruse that comforted her fears. Later, Elie and Tovah joined them at *Schloß Winzertal* for a small, but boisterous, celebration.

In 1921, they produced a brother for Michel. He was anointed with a Jewish name, but they would call him Stefan.

When Anno Kerber told them he wanted to retire. Max snatched the opportunity, and Lili Fieg Mayr was thrilled to be the owner of *Der Buchwald*, the bookstore with the perfect name.

# 19

*St. Jakob, August, 1937*

In Moosfeld, *Pfarrer* Nikolas Schönfeld lived in a tiny house next to the Church. In St. Jakob, he lived in a tiny room on the side of the Church. He landed in which ever bed was closest when his duties were complete. Lately, however, he diverted to *Grünen Baum* to jump into a card game with Sebastien and whoever else was around, or share a glass of wine in the comfort of the *kochecke.*

Viktor continued to show up at the bar, sometimes with Faber. "They ruin everything," Mathilde muttered, as she and Hannah served them more beer, pretzels and pickles.

Their other problem was Veronika. When she was free, which was increasingly the case, she came to flirt with Georg and tell him what card to play. He tended to her somewhat, but his usual entertaining banter suffered.

Late one Sunday, Niko, Georg, Hannah, and Sebastien were enjoying the warm evening under an apricot tree in the *biergarten.* Sebastien wondered aloud if anyone saw things the way they did.

Niko counted on his fingers. "Well, let's see. There's the four of us. Oh, And Andreas. Mathilde and Tobias. And Daniel."

"Willi hates the Nazis," Georg added.

"How do you know? Sebastien asked. "He doesn't talk."

"He talks to me."

"If we count Moosfeld," Sebastien continued, "there's Bernard. I'm not sure Sophie concerns herself with reality. Siegi is always good for a whack at *Der Führer*. As for Otto, who knows what he's thinking?"

"What about Elke?" Hannah asked, needing her friend to be beside her in this group.

"Ah," Niko said, "She used to be openly critical of Hitler's appeal. But not lately."

"She uses all her energy coping." Sebastien said.

In the beginning, Gerhard had enjoyed summer afternoons in *Grünen Baum's biergarten*. But when Viktor arrived and began throwing verbal arrows, his demeanor changed. He sat fidgeting, his expression subdued. He started leaving with Viktor. Not, Sebastien surmised, because he took pleasure being with his fellow mayor, but because he was tired of the dissent his friends failed to hide.

What Hannah kept from her husband was she, too, wanted to flee these septic encounters. Let Mathilde be the one to serve them and give them dirty looks.

One evening in early September, Georg asked Sebastien and Hannah if they could speak privately. There had been rumors, and Georg confirmed Veronika was planning their wedding. "I asked her to wait, because of Crush, but she showed up two days ago, excited she had found her wedding dress. She's already arranged for music and selected the flowers. This morning she said the food for the reception needed to be ordered."

"My God, Georg," Sebastien bellowed. "When is this supposed to happen?"

"Don't shout, Seb," Georg said. "You said you would be there for me."

"Of course we support you," Hannah hurried to say, "and Veronika, too."

"I'm just surprised," Sebastien said more calmly. This feels... hasty."

"She's always trying to please me, and it's nice to have someone to talk to about ordinary things. I already explained this. I want to be a normal person and get on with my life."

"And 'normal' is marrying a woman you don't love?"

George rose quickly, his chair scraping the floor. "I'm saying this is right for me." Sebastien and Hannah followed him to the door.

"Saturday, October 16," Georg told them as he walked out into the night.

"Oh," Sebastien called. "A week after your annual party?"

"No. *Instead* of my annual party."

•　•　•　•　•

Matilde had a new mantra. "She's a damned thief. She stole Georg, and all our fun."

"It's not really our party," Hannah commented.

"Every October for centuries, St. Jakob has celebrated the end of the harvest at *Winegut Maria Theresia*. It's *our* party."

Most of the town agreed. Everyone who would have showed up for the Crush festivities was invited to the wedding. Villagers grumbled about Veronika's nerve and having to bring paper schillings for her wedding dance.

"I heard them arguing," Daniel reported. "Georg said he didn't care what kind of good price Viktor gave Veronika, he wanted *Grünen Baum* to make the food for his wedding dinner and that was that."

Andreas stroked his silver beard. "George, one, Veronika, nil."

Veronika's wedding day began with perfect weather. Georg would come to the bakery, and the two of them would lead a procession to the church. She bought a parasol for the occasion that Elke would hold over her as they paraded through town.

"I don't want to be in the procession," Daniel declared.

Mathilde rolled her eyes. "You aren't the only one."

Sebastien and Hannah were at the winery, inspecting the array of food, when Hubert arrived for the Crush party. When he heard about the nuptials, he turned around and went back to Vienna.

From their pew, Hannah watched with fascination as Georg and Veronika exchanged vows. He seemed quite loving, holding her hand and kissing her gently.

"Maybe Georg brings out her best nature," she remarked as they walked through the forest to *Winegut Maria Theresia*. Veronika was again at the front, her long train and the petticoats beneath her pearl-studded dress slung over one arm, the other firmly in Georg's grasp.

Sebastien sighed. "I admire you, *liebchen*. Despite Veronika's bad behavior, you're giving her a chance."

She shrugged. It might be possible to forgive Veronika for the wretched way she had treated her since she arrived at *Grünen Baum*, but never for how she battered Daniel's spirit.

Guests wandered among the grapevines while others formed a crowd in front of the tables of food and two bars featuring Georg's signature wines.

"Who raided your private cellar?" Sebastien teased his friend.

"They're my wines," Georg bristled.

His defensiveness unnerved Sebastien. He suspected Veronika picked the expensive vintages to prove she was the most cherished person in Georg's life. But he acquiesced, and told his friend, "Your generosity makes each of us feel honored."

On the musicians' platform, Georg could be seen in tense conversation with Gerhard, who eventually called everyone to attention while Viktor and Faber emerged from the crowd and joined them. Veronika flew to Georg's side.

Ratzener's arm shot up. "*Heil* Hitler. I bring greetings from the National Socialist Party in Vienna. Salutations to Herr and Frau Wangermann." He hoisted his glass of expensive wine.

"Prost," the crowd responded automatically.

"I want to invite you both," he gave Veronika a little bow, "to bring your wine to Vienna. I'll introduce you to everyone you need to know."

Veronika clapped her hands. Georg remained stoic. "I don't mean to be rude," he said, "but the Viennese are already among my best customers."

Sebastien whispered to Hannah, "You know what that Hitler minion is doing, don't you? He's using the wedding to publicly connect Georg to the Party. He's boxing him in."

Georg gave Ratzener a thin smile, which the crowd took as a signal the celebration would go on. Sebastien and Hannah hurried to join the dancing, in hopes Georg would believe they were having a good time.

# 20

*Kahlenbergerdorf, September, 1937*

The Mayr family sat together for breakfast at their preferred gathering place, the kitchen table. Stefan casually remarked that a new girl had entered Kahlenbergerdorf's little school at the bottom of their hill.

Michel raised an eyebrow. "Did you talk to her, or stand there picking your nose?"

Stefan threw a spoon at him. The doorbell chimed.

Max opened the door to Klaus Kolbe and another man he had never met. Without being invited, they walked inside. "Max, I want you to meet Faber Ratzener. Periodically he will accompany me when I check on my more prosperous friends."

"What exactly are you checking? My business is fine."

"Way out here, you might need security."

Max knew the code: SS patrolling his property. "I assure you we're quite safe."

Ratzener was trying his best to look down his nose, which gave the taller Max an unpleasant view of his nostrils. The *standartenführer*'s voice dripped with arrogance. "The Austrian National Socialist party is interested in all Viennese with resources. Be flattered, Herr Mayr. You've been chosen to help us build a new Austria."

"I'm rather partial to the old Austria."

Ratzener frowned. "I assume you have a private collection of wines. Let's see it."

Max led the two men down the stairs to the chateau cellar. After he described a few wines, Ratzener picked up a bottle with an ostentatious-looking label. "How much is this one worth? If I'm getting free wine, I want to know how much it's costing you."

"Premium vintage," Max said.

Ratzener snatched another bottle of the same wine and headed for the stairs. Kolbe wagged a finger at Max. "Impertinence will not win the friends you need."

Max didn't flinch. "You know your way out." He brought a *Cabernet Franc* to one of the upturned barrels they used for private tastings, poured himself a glass and drank, not bothering to savor it.

When Michel found his father three-quarters of the way through the bottle, he couldn't help but laugh. "What are you doing?"

"Kolbe was here, and he wasn't alone. I need to relax. Fill me in on your life."

Michel took off his backpack and threw it on the ground. "First, I'll take the rest. We can't waste one drop of such an incredible vintage."

Max grabbed another glass and emptied the bottle.

Michel took a long swallow. "Anti-Semitism has infected many students at the University. Some of my Jewish friends have formed a committee to oppose National Socialism."

How ironic, Max thought, his mind fuzzy.

"They've decided to take action. A janitor who hates the Nazis gave us the key to the room with the school's printing press. Anti-Third Reich leaflets have been designed and printed, ready to be distributed all over Vienna. Everyone should be aware of what the Nazis are doing, especially against the Jews."

"How did they get that name, anyway?"

"Nazis? It's what people are calling them in the underground. You know how Bavarians call someone they think is only a stupid peasant by the name Ignatz? A journalist tinkered with it and came up with 'Nazi.' Brilliant, don't you think? Groups opposing the NS have been using it for years."

Max had sobered considerably. "Brilliantly derisive.""

Michel opened his backpack to reveal several banded sets of leaflets. He gave one to his father, who read it aloud. "*Attention Citizens of Austria! Do Not Be Fooled! Read the Truth about the Evils of National Socialism!*"

Max tossed it on the floor. "Who gave you these?"

"My friend, Remi Schnaitl. He's one of the leaders of the committee. Last week we say two young boys beating a woman with sticks, calling her 'a dirty Jewish slut.' Remi might be more militant than me, but he's doing what's right, just as you taught us. It's called resistance, Papa. I would think you would lead the parade."

"So you've joined them." Max muttered. They had preached compassion, and Michel had listened. "These leaflets—what if you're discovered using the printing press?"

"Well, this is where you come in. We need to move our work. Remi and I are working on finding someone with a printing press who feels as we do. Do you know anyone like that?"

Max stared, incredulous.

"Papa? Should I open another bottle?"

"No!" Max cried, his voice echoing off the walls. He paced in front of the rack that cradled their new red wines. "I have to think. Do nothing until we talk again."

Max started up the stairs, leaving his older son alone with his alarming new life.

Meanwhile, his younger son darted across the kitchen, having heard it all.

# 21

*St. Jakob, January, 1938*

With the start of the New Year, Georg announced they could now listen to the BBC for the truth of what was happening in Europe.

"English might be a problem," Sebastien remarked.

"Niko can translate," Georg said.

"I don't think so," the priest laughed. "Your English is better than mine."

"I was forced to learn when I started selling wine there. French and Italian weren't enough."

Hannah stared at him. "You speak four languages?"

"Some better than others. English was the easiest to learn."

I had no idea," Sebastien commented. "You're a linguist disguised as a grape stomper."

They gathered in Georg's living room, fire blazing, wine breathing, and Veronika enthroned on what was formerly her husband's favorite chair. He tuned into the station, which, though peppered with static, was still clear enough for him to translate most of what they heard.

The news did nothing to reassure anyone Hitler's tentacles weren't already unfolding in Austria. Chancellor Kurt von Schuschnigg was ordered to meet with Hitler at his mysterious private retreat in Berchtesgaden, but the prevailing opinion was Schuschnigg was powerless to hold on to Austria's sovereignty.

Veronika listened, too, her rigid posture betraying her annoyance. "Well," she said. "It's just talk. I don't know why you all bother."

"Vroni," Georg said patiently, gesturing toward the radio. "We finally have something other than Berlin coming out of that set of tubes."

Veronika arched one tailored eyebrow, reached for a bell on the table next to her, and rang it vigorously. A maid came in with trays of meat and cheese, bread, butter and jam.

"A bell?" Sebastien gave Georg a wry look.

"My husband doesn't realize how big this house is," Veronika said. "I can't be screaming at the top of my lungs for someone to bring me my coffee. Did you see how quickly the girl came?"

The radio broadcast did not come up again while they pretended to enjoy the sugary, rich cake Veronika had made. Eventually, Niko stood up. "Thank you, Georg. Thank you, BBC. And thank you, Veronika, you are a splendid hostess."

"I'll walk you all out," Georg said. "Why don't you stay here by the fire, *schatz*?"

Georg stopped them before they reached the cobblestone road that led out of the estate. "Gerhard has been after us to go see the Reich film *Triumph of the Will*. Maybe we should."

"Let's all go," Sebastien decreed. "For research."

Immediately, Hannah formulated a list of excuses to stay home. When Siegi mentioned they, too, could use an evening away from their children, Hannah invited her to leave them with Gabi and Benno. She would watch them all.

"Aren't you the wily one," Sebastien teased his wife.

"I don't know what you're talking about," she said. She hadn't confided her hesitation to anyone, worried they might think her cowardly.

Hannah had nodded off when the moviegoers, talking animatedly, burst in. She looked around. "Where are Georg and Veronika?"

"She made Georg take her home," Sebastien said. "She was tired of arguing with Niko."

The priest looked abashed. "I didn't mean to upset her."

"Yes, you did." He gently guided his wife to the table. "This calls for *schnaps*," he declared, and produced a bottle of the sweet apricot liquor and several glasses.

"It was quite spectacular," Gerhard said smoothly. "The man sitting next to me said he had seen it three times, and in one scene there were 700,000 people, and over a million took part."

"Good God," Sebastien groaned. "I'm not sure how they did it, but they made it look like Hitler was descending from heaven."

"The anti-Jewish rhetoric was obscene," Niko said.

Hannah nervously fingered her curls and tugged down her sleeve.

Gerhard was not to be put off. "You had to admire that scene with the workers, ordinary German people, carrying the tools of their trades, farmers, mechanics, welders, lumberjacks, even shopkeepers. A veritable parade of prosperity."

"Except they held their shovels and pickaxes like they were weapons," Elke said.

"They are weapons," Gerhard countered. "Against poverty and unemployment."

"The film was a Nazi fairy tale," Sebastien huffed. "They staged it all."

Gerhard stood and said to Elke. "Get the baby. We're going home." She rose, drank down Gerhard's unfinished *schnaps* and walked upstairs. When they left, Gerhard jostled Georg coming in.

Georg closed the door behind them. "What was that about?"

"That was Elke putting her foot down," Sebastien said. "I've never seen her like that."

"I wish I was that strong," Hannah said.

Niko laid a light hand on her arm. "Why would you say something like that?"

"Because you're all becoming warriors," she said. They were leaving her behind.

•    •    •    •    •

Daniel, who now lived with Veronika and Georg at *Winegut Maria Theresia,* was lonely in his new room, chosen by his sister, as far from their bedroom as possible. He escaped regularly, and was upset someone put boxes in his old room at the bakery. He begged Sebastien not to give away his job.

"What? We need you!" Sebastien exclaimed. Tearfully, Daniel told Hannah he didn't want them to think he didn't like them because he moved away.

"You haven't moved away," she told him. "You changed houses."

Daniel nodded and wiped his nose with his sleeve. "Georg is nice to me and wants me to stay, but I don't."

"He understands. Tie on your aprons and get ready for *mittagessen.*"

Sebastien invited Georg and Veronika to the *kochecke* that evening, claiming Mathilde had made the best *Sacher Torte* he'd ever eaten. Afterwards, he broached the subject of Daniel's distress.

"For some reason," he began, opting for diplomacy, "he's convinced if he lives with you and Georg, we won't need him anymore. That's why he keeps running away."

"Oh, no," Georg said.

"Silly boy," Veronika muttered.

"You're right, Veronika," Sebastien agreed. "How could he have gotten such an idea? Perhaps you could reassure him how valuable he is to us. Ask Willi to remove the boxes from his old room at the bakery so he might stay there overnight sometimes. Then he'll feel more content at *Maria Theresia.*"

"We can do that," Georg declared. "Can't we, Vroni?"

She shrugged. "I suppose that would be all right, as long as he doesn't get under our feet at the bakery."

Georg raised an eyebrow. "But you don't work there anymore. You put Willi in charge, and Elke is there every day until the rush is over."

"I have to check on them regularly," she countered stubbornly.

"They're completely competent." He stared at his wife, daring her to challenge him, as Hannah hoped that for once, Georg would have the last word.

•     •     •     •     •

As Sebastien and Niko spent more time together, Hannah's presence in their conversations dwindled. One night, he was very late joining her in bed. "You used to only talk to me at this hour of the night," she chided him, even as he pulled her close.

"Talking to Niko helps. I'm tired of feeling angry all the time. So many people have been sucked in. Our friends and neighbors, Hannah! They come to the inn and sit at the bar chatting about how Hitler will make them all rich."

"And Gerhard?"

"I hardly know him anymore."

"You spend so much time with Niko now, maybe he feels left out." She understood that.

"I think he has new friends. Viktor Lonauer, for one."

"They are the mayors of two tightly connected towns."

"You're right," Sebastien conceded. "But I can't help feeling I've lost him."

"Imagine how Elke feels. She's wondering what happened to the man she married."

Sebastien kissed Hannah's forehead, and left a trail of kisses down her face, around her neck, to her breasts. Fire arose instantly and for Hannah, melted any vestiges of conscious thought.

•     •     •     •     •

On the evening of March 9, Niko rushed in, excited about Chancellor Schuschnigg's plebiscite the following Sunday.

"This is good," Sebastien exclaimed over their late supper with Andreas. "The people of Austria can decide for themselves if they want to remain independent of the Third Reich."

On Saturday, March 12, from the pulpit of both towns, Niko urged prayer for Austria, and reminded the congregation that the next day, they had the chance to honor their homeland.

"I think they heard you, Niko."

"I hope so. Now we have to make sure they vote."

Sebastien and Hannah were looking forward to spending that evening at *Maria Theresia*. They had begun their walk to the winery when Georg drove up, Niko seated next to him.

"You must be the chariot we ordered," Sebastien said.

Neither of them smiled. Georg parked. Niko offered his arm to Hannah, who apprehensively accepted it.

Once inside, Georg said, "Turn on your radio. Who's still here?"

"Matilde and Tobias," Hannah said. "Andi, and Daniel, probably." She found all four of them still in the *wintergarten,* playing a dice game, which Daniel was winning. "You're needed in the *kochecke,*" she said without preamble.

"Is there a surprise?" Daniel whispered to Andreas.

"I'm not sure," he whispered back. "Come and sit by me."

Georg fiddled with the dial. "Hitler invaded Austria. From what I heard, he met little resistance."

"Instead, they were dancing in the streets." Niko scowled. "Viktor Lonauer arranged a demonstration of support in Moosfeld."

"Schuschnigg resigned, and the Germans have ordered the plebiscite cancelled."

They listened for the next hour, except for Daniel, who became agitated by the sounds of *Sieg Heil* repeated incessantly over the rumble of German tanks.

They hardly noticed that Elke, with Benno in her arms, had slipped into the room. She touched Hannah's arm, making her jump.

"I was listening too," she said brusquely. "Gerhard's in Linz. With Faber and Viktor."

# 22

*Kahlenbergerdorf, 13 March, 1938*
The University of Vienna cancelled classes for Adolf Hitler's grand entrance into Austria. Rules were announced: Most shops would close at noon, restaurants at four. All good Austrians were to hoist the swastika above their homes. Tossing flowers would not be permitted.

The Mayr family were sharing a somber breakfast of coffee and rolls when Elie Schett, his white hair flared out wildly, came through the kitchen door.

"There's a two-story-high Swastika flapping against your building."

Max tossed his butter knife on his plate. "Already?"

"That's not the worst of it. Someone painted '*Schmutziger Jude*' on the window of Bruno's shop." Filthy Jew.

Max's office was on *Hohermarkt*, near Lili's bookstore. Bruno Susskind, his wife Malke and their two young children lived above the delicatessen across the street, and occasionally Max, Elie, and sometimes their wives met there for a kosher meal.

"His door was ajar. I called out that it was me and not to be afraid. Finally, I went in. Their furniture was in pieces. They smashed every dish they own and all of Malke's flower pots. They stole anything of value and even ripped up their photographs. I know all his neighbors, but they wouldn't come to the door. Jews are hiding in their homes, thinking they're safe."

"A pogrom," Lili said, almost inaudibly.

Elie's eyes filled. "Young boys armed with rifles and bayonets squealed cruel epithets, like they were driving wild pigs out of the bushes to be slaughtered. Already people are begging me for help in coaxing passports out of the embassy. I've never seen such desolation and chaos."

"If Hitler is entering our city," Michel said, "I want to meet him at the gate."

Elie shook his head. "Vienna is engulfed in madness."

"I can find my way."

"Perhaps you can," Max said miserably. "But not alone."

After a seventy-five-minute wait in line at the station, Max and Michel boarded the tram toward the *Ringstraße*. At each subsequent stop, an immense crowd, including organized masses of school children, pressed forward to squeeze into the cars.

"We're going to greet Herr Hitler," a little girl told Max, toting a bouquet of flowers almost as big as she was.

Max coughed. "We'll be dead before we get there if no one can breathe."

The train seemed slower than usual, as if the impossible crush of passengers was weighting them down. "We need to get out," Michel said.

"Are you kidding?"

As the tram slowed, Michel shouted, "I'm going to be sick," and started toward the doors, Max clinging to the waistband of his pants. The doors slid open, and a battle raged between those already inside the car and those wanting to come on as the doors slid open.

"Stop pushing, you idiots," a woman yelled, "unless you want vomit in your hair!" In that split second of hesitation, Michel pulled his father onto the platform and through the advancing mob. They wove their way down the crowded boulevard. Church bells pealed all around them, and Michel unleashed his disgust. "A welcoming gift to Hitler from Cardinal Innitzer."

They were early, so when they passed an open pub, Michel ordered beer for them both. Five minutes later, a frenzied cluster of young men ran in, descended on the bartender and demanded to be served.

"Hurry! He's going to the *Hotel Imperial*!"

The bartender poured beer over several glasses, which were grabbed up instantly. Money tossed on the bar sank into a river of foam.

"Let's follow them," Michel said.

As they neared the *Hotel Imperial*, dense crowds seeped into every street, piazza and park like lava oozing over a doomed town. People ended up slammed against hastily formed barricades. Max was lucky enough to find a tree to wrap his arm around and Michel immediately scrambled up its branches, which almost disappeared under a mantle of hanging onlookers.

Max could see nothing through a sea of arms raised in tribute. A deep, rumbling sound signaled the motorcade as it came into view. The cheering almost eclipsed the roar of German bombers passing overhead.

"They're throwing flowers," Michel observed. "I guess adoration excuses them." Several people standing next to Max turned their heads to glare up at his son.

"There must be fifty more open cars behind Hitler," Michel continued, craning his neck. "He brought his whole Nazi family."

Hitler entered the *Hotel Imperial.* What followed was a bizarre series of appearances and disappearances by a confused-looking *Führer* on a third-floor balcony. Each time the hysteria started anew.

"He looks like Charlie Chaplin," Michel yelled.

A dark sky had descended when finally, a microphone was set up and searchlights focused on Hitler. It was an unusually brief speech. Shaking his fist, locks of his oddly trimmed hair falling into his face, his clipped mustache bobbing up and down like a yo-yo, Hitler concluded, "This love you are feeling, I have felt profoundly."

A woman next to Max swooned and he tried to catch her. She lay splayed over him.

"Adelaide," shouted a man with a Hitler mustache. "My wife," he explained with a shrug. Max dumped the woman into his arms while Michel dropped from the tree. This time he navigated his father through narrow streets, where they encountered not only jubilant Austrians, but families running, clinging to disheveled children, pushing carts of personal belongings away from the city central.

They slowed down on an unlighted street where tightly packed houses were devoid of life. They heard shouting and peeked around a corner. A man was being violently beaten while a woman wailed and begged them to stop.

One of the brown suited officers took out a pistol and fired shots at the feet of two young children, cowering behind her.

"My God," Max whispered, "it's the Susskinds."

"Run!" Bruno shouted to his wife, who grabbed the children's hands. The officer laughed and sent a volley of bullets into Bruno's back. Malke screamed and let go of the children.

"One dirty Jew down," the German shouted gleefully. He shot Malke, and she collapsed next to her husband on the street. "And two to go."

He pulled the trigger twice more. Turning to the other officer, he nodded. "I wouldn't want you to miss the fun." The second man stalked toward Bruno and began firing, moving to Malke, and then to the two little crumpled bodies, until they were dead many times over.

Michel had to wrench his father away. "Move. Papa!" While blood pooled under the little family who had been their friends, Michel kept Max upright as they ran.

# 23

*St. Jakob, 13 March, 1938*

The day after Austria served itself to Adolf Hitler on a soiled platter, Sebastien dressed Gabriele himself, hoisted her into his arms and waited impatiently in the family kitchen for Hannah to appear at the bottom of the stairs.

"We need to hurry. Niko is going to make it clear in his sermon today that Catholics are not required to capitulate to an evil regime. He told me last night, after you went to bed."

"He's a priest, Sebastien," she snapped. "It's not like he can reverse the invasion."

They were five minutes early. Customarily, the men waited outside, smoking, gathered in clumps in front of the wooden door, and filed in at the last moment. Niko had cancelled the early Mass in Moosfeld, so the stragglers were followed by a last-minute surge of parishioners.

He wasted no time. "I will not be saying *Guten Morgen*," he began. The bloated congregation that stuffed the aisles and crowded the choir loft settled down. "Because it is anything but a good morning."

Abruptly, the chirping of a few birds outside seemed unnaturally loud.

"Today, as we struggle to cope with the injustice that has accosted our nation, we will be talking about our responsibility as Catholics to resist evil."

Muffled comments rolled across the pews. Niko raised his hands together in the familiar gesture of starting the Mass. "Let us pray."

When the moment arrived for reading the Gospel, the crowd stood. Niko cleared his throat. "I would like to refer you back to last week's Gospel, the temptation in the Wilderness."

Herr Haas' squeaky voice rose above the stir in the congregation. "Who does he think he is? The pope?" This brought some snickers, and a few nods of agreement.

Niko planted himself in front of the people in the first pew. Two older women shrank back.

"After forty days and nights, the devil tempted Jesus to turn stones into bread and accept his gift of the Holy City. Jesus rebuffed him, saying the Lord will not be put to the test. Niko's eyes swept his flock. "My friends, we too, are being put to the test. The question is, what should we say to the devil who is tempting us?"

The faces that had shown puzzlement now registered shock. Were they supposed to answer him?

Next to Hannah, Sebastien was rocking the pew. "Calm down," she whispered to him. "Let someone else respond." But in this modest, centuries old house of God, no one was talking.

On her lap, Gabriele burrowed into Hannah's arms, put her thumb in her mouth, and, as she often did for comfort, fingered the soft lobe of her mother's ear.

Herr Haas stood up. "Aren't you going to read the statement from his Eminence, Cardinal Innitzer? It's supposed to be read from the church pulpit this morning."

Every face turned to the postmaster. Niko cleared his throat in an effort to retrieve his audience. "Thank you, Herr Haas. I will be dealing with that later."

"But we have the right to hear it," Haas insisted, "directly out of your mouth."

Niko turned and faced the altar behind him. "Is he praying?" Someone whispered loudly. "Are we supposed to be praying?"

"Leave him alone," Sebastien muttered. Hannah felt his fury growing and clenched her sleeping child. Gabi whimpered.

Niko addressed them again. "As the pastor of this Church and in Moosfeld, I am obligated to do what I must to tend to the spiritual lives of my parishioners." He stared at Haas. "I intend to do just that."

He finished the sermon he had planned, and the Mass crept along uncomfortably. When it ended, Haas flew from his pew and out the door. Sebastien took Hannah's arm and pulled her into the aisle. Struggling to soothe a perturbed Gabi, rudely roused from sleep a second time, she tripped on a floor runner and was caught by the man behind her.

Haas stood on the low wall around the Church and the village cemetery. He thrust a piece of paper toward the crowd like it was a declaration of war, "If you want to hear the words of your Church, this is what Schönfeld failed to announce today."

*"Austrian Catholics should greet Adolf Hitler and the Nazis by praying to the Lord God in thanks for the bloodless course of this great political change and to ask for a happy future for Austria. Of course, all orders from the authorities will be happily and willingly obeyed."*

"Signed," he concluded dramatically, "by a man who outranks him," his shoulder jerked toward Niko, "many times over. 'Theodore Cardinal Innitzer, Archbishop of Vienna, March 12, 1938.'"

The strings of tension had been cut; taking a moral stand was not their job.

•   •   •   •   •

Niko made his way to Moosfeld for the Mass at eleven. The first three rows were customarily reserved for parishioners whose families had either attended for centuries or made donations unequaled by the people in the fourth row and beyond. Haas sat with the elite.

Sebastien and Hannah also followed Niko to Moosfeld.

Niko began the same way he had in St. Jakob. "This day is far from ordinary."

Hannah felt relieved when he read the appropriate Gospel. But then, he hurled into the same cauldron of controversy he stirred up only an hour before.

Almost immediately, a man next to Herr Haas interrupted him.

"Our friend Adolf Haas has instructions from the Cardinal in his hand." Haas waved the letter above his head. "You can hear it now, or after Schönfeld finishes lecturing us."

Haas led the way down the center aisle, followed by the entire third row.

"How did he poison them so quickly?" Sebastien hissed. After some hesitation, a large group followed them, including Viktor Lonauer, dragging Otto along with him. Ernst ran after his father, and a scowling Siegi came next, a puzzled twin in each arm.

Niko continued, doing battle with the high-pitched voice reading of the Cardinal's letter outside and the ruckus that followed. Mercifully, the Mass ended, but Niko didn't greet his flock, something he'd done three times every Sunday for six years.

Hannah and Sebastien caught up with him walking through gravestones toward the back gate. "Niko, wait," Sebastien called.

He halted his retreat. "I asked too much of them."

"People forget," Sebastien insisted. "Next week, you can try something different."

Later that evening, Niko was already commiserating with Sebastien about a fresh approach for the following Sunday. Steps away, Hannah finished the cake she had baked, simply to have something to do.

Elke surprised them at the door. "I'm sorry. Benno's asleep and Viktor is on his way to our house." Siegi arrived next, flushed and wind-blown, as if she had run rather than driven Otto's old car from Moosfeld.

"I told Otto to put the children to bed. Viktor's friends were chanting, 'Sieg, heil!' I couldn't take it."

Niko stood to leave, and Sebastien followed him out.

"'What's that gleam in your eye?" Hannah asked her sister, slicing the cake.

"The other day, Veronika was in *Wachauerhof* with some friend of hers, and I overheard her talking about Georg."

Good. Siegi's gossip often took her mind off anything else. "In other words," Hannah said, "you were loitering at the next table."

"Something like that. She was really carrying on."

"How could anyone complain about the nicest man in Austria?" Elke wondered.

"Apparently," Siegi paused for effect, "He doesn't satisfy her."

"He gives her anything she wants," Hannah reminded them.

"He doesn't satisfy her," Siegi repeated, "in bed."

"Stop!" Hannah shrieked.

"Apparently, he never initiates anything, and when they do make love, he sometimes isn't able to...inflate."

Elke was a lot calmer. "I heard the same thing in the bakery."

"See?" Siegi said to her sister. "Veronika is wondering if he's a *Schwul*."

"Homosexual," Elke whispered, in case Hannah was uninformed.

"I know what that is," Hannah said.

"Well, I don't believe it for a minute."

Siegi shrugged. "He probably doesn't want to do it with *her*. I mean, I wouldn't want to do it with her."

Hannah and Elke could do nothing but laugh.

# 24

Max and Michel arrived in Kahlenbergerdorf just after midnight. Max's muscles burned as they started up the hill toward *Schloß Winzertal.*

Light poured out of almost every window of the chateau, and Lili, Stefan, Helga, Elie and Tovah rushed out. An hour later, they were still at the kitchen table, now dotted with wet handkerchiefs, swathed in grief and revulsion.

"Those sweet little children," Tovah sobbed.

Lili had listened, increasingly agitated, while Max and Michel described the Susskinds' heinous execution. "Have all the decent citizens of Vienna," she cried, "become possessed with Hitler's unfathomable hatred?" She took a breath, as if trying to contain her burst of ferocious emotion.

Stefan sat up. "Rabbi Elie says the Jews can only get food for one hour during the afternoon, and only when there's a surplus. We could secretly get food to the families."

"Absolutely not," Lili snapped.

"But Mutti," Stefan protested. "I'm not a Jew. The Germans won't bother an Austrian boy running an errand for his parents."

Max bowed his head, feeling acutely the rattle of nerves in the room.

Upon awakening the next morning, Max had a few seconds of oblivion before he remembered the scene on a dark Viennese street that would never leave him. He got up and walked into the kitchen to see Lili and Michel huddled together. I'm going to visit a friend," Michel said pointedly.

"You can drive my truck." He looked into Lili's eyes. "It's time." Max tried not to think while he climbed in and slammed shut the stubborn passenger door.

The Augustinian Monastery at Klosterneuburg was a jewel on the Danube with a nine-hundred-year-old wine operation. Michel parked on a patch of gravel in front of the abbey's cellar doors. Waiting for them was a monk dressed in a black woolen tunic and a cape with a pointed hood.

"*Pfarrer* Scholz, this is my father, Maximillian Mayr."

The monk arched an eyebrow. "I see you've finally succumbed to a very persistent son."

"Yesterday," Michel explained, "we heard Hitler talk at the Imperial Hotel. On the way home, we saw Jewish friends of ours and their children, shot in the back, for fun."

*Pfarrer* Scholz shook his head in disgust. "I'm sorry."

"I've had serious misgivings," Max said, "but if my son dares to confront the horrendous evil infecting all of Austria, his father should stand with him."

Scholz ushered them through broad oak and brass doors into the winery. "We're having a meeting shortly. You can join us."

"A meeting?" The courage Max had briefly felt evaporated. He and his son in a room full of resisters?

"Would you like a glass of wine? Oh my, what a silly question."

"No," Max said. Anything to calm down. "I'll try the Zweigelt."

Scholz chose a bottle from a bronze wine rack. Max eyed the label. "Heavenly, *Pfarrer* Scholz."

"It's Roman.

"I'm Max."

"Are you wondering how a humble monk could be challenging the Third Reich? When I was ordained in 1935, I was sent to teach here at Klosterneuburg. At the time, I was sympathetic to the National Socialists."

"I didn't know that," Michel said.

"Well, I'm confessing it now to your father. You happen to be in the room."

"In 1936, I was repulsed by what I heard in Nuremberg, especially the racial hatred. I came home with a new curriculum. Young people needed to be trained as guardians of Austria's moral center."

Max nodded gravely.

"My dear friend Dr. Viktor Reimann and I created the Austrian Freedom Movement and began gathering allies and initiating resistance here and there."

"When the printing press at the university didn't work out," Michel informed his father, "We came to Roman."

"We have one down in the least accessible area."

"Will your friend be at this meeting?" Max asked.

"Yes, besides Viktor, you'll meet two others, Fritz Lehmann and Otto Hartmann."

"It's good, Papa," Michel hastened to say. "They're actors. They know how to blend in anywhere." The winery doors rolled open and two men joined them.

"Where's Hartmann?" Roman asked.

"He'll be late," one of the men, every bit the model Aryan, informed him.

Roman introduced Fritz. The other man wore a rumpled suit and a hat over his eyes. "And Viktor Reimann, whom I told you about."

"He's not an actor," Michel added.

"We're off to rock bottom," Roman joked. He turned lights on and off as they descended 40 meters of steps; four levels of baroque cellar vaults. In the dampness and earthy smell, Max had a familiar thought: barrels, stirring with restless secrets in the fermenting wine.

"We're directly under the monastery. Put together, these tunnels would measure two kilometers." They came to a rock-walled room with five chairs. Roman remained standing, anticipating the arrival of Otto Hartmann, who strode in at precisely that moment.

"I don't have much time," the newcomer said, his tone petulant.

"You called this meeting," Roman replied. "Tell us what's on your mind."

Hartmann gestured toward Max and Michel. "Where did you find these two?"

"Trusted friends of mine who have decided they've had enough."

Viktor clapped his hands. "Good enough for me."

With one more wary glance, Hartmann said, "The events of the last several days have changed everything. Throwing around a little paper people are afraid to pick up, much less read, is as ineffective as it is minimal."

"Excuse me, Herr Hartmann," Michel said, "I've seen them tucked in pockets, under hats, even in baby carriages."

Fritz Lehmann, swimming in a huge black coat, spoke quietly. "I somewhat agree with you, Otto."

Hartmann nodded vigorously. "I'm not suggesting we go out tomorrow and murder some Nazis, but we need to make a more strident statement."

"Like what?" Roman shot back.

"Cut off their ability to communicate. Take out some of those trucks stuffed with brown-shirted hoodlums."

Though the flood of German and Austrian SS were busy seizing control of Austrian daily life, the blood thirsty SA were still a major presence.

"You want to create our own acts of violence?" Roman obviously disagreed, which kept Max from grabbing his son and running.

Hartmann sighed. "You act as if we are resisting childhood pranks. It's Hitler who is dispensing licentious acts of aggression."

Fritz patted Roman on the back. "Let's mull this over and reconvene in two weeks."

"Waiting only serves the enemy," Hartmann said curtly. "I'm late for rehearsal." The receding sound of metal beads rattling against light bulbs echoed his impatience. The others said their goodbyes.

"This was all quite unexpected," Roman said awkwardly.

Max peered at him. "Your friend Hartmann has made up his mind. Perpetrating violence is not why we are here."

Roman nodded wearily. "I understand, and I agree."

"You did not reveal our names to your colleagues. I appreciate that. But I'm not sure I can help you."

"Your assistance would not require the presence of the men you met today. Leave it to me to contain Otto Hartmann."

"What do you need?"

"To move the printing press. "I have to use the space for another purpose. I'm sorry, but I can't elaborate."

"I need time to think," Max said crossly.

"Of course," Roman said. "I propose we visit your winery together. I can suggest ways we can proceed. I will accept your decision either way."

Max looked at his son, and back to the monk. "Michel can coordinate the day and time."

"Thank you, Max."

"We'll see, Roman."

# 25

**_St. Jakob, March, 1938_**

Niko still had to say Mass every day in both Churches. "Only the children look me in the eye," he told Hannah. She showed him to a guest room on the second floor and said it was his whenever he needed it.

Another referendum was announced, a vote for allegiance to Hitler and reunification with Germany, to be held on April 20. In Vienna, Cardinal Innitzer directed his priests to urge the people in the pews to vote yes.

"I can't do that," Niko told his friends.

"Subtlety might be your best weapon," Andreas said. "Rather than fling your suggestions toward the pews, try gently rolling them down the aisle."

All week, Niko burrowed in at _Grünen Baum_, often with Sebastien at his side. The bellicose postmaster was making a nuisance of himself at the bar, while Hannah nervously eyed her husband contradicting him. "You can't out-shout Haas," she scolded him.

Niko's first Mass in Moosfeld was at 7:30, so he left to spend the night there. "He's ready," Sebastien told Hannah. But she couldn't shake the suspicion the week before had merely been a dress rehearsal for more trouble.

The next morning, they sat in the _kochecke_ with Andreas, Mathilde and Tobias, waiting anxiously for the time they would leave for the Church.

"Maybe we could chain Haas to his stool in the post office," Andreas said to lighten the mood.

At fifteen minutes past nine, they walked down the hill. They sat in front so Niko would feel their support. A bell chimed, and the sacristy door opened. The priest who faced them, however, was not Nikolas Schönfeld.

"Good morning," he said. "My name is *Pfarrer* Martin Vogl and I am your new pastor. *Pfarrer* Schönfeld was re-assigned."

If the congregation was shocked, they were quiet about it. A few were shaking their heads, as if they had sent a naughty child to his room. Vogl brought his hands together and spoke, his deep baritone hitting the walls and floors with the strength of a waterfall, spraying his new flock with entitled authority. "In the name of the father...."

The entire congregation watched Sebastien storm out.

Like a silent film, the lips of the man on the altar were moving, but Hannah heard nothing. Andreas sat with his head in his hands until the end of the Mass, when he led them into the aisle and without apology, pushed people aside to get through the door. Out of the corner of her eye, Hannah saw Gerhard follow Vogl into the sacristy.

Sebastien had slipped into a heavy coat of rage. "If he tries to hide, I'll hunt him down."

"We'll take Gabi," Mathilde said. Andreas and Tobias took her hands and swung her between them as they climbed the hill. Hannah listened to her innocent laughter and envied her.

Martin Vogl exited the sacristy and Sebastien charged toward him. The priest put up a hand. "Not today," he said briskly.

"Why not? Do you need to clean out his rooms, discard his belongings, burn his papers? If you work hard, it will be like he was never here."

Vogl froze, his white-knuckled hands clasping a fist full of black cassock. "There's no reason for sarcasm. *Pfarrer* Schönfeld could no longer fulfill his duties as pastor, and needed to be replaced immediately. There is no intrigue."

"*Pfarrer* Vogl," Hannah said, "I'm Hannah Brandl, and this is my husband, Sebastien. *Pfarrer* Schönfeld is a dear friend of ours, and his sudden departure surprised us very much."

"All I know is the Diocese investigated reports he had spoken inappropriately at last week's Masses and refused to read the mandate prepared by His Eminence Cardinal Innitzer. Despite any misgivings your husband might have, the Church chooses to show good faith and allow the new regime to progress."

"Where is he?" Sebastien snarled.

"They sent a car for him. I didn't see him leave."

"Abducted by his own Church because he suggests his congregation confront evil? *Pfarrer* Vogl, in the last five years, have you read a newspaper or listened to the radio?"

"Sebastien," Hannah said quietly, touching his hand. "Perhaps the *pfarrer* could come to *Grünen Baum* next week, and you can have a proper conversation."

"*Burgermeister* Eigner proposed the same thing," Vogl said. "When we are all calmer, surely we can come to a common understanding."

"I don't think so," Sebastien said. "But if Gerhard is eager to share a meal with you, I'll also bring a friend, to keep the sides even."

Days went by, and with Niko gone, Sebastien told Hannah he would never set foot in a Catholic Church again. "We're all grieving," Hannah told him the following Sunday, after she had attended Mass without him and watched him crawl through the day. He had driven to St. Polten to ask questions in the diocesan office. No one had heard of a priest being recalled. Some didn't know him, and those who did thought he was still dividing his time between two small towns near the Danube.

When Haas reappeared at the bar, Sebastien wasted no time in confronting him. "Did you run all the way to Dürnstein to inform on Niko?"

"Everyone heard his blasphemous words, Brandl. Why should it be me?"

After Andreas steered his son back to the kitchen, Sebastien pounded the table where chicken was being prepared. "I'm going to ban that other Adolf from *Grünen Baum*!" he bellowed.

"Who?" Daniel asked, grinning at the jiggling legs and thighs.

"No, you are not," Andreas said. "It had to be Haas. But this is not the time to alienate the rest of our customers with angry outbursts."

The next evening, Gerhard poked his head inside the *kochecke* door. "Come in, Gerhard. Sit down," Hannah said quickly. "We haven't seen you or Elke for days." Gerhard sat. Sebastien waited.

"Our new *pfarrer* would like to come to *Grünen Baum* tomorrow at noon. He wants to clear the air between you. I agree with him, Seb. You've taken the change way too personally. There were plenty of complaints about Schönfeld, even before."

"Before what? The invasion of our country by a brutal dictator?"

"What's done is done. We all have to adapt."

"Have you joined the Party?"

Gerhard hesitated. "You have to understand, as mayor I have to go along for the good of our town. You both have to join. The town looks up to the Brandls."

"You should try building a bar next to your house."

"Sebastien, I'm the only one trying here. Work on him please, Hannah," Gerhard muttered as he left.

Hannah didn't bother to hide her irritation. "I'm on your side. But find it in yourself to be civil to the new priest. Whether you like it or not, he's in our lives."

"That man means nothing to me. He's a Nazi puppet."

"Be reasonable. There are still many good Catholics out there, and many of them probably agree with you."

"But no one is talking!"

Lowering her voice, she said, "People are afraid. I'm afraid. And you can't discard Gerhard. You're angry because you miss him. And what about Elke? She's my best friend. And Benno? We thought he and Gabi would grow up together."

"I want it to be the way it was before as much as you do. But he's one of them now."

Hannah lifted a hand to her husband's agonized face. "Sign a truce." Perhaps they could all pretend.

Sebastien hosted Gerhard, Georg, and *Pfarrer* Vogl for a meal of poached fish, new potatoes, and *sacher torte* in one of the inn's private dining rooms and pleaded with Hannah to join them. "I need you with me," he said in a voice that usually worked on her.

"Maybe next time."

In just over an hour, he rejoined her in the *kochecke*. "How was it?" she asked, looking up from the menu she was copying for an anniversary celebration the next day.

"Oh, we had a tense conversation, but then the food arrived. They enjoyed the cod," And that priest loves cherry *schnaps*. He could barely walk."

How could a man who had entered a room fuming come out making jokes? "I didn't hear any shouting."

He picked up one of the finished menus. "We didn't throw any plates, as I recall."

"You always find a way out, don't you?"

The menu slammed to the floor. "Out of what? My anger? My sadness? I will never get over the loss of Niko, my friend, and ally." He took her face in his hands. "I couldn't bare it if you were afraid to stand by me. You're worried about our family. I understand, and I respect that, but I'm also worried about our country."

He embraced her as tightly as the boundaries of their skin and bones would allow. "Be with me," he murmured into her hair before he gathered the curls up in one hand and covered her mouth with his.

Hannah wanted to believe him, to not be alone, to know what was true for her still resounded in him. Between her legs, the familiar, powerful ache arched upward, making it impossible to do anything but submit to him, through the race up the stairs, the frantic discarding of clothes, the devouring of mouths. It was almost enough to forget.

•   •   •   •   •

On April 19, the eve of Hitler's referendum, Andreas suggested his son simply stay away from the polls. Hannah knew that would never happen. Sebastien Brandl wanted to be counted.

The next morning, they rode Apfel down to where a single voting table was set up in front of the Church. The presence of swastika-bearing soldiers, hovering over voters and taking their ballots out of their hands, was unnerving.

Unexpectedly, they heard Daniel's voice. "Wait for me!" He joined them in the line, glowing with excitement. Veronika was bustling after him, dressed in her finest, holding her feathered hat to her head with one hand and the layers of her red silk dress with the other.

"Daniel," she said harshly. "I told you to stay at the bakery."

Her brother recoiled. "Tell her Sebastien. I can vote, too."

Sebastien tried to smile. "You're both right, Daniel. You're lucky you don't have to vote, because this isn't fun at all."

Daniel crumpled in disappointment.

"You could help us by riding Apfel back to the inn." Begrudgingly, Daniel climbed on the horse and started up the hill.

"Where's Georg?" Hannah asked Veronika.

"He had some emergency wine meeting in Vienna," she huffed. "I told him they should not be thinking about wine on such an important day. I had thought we would vote for *Der Führer* together."

"Lucky him," Sebastien muttered.

"I assume you will be agreeable today?"

Sebastien smiled. "Oh yes, I'll do the right thing."

Veronika went straight to the head of the line, whispered something to the surly Brownshirt, and stepped to the table. The action halted while she made a spectacle of her vote. She marked her ballot with a flourish and handed it to a soldier, who looked at it, nodded, and gave her a tepid smile.

The Brandls waited quietly, not looking at each other. After a few minutes, Daniel reappeared next to them.

"I gave Apfel an apple," he explained with a grin.

"You should go home," Sebastien said, his mind elsewhere.

"Let me take you." Hannah said, jumping at the chance to escape.

Going anywhere with Hannah was enough for Daniel to abandon civic duty. They were almost at the bakery when a group of local police, with ragged swastikas pinned to their jackets that made them look desperate to belong, stood in their way.

"Have you voted, Fraulein?"

"She's a Frau," Daniel said.

"What's wrong with him?" the taller, blonder one asked.

"Nothing," Hannah said firmly. The bell on the bakery's white door jangled, and Chopin slipped into the yard.

"Could you fetch him, please, Daniel?" Hannah asked brightly. "Gabi is probably wondering where he is."

The other officer, short and stuffed into his uniform, took Hannah's arm and turned her around. When he deposited her back at the voting place, Sebastien was nowhere to be seen. The line was short, and soon the ballot lay before her.

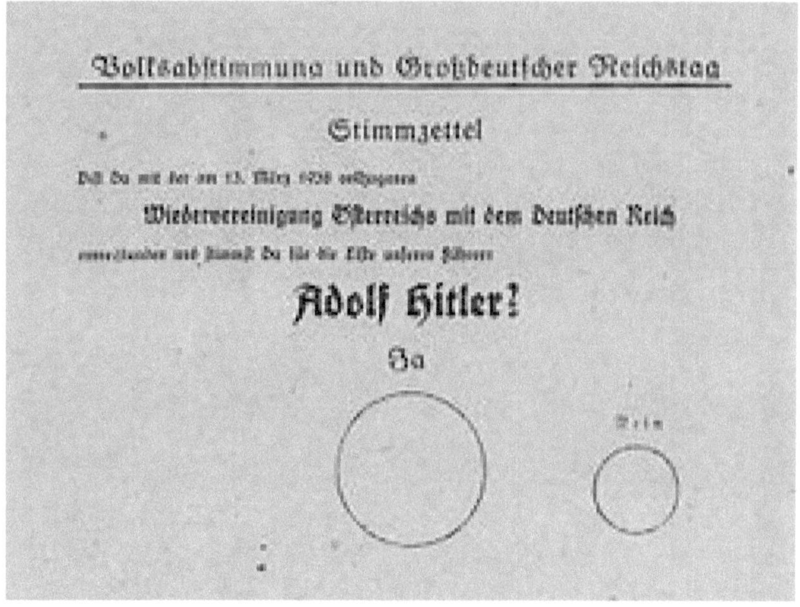


Hannah's stomach churned. Did she agree with the reunification of Austria with the German Reich and to vote for Adolf Hitler? It was as if her pencil had a mind of its own.

Later that night, Gerhard and Elke came by, looking for Daniel. "When we arrived to vote," Elke said, "Daniel was there, wandering around."

"When was this?" Sebastien asked.

"We didn't get down there until after eleven." She scowled at her husband. "I can't believe you made Daniel cry."

"He didn't belong there," Gerhard snapped.

"We sent him home, too," Hannah said, puzzled. "He came back?"

Sebastien locked eyes with Gerhard. "He was curious about all the fuss," he said. "You know how he likes to be in the middle of it all."

The two men, who at one time had been almost inseparable, continued to stare each other down. In the awkward silence, the drops of water dripping into the sink sounded like rocks rattling in a tin can. Elke finally went back to the bakery and returned to say Daniel was asleep in a chair.

# 26

Max and Lili Mayr had stayed home from the Referendum. *Sturmbannführer* Kolbe came by late in the day and Max lied, saying they'd voted early to avoid the crowds. When he asked how they voted, Max spread his arms and said, "How do you think?"

Max made a list of reasons why he should refuse to have anything to do with the printing press. But he kept coming back to Lili, Michel, and Stefan, and Elie and Tovah. The Susskinds.

Their people needed him.

Roman Scholz came to inspect the wine caves. On the lowest level, off a passageway lined with abandoned wine racks, they found a stale-smelling room, empty except for a few pieces of old equipment and curtains of cobwebs that fluttered when they opened the door.

"Is it big enough?" Max asked.

Roman nodded. "It's perfect."

He put off telling Lili until delivery day. Max and Michel took her into the room and announced the pending arrival of a printing press. She surprised them. She asked how it worked, where they would get paper and ink, and who would pick up the finished stacks. Max suspected her outrage over the cold-blooded murders of their friends had tempered her paranoia.

"Roman is doing a lot more than printing anti-Party materials," Michel said. "I'm fairly certain he's hiding people."

"Who?" Lili demanded.

Her son hesitated. "People who are being hunted by the SS. Clerics and dissidents. Our resistance is meager compared to Roman Scholz and a few of his fellow monks."

"There's nothing meager about contraband literature." Lili said.

After dark, Roman arrived with the press in pieces, hidden under tarps. He introduced Max and Michel to a couple in their early twenties, Rafe Klein and his girlfriend, Sigrid Jungmeier. He was medium height, scholarly looking, with dark hair and spectacles. She was slim, with alabaster skin and long blond hair cascading down her back. Lili joined them just as Rafe and Sigrid began to assemble the press.

Roman commented to Max, "It appears your wine caves are constructed in much the same way as the labyrinth at *Winegut Klosterneuburg*, I would guess you have five-meter-thick walls, with a meter of empty space, before you hit rock."

"That sounds correct," Max said.

Lili eyed the monk. "Who else are you hiding besides dissidents?"

He returned her gaze. "We are sheltering targeted Jews. "But I'm not asking you and your family to take that risk."

"You're saying we might get nothing more than a slap on the wrist for producing anti-Reich literature?"

"We have to do something, Mutti," Michel protested.

Lili pointed at the machine. "We are definitely doing something. And Stefan will have no part in this."

Rafe and Sigrid had stood silently during this exchange. Roman nodded at them and said, "These two know what has to be done and how to do it. Rafe can stay here for a while and teach you."

The young man smiled at Max. "Perhaps you have a cot? I can sleep here."

"Nonsense," Max said, glancing at Lili. "There's no need for you to sleep in an icebox. What about Sigrid?"

"She works at a restaurant during the day, and another job at night."

"My other job," she said, "is to do whatever Roman and Rafe need."

Max and Michel learned quickly. One of Roman's fellow monks delivered paper late in the evening several times a week, but never on the same day. Afterwards, Rafe and Sigrid worked through the night.

Max introduced Rafe to Helga and Stefan as a young man studying viticulture. Stefan knew immediately something wasn't right. He investigated and had located the printing press within a few days of its arrival. That night, he was in the room for a few moments before his parents, Rafe, or Sigrid noticed him. His tone was surprisingly businesslike as he pointed at the mounds of paper and leaflets in various stages of completion. "It looks like you need help."

Bundling the leaflets was a time-consuming task. Rafe shook Stefan's hand. "You're hired."

# 27

*St. Jakob, April, 1938*

As for his avoidance of the Referendum, Georg admitted he had taken the coward's way out. Sebastien bore him no grudge. "It was a brilliant move," he told his friend.

A week later, all the villages in Austria celebrated Easter Mass. Hannah told him that from the pulpit, *Pfarrer* Vogl announced that 99% of all Austrians voted yes to the Third Reich. In honor of the *Führer's* birthday the following Wednesday, April 20, Cardinal Innitzer ordered all Austrian churches to fly the swastika flag, ring the bells for a full five minutes, and pray for Adolf Hitler.

Afterwards, Veronika invited the village to *Bäckerei Crème* for a complimentary slice of Easter cake, in case anyone had missed the Nazi flag hanging from the bakery roof.

Still digesting Veronika's cake, the crowd came in later than usual for *Grünen Baum's Osterschinken*, the traditional Easter ham baked in bread with horseradish sauce. A large family waited for a table in the shade. Hannah hurriedly reset it with a new white tablecloth, silverware, and Tobi's bronze frog full of pink roses. She was taking their order when out of the corner of her eye, she saw Andreas waving frantically. Faber Ratzener, *Pfarrer* Vogl, Gerhard, a miserable-looking Elke, and Benno, calling for Gabi, came through the wide-open glass doors of the *wintergarten*.

Faber strode directly to the apricot trees. "We'll take this table," he said, waving his hand, as if shooing flies. The family struggled to collect their belongings, placate their bewildered children, and follow Hannah to the other side of the garden.

"I'm so sorry," she said helplessly.

"Sit with us, Brandl," Faber commanded, and to Hannah he added, "Get us beer, and some of that." He aimed a fork at an abandoned plate of *apfelstrüdel.*

They skipped pleasantries. Faber talked about Hitler's success. Vogl agreed with him, and even embellished. Elke hoped Gerhard would not grovel and Hannah prayed Sebastien would not explode.

The groveling, however, came down the steps with Veronika, trailed by Georg. "I'm so sorry we're late. Willi and Daniel couldn't see fit to clean up after our party for the village, and Georg insisted he had to change his clothes." Her husband plopped down next to Sebastien, "We were summoned," he murmured.

"Frau Wangermann," Faber said, "Compliments on the prominence of your flag." He pointed at Sebastien and Georg. "You both will follow suit."

Sebastien eyed him. "One flag is enough, Faber."

"We aren't children anymore," he barked. "From now on you will address me as *Herr Oberführer.* and listen carefully. Every business owner, farmer, and head of household in both St. Jakob and Moosfeld are required to attend a meeting in your restaurant on May 1. At that time, I will detail our expectations for village contributions to the success of the Third Reich."

Sebastien feigned puzzlement. "Why not hold it in Moosfeld? Viktor is dying to have a turn."

"You do understand, Seb," Gerhard said, "what is necessary for the wellbeing of our town?"

"I thought that was your job."

Twenty minutes later, a thunderous crash came from the kitchen. Andreas burst onto the patio and hurried to their table. "Sorry to interrupt, Faber, but we have a problem inside."

"*Oberführer* Ratzener, old man," Faber said crossly, and shoved his plate away. "By the way, Brandl, Viktor believes your wife is Jewish. By the town meeting, prove to me she's one of us."

•     •     •     •     •

The Brandls rearranged the restaurant into a meeting place. Andreas, Sebastien and Daniel moved most of the tables outside, and brought every chair in the building to line up in rows. Andreas, in a modest act of defiance, suggested that they needn't be neat, and though it went against his nature, Daniel went down each row, gleefully moving one chair askew.

Men filed in from both towns. A few women were also in attendance, sitting in the back.

In the front, Herr Haas sat clumped with others who had joined The Party, eager to hear how Faber Ratzener was going to improve all of their lives.

Sebastien stood to one side and watched Haas beckon Gerhard to the seat he had saved for him. Hannah sat in the chair next to her husband, with Chopin on her lap. He leaned down to her. "Gerhard looks like he's waiting to have a tooth pulled."

Behind Faber sat three more SS officers. Two of them stared ahead with steely eyes, ignoring the din in the room.

Georg joined Sebastien against the wall. "Those two, "he commented, "are trying their hardest to appear formidable. The other one is a bit of an oddball."

Sebastien grinned. The third man, short and rotund, twiddled his thumbs, looking inappropriately content. "They picked him up on the road and gave him a uniform."

The room came to order as the man many of them had grown up with raised his chin and addressed them. "Welcome, citizens of the Third Reich. I am *Oberführer* Ratzener. I'm stationed in Vienna and am here only to inform you of your solemn responsibilities. The *Führer* believes unification is Austria's fervent desire. Economic revitalization is about to begin!"

Hannah glanced up at Sebastien and Georg, who rolled their eyes in unison.

"Each of your farms or businesses will be assessed a percentage of crops and wares to be relinquished to *Der Vaterland,* of which you should be proud to be a part." A slight murmur rippled through the room. "This is your administrator, "Faber continued, "*Oberleutnant* Dietrich Pfortner."

When the thumb-twiddling officer hoisted himself off his chair, Georg leaned into Sebastien. "He's in charge?"

"He will command the assessment squad for both St. Jakob and Moosfeld, keep the records, and apply penalties for non-compliance. St. Jakob's patriots will deliver their donations here. Herr Brandl will store them as directed by the *Oberleutnant.*"

Hannah gasped in horror. Sebastien grabbed her hand and put his finger to his mouth.

"It's only been six months," Georg whispered, "and there are shortages in several areas. Clothing, shoes, fuel, firewood. Even toothpaste and mouthwash."

Gerhard jerked around. "Shh!"

"*Oberleutnant* Pfortner will work in liaison with my brother, Herr Viktor Lonauer, at *Der Wachauerhof,* in Moosfeld," Faber continued.

A farmer raised his hand. "I have a dairy farm. Are you going to measure how much milk I tug out of those teats?"

The crowd laughed. Faber ignored them. "The procedure for procurement and delivery will be explained after the assessments. Brandl, meet me in the back, and bring your wife. He raised his arm. "*Heil* Hitler."

A ragged echo came from the crowd.

Sebastien put his arm around a trembling Hannah and led her down the aisle. Lugging the family bible, Bernard and Sophie joined them.

Herr Hass was fawning over Faber. "I'm sure you are already aware of my prominent position in this town as the postmaster. And I've been a member of The Party for over a year."

"Good for you," Faber said. "Someone will contact you, Herr..."

"Haas. Adolf Haas. I'm going to suggest to our mayor we change the name of the plaza outside to *Adolfhitlerplatz.*"

Faber looked at him as if he was another species. "Take it up with Eigner."

Haas pulled Gerhard away, chattering jubilantly about his plan for elevating the town into a Nazi shrine. Faber poked a finger into Sebastien's chest. "Do you have the documentation I asked for?"

"Have you forgotten you grew up with my wife?"

Bernard stepped forward. "This bible has been in our family for over 100 years," he said as he turned to a page listing the births and deaths of generations of forgotten relatives. He pointed. 'Hannah Maria Maislinger, born October 14, 1916.'

"Why did you pick a Jewish name?"

"It's biblical," Bernard said. "1 Samuel."

"I thought it was pretty," Sophie added.

"Well," Faber sneered, "She doesn't look at all Aryan."

"Faber," Bernard began, unwilling to address otherwise the boy who regularly relieved himself on their barn wall. "There are several people in our ancestral line who weren't blond and blue-eyed. My guess is that you might find similarities in your own family."

Sebastien glared at the man he'd played *Fußbal* alongside in his youth. Neither town had enough for a side, so in a rare show of comradery, Moosfeld and St. Jakob fielded a team. "Are we finished?"

"For now," Faber said.

Bernard snapped the Bible shut and took Sophie's arm. "Please stay," Sebastien said to them. "We'll have coffee in the *kochecke*"

Faber strode off with a warning. "I won't forget you failed to include me in that invitation."

Hannah's eyes filled with tears. Bernard cradled her face. "We put it to rest, liebchen." He turned to his son-in-law. "Thank you, but after this fiasco, we want to go home." Bernard, Sophie, and the bible walked away.

Sebastien lifted Hannah's chin and kissed her. "Remember, I'll be here to take care of you whenever that goon darkens our door."

"They're taking over our cellar. That other one," she paused and pointed a shaky finger toward Pfortner, who was still standing by himself near the front of the room, looking around like he was wondering where everyone had gone. "He'll be here all the time now."

"We'll talk about that later."

"No, Sebastien, now," she insisted as they walked into the *kochecke*. Gerhard was waiting for them, red-faced and furious.

"Faber informed me someone in St. Jakob voted no in the referendum. Tell me you know nothing about it."

Sebastien shrugged.

"You stupid, misled man. I can't believe you are that selfish. You might as well of shoved the town in front of a train."

"I'm sorry," Sebastien said smoothly. "Not for my unwillingness to capitulate to a dictator, but for your discomfort."

"Discomfort?" Gerhard seethed. "Is that what you think this is costing me?"

"I said I was sorry," Sebastien bristled.

"Believe me, it won't be for you I remain silent."

Sebastien shook his head. "Gerhard, we've been friends…"

"Don't start. I'll take care of it."

"You aren't responsible."

Eyes wild, Gerhard pushed open the back door. "I said, I'll take care of it!"

•    •    •    •    •

In front of her small vanity, Hannah attempted to tame her curls. Sebastien sat propped up against the Tobias 'artistic wonder of a headboard.

The cellar was no longer on her mind. "I voted yes."

"You felt you had to," he said. "My job was to be a different voice."

"Why couldn't you leave town, like Georg?"

"Because that voice needed to be heard."

"I'm sure voting no made you feel righteous. But did you think about the risks?"

"I waited to slip my ballot in when lots of people were crowding around. I didn't want to make a personal statement. I wanted to represent those who desire to remain Austrian."

"There weren't many of those at the meeting." Hannah abandoned the hair brush and climbed into bed next to him. "What if someone else finds out?"

"We may disagree, but the Gerhard I know kept our secrets."

•     •     •     •     •

Veronika descended on *Grünen Baum* early the next morning. Daniel dashed into the *kochecke* to warn them, but she was right behind him.

"Good morning, Veronika," Sebastien said. "Join us for breakfast?"

"I've already eaten," she snapped.

"Something on your mind, then?" Hannah braced for fireworks.

Sebastien moved over and patted the banquette. "You're upset."

"I'm concerned my husband didn't vote. What if the authorities find out?"

"Are you going to turn him in?"

"Of course not. But I had to lie about it when Adolph Haas said he didn't remember seeing Georg at the polling place."

Sebastien changed the subject. "How do you feel about having to surrender your bakery goods to the Reich?"

"For God's sake, everyone has to contribute. Viktor says we'll hardly notice."

Hannah squinted at her. Since when had she become chummy with Viktor?

# 28

*Kahlenbergerdorf, August, 1938*

One late night, while bundling leaflets in the wine cave, Stefan reminded Max and Lili it was his turn to go to the University, like his brother. They had discussed it, but the thought of having both of her sons in a place that was sometimes violently anti-Semite made Lili want to lock Stefan in a closet.

"We both appreciate," Max began, "your desire to complete your education."

"But," Lili said, "we feel the situation at the University of Vienna is increasingly dangerous. Michel suggested we hire Rabbi Elie, who is also a professor, to teach you university level courses."

Stefan was intrigued. "Did you ask him?"

"Yes, and he loved the idea of becoming your private tutor."

Elie came the next day. Quickly, Stefan proved his thirst for knowledge insatiable, and his time with the printing press decreased considerably. "He devoured the material for an entire university course in three weeks," Elie told his parents. "Knowledge without wisdom is like water in the sand, puddles that will soon dry up and disappear. Your son is wise."

·　　·　　·　　·　　·

Max was in the winery, going over inventory when Michel approached him. "I have something I have to tell you. Remi told me about a plot to kill Hitler when he was in Vienna last June."

"How would Remi know that?""

"At first, he was in on it."

Max threw the papers down on an upturned barrel.

"It failed, of course. Hitler was riding through *Der Prater*, but he had changed places with his driver. They killed him instead of Hitler."

"Good God. Was Remi the one who pulled the trigger?"

"No, no. Before it happened, he went to some resistance meeting, he didn't give us details, and heard about it. He never went back. I'm sorry, Papa. I thought you should know."

Back in his office, Max's worry for his son burned even hotter in his gut.

•   •   •   •   •

One evening, Elie and Tovah Schett joined them for a late supper. Elie had an alarming report. German hatred and greed ravaged his community. Jews still in Vienna were desperate, either waiting in lines for food and exit visas, or in hiding.

"Roman Scholz has offered sanctuary to several of our families," Tovah said.

"I firmly believe," Rafe said, "that unless someone betrays him, he won't be discovered."

"What about those actors?" Max demanded.

"He and Otto Hartmann parted ways a week after you met him. Lehmann and Reiman are working with a different resistance cell. They don't know what Roman's doing."

"Those people came with stacks of *Mein Kampf* to *Der Buchwald*," Lili said, "rearranged my front window display and then told me I had to pay for them. I wanted to make a bonfire, you know, like the Nazis have done with thousands of precious books." She turned to the Schetts. "I have an assistant, now, Anno Kerber's daughter, Magdalena. She convinced me I had to keep at least one stack in view." Her voice faltered. "I hated myself for that."

Rafe put his hands on Elie's and Tovah's shoulders and knelt down between them. "We could help you get out."

"But many people are counting on me," Elie said.

Tovah shivered. "I have to admit, I'm afraid. But I won't leave before Elie says it's time."

# 29

*St. Jakob, November, 1938*

Listening to the BBC was outlawed throughout the Third Reich, and Veronika ordered Georg to get rid of the radio. It disappeared, relocated to the little office between the *Grünen Baum* kitchens. Every few nights, Georg, Hannah, Andreas, Mathilde, Tobias, and sometimes Daniel, huddled around it with the volume turned down low.

Despite her escalating anxiety, Hannah attended these furtive sessions. She needed to know what her husband knew. Her change of heart pleased Sebastien, but she feared if she didn't squeeze in with the rest, he would withdraw to some secret place without her.

They listened to the report of Hitler's invasion of the Sudetenland, his voice, as usual, both sinister and spellbinding.

"What does he want with that insignificant patch of land?" Andreas asked.

"Czechoslovakia," Georg and Sebastien replied in unison.

"What are you all doing?" Veronika demanded from the doorway. Too late, Sebastien reached for the radio dial. She was quick to point out they were all criminals and shouted at Georg, "Why would you put your wife in danger?"

Hannah sat back. It was a fair question. She almost envied Veronika, home, undaunted, doing whatever it was she did in Georg's beautiful villa.

Daniel spoke up. "Hannah and Mathilde are here. They're safe."

Veronika pulled Georg toward the back door, where Apfel filled the frame, surveying the scene. "I don't see any of you suffering under the new regime," she whined. "Instead, you sit in a huddle and complain. I say you're all ungrateful and reckless."

Georg mouthed a thank you to Sebastien and Hannah. "Excuse me," he said to Apfel.

Three weeks later, *Oberleutnant* Pfortner found Hannah folding napkins in the near-empty dining room. Since May, he had made a habit of taking a stool at Sebastien's bar and conversing with the usual clientele. He even told Hannah to call him Dietrich.

"Sebastien isn't here," she told him.

"Please tell him St. Jakob is on the schedule for assessments. They will be here on Sunday, the twelfth of November."

Her heart galloping, she nodded and went back to her napkins. Pfortner continued to stand there, reeking of day-old sweat and tobacco. Eventually, he lumbered out.

The date set, Sebastien had a plan. "You know what I've been thinking, Hannah? You've been worried about getting pregnant again. Maybe we should escape for a few days and concentrate on making it happen."

Astonished, Hannah said, "What about Gabi?"

"Do you want the list of volunteers itching to take care of her? I'm thinking Vienna. I've already called Hubert, and he can't wait for us to come. We'll leave on the Thursday before the assessors arrive and be back on Saturday to feed them."

"Go, we're fine here," Mathilde declared. "Tobi can step in behind the bar. And Hannah, your mother has told me many times she'd love to take a turn in the kitchen."

"There's a big party on Friday," Sebastien said, his eyes twinkling. "Bernard can be sommelier."

Sophie loved the idea of sleeping at the inn, and Hannah's guilt about leaving was somewhat assuaged.

On November 9, they got up early for Andreas to take them to the train in Krems. Hours later, they crossed the canal from Vienna's city center and arrived at *Hotel Stephanie*. Hans Bäder, the manager, greeted them.

"Welcome," he cried, embracing each of them. "Thank you for finally allowing me to repay your hospitality and generosity."

Sebastien explained he had met Hans while living in Vienna.

"Your husband and I shared an addiction to horse racing."

"A story for another time," Sebastien said swiftly.

Hans winked at Hannah. "But then he disappeared, so I followed his tracks to St. Jacob."

"And just before our wedding, he brought his family for a big Sunday feast."

"Your husband would not allow me to pay. I said he was welcome to bring his bride to *Hotel Stephanie* and be our guests for as long as he pleased."

"I'm not sure one meal equals two nights lodging in your lovely hotel," Sebastien mused.

"Never mind," the proprietor said. "Go on, visit your brother. Your satchels will be in your room waiting for you."

They hurried back toward *Café Hawelke,* stopping only to stare at a couple showing off their little boy dressed in a miniature version of Hitler's favorite suit. His hair was cut precisely like the *Führer*'s, parted on the left and plastered to his head, straight bangs sliced across his face at the same peculiar angle.

Hubert greeted them at the door a fierce hug. "Breakfast?"

"We'll take anything!" Sebastien laughed. "We were too excited to eat."

He led them to a corner table, warmed by a cast-iron stove, and returned with sliced ham and cheese, rolls, butter and jam, and cups of foamy cappuccino.

"I told Leopold about your coffee machine," Hubert said, "and he went right out and bought one. Even when we told Josephine it would boost business, she scolded us. Then I taught her how to use it, and she has at least three cappuccinos a day."

Josephine had snuck up behind them. "Oh Hubert, one. Maybe two." She put her hands around Hannah's face and kissed each cheek. "I still can't believe I can have one anytime I want."

The café came alive, and the Hawelkes bustled off to work. "Stay," Leopold called to Hubert, who poured himself a beer and sat down.

"Isn't it a little early, brother?" Sebastien teased.

"These days, anytime is good."

The conversation started pleasantly: *Grünen Baum*, Andreas refusing to slow down, adventures in the kitchen with Daniel. An hour went by.

"What's it been like for you?" Sebastien asked finally. We've heard terrible stories."

"From Georg?"

"Yes, have you seen him?"

"He comes by occasionally when he's in the city. He told me he saw people walking down the street, saluting people at random, or even raising their arms to one of the Hitler busts all over the city. Tragic, yes, but we had a good laugh."

Hubert went to the bar for another beer, and Sebastien signaled him to bring two.

"How is your friend, Maximillian?" Hannah asked Hubert.

"He's coping, as we all are," Hubert said. "When Hitler arrived, Max came into Vienna and saw him bragging about the love affair between him and Austria. On his way home, he witnessed the murder of a Jewish family he knew."

"No!" Hannah gasped. The familiar panic rose. "Do they come to *Café Hawelke*?"

"The Germans?" Hubert frowned.

Hannah didn't reply.

"Are you asking if we have Jewish customers? Of course. Although I'm not sure Josephine and Leopold are aware. They claim they know everyone, but sometimes I feel their job is to be acquainted, not connected."

Leopold glided by their table. "Where are you staying?"

"*Hotel Stephanie*," Sebastien replied. "The manager is a friend."

"That's in Leopoldstadt," Hubert said. "The Jewish quarter. It used to be a wonderful place."

Sebastien pushed on. "What does Mayr say about all of this?"

His brother smirked. "He says visiting his customers in Vienna feels like crawling around in a bed of worms."

"Could he be involved in the resistance?"

"I wouldn't know." Hubert rose to help Josephine, who was juggling five plates of sausage. "See you tomorrow?"

"Of course," Sebastien replied. They called out their goodbyes across the room. Hubert waved, but didn't escort them to the door.

On the street, Hannah grabbed her husband's arm. "You chose a hotel in the Jewish Ghetto?"

"*Hotel Stephanie* is beloved by the Viennese! They recommend it to their families and friends. And it's only two blocks from the canal."

Hannah waited for him to say more. There were other reasons he had chosen it. But Sebastien was resolute. Unlike herself, a harsh wind would not sway him.

She had other questions. "Why did you ask about Max and the resistance? Do you think Hubert joined, too?"

"If he did, I envy him."

"Why would you say that?"

Sebastien halted abruptly, his feet suddenly embedding themselves in cobblestone. "Don't you see? He's doing something!"

The wind blew ferociously and the temperature dropped. Hannah's tears became tiney icicles stuck to her skin. "What is it you think you can do?"

"I don't know. And now I have to actually help the bastards cheat our friends and neighbors out of what is rightfully theirs."

Hannah sighed and gave up. They resumed their walk. She bowed her head against the wind as they crossed the canal. When they finally arrived in their room, Hannah immediately went down the hall to take a hot bath. She lay back in the hot water and soap bubbles.

"Can I come in?" Sebastien said through the door.

"It's open."

He locked the door behind him and climbed into the tub. They touched each other everywhere, skin smooth and slippery under their fingers. Water and suds spilled onto the floor. Slowly, luxuriously, they came together beneath lingering white caps of soap, and stayed that way until the water was cold.

Later, she would reflect again on her husband's power to send the creatures of worry scurrying away.

•     •     •     •     •

When the weather seemed to have lost its edge, they ventured out again. Sebastien suggested they visit the site of their first night as a married couple. "We'll be there in time for a pastry and a glass of wine. We'll toast each other!"

They drew closer to the *Metropole*. A Nazi flag, the largest they had seen on any Viennese building, hung from the hotel roof down to the formidable front door.

"Oh, no," Hannah breathed out raggedly.

"It's still our place. Let's find our table in that sparkly dining room."

A cadre of SS officers, rifles ready, stood in front of the door, some conversing among themselves, others with concrete faces, eyes trained on every passer-by. Sebastien took a tentative step forward.

"What is your business here?" asked the one with an overwhelming moustache that looking like he had attached it that morning. If you're looking for someone you've misplaced," he snickered, "the line is in the back."

"We only want to have a slice of cake and coffee," Sebastien said politely.

"Oh, you do. "The dining room isn't open, at least not for you."

Sebastien looked at Hannah, expecting her to be crestfallen. But she was staring straight ahead. Several men had moved aside and revealed a gilded sign. *Geheime Staatspolizei.* Gestapo.

Sebastien steered her away held them to a controlled pace. "What did he mean, people you've misplaced?" Hannah asked.

"Their loved ones, I assume, who have disappeared. Look over there." Hitler youth in short pants carrying flags with swastikas and skull and crossbones marched by, followed by Hitler Girls Youth, leaping up and down in unison. Old women, backs bent under covered loads of firewood, and dwarfed by sticks protruding from under the burlap, staggered through their ranks without looking up.

Darkness descended. The skies opened and rain scented the night. The pavement glistened under street lamps. Cars passed by, stirring up new puddles. It was all soothingly normal.

Halfway back to the hotel, they passed a bookstore. "*Der Buchwald*," Hannah said appreciatively. The store was warm and welcoming, with nooks for people to read and a soft carpet on the polished wood floor for children to sit with a new book.

A woman approached them. "Are you looking for something special?"

"I imagine everything is special here," Sebastien said. Your store is a delight."

She smiled brightly. "How kind of you."

Promising to return the next day, they thanked the proprietress, who said she looked forward to it.

On the next street, they came to a sign in a store window, dimly lit by the street lamp.

*60,000 is what this person suffering from a hereditary defect costs the People's community during his lifetime. Fellow citizen, that is your money too."*

Sebastien leaned down and squinted at the print at the bottom. "The monthly magazine of the <u>Bureau for Race Politics</u>."

"What does it mean?" Hannah asked.

"More people to hate."

# 30

*Kahlenbergerdorf, November 9, 1938*

Max found Lili was in the kitchen, preparing stalks of white asparagus for *mittagessen*. Soup was already bubbling on the stove, and its savory aroma, along with that of fresh bread, almost brought Max to his knees.

He nuzzled his wife's neck. "I can't wait to eat."

"Michel is coming home with a friend from the university, and Stefan is bringing two friends from the village. And Elie, Tovah, Rafe, and Sigrid."

"She stayed here last night?"

"She stays here often, Maximillian. We're setting a table for twelve today in the dining room."

"Is that a hint?"

"No, but it's a good idea."

Dutifully, Max started pulling open cupboards and drawers. The Schetts arrived and Max handed Elie a stack of bowls.

"I don't think you put the spoons in the right place," the Rabbi observed.

They finished just as family and guests appeared all at once. Helga took one look at the table and frowned. "What have you done, Maximillian?"

"Elie did it."

"Papa," Michel said, "this is Remi Schnaitl."

Max summoned his gracious nature. "Hello, Remi."

"Good day, Herr Mayr," Remi said. "I'm going to tell my father you set the table."

"It's hardly a revolution," Michel said.

"It would be in our house."

"Mutti gives Papa chores all the time," Stefan piped up. "They have an arrangement."

Max threw his son a pile of cloth napkins. "Here," he said, "arrange these."

The atmosphere was light, with no mention of underground rooms or illegal literature. When they finished, Stefan whisked his friends upstairs, and Michel announced he and Remi were going tasting and set off for the winery. Tovah declared that after the endless plates of delicious food, they needed a nap. After they saw them out, Lili sat down heavily at the kitchen table and beckoned her husband to join her.

"I'm worried about them. Jewish leaders are being targeted by anyone with authority. But we are all in danger. People say they can tell a Jew by the way we look. The stereotypes have followed us throughout history. Things like dark skin, thick lips, and aquiline noses."

Max thought of the times he had identified Jews by those characteristics.

"There were Jews in my town who produced red-haired children. Red hair has meant Jewish for centuries. Our friends were already singled out and tormented before this current assault on Viennese Jews."

Max remained silent, knowing nothing he said would make a difference. He followed her down the hall to their bedroom. She closed the door. A shadow crossed her face, a ghost walking by.

"My heritage and our real names," she reminded him yet again, "must remain our secret."

"Lili, my love," Max said, fingering the thick braid of hair that fell over one shoulder. "Will Kielce never leave you?"

Lili walked to her armoire. "Did I tell you I'm planning to serve coffee and pastries at *Der Buchwald*?" He watched while she changed her clothes and pinned up her hair. Her beauty always amazed him, as did her lively mind.

They kissed goodbye at the kitchen door. "Why don't I drive you?" he suggested.

"Magdalena's at home tonight. I'm not sure when I'll be back."

Lili descended the steps and crossed the courtyard. Max heard her car start up and he waved, even though she probably wouldn't glance back, already thinking about books. And coffee and pastries. He worked in his office until the light streaming through his windows began to fade. Surprised it was so late, he started for the door.

The phone rang, and he retreated to his desk.

Tollner. A weed that came back every time Max thought he had yanked him out of their lives.

"Did you hear about France?"

"Two days ago," Max replied, "someone shot a Nazi celebrity."

"A Jewish someone, who was angry his parents were deported."

"I'd be angry too."

"It was a diplomat, Ernst vom Rath, and he died. Goebbels was his friend, and he's seized on the assassination to stir up every anti-Semite in Europe. People are out in the streets, demanding revenge."

"I can't believe how hatred metastasizes into feverish mobs."

"Don't go into Vienna tonight."

The hair on the back of Max's neck perked up.

"My guess is the SS and the Brownshirts are going to be only hours behind what's happening here in Berlin."

"Lili is in Vienna," Max said. "At her store." He glanced at his watch. "Unless she's on her way home," he added unconvincingly.

"Goering said Vienna must be *Judenrein* in four years."

Max exploded. "Cleansed of Jews? How dare he say that? It's not his city."

"Vienna belongs to Hitler," Tollner insisted.

"And I suppose that suits you."

"What do you mean by that?"

"I mean, you're a Nazi, but you call me and pretend to care. Does it make you feel better to throw a few secrets my way? Who are you anyway, Fritz?"

"You think I like what's going on?"

"Then why don't you resist? In your position, you could be of great help to the Jewish Community."

"Don't you get it? Jews are no longer welcome anywhere in the Third Reich. Believe me, the best thing they can do is leave. Far better than the alternative."

"What? Lining them all up and shooting them?"

"I hear things. Talk of forcing them into ghettos, sealed off from the Aryan world."

"How could they make entire families pick up and move?"

"They would have to leave everything behind."

"But how would they live?"

"I don't think they're worried about them *living*. You might not want to be seen with a Jew. The Reich has taken over every city registry and post office. They've got birth certificates and addresses. Lists have been made of possible sympathizers. I keep telling you, Max, they have eyes and ears everywhere. Join the Party."

Max slammed down the phone. The chatter in the kitchen came to an abrupt halt when he bolted through the door. He had to pull himself together.

"I assume Stefan's friends have gone home," he said shakily. "Remi, stay here tonight with Michel."

Helga came into the kitchen. "What's happening, Maximillian? I heard you shouting from my room."

"Because of an incident in Paris, there's unrest in the larger cities."

"What happened?" Stefan wanted to know.

'Not now. I'm going to call the bookstore and make sure Lili is on her way home."

He was back in under a minute. "No answer." He pulled his overcoat off a peg near the door.

"Stay here," Michel told his brother sternly. He and Remi followed Max down the stairs. "Tell us, Papa," he demanded.

"An important German diplomat was murdered by a young Jewish man whose parents disappeared. Goebbels, one of Hitler's closest associates, knew him well. He's made it a reason to go after Jews."

"Goebbels is the minister of Propaganda," said a voice behind them.

"I told you to stay upstairs," Michel said.

"I don't care," Stefan protested. "Papa is rushing out to get Mutti. I deserve to know why."

"I'm coming with you," Michel said.

"No!" Max strode to his truck and turned on the engine. "Stay here. He took one final look at the three young men. "Please."

They stepped back, and he roared away.

# 31

*Leopoldstadt, Vienna, November 9, 1938*

Sebastien sat up, disoriented. "What was that?" It sounded like firecrackers had gone off directly under them. But not ten seconds went by when the sounds mutated into sharp retorts, followed by the rumble of heavy vehicles and angry shouting.

"Guns," he yelped, "Get down!" After a moment he crawled to the window, Hannah right behind him. Massive trucks, some overloaded with what looked to be paramilitary, and others with men not in uniform waving rifles, sat in the middle of the street. Volleys of rifle fire blew out the windows on the building across from them.

Sebastien covered Hannah with his body. Bullets blasted the hotel windows, shattering glass across the room. Deadly shards pelted Sebastien's back and head. More bullets imbedded themselves in the ceiling.

They lay frozen until they heard the trucks move on, and the staccato of gun shots fade. Flames crackled. A woman wailed. A child called out for his father.

"Are you all right?" Hannah gasped. Glass rained off of him. Their heads rose. Men were pulling terrified residents out of the burning building across the street. A blue-lighted firetruck went by, siren blaring, its five occupants barely glancing at the conflagration.

"Wait," Sebastien shouted out the window, but the brigade moved on. He turned on a lamp and pulled off his nightshirt, wincing at the scattered pricks of pain.

Hannah put on her shoes and shoved away the glass as she made a path to the water bowl and towel on the dresser across the room. Trembling violently, she washed the wounds on her husband's back and arms, wondering if this Jewish hotel stocked bandages.

Sebastien was stoic. "How bad is it?"

"Three of the cuts are deep."

"Not too bad."

"Sebastien, please."

He stood and pulled on his pants and another shirt, which dotted instantly with splotches of blood. "I'm going downstairs. Just for a few minutes, I promise."

Hannah retreated to a corner and wrapped her arms around herself. She stayed in her cocoon until twenty minutes later, when she heard Sebastien's voice. Crawling to the window, she watched while he and Hans Bäder hurled buckets of water at the front door of the building. Inside, a wall of flame danced red and gold. She wanted to scream at him to come back to her. It would be useless; retreat would never occur to him.

A man, nightclothes on fire, emerged with two unmoving children in his arms, a boy and a girl. A couple rushed to him and set the children on a blanket someone had laid on the ground. Sebastien doused the man with water, and he howled like a wounded animal.

Hannah prayed. The girl's leg moved, She gasped for air and twisted frantically to look for the boy and call his name. There was a shout. "He's still breathing!"

Hannah retreated to her corner. Should she be helping too?

Sebastien finally returned, his face blackened, his lips blue. There were black smudges on his shirt, and dark stains from his still-draining wounds. The temperature in their room had plummeted, and Hannah wrapped the bed quilt around him and rubbed his icy arms and legs.

From outside came a cacophony of ominous sounds: Trucks, more gunshots, jeering voices, the cries of people running.

"I wish I knew what you were trying to prove when you picked this hotel," Hannah said. He gathered the quilt and shuffled to the window.

"Look at me, Sebastien."

The soft knock on the door was Hans. "Oh my God," he cried, surveying the glass on the floor. "I appreciate you coming with me, Sebastien, but you should have stayed here with your wife."

Hannah's senses deadened. The acrid smells of smoke and death, the keening of the injured, receded into the shattered walls of a room she was desperate to leave. "Where did you go?"

"Down the street," Sebastien said.

"I have a hotel full of Jewish employees," Hans said. "Most of them live in Leopoldstadt. So far, I've been able to shield them from the SS."

"But they must know," Hannah argued. "Why else would they attack your hotel?"

"I should have been more vigilant. Since March I was forbidden to offer a kosher breakfast. I suppose I thought that would be the end of it."

She glowered at him.

"They're razing Jewish homes," he said tearfully, "looting synagogues and setting them on fire. Glass is knee-deep in the streets."

Sebastien finally spoke up. "It's the Brownshirts, and gangs of Viennese who couldn't wait to shoot a Jew."

"This wasn't spontaneous," Hans said. "They created chaos, and then attacked."

Hannah began throwing their belongings into the satchels. "Why didn't the firetruck stop?"

"The Austrian police were also standing around, doing nothing. By chance, my family went on holiday to ski." He choked on a sob. "The snow was early this year."

He left, and Hannah seethed. "I don't understand you. Did you think you could take their guns away and tell them to go home?" She stopped to take a breath. "Why aren't you packing?"

He threw off the quilt. "I wanted to help."

Hannah stood up and faced him. "I know you can't stand to see someone suffer. But one man can't stand against truckloads of crazed killers."

"I wasn't thinking."

"That's not good enough, Sebastien. We're leaving."

He held up his pocket watch. "Four o'clock. We'll go when it's light."

Hannah shook her head furiously. "They'll see us."

"And we'll see them. Once we get over the bridge, we might blend in." He rummaged in his bag and pulled out all of the clothing he had left. "Put another sweater on under your coat."

More clothes would save them? Hannah fought through the fog in her mind.

Sebastien shoved the armoire against the door. "Less than three hours until dawn." He wrapped his bloody shirt around his hand and brushed the glass away from a spot near the wall farthest from the windows. "We'll wait."

They sat down, Hannah clutching the satchel on her lap. Gently, Sébastien took it from her. "We'll leave this here," he said. "We can't look like we're running."

Surrender. Leave everything. "Where will we go?" she managed to ask.

"To Hubert. Hopefully, he can get us out of Vienna."

# 32

Dense overcast hid the moon, and the road to Vienna was quiet and dark with menace. Nearly at the city limit, Max heard a loud bang. His truck jerked to the right and skidded off the road. Cursing, Max saw that one of his tires was not only flat, but split in half.

The lantern he kept stowed behind the seat had somehow disappeared. He yanked out the spare from the back, and working by feel, loosened the first of six bolts and set it on the ground. It immediately rolled down the slight embankment. Scrambling after it, he sifted through dirt and weeds until his fingers found it. The rest of the bolts went into his pockets. His eyes slowly adjusted.

The new tire was stiff, and the bead uneven on the wheel. He debated deflating it to correct the problem, but it was almost 8:00. He replaced the bolts, working with one eye on the road in case Lili's car, a new red and black Steyr Baby 55 he had surprised her with for her birthday, came along.

He tossed the old tire into the truck and climbed into the driver's seat. The starter button stuck, and the vehicle refused to turn over. After a few minutes of furious attempts, Max slammed his fists on the steering wheel. The truck came to life.

He drove toward the city center until the Austrian police blocked his way. When they shouted at him to turn his vehicle around, he abandoned it and ran.

Seven blocks later several truckloads of soldiers came up behind him, waving rifles and shouting, *"Judenrein!"*

One voice rose over the others. "An eye for an eye!" Others answered, "One hundred eyes for an eye!"

Smoke rose in the distance. As he got closer to *Der Buchwald*, the sky flashed with exploding flames.

"Max?" Tovah Schett stood in the street just ahead of him. She flung herself into his arms. "Her store is on fire," she cried. "There were men with torches and guns. Elie told me to run."

He had never moved faster in his life. Three blocks to the bookshop, then two, and he was pushing through a crowd and calling his wife's name. Two men stepped in front of him, rifles pointed at his head.

"Move aside," Max ordered them fiercely.

"You're too late," one of them sneered.

Max pushed the rifle away. "Where's the fire department?"

"They aren't coming," his tormenter said.

He ran down the alley next to the store, feeling the intensity of the fire sear his skin. The back door was open and Elie stood near the doorway. Max charged forward.

"No," Elie shouted. His face was black, and he was swatting at his burning coat sleeve. Max pulled off his own coat, pushed his friend to the ground and rolled him across a patch of dirt. When Max struggled to untangle himself, Elie held him in a fierce grasp.

"She's gone."

Max fought him furiously. He leaped toward the door, which was off its hinges, and an eruption of fire knocked him off his feet. Elie dragged him away. Max's cries of denial pierced the heavy black air.

"It's my fault," the Rabbi wailed. They crawled away over rocks and broken glass. He stared into Max's vacant eyes. "A gang of angry men were raging through the streets near our temple. I found some terrified children, and I sent them to the bookstore. I knew she would care for them. But the men must have followed. When I got here," he raised his blistered hands to his cover his face, "it was an inferno."

They staggered to a patch of unscorched grass and collapsed. "I ran to the back door and went in," Elie continued. "Two of the children were right there, so I pulled them out and went looking for the others. And then I saw her, her body covering a little girl. Somewhere inside, there are two other children."

Elie wept uncontrollably while Max sat, numb, still disbelieving. "Was she alive?"

"A beam from the ceiling had fallen on them."

A husband's agonized sounds of despair rose into the squalid night.

The beasts had moved on, tracking other prey. Only the back wall of her store remained, the rest, by now, a smoldering pile of embers. There would be no retrieval of bodies. Lili, the child beneath her, and two others, none of them more than eight years old. Their cremation was complete.

Elie lurched into the street, calling for Tovah. When they returned, they held Max and recited the prayer for the dead.

The two surviving children crawled out from under Lili's car. They clung to Elie and Tovah, whispering questions about their companions.

"Lili gave her life to save five children," Tovah agonized. "Two of them lived, Max." But he was beyond solace.

"We have to take them home," Elie said. "And I have to tell the other families."

Tovah shook her head. "Max can't be alone."

"No," Max said unevenly. "Go with your husband. Tell them all I'm sorry."

"How will you get home?"

"I'll manage," he said. He embraced them both, and then the children. Later, he left Vienna in the red and black Steyr Baby 55, unable to see the road through the constant cascade of tears.

# 33

*Leopoldstadt, November 10, 1938*

In their bullet-riddled room, Sebastien and Hannah waited for dawn. The sun finally rose, barely visible behind a screen of smoke. They crept down to the lobby, and Hans ushered them out of the hotel through a back door and into an alley. They followed the path toward the bridge until it ended and they had to move to the street. Various modes of transportation were at a standstill. Sebastien yanked Hannah into a doorway.

Only one truck moved forward, crunching the broken glass. Two Brownshirts fired into the air from the truck's cabin, and cursed at people to move out of the way.

"Don't move," Sebastien said into Hannah's ear.

The truck straddled the sidewalk and rumbled toward them. They flattened themselves against the door. Boys, hardly grown, sat with their legs hanging through slats in the back, laughing and chanting. "Maggot Jews!" One of them caught Hannah's eye and pointed a rifle at her.

"No," Hannah screamed. He laughed and took several shots at the wall above her.

They sprinted toward the canal bridge. A block away they could make out its cornerstone, and two bloodied bodies propped up against the bricks. Sebastien pulled Hannah's head into his shoulder and kept moving, stepping over their skewed legs. Out of one eye Hannah saw a woman, her eyes open and mouth gaping hideously. Rivulets of dried blood creased her swollen abdomen.

"She's pregnant!" Hannah screamed.

"We can't help, Hannah." He dragged her forward across the bridge and onto the street that would take them to Hubert. Away from the canal, the chaos waned.

Leopold met them at Café Hawelke's door. "Hans Bäder called. Thank God you made it back to us." Josephine came to wrap her arms around Hannah.

"Where's Hubert?" Sebastien asked, still coughing up smoke.

"He's not here. I thought maybe he went after you."

Hannah's eyes glazed over. "We saw a pregnant woman. They killed them."

"Sweet Jesus," Josephine said, crossing herself.

Leopold led them to the same corner table they shared with Hubert the day before. Josephine brought coffee and rolls, but neither of them gave them a glance.

Sebastien ran a trembling hand over sticky clumps of hair, stiff with dried blood. "We need to find my brother."

Leopold pulled a folded piece of paper out of his vest pocket. "He left this."

"It says to leave immediately and follow these directions to the *Hütteldorf* train station," Sebastien told Hannah. "He's given us a list of streets to take, where to turn, even landmarks. We should go, now."

Josephine rolled up the bread in a cloth napkin and tied it. "You have to eat."

"Please tell Hubert to call *Grünen Baum*," Sebastien said.

"And please call here when you get home," Leopold said, directing them into the kitchen. "It's what he will want."

They lunged out the back door, startling two women holding empty baskets.

"They're here for Hubert," Leopold said. "I'll take care of them."

Following his brother's instructions, they walked unhurriedly. They passed the charred rubble of several buildings and Hannah's hand flew to her mouth.

"Isn't this where the bookstore was?"

They stood for a moment, surveying the ruins. "I'm sure it was empty," Sebastien said, the wounds on his back screaming.

Hubert hadn't sent them to the nearest train. "He must have his reasons," Sebastien said when they passed a sign for the *Westbahnhof*. Instead, they walked southwest through narrow streets and alleys. They heard rifle shots and cheering coming from the boulevards. When the sounds of madness lessened, they rested on a bench and devoured Josephine's rolls.

Almost two hours later they reached the *Hütteldorf* Station in Vienna's *Penzing* district. They had just missed it. Sebastien frowned at the schedule on the wall. "This line stops at every silly little town. It will take hours to get back to Krems. When at last they fell into their seats, weariness overwhelmed their lingering fear and they slept.

Hannah's stomach awakened her, roiling with both hunger and a day besieged by tension. She poked Sebastien. "How will we get back to St. Jakob?"

His eyes popped open. "We can hire a car in Krems."

"Do we have enough money?"

"Let's hope someone has heard of Andreas Brandl."

They arrived in Krems, and Sebastien insisted they go first to a restaurant owned by a friend. "He'll let us pay later." He downed two beers while they ate *Bratwurst* in silence.

The first taxi they approached refused them outright. "You don't look like you have enough money to hire a horse, much less a car."

Sebastien smirked. "Apfel, where are you?" When Sebastien explained to the next driver he couldn't cover the bill until they returned home, he simply grunted, and gestured for them to climb in. Hannah felt her muscles release, and beside her, Sebastien slept again.

•   •   •   •   •

The lights on the front of the inn were out.

"Papa must have closed," Sebastien said. But Andreas rushed out, threw money at the driver, and pulled them inside to the *kochecke*, where Bernard and Sophie, holding Gabi in her lap, Mathilde and Tobias, Daniel, and, unexpectedly, Siegi and her children, were just finishing supper.

"Why are you home?" Daniel asked.

Hannah burst into tears.

"What's happened?" Bernard cried. When Sebastien took off his coat, Mathilde and Siegi screamed.

"It looks worse than it is," he explained.

Hannah shook her head in exasperation and wiped her cheeks with the sleeve of her sweater. Mathilde ran for supplies.

"Where are your things?" Sophie asked.

"We had to leave them," Hannah said.

Georg and Veronika came through the kitchen door.

"Have you heard anything?" Sebastien asked.

Georg relayed the scant amount of information he had about the murder in Paris and the pogroms in Germany and Austria.

For the next hour, Gabi sat quietly on Hannah's lap and played with a napkin ring. Even Ernst and the twins were solemn, toting the books their mother gave them into the office. Sebastien told the story, but Hannah interrupted him with the graphic details he left out. Even Veronika was subdued.

Sebastien sighed. "I stopped in front of a home that must have been burning for a long time. A family stood watching. The bright glow, the burning embers, and then next to nothing. I could see what was left reflected in the eyes of the children."

About midnight, Georg stood. "Get some sleep," he told Sebastien and Hannah. You've been through hell."

"Worse than hell," his friend conceded.

"I'm sorry," Veronika said to Hannah. Georg took her hand, and they left.

# Part 3

*"Has the likes of this happened in your days or in the days of your fathers?*
*Tell your children about it, and let your children tell theirs, and their children the next generation."*

**–Joel 1:2**

# 34

*St. Jakob, March, 1939*

Sebastien was already downstairs, but Hannah wasn't ready to get out of bed. During the night, she dreamed of running far away from Austria. Awake, she clung to the fantasy.

Later, she was preparing for *mittagessen* when Siegi dashed in and told her to have everyone meet her in the *wintergarten* at four o'clock that afternoon. It was unusual, but so was Siegi.

Sebastien pushed two tables together. Hannah served coffee and an array of sweets. Siegi had to raise her voice to get their attention.

"Otto's been conscripted." Conversation ceased.

"A truck came and picked him up along with two others, so Papa and I followed them." She slapped away tears. "He went through a line of doctors. Otto said he told them he couldn't see without his glasses, but it was all too quick. They exempted no one."

"But he still might get a desk job," Sophie offered.

"They gave me eighty German marks. I told them my husband was worth a lot more than that."

"That's 120 schillings," Daniel commented.

"I can't stay at *Der Wachauerhof.* It's impossible to mop his dirty, greasy floors with three children pulling at my skirt or chasing each other. Even with Otto there, he called me a useless cow."

"He called me that all the time," Hannah said.

"Bring the children and live with us," Bernard said.

"Or stay here for a while," Sebastien said. "Gabi loves her cousins."

Siegi turned to her mother. "Thank you, but I think going to the farm is what I should do. If you can help with the children, maybe I can get a part-time job." Her mouth turned up. "But you'll have to stay alert, or they'll lock you out of your own house."

"I'll give them chores," Bernard said. "They'll be too tired to be naughty."

"We always need help around here," Andreas said. "Come in whenever you want to. And, please, stay here tonight."

She nodded gratefully and fiddled with her wet handkerchief. "Willi said I could work at the bakery."

Mathilde and Hannah's eyes widened.

"Viktor won't be happy," Bernard remarked. "He's losing free labor."

Sophie sighed. "It's about time."

Hannah hugged her mother, who never said things like that.

•　　•　　•　　•　　•

"Brandl, open up!" Hannah was gulping down breakfast. She was in no mood for Viktor Lonauer.

He charged past, pointing a finger at her. "Go get him!" he bellowed.

Sebastien flew through the *kochecke* door. "What's all the shouting? Oh," he said. "Hello Viktor. There's a little coffee left."

"Where is that worthless woman my idiotic brother married? The cook didn't show up this morning, so I went upstairs and pounded on her door. I don't know why the army would need Otto. If they give him a gun, he'll shoot his own foot. I don't care if he's gone. She's not walking out on me."

Sebastien took a languid sip of coffee. "How much are you paying her?"

Viktor's face moved within an inch of Sebastien's. "You forget I give her and those brats a place to live."

"She's making other arrangements."

The sound of little feet could be heard coming down the stairs. Hannah dashed up the steps and grabbed them. "Let's go upstairs and find Mutti."

"I'm hungry," Ernst shouted.

"I want strawberries," Anke declared. "Raspberries!" Juli joined in.

Siegi stood at the landing. "Do I get to pick, too?"

"Viktor's here," Hannah said. "The cook is missing and he can't go on without you."

"He's still got Gertraud."

Mathilde appeared. "Someone isn't pleased down there."

Siegi said. "I don't want to burden you, Tilda, but would you mind taking my children around the other way to the restaurant and get them some breakfast?"

"Oh, poof. That's easy." Mathilde hoisted both twins into her arms and smiled at Ernst.

"They want strawberries and raspberries," he chirped. "I want chocolate."

"I think we have all those things," Mathilde said conspiratorially,

Hannah and Siegi plastered smiles on their faces and returned to the *kochecke*. Siegi walked right up to Viktor. One eye twitching furiously, he spat, "You ungrateful bitch."

Siegi smiled. "Who's minding the kitchen? Let me guess. Gertraud. Aren't you worried she might poison your customers?"

"First, one Maislinger, and then the other. Useless cows."

"See?" Hannah exclaimed. "He has no imagination."

Sebastien took Viktor's arm. "Time to go."

Viktor wrenched away. "I'll go when I'm ready." He jabbed Siegi's arm. "I'll give you ten minutes to get home."

"I don't think so. And keep your finger to yourself."

He cursed. "Unless you return immediately and do your job, your possessions are all mine." Viktor goose-stepped through the door. They burst into laughter.

"I don't want his grungy old furniture anyway," Siegi said.

The sisters took the children to the *wintergarten*, cozied them on sun-warmed cushions, and gave them paper and fresh boxes of crayons. Elke came over to watch them. Benno happily climbed in next to Gabi and took a red crayon out of her hand.

"Amazing," Siegi remarked, watching her niece. "She just sits there and lets him do that."

"They have an understanding," Hannah said.

The two sisters drove to *Der Wachauerhof* and began to pack up the family possessions.

"Take the plates and bowls, and all the silverware," Siegi directed. "But leave the ugly vases and that horse."

"It's bronze," Hannah commented.

"Oh. Could I sell it?"

They were in the children's room when they heard the apartment door open. A moment later, it closed again, followed by the wiggle of the door knob.

Siegi threw down an armful of shoes. "I'm going to kill him." They shouted and banged on the locked door until their hands hurt.

"Why doesn't someone hear us?" Hannah panted.

"Viktor probably told his friends at the bar it's just a couple of hysterical women. To those stupid dolts, an acceptable explanation."

"Did Otto leave some tools?"

"He could tell you the history of the screwdriver but I never saw one in his hand." Siegi dug through her sewing basket for anything that might pick a lock. She fiddled with it for so long, Hannah decided to keep packing. "Why doesn't your door lock from the inside?" she called from the bedroom.

"Otto's mother locked them in when they were bad. Otto didn't hear me all the times I told him to change it." Siegi hurled the crochet hook across the room, along with the seam ripper and a knitting needle. "Maybe when Sebastien comes with Papa, he can throw Viktor down the stairs."

"That's possible," Hannah stated wearily.

Finally, they saw Bernard's truck parking in front of the restaurant. Viktor stormed out. Voices were raised. It only took a moment to hear boots thundering up the stairs.

"The bastard locked us in," Siegi bellowed. The door shook as they rattled the doorknob. "Look for the key in his pocket."

From the window, Hannah and Siegi saw Viktor slinking to his car. Siegi yanked up the window frame. "He's getting away!" Somehow Sebastien was there in time to wrestle him from behind the wheel.

"I'll have you arrested!" Viktor roared, kicking his legs and trying to bite Sebastien's arm. They rolled in the dirt and gravel. Sebastien ended up on top and pinned him to the ground.

"Get off me!" the captive howled.

Bernard brought a friend he found at the bar. "Let me help," the newcomer said, clearly drunk. And immense. He sat down hard on Viktor.

Bernard fished the key out of his pocket. Hannah and Siegi cheered and ran to the door to greet the rescue party.

"Papa," Siegi squealed. "That was like a movie, you know, one of those American westerns where they tie up the outlaws and save the women."

Bernard gave her an incredulous look. "When have you ever needed to be saved?"

"I'm not sure how long he'll stay subdued," Sebastien said.

"He's the mayor," Bernard reminded them. "When he can breathe again, he'll start shouting for help."

Siegi poked his arm. "Who's your friend?"

"Oh, that's Vincenzo. He's from Italy, but he's lived in Dürnstein for years."

"He's enormous."

While the four of them loaded the boxes, Viktor threw out threats.

Sebastien called down to him. "We'll explain how you've been raiding the cash drawer and bilking your own business for hundreds of schillings."

Viktor spit into the dirt. "No one in this town will believe you over me, Brandl."

"Maybe. Except for Otto, bless him. He kept track. It's all written up and safely stashed somewhere, in case the day came when he and Siegi needed evidence."

"Otto doesn't have the nerve to betray me."

"You underestimate your brother. He's more organized than he looks."

Siegi shook her head and grinned. "I didn't know he'd done that."

Viktor squirmed, to no avail. Sebastien walked down the stairs and crouched next to him.

"Siegi moves out and no one says anything. Do we understand each other, Lonauer?"

Viktor made nasty sounds.

"Good," Sebastien said. "Let him up," he told the large Italian. "Thanks for your help."

"I wanted to punch the bastard," Vincenzo said with a tipsy smile, "But this was better. *Grazie*!"

"Come by *Grünen Baum*," Sebastien urged him.

Viktor shook off the dirt. "You'll never see me coming, Brandl."

Sebastien looked at Hannah and smiled. In that moment, the sweet scent of victory overpowered the noxious odor of menace.

# 35

*Kahlenbergerdorf, May, 1939*

Max hurried down the stairs. His youngest son was shouting at whoever was standing at the front door. "Are you an idiot? There's nothing left. Why would you need the key?"

Max pulled Stefan back and faced Klaus Kolbe. "There's no reason to upset my son. We are all still grieving."

"He wants the keys to *Der Buchwald*," Stefan snarled.

"You want the key to a pile of ashes, rubble, and the bones of the innocent?"

"I've been wondering," Kolbe said, "why a group of Jews ran to your wife's bookstore for protection."

"A group of children."

Kolbe cleared his throat. "The Reich has requisitioned the property and I must collect any documents, and of course, the keys. I came to you personally, as a favor." He crooked a finger at Stefan. "Others might find your son's insolence troubling."

Stefan gave him a last look of distain. "I'll be close by, Papa, if you need me."

Kolbe chuckled. "Was that a threat? Young Mayr has grown quite a mouth."

"Wait here, Klaus," Max said. "I'll get what you want."

"It's *Sturmbahnführer* Kolbe."

Max stalked to his filing cabinet and pulled so hard on a drawer the cabinet threatened to come down on top of him. "Get control of yourself," he muttered.

Six months after *Kristallnacht,* as they were calling the night when layers of jagged glass covered the streets, the Mayr family still anguished over Lili's horrifying death. When Max had arrived home that night, alone in his wife's car, his sons ran to him. In agony, he told them they no longer had a mother, and how she died. They knelt next to their father, and three anguished hearts made rivulets of tears in the dirt.

They held Lili's memorial in the tiny chapel that had been on the property for centuries. Only the Schetts, and Anno and Magdalena Kerber were in attendance. Terribly conflicted, Max asked Roman to say the funeral Mass, for the sake of his sons, who continued to believe they were marginally Catholic, despite infrequent participation in the rituals. Nevertheless, Max could hardly bear the deceit. As Michel gently led him away, he looked back and felt a degree of consolation. Elie was reciting the *Kaddish* over his wife's ashes.

There was no shortage of loved ones taking the blame for Lili's death: Max, whose car broke down. Michel, who felt he should have gone with his father. And Elie, who sent children to Lili for protection, only to be consumed by a fire set by Hitler's henchmen.

Four months went by while Max brooded about his next move. On some level he knew vengeance was compelling motivation for reckless acts, yet it was winning over reason. The battle exhausted him. He was running, but going nowhere.

It was Stefan who moved him with a simple question. "When are we going to do something?"

That evening Max rushed into the kitchen, where his family sat with Rafe and Sigrid. Stefan looked up in surprise; and felt an electric charge circling the air around his father.

"Rafe, tell me about Roman's operation in his wine caves," Max demanded.

"He hasn't wanted to involve you."

"I'm ready to be involved."

"When Roman started hiding Jews," Rafe began, "they stayed only a night or two before moving on. Now he and two other monks are sheltering dozens of people, creating false documents, and struggling to find other places they can hide."

It took one day for Roman Scholz to be on their kitchen doorstep, accompanied by Elie Schett.

"I understand Rafe told you what we need," Roman said. "Besides the Jews desperate for a place to hide, there are thousands standing in emigration lines every day."

"Every Jew in Vienna," Elie said, "is reaching out to a relative who might sponsor them."

"What about Switzerland?" Max asked.

"It's a small country," Rafe said, "the holes in that fence are closing up. It's infuriating. With a little imagination, Viennese Gentiles could help their Jewish neighbors instead of simpering along after Hitler."

Elie exploded. "They *choose* not to help! Most of them would offer up a Jew for any bit of favor from the Reich."

Max bristled. "Tell us what to do."

"Are you sure, Maximillian?"

Max gazed at his sons, and his eyes filled. "Lili admired you, Roman. The night before she died, I admitted I felt inadequate, printing leaflets while you were saving lives. She told me something her father said: 'Hide one child in your coat, and you save yourself. Hide two and you alter the universe."

"There is no score card," Roman agreed, and charged ahead. "First, use the model of what we did at Klosterneuburg. Since you have the same configuration of walls and air ducts surrounding our winery, if you're raided, they'll have a place to hide."

"The meter of space between the walls," Max said. "Enough for an adult to stand in."

"Yes. In fact, I've seen people crammed into much smaller places—a mere crevice, or under a floorboard."

"So, we design a way for them to move from a room into the walls."

"Next, we need your printing press for false documents. If we could create German marks, we would. Maybe later," the monk said with a smirk.

They chose a room on each level of the wine caves, and a lengthy discussion about disguising their entrances ensued, until Michel raised his voice. "I can do this."

"And I can help," Stefan declared.

Roman clapped his hands. "Good, you two are in charge of trapdoors and hidden panels. Rafe will prepare the printing press for what we need."

"No more leafleting?"

"More than one thing at a time will make us sloppy."

When Roman left, Elie raised his hand.

"Speak, Elie," Max said. His friend's constant contrition was wearing on him.

"I visited some Jews hiding in Klosterneuburg. A woman pulled me aside. She said the worse thing was the absence of privacy, not even to relieve themselves. Do you think you could, perhaps, put a sheet up?"

Max was contrite. "That's a wonderful suggestion." He embraced his friend. "Enough. Guilt does not bring Lili back to us, or punish her executioners."

The blockade between them crumbled, and they could finally part without the burden of remorse.

# 36

*St Jakob, November, 1939*

The anniversary of *Kristallnacht* arrived, and Hannah cut her hair. She snapped the scissors through large clumps of curls before she could change her mind. Sebastien found her in their bedroom, holding Chopin, studying her new look in the mirror.

"I like it!"

She glanced up. "Do I still look Jewish?"

"Is that what this is about?" He fingered her curls. "Nonsense. You look glamourous."

She felt ashamed; she was acting like the Jews were the enemy. Yet the specter of fear continued to skulk about her brain.

That night Sebastien reverently touched her hair.

"You know, Sebastien," she said. "I used to think God visits everywhere else," she sighed, "but lives in Austria."

Sebastien didn't respond.

Had her husband decided God lived nowhere at all?

•   •   •   •   •

The newest whispered fear around St. Jakob was conscription. Austrian males were being forced into the army of the Third Reich. Hannah put it out of her mind until Finn Bender was ordered to report to Enns for basic training.

Siegi told Hannah, several times, how worried she was that Willi Reiter would be conscripted. Hannah tired of reminding her it was her husband, already endangering his life for the wrong side, she should pray for.

Tomas the Fiddler was next.

"Tell them you're a chef. That should keep you off the front lines," Andreas advised him.

A week later, Veronika accompanied Georg to the inn for *mittagessen*. When Sebastien and Hannah greeted them at their table, she demanded to know why "the great Sebastien Brandl" had been spared.

"Because they're forcing him to work for the Reich in his own home," Georg said.

"And what about you?" she barked at him. "What are you doing for the war effort?"

"Really, Veronika," Sebastien said. "Do you want to run the winery? It's a little more complicated than baking muffins."

Hannah leaned over to Veronika. "We should be grateful."

"No," Georg brooded. "Veronika has a point. They need Gerhard to be the Nazi mayor, and Sebastien to gather the spoils. What about me?"

"It's obvious," Sebastien said. "They're convinced only you can produce wines worth stealing." It was true; every SS officer passing through the Wachau Valley waltzed in and helped himself to an armload of bottles.

In the next weeks, Georg lost two of his most dependable workers and a server at *Grünen Baum* disappeared overnight.

In Tomas's absence, Hannah concentrated on her cooking lessons from Andreas, Mathilde and Sebastien. Food preparation occupied entire mornings, which she enjoyed. But Sebastien, more and more, was absent.

One day Hannah stepped out of the kitchen long enough to look for him in the restaurant, the *biergarten*, and even in their bedroom upstairs. She found him in the cellar, which ran the entire length of the family wing. Besides the roomy space Pfortner had ordered cleared for the donations, they had their own wine cellar, an enormous auxiliary pantry, and another cooler, Nazi commandeered, for additional refrigeration.

There were two other narrow rooms, empty except for unused kitchen items. Sebastien had taken one of them over and crowded in a desk and two old chairs. Lighting came from a kerosene lamp hanging from the ceiling. A *Grünen Baum* blanket was folded neatly over the back of his chair. He was hunched over the desk, moving his pen methodically, like a monk scripting a scroll.

"When did you do this?" She asked, trying not to reveal the exclusion she felt.

Sebastien leapt out of the chair, his pen flying. "Hannah! Is something wrong?"

"Not with me," she said flatly. Ink had splattered on the floor, and Sebastien stepped in it bending to retrieve the pen. "Tell me, Sebastien, who are you hiding from?"

"I'm not hiding. I needed a space where I could be alone."

His deceit unnerved her.

"*Schieß*," Sebastien muttered, turning his papers over. "I wasn't ready to show you what I've done here. I wanted to make it more...welcoming. You know how I get moody about everything that's going on? Niko always kept a journal to express things he might not want to say out loud. He was right. When I'm agitated, writing calms me down."

"Show me."

"Sometimes angry thoughts come out on the page. You'll be ashamed of me."

"I thought we didn't keep things from each other. I feel like a fool, searching the inn for you while you're in your secret room scribbling down feelings you won't share with me."

"Be patient with me, *liebchen*. It's amazing how much better I think with a pen and paper in my hand. I'm actually coming up with new ideas."

"You mean more ways to fight them." She looked him in the eye. "Do you love me?"

"Of course!"

"And do you love our daughter?"

"How can you ask me that?"

"I don't feel protected by you anymore. If you love us, why won't you behave in a way that keeps us safe? Resist, resist, resist! I'm tired of that word. I understand your anger, but every single day you say the wrong thing to the wrong people at the bar."

"I'm sorry. I didn't know how worried you are."

How could he not know?

"I'm telling you I will never do anything to endanger our family. Never. I promise."

Sebastien hardly left her side for the rest of the day, and spent more time with Gabi than he had in weeks. Hannah went to bed feeling calmer than she had since Vienna. He caressed her, his fingers moving over her body, lingering in places that would pleasure her. She let him do it all. She deserved that much.

She woke before her husband. As she regarded the man she loved, thoughts of the day before crawled into her memory like ants in a pantry, leaving a black trail of doubt. What had he written on those pages, each word a hazard, prickling with threat.

•　•　•　•　•

St. Jakob was in an SS zone, where the German administration installed itself, abolished the local governments, and by the end of 1938, inserted a network of Nazis to occupy almost every city, town, and one-road hamlet.

"The schoolteacher teaches only sanctioned curriculum." Sebastien complained to Hannah. "That priest supports the Reich from the pulpit. The mechanic fixes German cars and trucks, the village tailor mends their foul uniforms, and the doctor and dentist see the Germans before our own sick children, all without charge.

More and more uniformed Nazis were occupying tables at *Grünen Baum*, especially at night. When they drank too much and couldn't seem to remember where they lived, they demanded rooms in the inn, and left them in a disgusting state.

The Brandls were told they could only consume their rations. Their pantry remained full, however, to serve SS, other Nazi officials, and favored members of the Party. Too lazy to check who was who, their menu remained presentable.

The assessments had long been made. Pfortner was in charge, watching for any abnormality in the collection process. Farmers "donated" grain, fruits, and vegetables, and milk, as well as cows, chickens, and pigs. The town butchers were expected to slaughter the animals and hand over the best cuts to the local upper echelon of Nazis.

Veronika donated bread "to the war effort" without complaint. Meanwhile, Daniel hoarded pastries in a place "those people can't find."

Sebastien, Georg and Andreas held clandestine meetings to devise ways to cheat the Germans out of some of the goods and livestock they appropriated. Hannah, again torn between knowledge and ignorance, listened in. Sebastien made a list of trustworthy farmers and villagers. But Georg drew lines through some of the names.

"These men have large families to feed," Sebastien argued.

Georg was firm. "We can't include anyone whom we've seen being too friendly with Pfortner or heard praising the Reich. Even if they say they are just protecting themselves."

They visited the ones who made the list.

"What did you say to them?" Hannah asked anxiously.

"I simply suggested to one dairy farmer he move some of his cows elsewhere. He understood, and said he had an empty silo. I told him to make sure they were well fed and dozing when the Germans came. Another villager, even before I opened my mouth, confided he had a place to hide some of his chickens."

Hannah wondered how anyone could keep a chicken quiet.

They advised a few farmers to find new storage places for some of their grain, or their apples, or eggs, only enough for their family for a few days.

They strategized sabotage at *Grünen Baum*, the collection place. Pfortner was always there to inventory what came in, and from whom. Late one night, long after the *Oberleutnant* had made his list and joined the SS officers for a drink in the restaurant, Sebastien and Hannah sat amidst the cartons and boxes.

"I might be able to take some of this back," he said.

"What do you mean?" she asked.

"Everything is put in separate piles according to donor, so Pfortner can monitor compliance. I could reassemble them, put the apples into one pile, the beans into another, the bakery goods, the eggs in the cooler. That way he won't be able to identify shortages. He was shoving all the sacks of grain into one corner when Hannah slipped out.

"What have you done here?" Pfortner wanted to know the next morning.

"I've organized everything for transport." Sebastien said cheerfully.

When two trucks arrived for the collection, the officer in charge praised Pfortner. "The potatoes are all in one place!," he said, surveying the new arrangement. "Good thinking, *Oberleutnant*." Pfortner told Sebastien to carry on, and Hannah could breathe again.

Since the farmers were required to give up a percentage of their products, harvest times meant more fruits or vegetables in the piles, which made it easier for Sebastien to remove a few for "redistribution." When they awakened at dawn, a few days each week, a farmer or villager would find several peaches and some potatoes, or a head of lettuce and half a loaf of bread on his back doorstep. As Georg had predicted, no one mentioned these gifts around town. But the ruse produced so little, for only a few families a day.

Sebastien started removing a cup of grain out of each sack. One night he was so tired, he failed to adequately hide the extra sack, only two-thirds filled.

Pfortner noticed, and Hannah fought to hide her panic.

"I'm not sure you counted correctly yesterday, *Oberleutnant*," Sebastien said hastily. "You might have missed one."

He picked up the extra sack. "Who's responsible for this, Brandl? It's not even full."

"I warned all of the wheat farmers to fill them to the brim or face the consequences," Sebastien said firmly.

Pfortner grunted and waddled up the stairs.

Sebastien wiped his brow and took Hannah's hand. "My stupidity is baffling."

"You're playing a dangerous game," she said curtly.

"But we're helping people."

She pulled her hand away. "I'm sure two peaches is sufficient for a family of eight."

# 37

*Kahlenbergerdorf, January 1940*

The Mayrs began with the room at the bottom. The smell of mildew wasn't as strong as they feared, as the air ducts pulled in enough outside air. They covered the old door with matching planks, and Michel used the artistry he didn't know he had inherited from his Polish father to hide the seams on a smaller door in the shadows. To enter from the outside, they would poke a thin nail through a natural hole in the wood to unlatch the door.

In the week that followed, they brought in cots, blankets, towels, plates, cups and utensils. They curtained off each of a pair of chamber pots.

"Could two families live in here?" Michel asked.

"More," Rafe said grimly.

They dug a hole in the floor and working in shifts all night, chiseled through three meters of rock until they had carved a tunnel to the one-meter space between the walls. Using discarded wood from a shed, aged with gouges and wine stains, they laid a floor in the room using old iron nails. Michel built a trapdoor above the hole. When he finished, the break in the floorboards was almost invisible, but they moved a bench over it. Although it was heavy, it could slide away, and then pulled back to cover the trap door once inside the tunnel.

In the passageway, they positioned a wheeled rack laden with wine bottles in front of the door and awaited Roman's inspection. A week later, he arrived at midnight, having hiked for two hours through forests and grapevines. He pronounced the room more accommodating than anything under the Abbey. Michel opened a bottle of Riesling.

"Let's talk about the tunnel between your house and the winery," Roman said as they savored the wine and a moment of success. "Make the entrances look old and out of use. If anyone wants to investigate, leave broken equipment and boxes at both entrances, which would buy time on either end. But only use this tunnel as a last resort."

He accepted a second glass. "Tell me about the ladder tunnel."

"Stefan and I concealed both the entrance from the cave and the exit up the hill, "Michel said.

"It comes out in a forest between two sections of vines." Stefan said proudly. "It's well hidden with brush. The woods run up and over the ridge."

Roman gave Stefan a nod of approval. "Rafe will be in touch with the Monastery and alert you when to expect the first family."

The only possibility on the first level was a room not connected to the outside walls. On one side, a hollowed-out fireplace held a grill and an old charred log. Rafe reached up and opened the flue. "A person could fit in here," he said in a muffled voice. "We could chisel some footholds into the sides to straddle the chimney and make their way up."

Max looked at Stefan. "I suppose you know where this comes out."

"It doesn't. The opening is on a terrace with Veltliner grapes, but it's filled up with cement."

"But maybe we could chisel an opening for air," Rafe said. "Then, as a last resort, four or five people could hide up in the chimney. They'll have to be able to lock the flue from the inside."

Michel nodded. "I can do that."

"Nevertheless," Max said, shaking his head. "To escape from this room, people will have to go up the ladder tunnel."

"Or go down to join the group in the walls."

After they concealed the entrance to the room, they fronted it with two barrel tasting tables with candlesticks grounded in melted wax. They hung a disabled lantern from a crossbeam.

Roman ruffled Stefan's hair. "Have you considered the square opening at the bottom of the old barrels? You've gone in, right? One shoulder at a time, to scrape the sludge off the walls?"

"Two children could fit in there," Stefan agreed.

They christened the hiding space with the wall escape *Das Pumpenraum* and the room with the fireplace became *The Besenkammer*. The Pump Room and The Broom Closet. Max directed his employees to leave by five in the evening, a gesture they appreciated. If they needed to meet, it would be very late at night. Roman and the monks who had constructed the safe rooms at the Abbey were busy with four Jewish families and two dozen other refugees.

•   •   •   •   •

On March 5, at three in the morning, Roman Scholz arrived in the courtyard of *Schloß Winzertal* with the first family, including two young girls and a howling baby. Michel and Stefan settled them in the Pump Room and showed the way into the walls. Stefan took the baby from his exhausted mother and tried singing, tickling, and making funny faces until the little one was choking on his own tears.

"Do not befriend them," Roman said. "More will be coming. Treat them as guests."

Two families came in the next transport. A man and his elderly grandparents joined the first family in the Pump Room. The Bergmanns, a couple with two children, were stashed in the Broom Closet and taught how to maneuver the flue and climb the chimney. Isaac Bergmann was eager to tell their story. He worked at a bank, and his wife, Muriel, taught promising young chefs at a celebrated cooking school in Vienna. Their daughter Libby still dreamt of becoming a doctor, and their son Emil was determined to be a professional footballer.

Michel again had to warn his brother. "This isn't a neighborhood we've created down here. It's a dungeon with a limited amount of food, uncomfortable beds and a chamber pot that registers every tinkle and plop as it's being filled."

Nevertheless, Stefan exchanged a few friendly words with Emil whenever he came to empty the chamber pots.

Without warning, the first family was secreted away to another destination in the middle of the night. Seven new terrified guests replaced them.

In Kahlenbergerdorf and a few other insignificant villages, rationing had not yet been implemented, although restrictions were looming. Max sent Rafe and Sigrid to buy extra food necessities, like flour, rice, sugar, salt and potatoes in the markets of other towns. They kept perishables, such as meat, milk and eggs, in a locked cooler in the chateau cellar.

During Crush, Max employed his usual pickers, but none of them needed to be in the cellars. Max put a halt to wine-tastings, unless arranged by Kolbe. In the winery, he let everyone go except for his foreman and another man who had worked for his father.

•     •     •     •     •

On July 22, Roman Scholz was arrested. Caught in the city, Rafe didn't return until late the next day to give the Mayrs the news. Michel was in tears. Stefan was enraged. Max was thoroughly rattled.

"It turns out," Rafe said, "that Otto Hartmann is a German spy. Roman had nothing to do with him for over a year. But all the time he was working for the Gestapo and covered his treachery by pretending to plot an assassination attempt, which was then conveniently abandoned."

"When we met him," Max said shakily, "he was pushing for violent revolt. Roman would have no part in it."

"You realize the men you met were a small committee leading a large movement. Nearly 200 members of the Austrian Freedom resistance were arrested and interrogated."

Max gasped. "I had no idea there were that many people involved."

"Hartmann doesn't know who you are."

Max would never be convinced.

"Last month," Sigrid said, " Roman's group joined with another led by Karl Lederer. Both of them are in the hands of the Gestapo. Hopefully, Reiman and Lehmann escaped the purge."

"What about you?" Michel asked.

"Roman went to extreme measures to keep us unidentified."

"And the Jews he was hiding at Klosterneuburg?"

Rafe winced. "It wasn't good. The Gestapo raid was about collaborators, but instead they found all but one of the Jewish families. They shot the men and deported the women and children along with 123,000 other Jews rounded up in Vienna."

"One family was saved. They're stranded in the cellar," Sigrid said.

"Eleven people. Four monks were arrested with Roman. That left two others who were working with him but managed to hide, and this morning, they finally made contact."

That evening, Max sat alone in his darkened study. He felt a formidable collection of emotions: grief for his friend Roman, anguish over the plight of the Jews caught in the depths of Klosterneuburg, and dread, cold and insidious.

# 38

*St. Jakob, August, 1940*

Hannah's sense of humor was failing her. When Elke and Siegi, children in tow, joined her for coffee in the *kochecke* late one afternoon, she looked forward to a laugh. But as soon as they settled at the table, the back door opened and Veronika peeked in.

"Oh," she said. "You're all here together."

Hannah waved at her to join them.

"Thank you," she said as she plopped down on the banquette. To their surprise, she started to cry and announced that she was "terribly, terribly unhappy."

Siegi sighed dramatically. "What's the problem? It can't be your wonderful husband."

Veronika pulled her white lace handkerchief from the sleeve of her coat and blew her nose several times. She pinched the dirty cloth and held it up, as if expecting someone to take it away to be washed.

"He's never home in the evenings," she pouted, "He's always here."

"At least he's in town," Siegi reminded her.

Veronika didn't acknowledge Otto's absence and launched into other grievances.

"I'm tired of telling people we haven't had a baby because God hasn't blessed us. How is that supposed to happen," she snorted, "if he doesn't spend much time in bed?"

The words burst out of Hannah like popcorn in hot oil. "He comes home late and doesn't go to bed?"

"No!" Veronika cried. "He comes home, and he comes to bed." The skin above her tight collar reddened. "But then, well, he's not much of a man."

A pall of collective humiliation hung in the air. Daniel chose that precise moment to shove the door open and race toward them.

"Guess what? Georg said I can have a dog. I really want a dog."

Before Veronika could crush him, Elke jumped in. "What a wonderful idea!"

Veronika dismissed his announcement with a wave of her hand. "That's ridiculous. You can hardly take care of yourself, much less an animal."

"Yes I can!" Daniel crossed his arms defiantly.

"Why are you so mean?" Elke asked her sister.

Veronika stood and flounced her skirts. "I'm not sure why I came here. I'm going to *Der Wachauerhof.* I'll find more sympathy from my friends there." The door shut with a thud.

Daniel wiped away a tear. "She's been going there a lot."

Hannah, Siegi and Elke gawked at him, curiosity sweeping away the dregs of discomfort.

When Veronika next appeared at *Grünen Baum* a month later, Georg was there, but she marched straight up to Sebastien.

"I need to talk to you."

Sebastien pulled out a chair for her. She shoved it back. "Alone."

Georg was scowling, but he gave Sebastien a curt nod.

"What's that about?" Andreas asked. "If it's important, she should be talking to her own husband."

"That would be me," Georg said under his breath. Hannah decided it was a good time to open one of the bottles he brought.

For twenty minutes, they drank superb wine, but the conversation was stilted and tense. Georg finally pulled his lanky frame off the banquette. "Tell Seb goodnight for me, please."

"What about Veronika?" Hannah asked.

"She's got her own car. Hopefully, she can drive back without running into anything."

He stood just as Veronika reappeared, followed by Sebastien, his face blank. She approached Georg and put her hands on her hips. "I've talked it all over with Sebastien. You dragged me into this marriage, but you're not the man we thought you were."

Sebastien was making himself busy pouring more wine. Hannah reached for another glass for Veronika, but he caught her hand. "We won't need that."

"Veronika," Andreas said. "Why don't you sit down."

She continued to scowl at Georg. "We're wondering if you're a man at all."

Georg lowered himself back into the booth. "All right, Veronika. Let's talk about Nikolas Schönfeld."

For a fleeting moment, she looked flustered.

Georg padded the seat beside him. "Andi is right. You should sit."

"I'm leaving," Veronika said, already halfway to the door.

Sebastien grabbed her sleeve. "What did you do, Veronika?"

She wrenched her arm away, but Sebastien set down the wine bottle and leaned in. "Tell me. Now."

"You can't talk to me like that. Georg!" she barked. "Do something."

"But you're not finished," her husband said. "Last night Herr Haas told me he'd seen you coming out of the chancellery office the day before Niko disappeared. I always thought he was to blame."

"He was the most obvious suspect," Andreas said.

"Veronika," Georg said, his voice unfamiliarly dark and foreboding, "was it you who ran all the way to Krems to tattle on *Pfarrer* Niko?"

"Haas was going in to complain too. And I'm sure there were others."

"Why, Veronika?" Sebastien raged. "Niko did nothing but befriend you."

"What that so-called priest said was blasphemy!"

"Do you even know what blasphemy is?" Georg shouted.

"The monsignor said it, not me."

Sebastien bolted toward her, but Georg stepped in front of him. "I'll take care of this." He gave Veronika a firm shove toward the door. "Go get your things and get out of my house."

She flailed at him, her blows bouncing off his shoulders and chest. "You can't tell me to leave. I said it first!"

A giggle escaped Hannah.

"Georg wins, Veronika," Sebastien spat. "And, to be clear, I said nothing to support your malicious complaints."

When Andreas clapped, Veronika swirled and lowered her gaze to him. "You fool."

"That's it," Georg roared. "I'll follow you home. I can't imagine what you'll claim for yourself while you pack."

She looked at the floor and lifted her skirts, as if dirt from the floor would jump up soil them. "The nice things are mine. You can keep the dog."

"Daniel got his dog?" Andreas exclaimed "What's his name?"

"Schnapsi," Georg said.

"A wonderful name!" Andreas exclaimed. "Do you get to keep Daniel, too?"

Veronika let out a piercing whistle. "Georg! "You will build me a new house!"

She disappeared, and Andreas said, "I didn't know she could whistle like that."

Georg smiled. "What a good idea. Where shall I move her to?"

Hannah beamed. "Is Vienna far enough?"

•　•　•　•　•

The morning after Georg chucked Veronika out of his house, an extremely agitated Daniel arrived at the inn and found Sebastien and Hannah.

"Vroni woke me up in the middle of the night and told me to pack all my things because we were going to a hotel in Moosfeld." His chest jerked up and down as he fought off a sob. "I got Schnapsi and locked us in my room."

Smart, Hannah thought.

"She stood outside and told me she had a big surprise for me I would like. I didn't believe her. She wanted me to open the door so she could grab me."

Hannah put her arm around him, and he gave them a thin smile. "I heard her car start. She drove away."

"Good," Sebastien said.

"Georg told me he would work it out with my sister." His voice wavered again. "But Veronika doesn't like to work it out."

Hannah fed him a breakfast of pancakes with strawberries and cream, sausage, and eggs. Sebastien made him hot cocoa. "Maybe she'll let him stay with Georg," she said.

Georg wasted no time. For all the wine he had given his neighbors over the years, a construction crew materialized in no time. By the end of August, Veronika's house was ready for occupancy. At Veronika's insistence, it was one street down and around the corner from the bakery, with only a partial view of *Grünen Baum's* roof.

Still promising a special surprise, Veronika dragged Daniel to the new house. Hannah offered to help him move his belongings into his room, and was surprised when Veronika allowed it.

"After all the fuss he made? You can deal with him."

"She's letting me keep Schnapsi here," Daniel told Hannah while she made Daniel's bed.

That didn't sound like Veronika.

# 39

*Kahlenbergerdorf, October 1940*

After Roman's arrest, Max's anxiety invaded his bones like a cancer. Even though the cellars at Klosterneuburg had been compromised, Jewish refugees continued to make their way to the Abbey. The monks needed help. Max, with eighteen souls, was at capacity.

He formulated a plan. On his way to discuss it with Rafe and his sons, the telephone rang in his office. He sensed it was Tollner, who would soil his thinking. And yet, he needed to know.

"Have heard your friend was promoted? He's now *Obersturmbannführer* Klaus Kolbe."

"A senior assault leader," Max said. "Is he going into battle?"

"Who knows where they came up with all these titles? But he's pretty important. Here's an idea. Buy a German car and let him see you driving it."

Max had a Mercedes he had abandoned behind the winery. He drove Lili's car.

"And for God's sake, join The Party!"

"What else?"

"Remember when I told you two years ago Hitler ordered the confiscation of six extensive properties in Germany and Austria? Himmler never talked about it and nothing came across my desk until a few months ago. They are all psychiatric hospitals."

"Why are you telling me this?"

"I thought it was interesting."

"Fritz, every time you call me, you pretend to be on the right side. Teasing me with bits of information is not an act of opposition. You're in Himmler's office, for God's sake. There's a resistance movement in Berlin that could help you get very creative."

"How do you know about the resistance?"

Max swore silently. "It's not as secret as it should be."

"I'm warning you, my friend."

"Are we actually friends anymore?"

"I'm risking my life talking to you."

"So don't call me anymore!" Hang up on the coward, Max ordered himself. He sat smiling at the phone.

Rafe, Sigrid, Michel and Stefan approved Max's plan. His first destination was Gottweig Abbey, a magnificent edifice with a medieval winery, high on a hill overlooking the Wachau Valley. The current abbot, Jurgen Auer, started visiting *Schloß Winzertal* when he was in seminary in Vienna. He ushered Max into his luxurious apartment in the monks' residence while apologizing for the lavish décor.

Max laughed. "It's permitted to be comfortable."

"It's atrocious. If this building wasn't full of young monks, I'd join them in my own little cell and turn this thing into a museum. Would you like a beer? I ran out of *Winzertal* wine months ago."

"Why didn't you call me? I would have been happy to visit sooner, with several cases in my pocket."

"I've been busy. The Germans crawled through here several times. They helped themselves to the gold chalices, and anything else in the Sacristy that glittered. Thank God they didn't touch the library. 150,000 books and manuscripts saved from one of their funeral pyres."

They drank a beer together and reminisced about better times. "It's always a pleasure to talk to someone else who hasn't fallen into lock step," Jurgen told Max.

"That's why I'm here."

"Tell me."

"The information I'm about to give you is dangerous, and if you find it in your heart to help me, the meter will rise."

Jurgen smiled. "If you're going to propose a way for me to resist those lunatics, I'm in."

"My wife was murdered during *Kristallnacht*," Max began quietly. "Five Jewish children ran to her shop for protection, and they burned the place down with Lili and all but two of the children inside."

"Oh Max, I have no words."

"There's more." He described his friendship with Roman Scholz and the journey of resistance he and his sons had taken.

"The Provost at Klosterneuburg, Alipius Joseph, is a close friend," Jurgen said. "He told me what Roman and his monks were doing, and about the arrests. What happened to the refugees hiding in the wine caves?"

"The only survivors, a Jewish family of eleven, concealed themselves in a gap in the outside walls."

"God bless them."

"We have eighteen people at *Schloß Winzertal*. We try to keep them comfortable, but there's no space to sleep or move around. A chamber pot behind a curtain. The stench is constant."

"You need more hiding places."

"Yes."

Jurgen stood. "Follow me."

They circumvented the massive abbey and arrived at the winery door several minutes later. Jurgen showed him the single cavern one floor down from the production area and tasting room. Max understood immediately his friend had no suitable hiding place. "Do you know of other Abbots I might approach?"

"None I could be sure wouldn't turn you in. But couldn't I disguise two or three men as seminarians? And perhaps their wives, an extra hand in the kitchen or helping to clean the abbey?"

"Yes! I've got a couple of men posing as workers at *Schloß Winzertal*. We had to give them a crash course in grape picking and fermentation." Max smiled at his friend. "You are as I remember you, noble and kind."

"I feel the same way about you." Jurgen gathered him into an embrace. "Actually, I haven't felt this energized in months."

"A man named Rafe will be in touch with you."

His next stop was Mautern an der Donau, a town on the Danube River that was home to the winery *Nikolaihof,* a Celt holy site that produced wine in 800 B.C. Owned for generations by the Saahs Family. Max and Nicholai Saahs had been friendly rivals for years.

Walking through the ancient, vine-covered entrance, he was challenged by a trio of young German soldiers.

"I've come to see *Herr* Saahs."

One of them raised his rifle. "He sold the property to the *Wehrmarkt* two years ago. You can be on your way."

Max looked past him, and saw that the courtyard was no longer well-kept, its long tables warped from remaining uncovered during the winters. "Do you know where I can find him?"

The other rifle came up.

Relieved that he arrived back at the Steyr Baby without a bullet in his back, he turned toward the bridge that would take him to the other side of the river, and the village of last resort.

# 40

Even with a scruffy brown dog entertaining the staff, Daniel was more subdued than usual when he was in the *Grünen Baum* kitchen. One day Mathilde made Daniel his favorite cake, and Hannah offered to take it to him. She and Apfel arrived to see Daniel dragging a heavy satchel towards a van parked nearby. Schnapsi danced around his feet.

"It's a vacation!" He cried. "Veronika's surprise is a vacation! Will you watch Schnapsi for me? I can't take him on the vacation."

"Time to go," the driver said.

"This is Pepi," Daniel said. He picked up Schnapsi, kissed him several times, and handed him to Hannah.

Hannah clutched the squirming dog. "Let's wait for your sister."

"She's sending me to camp," he said, standing by the door of the van, fidgeting.

"But it's getting colder, Daniel. Camps are for summer."

"It doesn't get cold at this camp."

"Let me go get Elke."

"I can go by myself. But you can kiss me goodbye."

Hannah smiled uncomfortably at Pepi and kissed Daniel's cheek.

"Don't worry about him, Fraulein," Pepi said.

"She's a *Frau*," Daniel corrected him

"Fine. We have to go now. I have to pick up another passenger."

"Wait," Hannah said, still wary. "Mathilde made you a *Sacher Torte*."

Daniel took the box, his smile faltering. "Thank you, Tilda. I'm going to miss everyone when I'm on my vacation." He got into the back seat. "Bye, Hannah. Bye Schnapsi. Bye, Apfel." Pepi closed the door. Hannah waved, but it was hard to see Daniel behind the blackened windows.

Back at the inn, Sebastien was standing in the doorway, talking animatedly with the butcher about cuts of meat still available to order. He clapped the man on the back and walked out to meet his wife and the wriggling dog.

"Hello Schnapsi. Did Daniel like the cake?"

"I think so. But Sebastien, did you know Veronika's surprise was a vacation? He was getting into a van and going to some kind of camp."

"A camp? It's October."

"That's what I said. Veronika wasn't around, so I tried to convince him to wait. But he was pretty excited, and the driver was in a hurry to pick up someone else." Her eyes filled. "And now he's gone."

They were still in front of the inn when Veronika appeared, walking swiftly toward them. "What have you done with Daniel?" she asked testily, as if they were holding her brother hostage. "He has to come home right now. He's going away for a few weeks, and the car will be here any minute."

"He's already gone," Hannah said, rattled. "You told him to wait for a driver named Pepi. I tried to keep him here until I could find you."

"Did you make sure he took his coat?"

"I didn't see it. Maybe he stuffed it in his bag."

"What kind of camp is running now?" Sebastien demanded.

Veronika ignored him. "What were you thinking, Hannah? You should have made him take his coat." She started up the street, without the dog. Sebastien was about to go after her when he heard an urgent voice calling his name. Mathilde flew out the door. "Sebastien, your father fell and we can't get him up."

Veronika forgotten, they ran to the porch.

"His eyes are open but he can't talk. He's in the *kochecke*."

Sebastien found his father on the floor, arms and legs splayed awkwardly, breathing in short gasps.

"Papa, what is it?" He cried. Andreas stared at his son with blank eyes.

The town doctor, Anton Kronberger, arrived, along with Elke, carrying both Benno and Gabi. Mathilde closed the restaurant. She and Tobias, Sebastien, Hannah, Elke and the children waited while he examined Andreas.

"Your father had a stroke," he said grimly. We need to get him to University Hospital to evaluate the severity of his condition." When the ambulance arrived, Sebastien and Tobias helped the driver put Andreas on a stretcher and carry him to the back of the vehicle. Sebastien wanted to go with him.

"Why don't you follow us," Dr. Kronberger said kindly, "Let us do our job."

Hannah was barely in the passenger seat when Sebastien pounded the accelerator. They caught up with the ambulance only a kilometer down the road. "Why can't they drive faster?"

Hannah caressed the back of his neck and prayed.

Fifteen minutes later they arrived at University Hospital in Krems. Sebastien took his father's hand as they wheeled him inside. Elke, Mathilde and Tobias rushed through the doors. "We'll sit with you," Mathilde said. "Siegi has the children. And the dog."

After a considerable wait, a white coated man introduced himself as Dr. Lang. "I'm a neurologist." Herr Brandl has had a massive stroke. We've given him some sedation to calm him down."

"I want to see him, "Sebastien said.

"Talk to him. Even if he can't speak, we're fairly certain he can hear you." He led the group up some stairs and down a hall to a room with two beds. Andreas was in the one next to the window.

Sebastien put his mouth to his father's ear. "I'm here," he whispered.

Dr. Lang came up behind Hannah and laid a gentle hand on her shoulder. "I'm afraid the damage is irreversible." She put her arms around her husband and wept with him.

Hubert was home by the next morning. Bernard came immediately to *Grünen Baum* to tend bar, and Sophie to mind Gabi. Mathilde took over the kitchen and Tobias and Siegi waited tables. Georg promised to care for Schnapsi until Daniel returned.

Sebastien, Hannah and Hubert agreed to take turns staying with Andreas, but most of the time all three of them ended up there, unwilling to leave him for very long.

Two days went by before Hannah noticed Hubert was walking with a slight limp. "What happened to your leg?"

"*Kristallnacht*," he said. After I left *Café Hawelke*, a band of ruffians jumped me, and smashed my knee with a bully stick."

"Why on earth," Sebastien began.

"They were drunk," Hubert said dismissively, "fired up about Hitler, and angry at everyone."

Dr. Lang came in. "You can take him home if you'd like," he sighed. "I don't think it will be more than a few days. His breathing is a little less rattled, but he can't eat, and he's not responding to any of our physical prompts. If I were you, I'd pray God will take him soon." Hannah took Andreas' hand. Hubert kissed him tenderly. Sebastien collapsed across the bed.

Mathilde prepared Andreas' room with extra pillows and blankets, flowers, and Tobias' candles, which glowed softly while they tried to make him comfortable.

Hubert took charge of the inn's daily routine, and the steady flow of visitors who arrived to say goodbye to St. Jakob's most beloved citizen. They had to force Sebastien to leave his father's side to eat or sleep.

Ten days went by. "I feel guilty," he confided to Hannah and Georg.

"No, Sebastien," Hannah protested. "You're the most devoted son any father could have."

"I was selfish, running away and leaving him to run the inn by himself."

"He wasn't alone. And he understood what you needed and blessed your journey."

"You know," Georg said, "My own father was annoyingly quiet. I deliberately agitated him, just so he might speak more than one word at a time. Eventually I invented another father. I decided what he looked like, what he did for a living—he was never away selling wine—and the games he played with me. I remember being very excited about this day-dreamed father."

"Oh, Georg," Hannah murmured.

"But one day I realized, *your* father was as close as a walk through the woods, and he talked to me and was interested in my life. And he treated me with such kindness, like he did you and Hubert."

Sebastien took Andreas' hand in his own. He caressed his knuckles, his palms and his fingers. Andreas' breaths became short and shallow. When they stopped, Sebastien put his lips to his father's.

"Goodbye, Papa."

Hannah prayed Andreas had felt his son's adoration, and heard every word.

# 41

As he drove, Max fought his nerves. But when he passed through the village and entered the vast wine estate, owned by not only a friend, but without a doubt, an ally in resisting the Reich, he felt a spark of hope.

The wine cellars were quiet, so he approached the front door of the villa and knocked loudly. Georg Wangermann lunged at Max and wrapped him in a bear hug.

"What are you doing here?" He cried. "Come in!"

Settled on the veranda with lemonade and pretzels, Max first told him about Lili, and about his leap into the resistance. "I'm rather desperate. Is there any way you could conceal a family or two in your cellars?"

Georg took the challenge in stride. "You're lucky. My wife recently left."

"Oh, dear."

"Oh, no. I helped her move out. Believe me, in the midst of Austrian tragedy, it was a minor, yet essential, victory. Let's go wine-tasting."

They strode through the winery's party room and went directly to the wide rock steps behind the barrels. Max was already asking about the ventilation system when they reached the first level of the cellar vaults.

"The walls are about three meters thick," Georg said.

"And then?"

"A space between them for air, about a meter wide, and the rock wall."

"Excellent!" Max exclaimed. "In one of our rooms we added an undetectable trap door and chiseled a tunnel into the air space. I've brought drawings with me."

Georg pondered this for a moment. "You, know, Max, I consider our relationship to be close, but we built our friendship around wine. I knew you were married, but I didn't know your wife's name. I thought you must have told me and I'd forgotten, which seemed very rude of me. And you never spoke of children."

"Lili wanted their identities to remain private. It became my reality. When we joined the resistance, I appreciated her vigilance." Max smiled. "Can we get back to the excellent possibilities your caves present? Do you trust anyone enough to help you?"

"I can work that out."

They both looked up, startled to hear a female voice shouting Georg's name.

"Is that, by any chance, the evicted wife?" Georg asked. "She doesn't sound pleased."

"Her perpetual state. I'll go see what she wants."

He returned minutes later. "Veronika seems to think I'm needed at *Grünen Baum.* The patriarch of the family died, and the funeral is tomorrow."

"That would be Andreas Brandl. Terrible news. I met Sebastien and his wife in Vienna, on their honeymoon. They were visiting his brother, whom I know well."

"Sebastien mentioned they met a close friend of Hubert's, but no details that I can recall. Overcome by the honeymoon, I suppose. Can you wait? Open any bottle you want. There's food upstairs."

A moment later Max heard again the irritated voice, and Georg's sharp retorts. He thanked God that, whoever she was, she had abandoned such a good man.

•　　•　　•　　•　　•

At *Grünen Baum,* Hannah and Mathilde were mired in details for the reception after the funeral. Willi and Elke were providing all the bread and pastries from *Bäckerei Crème,* and Veronika had discovered her sister had not given Sebastien a bill.

"This is what we do, Veronika," Georg said. "I provide the wine, the bakery provides the bread, like your father and mother did. Someone else will bring flowers. Did you get a bill for the huge gathering after your father's funeral?"

"I can't afford to give away several days' worth of baked goods," she said.

A week after his father's death, Sebastien was still moving at half-speed, unable to juggle people and restaurant needs at the same time. But now he peered at Veronika.

"We can pay."

"You will not," Georg said. He loomed over Veronika, a perturbed lion ready to dispatch a field mouse. "I built you a house. I give you plenty of money, which I assume you don't put into the bakery or share with your siblings."

"It's the principle," she whined.

"Yes. It is the principle. We take care of our friends."

"Well," she said, moving out from under him. "Of course, I want to help. I'm devastated about Andreas. But Elke should have at least shown them what the bill would have been."

"Veronika," Hannah said, "we appreciate your generosity. You know how Andreas loved your apricot pie."

"There will be four apricot pies," Veronika sniffed.

"That's very thoughtful."

As Veronika trailed out, Georg gave Hannah a look. "Don't patronize her."

The funeral Mass was noisy. Soft chatter, weeping, and sniffling punctuated the entire ritual, enough to frustrate *Pfarrer* Vogl into stumbling through his sermon. The church was only large enough for six people to crowd together in a pew. Sebastien attended the funeral for his father. He and Hannah insisted Mathilde and Tobias sit with them in the front row, and Gabi held out her arms to each of them, her turn to provide comfort. Behind them sat Georg, Gerhard and Elke with Benno, and Hannah's parents. Siegi and her family came next.

On the other side, the entire staff of *Grünen Baum* and a considerable group of past employees took up many rows. Behind them all, friends, acquaintances, and a small cluster of Brandl relatives, many of whom travelled long distances, filled the rest of the pews, the aisles, and the choir loft. Others stood outside.

Viktor sat with his mother and *Oberleutant* Pfortner. Hannah heard the SS Officer sniffle. Viktor shook his head in disgust.

The last person to receive communion had both Sebastien and Hannah staring. "It's Hubert's friend," she whispered. "Maximillian Mayr."

Back at the inn, the tables filled quickly, inside and out. Servers who had been at *Grünen Baum* at least a generation ago seamlessly joined the staff. Mathilde and Tobias' grown son, daughter, and their spouses helped to clear the tables. The bounty of food seemed endless. No glass went empty.

Conversation grew to a gentle roar. The number of well-wishers overwhelmed Sebastien and Hubert, yet they spoke with everyone. Stories of Andreas and Amalie Brandl were endlessly shared. Chopin lounged on the patio steps near a photo of Andreas, unperturbed by people stepping over him. To the delight of the children present, Apfel wandered the *biergarten.*

Dietrich Pfortner came to offer his condolences and hastily exited. Viktor, Hannah noticed gratefully, was absent. "Where's Veronika?" she asked Sebastien as they passed each other in the *wintergarten.*

"Does it matter?" Sebastien grimaced. "I can't believe I said that."

They were both still outside when they heard the screaming. Sebastien sprinted up the steps and into the restaurant just as Veronika staggered in, waving a piece of paper.

"He's dead! He's dead!"

A crowd formed around her, wondering who died. She thrust the paper in front of her and howled. "Daniel," she screeched, turning on Hannah. "And it's your fault! You should never have let him go."

Georg had joined them, with Max Mayr. He took the paper and with a trembling voice, read:


*We are sorry to inform you that Daniel Reiter has succumbed to pulmonary tuberculosis. He became ill shortly after arriving, and although we have some of the Reich's best doctors on staff, he was too weak to survive.*

*Since this is an extremely communicable disease, it was necessary to cremate him immediately. You will receive his ashes and effects in several weeks.*

*Sincerely yours,*

*Georg Renno, Deputy Head Doctor*

Veronika's keening cries reverberated across the dining room walls. Sebastien and Hannah clung to each other. After a few moments, Max took a step toward Hannah. "I'm sorry," he said softly. "Hubert bragged about Daniel, how remarkable he was in the restaurant, and how everyone was so fond of him."

Behind Hannah, Elke stood alone, her face white with rage, eyes fixed on Veronika. She took the letter from Georg.

"Where did you send him?" Elke demanded.

"I didn't send him," Veronika whimpered. "He was invited."

Sebastien moved next to Elke. "But you arranged it."

"Two men came to the bakery. They said the Reich would like to help people like Daniel. They said he could go to a special camp, and promised he would be happy there."

"Or you would be happy while he was gone," Elke said.

"How can you say that? I loved Daniel!"

"Would you mind if I made a phone call?" Max whispered.

"In the reception room," Hannah said. He disappeared down the hall in a run. Tollner answered on the third ring.

"Tell me more about the six psychiatric hospitals," Max said without preamble. "Are any of them in Austria?"

"Why do you want to know about that? I can't talk right now, Max."

"Yes, you can."

"Wait." Max heard Tollner moving around. He finally spoke, his voice guarded.

"They were for a sterilization program directed by Hitler's own *Doktor* Karl Brandt."

"And the victims?"

The people who had been in the hospitals they took over."

"That's all?"

"I don't know," Tollner said testily. "From what I've heard, they've made a registry of all people with congenital disabilities or mental illness."

"This is how Hitler intends to purify Aryan race? Keep them from procreating?"

"That's not necessarily a bad thing, Max. How could any of them take care of a child?" He paused. "But between you and me, Hitler would rather get rid of them all. The only Austrian facility is Hartheim Castle."

"In Alkoven?"

"How would I know that? There are thousands of castles in Austria."

Max hung up, made one more phone call, and returned to the restaurant. Georg stood behind Veronika, his own tears spilling silently. Hannah held Elke as she sobbed. Sebastien hovered over Veronika while she alternated between blubbering and raging against Hannah.

"It's not Hannah's fault," Sebastien growled. "He got sick."

"Daniel's never sick," Veronika wailed.

Both Sebastien and Georg abandoned Veronika and joined the circle around her sister. Max knew intimately the intensity of their grief, and wished he had met this cherished young man.

Eventually, Georg offered to take Veronika home. With a final vile glance at Hannah, she permitted him to help her out of her chair and hobble out of the restaurant.

Mathilde coaxed Elke to sit down, and she and Tobias tended to her lovingly. "Someone has to find Willi," he said.

"I saw him go out with Siegi and the children," Mathilde said. "I'll get them, and Tobias can fetch Gerhard."

Hannah knew the last thing on Elke's mind was her husband.

Max approached Sebastien and Hannah. "Excuse me," he said. "Could we speak privately?"

They went into the *wintergarten,* the room's light and warmth having faded with the news. "I know where Daniel died," Max said. "If we go there, we might find out what happened."

Sebastien stared at him. "You think the doctor lied?

"I'm sure of it."

"Can we go right now?"

"Tonight. We should only be gone a day or two."

Sebastien announced that Max was taking him to see someone who may know more about Daniel. Hannah couldn't form a coherent thought. Max took out his handkerchief and handed it to her. "You're not responsible."

First Andreas, and now Daniel. What happened to the uncompromised joy with which they once lived their lives?

Sebastien turned to his brother. "You'll tell Georg?"

"Go," Hubert said. "We'll take care of everything."

# 42

Max drove them to *Maria Theresia*, where he tossed his bag in the back seat next to Sebastien's. They headed north along the river toward Krems, and then turned west. The narrow road was full of curves, passing through farmland and forest without a glimpse of a village to break the monotony.

Max sped along in silence, sensing Sebastien was not ready to hear the details of his phone conversation with Fritz Tollner, and only beginning to comprehend that this beloved Daniel, at once a friend and younger brother to him, was gone forever.

After almost two hours, a sign popped up along the road. Konigwiesen. They stopped to relieve themselves and have something to eat.

Sebastien steadied himself. "Tell me everything."

"I have a contact in Berlin. A while ago he told me the Reich had taken over six psychiatric hospitals. I called him for more information. Five of them are in Germany. The sixth is in Austria. Hartheim castle. Do you know it?"

"I don't think so."

"Hitler instituted a sterilization program for persons with mental illness or any other kind of disability."

"Are you telling me Veronika sent her brother away to be neutered?"

"She probably believed it was a camp for the disabled. The Nazis find their victims through municipal lists, doctors' records, anywhere they can uncover the whereabouts of 'unworthy' citizens of all ages."

"Unworthy?"

"Unworthy of life."

"Hitler is murdering them?"

Max put a finger to his lips, and Sebastien sank back. The bartender and a young woman were staring at him in horror. "Finish your drink," he muttered. "Let's not give them a chance to memorize us."

They drove for two more hours. "Hartheim," Max said, pointing to an imposing stone castle, unadorned except for polygonal corner towers and a larger central tower. They observed lights in some of the upper windows and guards at the gate.

"Aren't we going to stop?"

"Tomorrow," Max said. "I have friends in Alkoven who may have information and a way inside." Max pulled up in front of a small house only two blocks from the castle and turned off the engine. "Listen, Sebastien. You must never reveal to anyone what you know about me and what you will learn tonight. There are many good people who are resisting, and their survival depends on complete discretion."

"And you're one of them?"

They started up the path toward the house. "Did you understand what I said?" Max asked as he raised his hand to knock.

Sebastien nodded.

A light came on. The door opened and a friendly face peeked out. "Max! Welcome."

"Hello, Leopold, I appreciate you allowing us to come. He introduced Sebastien. A young boy squeezed in next to Leopold's leg.

Max bent down. "And Lukas. When I met you, you were not this tall! What happened?"

"I ate a lot, Herr Mayr."

"I think I remember sending you to bed an hour ago," Leopold chided the child. "If you scamper up those stairs right now, I won't tell."

He led Max and Sebastien through a closed door into a kitchen. "We're in the back." Through the half-drawn curtains of the door outside, a woman sat at a candlelit table on the grass. As they joined her, Leopold said soberly. "Knowing what we are doing puts you at monumental risk."

"I'm already at risk, Leopold," Max said. "I can't speak for my friend."

"Is the truth about Daniel out there?" Sebastien asked.

Leopold nodded. "You've come to the right place."

He made introductions. The woman's name was Helene. After a moment of silence, Leopold said to her, "you can trust them." She didn't respond.

Helene's brother joined them. "Franz Sitter," he nodded to Max and Sebastien.

"Up until recently, Franz worked at Hartheim," Leopold said.

Max saw a ripple of anger cross Sebastien's face, as did Sitter, who locked eyes with him. "In two days, I'm off to the front."

"I'm sorry," Max said.

"I chose the front. Anything is a better alternative than losing what's left of my soul."

"Franz, as long as you're here, and I know this is a cruel request, could you tell Max and Sebastien what you experienced? Sebastien's friend was a victim."

"I was a caretaker in the Health and Nursing Institute. One night they summed me to Reich headquarters in Linz and informed me I had an emergency service obligation. I was to transport the mentally ill to an unknown destination."

He accepted the beer Leopold handed him and took several long swallows. "I signed a statement of silence, and the next day I accompanied my first group to Hartheim.

"When I asked why they denied food and water to my passengers during the long drive, the head doctor said it wasn't my concern. After a few weeks I was ordered to help them disrobe for the shower room as soon as they were inside.. I didn't know I was preparing them to be gassed until an orderly told me it was his job to untangle the bodies and clean up the excrement."

Leopold said, "Many people in our town smelled something foul coming from the chimneys at Hartheim shortly after the trucks arrived. A fire engineer was sure it was burnt flesh. Leopold and I went to the castle and walked the path behind it. What we first thought were rocks in the road were bones. Our shoes were black from the ashes they spread out at night."

Max watched Sebastien wrap his arms around himself, grappling for control.

"It caused quite a commotion in our town. They tried to make us believe contaminated oil caused the odor."

Sebastien swallowed a sob, and they fell silent. After a while, Helene said, "Thousands of others have suffered the same fate as your friend."

"We've formed a resistance cell," Leopold said. "Helene has access to a printing press and large reams of paper. Our plan is to unveil this horrific evil by leafleting Alkoven and then moving on to other towns as far away as Linz. But we have to wait a while longer. We don't want our detailed knowledge of the atrocities at Hartheim traced back to Franz."

Sebastien drew his sleeve across his face and stared at the wet fabric clinging to his arm. "His name was Daniel Reiter. I can't bear the thought of what they did to him. He must have felt alone and afraid, and confused his sister would send him there." He explained that Hannah saw him last and felt something was very wrong.

"I have to pick up some papers that will help my wife and children get extra rations, so I'm going there tomorrow," Franz told him. "Come with me. Nazis keep meticulous records. I can at least confirm Daniel was there, and that he was gassed."

"They told Veronika in the letter she would be receiving his ashes in a few weeks."

Sitter stood, as did Helene. "You don't need to tell her this, but they shovel mounds of ashes from the incinerator and put them in piles. I know, because I had to take the lists of names and assign each one to an urn claiming to hold that victim's ashes."

Max shook Sitter's hand. "Thank you. For the truth. And for your incredible bravery in leaving."

"I don't think the SS will come looking for me at the front. They'll tell themselves I'm already dead."

Max and Sebastien walked three blocks to the nearest *Gasthaus* without speaking. The restaurant smelled like fried fish. The light in the hallway was out, and they had to feel their way to their rooms.

In the morning, they waited impatiently for the Gasthaus to open for breakfast. While they ate stale rolls and sipped weak coffee, Max asked Sebastien about the Nazi spoils in his cellar.

"I can only steal back enough to return to one or two families every few days. A rather peculiar *Oberleutnant* named Dietrich Pfortner stands over me and counts everything."

"Who knows about this?" Max asked.

"Only Georg, Hannah and I. We leave packages on back doorsteps."

"They have to suspect it's you."

"They're hungry. No one has said a word."

Max slathered more butter on his roll. "You don't know who will expose you, even accidently. Worse, if an SS officer gets a whiff of even one slight discrepancy, they will threaten the entire town until someone talks."

"I know that. But look what Leopold, Helene and their friends are doing."

"It's formidable, I agree. But you resist the Reich every day you confiscate a single egg."

His sentiment didn't pacify Sebastien. "It will take a lot more to avenge Daniel."

Max pushed away the cold remains of his breakfast. "When they murdered my wife, I was so angry I wanted to storm the Gestapo."

"But you joined the resistance right away. Is that how you know Leopold?"

Georg eyed him. "No details, Sebastien. Someone close to me had already gotten involved. He led me to a monk in Vienna, who taught me mutiny is only possible if I quell my rage, lest it become malignant. Act only when you are sure beyond a doubt you have considered everything you could lose."

"Sitter has a family, and look what he's risking because he listened to his conscience."

Max sighed. "Here's some good news. In some remote places in Austria, the original pleblecite called by Dollfuß on March 13 went on as planned because no one had heard Hitler had replaced it with the referendum on

April 10. In the village of Innervillgraten, 95% of the people voted to maintain the republic."

"I've always wondered what would have happened if that vote had actually taken place."

"The news came, but on April 10, 43 of the 200 people living in Innervillgraten still refused to accept the *Anschluß* and voted no."

"Forty-three Austrians," Sebastien whispered, "who weren't alone."

•   •   •   •   •

Franz and Helene were waiting for them. Black smoked billowed from Hartheim's chimneys, and when ashes flecked his coat, Sebastien fingered them tenderly.

Max covered his nose with a handkerchief. "I take it we can't go in."

"No visitors," Sitter said. "Helene will take you back to Leopold's house. I'll get the ration card, and then take a chance the records room is empty."

Leopold waited with them at the table in his back yard.

"I don't know what I'm going to tell everyone," Sebastien said despondently.

"Wait until Franz gets back," Max said. "You need more facts."

Sitter finally arrived, beads of sweat lining his forehead. "I'm sorry it took me so long. Dr. Lonauer tried to change my mind. He offered me a raise, as if this was some normal job where money made a difference. As if killing people was..."

Sebastien interrupted him. "Did you say Lonauer?"

"Dr. Rudolf Lonauer."

In Sebastien's face, Max saw a surge of emotion that frightened him. Sebastien wrenched himself from his seat and let out an ear-splitting scream.

"Herr Brandl," Helene snarled. "You just made this house the talk of the neighborhood. Shut your mouth and sit down."

# 43

Sebastien gulped for air. "I'm sorry," he managed.

"Rudolf Lonauer," Sitter reminded the others, "is the medical director at Hartheim, and he's also in charge of records. I'm lucky he wasn't upstairs when I searched the files. He's a monster."

"I know him," Sebastien wheezed. "He's from Moosfeld, where my wife was born. One of his brothers, Otto, is married to my wife Hannah's sister."

"Oh, my God," Max exclaimed.

"The oldest brother is the Nazi in charge of our area, and he put another brother, Viktor, in charge of tormenting me." Sebastien put his head in his hands. "What about Daniel?"

"He arrived here the same day your wife last saw him," Sitter said. "He was dead within the hour."

"But Rudolf must have recognized his name!"

"He's such an ardent follower of *Der Führer*," Sitter said, "he wouldn't spare someone he knew once, much less a young man deemed imperfect by the Reich."

"Sebastien, let me remind you," Max said. "Daniel's sister, Veronika, sent him to Hartheim. When we left, she was blaming your wife."

"Veronika didn't bother to consult anyone. We would have questioned a couple of strange Germans, showing up on her doorstep, promising Daniel a vacation."

"I must go," Sitter said. He looked at Sebastien. "I'm sorry for your loss. Let me say this to you: With my whole being, I regret the time it took me to listen to my conscience and admit my complicity in Nazi atrocities. Those days are a mark on my soul not even the most gracious God will forgive." He slipped through the door, followed by Leopold.

Sebastien wept again, surrounded by concerned faces. In a few minutes, Sitter was back.

"Sebastien, I forgot to tell you. I saw a strange notation next to Daniel's name."

"What do you mean?"

"They sort prisoners by their afflictions. Daniel was classified as mentally ill. But he was also labeled a criminal and threat to the Reich."

"That doesn't make sense," Sebastien said. "What was his crime?"

"Treason."

.    .    .    .    .

Max shoved Sebastien into the car, where he ranted incoherently as they drove away.

"Perhaps it wasn't an official notation," Max suggested. "Anyone could have added that, perhaps as a cruel joke."

"I don't understand. Daniel was talented in so many ways. But he was also naïve and childlike. Hitler was bad. The people he loved were good. While we were sinking into despair, his world remained joyful. What could he have done to be accused of treason?"

"The Reich throws that word around whenever anyone objects to anything. Unless you support Hitler, you're a traitor."

"Pfortner liked Daniel," Sebastien recalled, "even suggested they play cards once in a while. Other than supervising me and counting every tomato, our local Nazi doesn't have much to do."

"Did by some chance Daniel vote in the referendum? Voting no would have gotten him into trouble."

Sebastien launched himself from his seat, buckling against the grill in front of him. "Oh, my God. Oh, no, no, no."

"What is it?"

"This did not happen." He gripped the door handle. "Please tell me it didn't happen."

"Let go of the door," Max cried, and then softened his tone. "It's all right, Sebastien. Let me help you."

Sebastien rocked back and forth, until the words finally made their way out. "The person who voted no was me."

"So," Max said slowly. "Someone reported that it was Daniel?"

"Not someone. Daniel's brother-in-law. He took care of my 'error' by giving up Daniel."

"You can't mean Georg Wangermann."

"No, no. Gerhard Eigner, married to Daniel's sister Elke. He's a Party member, no matter how often he claims that as the mayor, he had to go along. Besides Hannah and Georg, he was the only one who knew. He was furious, and accused me of endangering the town."

"Perhaps. But yours was a brave act of defiance that Lili and I couldn't muster. You think your friend deliberately blamed Daniel? Maybe he thought his innocence was apparent, and the vote would be ignored."

For the next hour, Max said nothing, but periodically reached over and touched Sebastien's shoulder in a futile effort to comfort him.

•   •   •   •   •

Hannah heard the truck pull up. She had been busying herself in the reception room to watch the road, and hurried down the walk.

Sebastien got out. Without acknowledging her, he yanked his satchel out of the back of the truck.

"Sebastien!" Georg shouted. "Think before you act!"

"I've had several hours to think. I'm ready to act." He charged past Hannah, opened the door to the Inn and tossed the bag inside. "Is someone watching Gabi?"

"Siegi."

"Good. We're going to visit our Nazi mayor."

He gripped Max's hand. "I will never forget you, or your friends."

"Don't take this on yourself, Sebastien. The Reich did this to Daniel."

"Many people shoved him into the gas chamber. But I was first in line." He started down the street.

"Go with him," Max said to Hannah. "I hope we see each other again."

Hannah caught up with her husband and grabbed his arm. "Tell me what happened," she panted.

"I can't say what I'm going to say twice."

They reached the Eigner house. Sebastien pounded on the door, which Elke opened. Her hand flew to her heart at the look on Sebastien's face. "What's wrong? Has something else happened?"

"I need to talk to Gerhard."

"He's with Benno and Willi." In the kitchen, Willi was making faces at the giggling little boy. Although Hannah rarely saw Willi outside the bakery, and he came in and out of the inn almost unnoticed, Elke said he was not shy around his nephew.

Without greeting any of them, Sebastien said. "Willi, can you take Benno to visit Gabi?

"I suppose I could," Willi said.

"Please," Sebastien said. "What I have to say should not be uttered in front of a child."

Willi took Benno's hand. "Let's go visit your best friend."

"At least you can sit down, Sebastien," Elke said when they were alone. "Would you like a beer?"

Hannah gave him a shove. "Sit, Sebastien. You're being rude."

When they were seated, the gaze he leveled on Gerhard was meant to burn through him. "Who did you tell that Daniel voted no?"

Elke gasped. "What?" Hannah grasped her chair and moaned.

"Was it Faber? Or Viktor, who you knew would go running to his brother."

"They both knew about the vote. Of course, they suspected you. I had to come up with something or the town would suffer. I told him Daniel didn't know what he was doing. It was like a child playing with a pen."

"Daniel could read," Elke said tersely.

"Who would blame a person like Daniel ?" Gerhard protested. "I thought I'd convinced Viktor no real harm was done. He certainly acted as if he agreed."

"Let me explain this to you, Gerhard," Sebastien said. "Hitler branded Daniel, and others like him, as threats to the genetic purity of his new Aryan Empire, and therefore, not fit to live. Those in Austria were taken to Hartheim Castle in Alkoven. When they arrived, their belongings were thrown in a pile and they were told to undress for the showers. When they'd shoved all of them in, they pumped gas into the room." His face contorted. "It wasn't a peaceful death."

"The poster in Vienna," Hannah whispered.

Elke exploded. "Veronika arranged for him to go!"

Hannah swallowed. "She couldn't have known."

"Something else, Gerhard," Sebastien bore down on the man who had been his friend. "Because of you he wasn't only executed as a misfit, but as a traitor. Even if anyone cared to show compassion, he was doomed."

"How do you know that?"

"Because I went there. Daniel's death was recorded. Hartheim is a killing center where they perfected the gas chamber, so they can exterminate many Daniels at the same time."

Gerhard's face turned to stone, and he said nothing.

"How unfortunate you didn't tell any of us. Instead, you ran to Viktor, who told Faber, who undoubtedly got some reward for reporting him."

Gerhard pounded the table. "I wasn't the one who voted no!"

"No, it was me. And my part in Daniel's death will haunt me for the rest of my life. But I never thought for a minute you would betray your wife's brother. I would have confessed before I let you make such a heartless decision."

Elke stood. "I'm going to get Benno. Gerhard, I expect you to be out of this house by the time I get back."

"What?" Gerhard bellowed. "He's the one who put the town in peril. And you can't throw me out of my own house."

"Come to the inn," Hannah said.

"You are not leaving. When you are more rational, we'll talk."

"I'm too busy mourning my brother to be rational. I think of him, alone and afraid. And my own husband was responsible for his final moments of agony."

"I accept the blame, too," Sebastien interjected, his smoldering eyes never leaving Gerhard's. "But I wasn't the one who signed his death warrant."

Gerhard stood to face him. "I did it for you, and the whole town."

"No, you did it for you. You wanted to show off your loyalty to Ratzener. You needed me to stay silent so business could go on as usual. Daniel was convenient."

Elke returned with a valise. "I can come for the rest later."

They left Gerhard standing in the middle of his kitchen, denying his own fatal decisions: He had discarded his conscience, embraced expediency, and murdered an innocent young man who trusted him like a brother.

·   ·   ·   ·   ·

For many months, Sebastien wore his misery like a shroud. The death of his father and his guilt over Daniel left him somber and disinterested. Still troubled with her own worry that she was at least somewhat to blame, Hannah found it difficult to comfort him.

The small group of people who knew the truth adopted a tacit vow of silence. The past could not be undone.

When Willi was drafted, Sebastien had to be coaxed into hosting a little gathering to say goodbye. Hannah tolerated his indifference while she consoled her sister. "He won't come home, either," Siegi said. Hannah reassured her both Otto and Willi both would return. The lie lay heavy between them.

Elke was left with the bakery. She was used to getting up at four, leaving Benno at the inn to sleep in the little bed they moved into Gabi's room, and meeting Willi to bake bread and pastries. After a few hours in the front of the shop with her brother, she went home to watch Benno and Gabi while the Brandls served the midday meal. Willi handled the bakery alone until they closed later in the afternoon.

That routine was over. "Veronika will have to work at the bakery," she told Hannah, who couldn't wait to see Veronika back in a stained apron.

Elke didn't know how long she and Benno would be living at the inn, but for now, with people to care for him, she plotted a new routine. She informed Veronika she would get up an hour earlier to bake, and after that, handle the customers in the front, until eleven, when she would return to her son and help at the inn to pay for their keep. Veronika would relieve her until closing.

That night, after the children were in bed, Elke sat with Sebastien and Hannah in the *kochecke*. "She said she wouldn't do it. You should have seen her when I suggested we hire two more people."

"Wait," Sebastien said. "Is she being paid even though you and Willi were doing the work?"

"My parents gave her the bakery. She has the deed. We're the help. Today, at eleven, she was waiting outside. She pounced on me about my irresponsibility and her sacrifice, taking care of Daniel."

"The nerve," Hannah remarked.

"I reminded her Daniel would have been a big help to me, if she hadn't sent him away."

"Time to face the truth, Vroni," Sebastien muttered.

Veronika lasted a week. She hired a baker who needed a job and didn't quibble at meager wages. Elke had to train him, but he was quick to learn. She gave him a raise and hired a neighbor to work the counter in the afternoon. When Elke relayed all of this to Veronika, she feigned disinterest.

•　　•　　•　　•　　•

By the summer of 1941, Hannah noticed Sebastien reconnecting with his customers at the bar. Veronika continued to blame Hannah for Daniel's fate, and suggested Sebastien could buy his bread elsewhere.

"I'll say who can buy our bread," Elke told her sister.

One night after they had put on their nightclothes and were ready to go to bed, Sebastien said to Hannah, "I have something else to tell you. I had to wait a while, because I didn't know what I was going to do about it. Now I realize I can't do anything."

Hannah shuddered. What else?

"The man who ordered Daniel's execution was Rudolf Lonauer, the brother of Faber and Viktor. And Otto."

Hannah gripped his arm. "What?"

"Franz Sitter told us before we left for home. Listen, I've thought about this for a long time. I would like nothing more than to shove this into Viktor's face and tell the world. But I have no way to prove it. If I threaten him, Faber will make it his mission to make every moment of our lives excruciating."

Hannah wanted to scream. She was afraid, and it was her husband who inhabited her fear. But at least he had chosen her to confide this new hideous detail of Daniel's death.

"We keep the secret," she said.

He embraced her more furiously than he had in a long time. And afterwards, mercifully, sleep came.

# 44

*Kahlenbergerdorf, February, 1942*

Max Mayr and his sons had been hiding Jews in their wine caves for a year and a half. They retooled the printing press to make false papers. The forger lived nearby, and without notice, the little man with the pock-marked face slunk in at night and worked until dawn.

Using the documents he produced, they moved a family of four into Helga's little house next to the ruins of Lili's bookstore. Max employed two sets of Jewish fathers and sons in the vineyard. The printing press created possibilities for Jews to get out of Vienna, and the winery hid a small number who couldn't take that chance.

A multigenerational family of nine moved into the Pump Room. When it was there turn to move on, the Bergmanns were left behind because Libby was sick. Thirteen frightened people co-existed with little complaint. Every other week they practiced hiding in the walls and the chimney. They were all shown the route to the ladder tunnel.

Several times, however, Kolbe and his SS friends came very close to discovering the printing press. Stefan's jar of spiders sent them scuttling away just in time.

"How did you manage that?" Michel asked his brother.

"I sent the spiders down the passageway and hid in a wine barrel, like we talked about. I closed the little door and straddled the walls until they left."

Despite Stefan's ingenious scheme, Max told Michel to dismantle the printing press. If the monks didn't have another place for it, they would bury the pieces. The decision devastated Rafe. Tens of thousands of Jews remained in Vienna, trapped in their homes with no work and scant provisions. Poverty and disease were rampant.

A week later Kolbe informed Max that *Oberführer* Ratzener had chosen *Schloß Winzertal* to host a party for elite Viennese supporters of the Reich. Max was to put his best wines aside.

"It's bad enough he barges into the winery whenever he wants to," Michel stewed. "Imagine a room of drunk Nazis wandering off to explore."

Stefan cornered his father and Michel to ask why the mandatory conscription order left them untouched. Max had wondered the same thing. He was sure Kolbe would not intervene. Fritz Tollner was too much a coward to look out for his sons. "We have a plan," Stefan said, "just in case." Max also had a plan. The entire family would have to disappear, permanently. The sound of quick footsteps coming up the stairs ended the conversation. Rafe joined them at the table.

"I've just come from Vienna."

With all the precautions they took, Max wondered what could have taken Rafe into Vienna in plain daylight.

"It's bad news. Elie and Tovah were picked up last night."

"God, no," Max said, recoiling as if he'd been shot.

"Roman had been the contact with Elie. After his arrest, Johannes Veit took over. Last night he was at their house for a meeting, and Elie convinced him to spend the night because it was too late for him to be alone on the streets. About three in the morning, he heard cars screeching to a halt outside. He went into the hallway just as Elie was coming out of their bedroom. He sent Johannes to hide in a closet.

"The Gestapo."

"Johannes listened to them rampage through the house and Tovah being ordered downstairs. He heard the front door bang shut and crawled to a window. They loaded them into the back of a black car, still in their nightclothes."

Michel stood up and kicked a chair across the kitchen. "He and Tovah were heroes," he cried.

During the last year, with a carefully selected group of friends, the Schetts smuggled food and supplies collected by the resistance to dozens of starving Jewish families. Elie delivered false papers and worked with the underground to deliver hundreds of Jews out of Vienna.

Stefan wept for his teacher.

Max put his arm around him. "I remember when he told you that education led to truth."

"And truth," Stefan murmured, "is the soul of resistance."

They moved through the day in a haze of misery. Max again slipped into his mourning coat. Rafe advised against telling their guests what had happened to their beloved Rabbi and his wife. "They'll lose hope," he said, "the only thing that gets them through each wretched day."

Weeks went by. An onslaught of jagged emotions left Max bruised and battered. But it was fear that possessed him with demonic intensity. He couldn't shake the feeling they were about to be discovered. Kolbe was visiting more often and had abandoned any pretense of friendship. By the middle of March, Max shifted his focus to a plan for escape. He was sitting at his desk, smoking a cigarette, considering all possibilities, when he received a call from Fritz Tollner, whom he had not spoken to since Andreas Brandl's funeral.

"I didn't expect to hear from you again."

"This will be the last time," Tollner said.

Max swallowed a groan. What in the hell was he doing, anyway? He didn't want to talk to the spineless Nazi.

"I'm calling because it might be too late for you to join The Party. You are too prominent a citizen to be overlooked."

"I've been thinking about it." Max clutched the receiver, which felt too heavy to hold. Could he have joined without compromising his integrity? But this was no time for remorse. He could no longer allow Tollner to assuage his conscience by sitting in his place of privilege, serving his slimy boss, and then warning Max of atrocious crimes he himself sanctioned.

"One more thing," Tollner said in a voice that flirted with excitement. "Hitler set up a conference at a villa in Wannsee and sent everyone but himself."

"Why didn't Hitler go?"

"He sent Reinhard Heydrich to present his next plan. He's calling it 'The Final Solution.'"

"Tell me again who Heydrich is."

"I assume you know what was happening at Hartheim. Heydrich was in charge of developing gassing technology. Since they stopped the program last year, he's been building gassing trucks and outfitting many of the so-called work camps with gas chambers."

Inconceivable evil. Max's heart pounded.

"Heydrich declared 11,000,000 Jews in Europe, including those in allied and neutral nations, fall under the provisions of The Final Solution."

"He wants to kill every Jew in Europe?"

"Deportation means extermination. And of course, anyone caught helping a Jew suffers the same fate."

Max glanced at Lili's gift, the painting of his two Jewish sons. They had to get out, now.

# 45

*St. Jakob, February, 1942*

At least once a month, Sebastien left the inn for several days. It was always the same: it was difficult to find locally whatever special food the Germans demanded or truck part they needed. Hannah grew tired of his excuses, which no longer sounded reasonable to her distrustful ear.

Between his absences, Hannah found him increasingly restless, and sometimes angry at the staff for insignificant mistakes. But on the night of Hannah's celebration for Elke's birthday, Hubert showed up in the *kochecke* and broke the malevolent spell. And yet, his brother had barely hoisted his wine glass before Sebastien demanded to know what was happening in Vienna.

"The rich," Hubert reported, "complain they can't survive on one unrationed meal a day. They have no idea how many Viennese would be happy with that amount of food for an entire week. Shelves are empty. No butter, flour, fish or fruit. Confectionaries create dummy packages of chocolate made of *papier-mâché*. We haven't had real coffee in the café for a year."

"How do they feed their children?" Hannah asked.

"I don't know. When the mark replaced the shilling, earnings decreased by one-third. And even if they wanted to, it's against the law for employers to supplement wages. Only Party members get the factory jobs, making war supplies."

"And the Jews?" Sebastien asked.

Hubert glanced at Hannah and said, "I've seen lines of families waiting to be loaded into boxcars going to labor camps, never to be heard from again."

Hannah's stomach clenched, a reaction she was familiar with.

"I decided to leave. Leopold and Josephine will probably have to close the café anyway."

"We could use your help," Sebastien said.

His brother shifted in his seat. "I'll work *mittagessen*. Otherwise, Georg needs me. Many of his employees have disappeared, so I'm going to stay with him and come back and forth."

"Were they Jewish?"

"I wouldn't know, Sebastien. Anyway, *Grünen Baum* is swarming with Germans. It will be safer for me at the winery."

"You need to hide?"

"I had some trouble in Vienna. I might be on a list or two." Abruptly, Hubert stood up and gathered his coat and hat. "Do you mind if I borrow Apfel?"

"Of course not."

"I'll be here tomorrow." Without a parting embrace, or bidding them goodnight, he was out the door.

Sebastien couldn't sleep. "I don't understand. Why wouldn't my brother stay here and go back to the winery when Georg needs him? The harvest isn't for months."

Hannah snuggled next to him. "Maybe he likes Georg more than us," she said.

"This is so wrong."

Hannah smiled. Sebastien sounded like his old self.

Calm lasted for a day. Hubert returned as promised, but stayed at the stove, one eye on the door. Siegi came into the restaurant with her children while Sebastien and Hannah were serving Faber Ratzener and a rowdy group of SS officers, spread out over two tables in the middle of the room, more belittling and argumentative than ever. Ernst ran into Hannah, causing several plates to wobble in her arms. Sebastien picked up the twins and walked them all down the hall to the *kochecke,* but then he was back, beckoning his wife.

"What's happened?" she asked, sure Bernard or Sophie had fallen ill.

"Otto."

Mathilde was already on duty. "Uncle Hubert is here!" She told the children, gathering them up and leading them away.

Siegi didn't seem to notice. "Hubert's here?"

Hannah glanced at her husband. "He came last night."

"Shock," Sebastien said under his breath. "Siegi, do you understand what's happened?"

The Siegi they knew was absent. "Faber came looking for me," she whispered. "Otto was reported dead in France. I didn't even know he was in France."

Hannah sank into a chair. They had all clung to the belief that Otto's bad eyes would save him.

"Faber is out there carousing, as if nothing happened," Sebastien muttered.

Siegi shrugged. "Faber didn't like Otto."

Hannah wrapped an arm around her sister. "Do the children know?"

Showing the first bit of emotion, Siegi crumbled. "Can you tell them?"

"If you want me to," Hannah said. "But let's sit here for a while longer. They're fine in the kitchen with Mathilde and Hubert."

"And Tobi," Sebastien said. "He'll have an art project for them." He called the children his *Kleine Künstlern.*" Little artists.

Later, when the children were returned, Hannah told them their Papa was in heaven with Opa and Daniel. Ernst ran into Sebastien's arms. The girls, tearful and bewildered, climbed into their mother's lap and patted her on the back.

·　　·　　·　　·　　·

A week later, the familiar Siegi was back. After the last of their patrons had left and the restaurant door locked, she joined Georg, Hubert, and the Brandls around their table.

She shoved her sister over with her hip and sat down. "I have news. Willi wrote his unit is inactive for the moment."

"Where is he?" Sebastien asked.

"France." She frowned. "I guess he isn't where Otto was."

"He's writing to you?" Hannah asked.

"Because I write to him. What's wrong with that?"

"Nothing," Hannah said. "I didn't know you two were corresponding."

"Well, we are." Siegi took a few gulps of wine.

"Does he write to Elke? Or Veronika?" Hannah pressed.

Siegi reddened. "I don't know! Why don't you ask them?"

As if on cue, Veronika burst through the back door. She stopped short when everyone laughed.

Hubert led her to a chair. No one was in the mood for histrionics. "Here," he said soothingly. "Have some wine. Good news, Willi's in France, but not having to fight at the moment."

She frowned. Obviously, Veronika didn't know Willi was in France, and had other things on her mind. "I wanted to remind you, Sebastien, we are all required to celebrate *Der Führer's* birthday. We're going to bake something special."

Hannah rolled her eyes. Elke would do the baking.

"You know," she continued smugly, "in Vienna, if the weather is nice, people go around saying it's a Hitler Day. Sunny and beautiful is Hitler weather."

"How odd," Hubert remarked.

"It's a sign of support. "If you don't show support, you're switched off."

"Switched off?" Georg wondered. "Veronika, where are coming up with these things?"

"She's right," Hubert said. "That's what they label people who aren't complying with Nazi ideals of racial and social conformity."

"I wonder how many people choose to support the Reich," Georg asked, "and how many are simply too scared to do otherwise?"

Veronika thought for a moment. "What's the difference?"

"Believing and pretending. Neither one is helpful." Sebastien said sarcastically.

"I understand what she's saying," Hannah said. "It's all about appearances. Not wanting to be...different."

Veronika frowned, as if wondering if that was what she had said. "The streets in Vienna are a lot cleaner than they used to be."

As if exhaustion descended on them all at once, they ignored the implications. It was time to drain their glasses.

The next morning, Hannah tiptoed after Sebastien down to his cellar hideaway. The lock on the door was new, and she watched him pull a key from his pocket.

"Do you think someone will come in and read what you're writing?"

He whirled around. "Hannah! You startled me."

"Well?"

"I don't trust Pfortner," he said. He took one step into the room. "See you later?"

She had been dismissed.

# 46

*Kahlenbergerdorf, April 1, 1942*

The first thing Max did was contact a Swiss winemaker he trusted. Did he know where the holes were in the border? Reluctantly, his friend gave him one location. The monk Johannes Veit, still chastising himself for simply watching Elie and Tovah disappear into one of the dreaded black sedans, volunteered to test two supposed safe routes on back roads. Departure from *Schloß Winzertal* was set for April 18.

Max never considered their own passports would be a problem, and was furious with himself for destroying the printing press before he'd secured the forger's masterful facsimiles. With Rafe and Sigrid present, Max told his family it was time to flee Vienna.

"I agree, Papa," Michel said. "I hate to abandon the resistance, but we have Stefan and Oma to think about."

"And our guests," Max said, frowning.

The four Bergmanns were still in the Broom Closet. Eighty-year-old Rena Mendelssohn had been hiding in the Pump Room for over two years. Josef, her husband, had pneumonia when they arrived and died shortly after. She was one of the last people to receive false papers from the printing press. While other refugees came and went, Rena graciously welcomed the new arrivals, as she once did in their lovely home in Vienna.

Max was not about to strand anyone. They spent hours at the kitchen table, plotting the evacuation of everyone still on his property.

With his usual mixture of ingenuity and carpentry skills, Michel built a compartment under a false bottom in Rafe's truck.

"The night before," Max said, "we'll drive it up the hill to the spot where the ladder tunnel ends. The Bergmanns will climb up in the dark and wait for Michel to help them into the compartment. You'll continue up to the top and take the dirt road down to Mauerbach," Max directed his son, "and then proceed onto the first route Johannes mapped out."

"They'll be lined up like sardines in there," Michel said. "I'll probably have to make a stop before we cross the border." He swept a hopeful gaze around the table. "We'll meet again in Switzerland."

Max resurrected the German-made Mercedes and would drive with Stefan, Helga and Frau Mendelssohn, the Steyr Baby 55 left behind.

Michel was staring at Rafe. "I've never asked you if you have viable papers."

"Sigrid is a Catholic. I'm a Jew with a false identity. Roman made sure of that."

"I didn't know," Max said.

"You still don't."

Max unearthed his father's hunting rifle and taught his sons how to use it. "Just in case," Max kept saying, as they fired at a target tacked to a tree deep in the forest. Any trace of their innocence was now imbedded in brown bark; it was time to tell them who they really were.

They sat together on the leafy forest floor while Max gave them an edited version of their mother's story. He finally got to the heart of the secret.

"Michel, the name you were born with is Moshe Fieg, after your father."

"What do you mean?"

"Your mother's real name was Ester Fieg, and she cherished the name they gave you. Your father and both her parents were beaten to death while she watched, only steps away, with you in her arms. She carried that terrifying image with her from Poland. She asked me to help her bury your names and real identities so deeply, no one would ever be able to hurt you or any other children she bore."

"You're telling me I'm Jewish."

"Yes."

"And Stefan, too. The truth could condemn us, Papa."

"Yes." Max put his arm around his youngest son's shoulder. "Your Jewish name is Sivan."

"Was I named after somebody?" he whispered.

"No," Max said with a slight smile. "Your mother thought it had a beautiful sound."

Stefan wrenched away from his father. "Michel isn't really my brother," he said angrily.

"Of course we're brothers," Michel said, going to him. "Think of it this way. Mutti chose two names she loved for each of us."

Max sighed. "Except that one of them cannot be spoken aloud, until this insidious evil has been defeated."

Max consoled them as they wept, and then left them alone with their immutable promise to keep Lili's secrets.

•     •     •     •     •

With one week left, they sat around the kitchen table, looking for flaws in their escape plan. Michel, as was customary, brought up two bottles of wine for the meeting.

"I'm the son of a winemaker," he grumbled. "I think better with a glass in my hand."

Stefan didn't join in the laughter. Michel was not the son of a winemaker. The new reality poked at him and left a trickle of blood that he and his half-brother no longer completely shared.

From below, they heard pounding on the front door, and they scattered while Max opened it to Klaus Kolbe, the last person on earth Max wanted to see.

Max told Kolbe to follow him up to the kitchen, where only Helga remained.

"Next Monday is the birthday of our great *Führer*," Kolbe began, "and the annual celebration all over the Reich. I told you *Schloß Winzertal* was on our list. The event will be in your winery, next Sunday the nineteenth, the day before the festivities in Vienna."

"How many guests, Klaus?" Helga demanded. "Are we serving food? You'll have to give us the details if you expect this to happen on such short notice."

Despite her blatant lack of respect, Kolbe said, "You will comply with my orders, Frau Mayr. The invitations are out."

"We didn't get one," Max said.

"Obviously. You're staff."

"Think of it this way, Papa," Michel said after he'd gone. "Kolbe and his fiendish friends will be here celebrating on Sunday night. We'll make sure they have a lot of wine, or beer, *schnaps*, or any other liquor we can pour down their throats. Between their pounding heads and the damn birthday, they won't come back on Monday."

Not convinced, Max said. "We won't be ready. It can't look like we're leaving."

"I already packed my suitcase," Stefan said sheepishly.

"Unpack it. We'll have to get up very early on Monday.

"Let's hope they've scuttled back to the pigsty by then," Michel said wryly.

# 47

Sebastien's disappearances often lasted a week, so Hannah became the one to accept the Nazi spoils from their neighbors. Suddenly, it was her fault their neighbors' doorsteps were empty.

He hadn't been there when they announced severe cuts in consumer food allotments. *Oberleutnant* Pfortner gave out new ration cards in St. Jakob and Moosfeld. When Sebastien returned the next evening, Hannah was examining them. He put his arms around her and kissed the top of her head. Despite her aggravation, his affection moved her, as it was bound to do.

He read the new restrictions on meat, butter, margarine and bread. "This can't be right. They act like this is their own kitchen. They'll starve if we have to follow these guidelines."

"That's bad news and good news," Hannah said. She couldn't help herself. Hungry for him, she pulled him down for a long, sensuous kiss. "Let's go to bed," she whispered. The days between lovemaking had become longer, and more often than not, Sebastien wasn't the initiator. She didn't like her new role.

That night, he received her eagerly. They explored each other's bodies, familiar with every spot and crevice. They kissed, and tasted.

"Hannah," Sebastien whispered. "I never want to be without you."

Her contentment vanished.

And yet, you go.

•    •    •    •    •

On the day Hubert didn't arrive for *mittagessen*, Sebastien and Hannah were so busy with an overflowing restaurant, the usual Nazi tables, and people from neighboring villages, they didn't notice until Mathilde sounded the alarm she was falling behind. Sebastien went into the kitchen to cook and Hannah handled all the orders, along with the newest server, who apparently had fabricated his prior restaurant experience.

Luckily, they had Tobias to take over the bar. Tobias' presence bolstered them all, especially after the loss of Andreas and the staff members kidnapped by the German army.

When it was over, they sat in the empty dining room at a table, still messy with dirty plates, and took lengthy swallows of beer.

"He'd better have a good excuse," Mathilde said.

They heard the front door open and bang shut. "We're closed," Sebastien said irritably. But it was Hubert who rushed in. "Georg has been arrested," he stammered.

Sebastien stood up so quickly he almost fell into Hannah's lap. "What happened?"

"Pfortner came with two other SS officers. They said they were taking him in for questioning. Pfortner actually looked uncomfortable, but the other two grabbed Georg and threw him into the back of a car." Hubert blinked back tears. "He didn't even have his shoes on."

Sebastien was already leading his brother out. The nearest Gestapo headquarters was in Krems. The tires on Sebastien's truck kicked up a cloud of dust as they sped away.

Two hours later, he had only ambiguous news. "We think he's there."

"They said it was against regulations to tell us," Hubert said dismally.

For the next five days, Hubert went to Krems to ask about Georg. "If I pester them enough, I'll get some answers." His thin frame became even thinner.

Late in the evening of the sixth day, Sebastien and Hannah sank onto a banquette in the *kochecke*. Neither of them spoke. They had used up all their words on worry. Suddenly, Schnapsi scuttled through the open back door, followed by Hubert and Georg. Hannah shrieked and ran to embrace them both, Sebastien right behind her.

While Hubert had lost weight, Georg looked like he'd gained ten pounds. "They kept feeding me, even when I said I'd had enough," Georg explained. "The Gestapo want people to think some of us are being treated well while being held in a dungeon."

"Guess who drove Georg home," Hubert said.

"Ratzener," Georg laughed. "He ranted and raved about Hitler's latest warning: 'Those who do not live up to their wartime duties will be mercilessly purged.'"

Hannah tensed. "Was he talking about you?"

"He was talking about me," Sebastien said. His words still hung in the air when Tobias came in, followed by Faber and Viktor. Schnapsi barked frantically.

"I'm sorry," Tobi said. "They insisted."

"Nice to see you again, Wangermann," Faber said. "I had a meeting to attend to in Melk, but I knew this is where you would run. "Schnapsi sniffed his leg and Faber pushed him away. "Do something about this dog."

Hannah put him in the hall. But that didn't stop him from continuing to protest.

"Have a seat, Faber," Sebastien pulled out a chair. "You, too, Viktor. I'm surprised to see you here."

"He meant *Oberführer,*" Hannah heard herself say.

"My brother didn't want me to miss his announcement," Viktor said, looking fiendishly pleased.

"I'll stand," Faber said. "What I have to say won't take long. *Weingut Maria Theresia* is my new summer home. Wangermann, you will be my personal sommelier." He pointed at Hubert. "And since Brandl doesn't need you, you'll be my chef. When I'm in residence, members of The Party will join me to rest and relax. *Der Führer* encourages us to take care of both our physical and mental health."

"Despite the fact you've appropriated my home, I still have a vineyard to run," Georg said sharply. "Summer will be busy."

"That's why I haven't sent you to the front. And I'll even make it easy for you. Move your things into the wine cellar. Take the dog. You can both get an early start in the morning and still tend to my needs."

Georg looked at Hubert. "I'll find us a couple of cots. We can pretend we're camping."

"Schnapsi will love it."

Sebastien laughed. Hannah covered her mouth, and Georg looked at the floor and grinned.

"I'd sober up if I were you, Brandl," Faber continued. "Pfortner tells me you sometimes fail to take your job seriously."

Innocent was one of Sebastien's best faces. "I don't know why he said that. Everything is ready for you to steal right on time."

Faber made a point of swiping at his nose. "I also hear from the *Oberleutnant* that you often disappear and leave your wife to do your job. Where do you go?"

"The grocery list I'm given from your friends is long. St Jakob is a simple village. We don't have all the ingredients I need to prepare the elaborate meals they demand."

"Send Pfortner."

"Will he pay, then?"

"Schieß! I don't have to time to trifle with a town no more important than a chicken coop." He turned back to Georg. "One more thing. Remove your signs. I'm changing the name to Weingut Linzer," in honor of the town Hitler has chosen to become the centerpiece of the Third Reich."

"A grand idea," Viktor cackled.

Faber eyed his brother. "You should think about doing the same thing."

"Everyone is used to *Der Wachauerhof*," Viktor said peevishly.

"That may be true, but Nazi leaders would look more favorably on a name like *Braunauhof*, after *Der Führer*'s birthplace. Or how about *Gasthaus Klara,* after his mother?"

"I'll think of something!" Viktor barked, humiliation seeping out of him.

Gabi and Benno chose that moment, or were conveniently sent, Hannah decided, to visit.

"Papa, Benno needs chocolate," Gabi declared.

Sebastien scooped her up. "Only Benno?"

"He can share with me."

"I want my own," Benno said.

"Two orders of chocolate, coming up!" Sebastien added Benno to his arms. "Sorry, Faber."

"He meant *Oberführer,*" Hubert said.

Faber rose and snarled at them. "You have my orders. *Heil* Hitler!" Hannah froze. Georg and Hubert waved at him. Sebastien shrugged, his arms full.

# 48

*Kahlenbergerdorf, April 19, 1942*

On the afternoon of the Nazi event, two SS officers arrived with boxes of ingredients unavailable to most Austrians. Helga hired her usual helpers from the village to prepare a large variety of hors d'oeuvres. "I thought about poisoning the food," she told Max. "But then I thought that would be too messy."

"What do you mean?"

"Where would we put the bodies?"

"Mutti!" Max exclaimed. "You are wicked."

The young women trooped in, and Helga was back to cooking and planning assassination.

Several SS officers arrived to inspect the room. "It's so Austrian," one of them observed.

"We thought that's what *Obersturmbannführer* Kolbe wanted," Michel said pleasantly.

Everything in the room was red and white. The tablecloths were red and decorated with rosettes of meringue made to look like *edelweiß,* and perky little red poppies flowing over the sides of baskets set between red and white candles. Even they objected to the Austrian décor, it was too late to redecorate.

Guests poured into the winery. Servers stood at tasting stations around the room. The women studied each other, comparing hairstyles and attire. Not bothering to taste, some men took more than one bottle and sat down.

Silver platters of Helga's hors d'oeuvres were passed through an unappreciative crowd.

Kolbe and Ratzener slithered through the winery doors, causing a sizable commotion.

"Where are the trumpets?" Stefan asked. The Mayrs didn't have to feign respect; everyone else was giddy with uninhibited adulation.

"*Heil* Hitler," Max mumbled. Ratzener and Kolbe returned his greeting, Kolbe with a triumphant smile on his face. "Welcome to *Schloß Winzertal*," Max said. "Please, come taste my best wines." He motioned to his sons, who each picked up a bottle.

"I wasn't going to salute," Stefan whispered.

An hour later, Ratzener walked to the stone steps. Max hurried over. "Can I help you?"

"I assume you keep the most valuable vintages locked away." Max followed him, his stomach in knots. The lights had been extinguished. The Jews were in the walls.

"I can get you other varietals to try," Max said.

"Fine. And for God's sake, turn on the lights."

Max gave a lantern to Ratzener, who, with confidence in his step, continued down to the cave. As if he knew exactly where he was going, he stopped outside the Pump Room.

"This is cozy," Ratzener said with a sneer. "Is this where you brought your mistresses?"

Max took a bottle off the rack and set it on one of the barrel-tops. "One woman was enough for me," he said, handing Ratzener a healthy pour.

"I heard she died. What a pity. And on such a glorious night for the Reich."

Max had to keep from crushing a bottle over Ratzener's head. "We miss her very much," he said evenly.

Ratzener drained his glass and pointed to the rack. "That was adequate, but you can do better." Max opened another bottle and again was generous. Ratzener launched into a testimony of Hitler's genius. A lantern came around the corner. "There you are, Papa," Michel said. *Obersturmbannführer* Kolbe wants you to talk about the wine."

"I'm sorry," Max said, seizing the bottles and stepping away. "Please, bring your glass. These rare wines are my gift to you."

"If these are your best, they should have already been upstairs," Ratzener said.

Back in the winery, the crowd again cheered Ratzener heartily, as if he had just scored the winning goal in the World Cup, instead of what amounted to a heist. Max described the wines in terms they pretended they understood. When he finished, the noise in the room went up several notches. One thoroughly inebriated group slurred the words to Nazi-approved songs.

Max told his sons to go to bed. Hours later, he helped the last of the drunken guests stumble into their cars. He stood alone in the courtyard and allowed himself a moment of satisfaction. They had entertained the vile Nazis while five objects of their hatred breathed fresh air below them. He took out his watch and turned it to the moonlight. Saying goodbye to the home of his proud Austrian ancestors was only four hours away.

# 49

Sebastien prepared plates of spaghetti for Georg and Hubert, who had made themselves comfortable in the *kochecke*. They sat with their heads together, chatting, the dog asleep beneath them.

Afterwards, Sebastien brought out the peach *schnaps*. Hannah couldn't take her eyes off Georg and Hubert; she envied their lightheartedness. As if there was no war, no Nazis stomping on their lives, and no problem with their pending eviction.

"You know," Georg said to Hubert. "It's cooler in the winery during the summer."

"That's good," he replied. "Our bedroom can get quite warm."

"I've been meaning to buy another fan." They grinned at each other, and then slowly turned their smiles on Hannah and Sebastien.

"Are you shocked?" Hubert asked.

"I'm, uh, confused," Sebastien sputtered.

"I'm shocked." Hannah conceded.

"You can say it," Hubert said, pulling his chair even closer to her. "You're horrified. We didn't expect you to be comfortable, at least until we told you more of our story."

"Seb," Georg said solemnly. "We couldn't go on hiding our secret. Someone has to know who we are, and what we mean to each other. We've spent practically our whole lives pretending to be normal, and we hope that maybe, in the future, you might understand."

Hubert nudged him. "We're quite normal."

"I'm sorry. You're quite right."

Sebastien gulped down his *schnaps*. "The story?"

"One night," his brother said in a voice full of delight, "when Georg came to Vienna, I asked him to come with me to my friend's cozy café."

"We talked, honestly," Georg said, "and I felt like I'd been lifted out of a swamp." Neither Sebastien nor Hannah missed Georg's hand move to cover Hubert's, who took up the story again.

"We had a nice supper and a couple of beers. It got very late, and we were still talking. My friend told me to lock up when we left and leave the key on the ledge above the door." He shrugged. "He likes me."

"He certainly does," Georg interjected.

Hubert's eyes twinkled. "Anyway, we turned off the lights and brought candles from the other tables. We opened some of his wine."

"And put the money next to his cash register with a note," Georg hastened to add.

Hubert threw his arm around Georg's shoulder. "We stayed the entire night!"

"Just before dawn, a young man came in from the back. He started mopping the floor, and we sat at a table and lifted our feet while he cleaned under us."

"We were invisible," Hubert said. "Do you understand?"

Sebastien hesitated. "It all sounds very…"

"Romantic." Hannah waved a hand in submission.

Sebastien leaned forward. "The night of *Kristallnacht*…."

Hubert's smile vanished. "They arrested me on suspicion of being a homosexual. They stripped me, and paraded a terrified, naked young woman in front of me. They were testing my response, or lack of it. I don't know what happened to the girl."

"How did you get away?"

"A moment of pandemonium, when they were moving too many prisoners from one side of the jail to the other, I walked away."

"This explains a lot of things," Sebastien mused.

"What?" Hannah demanded.

Sebastien sighed. "Veronika."

Hannah hadn't thought of that, and couldn't help but sympathize. Georg took no offense; whatever happened with Veronika no longer mattered.

They stood to leave. "I hope this knowledge doesn't put undue pressure on you," Georg said. "It certainly takes a lot of pressure off of us."

After watching them together, they couldn't deny Georg and Hubert were in love. "We can relate," Sebastien said, when they were in bed. The shock had worn off. What possessed them now was immense curiosity about an unimaginable relationship.

Hannah said, "I keep picturing two very tall men cuddled up together under a pile of blankets."

"Oh. I'm not ready for that."

The next morning Sebastien got up early and told Hannah he had a few errands to run. Later, she wondered if he had kissed her good-bye.

Four days went by. A cauldron of rage and disappointment burned inside of her. When obsession wore her down, she spent an entire morning searching for the key to Sebastien's room in the cellar.

At noon, she served food and avoided conversation, and at three o'clock, resumed her search. She climbed down the cellar stairs, rattled the lock, dismissed the idea of breaking in, and dropped to the floor in frustration. A pair of gloves sat next to her. She picked one up and threw it. The key came tumbling out.

She went quickly to his desk and examined a pile of papers, folded into fours. On the front were a variety of anti-Nazi declarations and a crude cartoon. Sebastien was designing leaflets for the resistance. And, she was sure, delivering them.

She yanked out each of his drawers and rifled through more papers, train schedules, and maps, marked with a pen. She examined one of them; the line ended not in a town, but at a bridge. Next to the mark he'd written, "Leopold." She didn't find the journal.

*You wouldn't want me going to Vienna, would you?*

A coat lay on his chair. She seized it and felt the pockets. Nothing. But sitting on the seat were more leaflets, tied together with a string. On top, Sebastien had written a note.

*Helene 11 o'clock Tuesday.*

She went upstairs, and told Mathilde if Sebastien returned, to send him up to their room. An hour later, he was home, with a single box of Nazi cravings.

"I'm sorry, liebchen. I had to go to three towns to find sardines, of all the silly things."

She held up a fistful of leaflets.

He took a breath. "I can explain."

"No, I don't think you can, Sebastien. You've ruined everything. Throwing rocks at them would be safer than handing out these."

"All right, then. I don't know what to say."

She tossed the leaflets on the floor. "It appears you know exactly what to say. Who are you working with?"

"Some friends I met when I went to Alkoven with Georg. Don't you understand? I couldn't sit on my hands any longer!" He reached for her. "Please, liebchen, listen to me. I'm relieved that I don't have to lie to you anymore."

She turned her back on him, too broken to ask about the woman.

# 50

"Papa!" Michel shook his father, who was asleep in his clothes on top of his bed.

"*Schieß*." Max sat up so fast he saw stars. "What time is it?"

"Just after six."

"Are you packed?"

"Yes. We thought that's what you were doing."

"I'll catch up in ten minutes." Max raced around the room, throwing a few articles of clothing and toiletries into his duffle bag, along with a photo of Lili and her favorite hat. Michel brought him his boots. "Oma said you should wear them."

He joined his sons, Helga, and Sigrid in the kitchen. Coffee and the last of the rye bread waited at his place.

A door slammed. "Three SS cars are coming," Rafe called out as he pounded down the stairs from the bedroom where he had been surveilling the road.

Max blanched. "This can't be happening."

Rafe pulled Michel out of his chair. "You have to move." The truck was already at the tunnel opening, the Bergmanns waiting to emerge.

Michel shook his head. "I'm not leaving Papa to deal with whoever that is."

Sigrid stood. "I'll take them. Maybe Helga should come, too."

"She's right," Rafe said. "With her in the passenger seat, you'll look less suspicious." Helga was already heading for her room.

"Best leave your suitcase," Sigrid called.

Helga frowned, but allowed Rafe to rush her out the kitchen door. He handed his keys to the fury-eyed, tall blond woman the Mayrs had come to love almost as much as he did. He looked into those eyes.. She returned his gaze and touched his face. "No time," she said, and the two women were gone.

"All of you," Max said. "Go to the caves and hide with Rena in the wall. You'll have to take the tunnel from the chateau cellar."

"Rafe can take Stefan," Michel said. I'll stay here and put the wine rack back against the entrance."

"I want to stay with you," Stefan cried.

Tires rumbled across the courtyard.

Max embraced his youngest son. "Go with Rafe!"

When they were out of the kitchen, Max took a few steps toward the window. The black cars sat idling, Klaus Kolbe in the driver's seat of the one in front.

A minute went by. Max closed his eyes and played through the escape: the Bergmanns folding into the compartment under the truck, his mother in the front seat next to Sigrid, the truck disappearing over the hill. Rafe and Stefan, and a Jewish widow, already in the walls.

The sound of car doors slamming brought him back.

"Mayr!" Kolbe shouted. "You can't hide. Don't make us drag you down here."

"Run," he told Michel as he came back into the kitchen.

"What are you going to do?"

"Distract them. Go out the front door and hide in the forest. I'll find you when I've gotten rid of them."

"You have three seconds, Mayr," Ratzener shouted.

Max opened the kitchen door and motioned Michel away. He stepped out, closed the door behind him and descended the steps, trying to order his frantic mind. Behind Kolbe and Ratzener, a squad of SS formed a ring around the courtyard. They raised their rifles and took several steps forward. Max hoped Lili would be there, waiting for him.

•    •    •    •    •

When Rafe unlatched the Pump Room door, Rena Mendelssohn was standing in the middle of the room, wearing her coat and hat. "Time to go?" She asked pleasantly.

"I'm sorry, Frau Mendelssohn," Rafe said. "We have unexpected visitors and we need to get into the walls right away." He opened the trap door. "Are you going to be all right, crawling through the tunnel?"

"I've been practicing." She got down on her hands and knees and shoved her little bag into the opening. "Got to take this," she muttered. "Leave no evidence."

"You go next," Stefan said to Rafe, "in case she needs help."

"You know how to close it up from the inside?"

"Of course. Go," Stefan directed. He waited until he was sure they were in the walls to drop the trap door back in place, shove the bench over it, and sprint back up into the tunnel. Very quietly, he repositioned the wine rack and crept into the kitchen. Michel was kneeling at the window, peering outside, gun in hand.

Stefan touched his brother's shoulder. Michel jerked, and quickly lowered his head.

"What are you doing here?"

"Would you have left me and Papa to face those bastards alone?"

Michel relented. "They know Papa was working with Roman, and about the printing press. They're pushing him to admit he's hiding Jews scheduled for deportation. Kolbe sent men to search."

Michel reached up and cracked open the window pane. They listened, but no one was talking. Stefan tried to peek over the sill, but Michel pulled him down.

"Who turned us in?"

"My guess is Otto Hartmann. Ratzener has been threatening to kill us all if Papa didn't give up other members of the Resistance."

Outside, they heard the search party return. "Jews have been here," one of them said. "But they're gone."

"They must have found our rooms," Michel whispered. "Thank God the Bergmanns got away, and Rafe and Mrs. Mendelssohn are in the walls," he poked his brother, "where you should be."

Side by side, they lifted their eyes over the sill.

"You're nothing but a *Judenknecht*, Mayr," "Ratzener said. Lackey for the Jews. He turned on Kolbe.

"You should have figured this out long ago. Your weakness allowed him to spread the Jewish plague right under your nose." Ratzener poked Max in the stomach with his gun, backing him into the wall. They could no longer see him.

"Go find the sons," Ratzener ordered. "And the grandmother."

"They have nothing to do with my activities," Max said.

"Oh no, you have perpetrated a family deceit. Your sons work for the resistance. You and your wife collaborated with the traitor Schulz, whose hands were especially filthy. But we emptied his hiding places for Jewish scum, and we'll empty yours, too. Whatever else your family is up to, the Gestapo will get out of your sons."

"Run!" Max screamed. The next sound was gunfire.

Michel leapt to his feet. "Go, now, Stefan, into the forest," he hissed.

"But what about Papa?"

"Go now!"

Stefan crawled across the kitchen. He looked over his shoulder to see Michel step out onto the landing and raise his gun. Two more shots rang out. In the next instant, his brother's body pivoted down the stairs.

A voice said, "*Herr Oberführer*, it looks like a vehicle went up the hill."

"Go after it, you imbeciles," Ratzener commanded. "I want the other son. Kolbe, you're with me inside."

Stefan ran through the chateau, out a side door, and into the forest. He kept running until he couldn't anymore. Panting, he listened. Nothing.

He slid to the ground and crawled behind a tree, sobbing wildly, pounding the dirt with his fists. When he finally raised his head, questions pummeled him. Were they still alive? Did they need him? The decision came easily. He ran back the way he had come and entered the chateau. He crossed the kitchen and crouched in front of the window.

Car doors banged. "We found him," shouted an officer. "He and the old lady were trying to escape. Another woman was driving the car, and we pulled three more people out of a box built under the truck." He paused. "Alas, *Herr Oberführer,* they tried to run."

"So you took care of them," Ratzener said with a vicious laugh.

"We kept the women alive, in case they can tell us something."

Stefan's mind was a blur. The Bergmanns were dead. He watched Sigrid and Uma, both blindfolded, being pulled from one car and thrown into another.

"Take them to the *Metropole,*" Ratzener ordered Kolbe. "Unless you think you might lose them on the way"

"No, Herr *Oberführer,*" Kolbe. He hurried to join the officer taking the women to face the Gestapo.

"You," he pointed t the two remaining men. "Go back and get the body. Bring him here and line them up. We'll let them rot here for a few hours."

Ratzener disappeared into the last car.

Stefan crawled to the door, pushed it open, and forced himself to look down the steps.

His father was slumped against the wall. Michel lay crumpled a meter away. Stefan cried out and careened down the stairs. His put his hand on Michel's back and smoothed down his shirt. His fingers found a hole, and he jerked back.

"Michel," he whispered, bending over him. And then he felt it. A tiny breath. "I'm here, Michel!"

His brother made a faint sound. "Papa?"

Stefan forced himself to crawl over to his father. His eyes were open and blank, his body bathed in red.

"They killed him," he whimpered.

Michel's voice was a soft rattle. "You can't be Stefan Mayr." A drop of blood appeared at the corner of Michel's mouth. "Not safe. Be somebody else."

Stefan felt his brother's strength drain from his body and blend into the scarlet pool beneath him. "Michel!" He grasped his brother's face and glanced around frantically, as if a doctor might be hiding in the trees.

Michel's eyes fluttered closed.

"Stay with me!," Stefan pleaded, "I don't want to be alone." This is a dream, he thought, blinking his eyes furiously to wake up. But the sound of the car returning from the hill assured him the horror was real. With one more tormented glance at his family, he ran across the courtyard to the winery and crouched behind one of the decorative barrels in front of the entrance.

He watched as they pulled his father off the wall to the ground. They dragged Michel over. The car door opened and another body was tossed next to them.

"The destruction of the Mayrs is complete," one of them said.

A strangled word came out of Stefan's mouth. "Emil."

Stefan felt eyes moving in his direction, and then he was running, mindlessly, stumbling through the grapevines, abandoned, nameless.

# Part 4

"There is no greater agony than bearing an untold story inside you."
–Maya Angelou

# 51

*Winegut Maria Theresia, July, 1942*

Stefan had been hiding in the woods all night. With no moon, the landscape was pitch black. When the sun rose, he beheld vines, and ached with memories.

His twenty-one-year-old mind felt trapped in a decomposing body. Three months of walking, scrounging for food, hiding behind fences, in ditches, diving into bushes, not breathing, weeping when the danger had passed. "Jews value the preservation of life above everything else," Rabbi Elie had told him. For everyone he had lost, he couldn't give up.

The large, white-washed sign read *Weingut Maria Theresia*. He walked through rows of grapes. He could see the villa and the stone and timber winery. Stefan knew how to hide among wine bottles; there would be food, and running water to drink and pour over his swollen feet and festering scratches.

The door was ajar. He crossed a room crowded with rows of wood-carved tables and chairs. Like ours, he thought. He was accosted by stinging images of the night before they came for his father, the night they laughed together, foolishly believing they had outsmarted them.

He found the stairs to the cellars below. At the bottom he waited, listening, feeling the familiarity of cavern walls and winding passageways. He heard footsteps and fled around a corner. Two men came into the open and headed for the stairs.

Antiquated wine barrels hovered over him. At the end of the row, one of them sat back in a hollowed rock. Stefan studied it. He couldn't squeeze around the sides, but neither could anyone else. Bracing one foot on the wall, he climbed up the barrel, pulled himself to the top, and dangled his legs over the back. It would be tight. He gave himself a push and accumulated more abrasions as he fell to the ground. But he leaned his head against the wall and allowed himself a moment of calm.

He was unaware of how long he had slept when bobbing lights and low voices awakened him. It was the same two men, and to his immense relief, they passed by, caught up in a conversation about wine.

He slept until hunger roused him. Upstairs, he found a compact kitchen adjacent to their party room. He turned on the water faucet and leaned in to drink. The water splashed his face and spilled out of his mouth as he gulped it down.

The kitchen was full of treasures: Two crates, one with an onion, several potatoes and a head of lettuce, the other almost full of oranges and apricots. He helped himself to one of each.

The kitchen became his nightly destination. Food continued to be plentiful, which puzzled him. Perhaps the winemaker had scheduled a tasting, or been forced into entertaining local SS. That thought cut short the meal he was enjoying, and he tore down the stairs and over the top of his barrel.

One evening, wandering new passageways, he came to a softly glowing lantern. I wonder, he thought. He looked for telltale signs on the walls, felt for seams and hidden latches, and it didn't take him long to find the hole. He pushed at it, felt for a fingerhold. He heard the murmur of voices and the release of a latch, and was gone in an instant.

All night he wondered, how many people hid behind that wall? He thought of his mother and brother. Were they his people?

And how only two men could run a winery? His curiosity led him to slip out of his hiding place and follow them, only to realize they were delivering food.

He found an old cushion and folded it to fit on the ground behind the barrel. The quality of his sleep improved. Good food was healing his spirit as well as his body. A taste of security unearthed an old ally. Confidence. If he had counted correctly, he had been hiding behind his barrel for thirteen days without incident. He might stay longer.

Two nights later, Stefan was in the kitchen when the lights came on. He hadn't heard them approaching, and now they were half-way across the room. A head appeared around the door.

"Hubert, I think we've found our thief."

Stefan tried to run, but two pairs of arms immobilized him. He cursed himself. Smugness had consumed his vigilance.

They were both tall with ragged beards, as if for them, too, a shave was no longer an option. One of them smiled. "If you promise not to make a run for it, we promise not to give you a bill."

The other one said, "I'm Hubert and this is Georg. Do we have a deal?"

Stefan nodded. He would bide his time until an escape route showed itself.

"How about some wine? Or is beer your chosen refreshment?"

"Wine."

"Oh good," Hubert said. "You can talk."

Stefan accepted a glass of St. Laurent. He twirled the red liquid around in his glass. "A lighter body than other reds. Notable, yet soft tannins."

The two men burst into laughter.

"I worked on a winery near Salzburg," he lied.

"Which one?" Georg asked. "Red wine is still young and naive in Bavaria."

The price of showing off, Stefan scolded himself. "You wouldn't know it. It was insignificant, I mean, compared to yours."

"Why are you hiding in our winery and helping yourself to Nazi food?"

Stefan stiffened. "Nazi food?"

"Yes," Georg said ruefully. "I'd invite you in, but Hubert and I and our dog have been sleeping on the porch behind the winery. Most of this food is for the selfish Nazi bastard who confiscated our house."

Stefan was intrigued. "Are you brothers?"

Stefan noticed their shared smile.

"Partners," George said. "We delight in pouring mediocre wines down Nazi throats. None of them have the beginning of a taste bud."

Who were these two men? For the first time since he'd fled the carnage in the courtyard of his home, his taut frame loosened.

Hubert refilled his glass. "If you're hiding, you must be running."

Stefan had spent some time behind the wine barrel concocting a story that might not get him arrested. "I was stealing fruit off my employer's trees. He reported me."

"Curious that you ran east," Georg said. "You've been wandering around since then? Taking advantage of winemakers?"

That would have been much more pleasant than hiding in ditches. "Not exactly."

Georg said, "You seem fairly industrious. Can we get you a blanket? I can only imagine where you've been hiding."

"That's my secret."

"Or, we could take a stab at trusting each other," Hubert said firmly. "What's your name?"

He didn't know anymore. It couldn't be Stefan Mayr, and his Jewish name, Sivan, was even more dangerous. He had to give them something. Emil, he decided, as if fate demanded it.

He slept fitfully, wary of the breakfast meeting they had proposed. He had no choice but to trust them, at least until he determined his next move.

"We have a plan," Georg said over coffee, bread and jam. "Sorry, Emil, no butter."

"A friend needs help in his restaurant," Georg said. "Washing dishes, that sort of thing. He agreed to take you on."

"The Germans are looking for me," he said. He didn't want to move from behind the barrel.

"Are you Jewish?"

Betrayal slid easily across his tongue. "No."

"Maybe you've out-run them. We told Sebastien you would prefer to stay out of sight."

With sudden clarity, he understood if they were hiding Jews, they had to send him away. He wasn't about to tell them he had known since he arrived.

"Most days," Hubert said, "I'm the chef. I'll tell the kitchen crew you're Georg's cousin who needs a job."

Georg nodded. "We're leaving in an hour, before they serve *mittagessen*."

"Where is this restaurant?"

"In our village. We can walk there."

"How many people in the village?"

Hubert laughed. "You sound like a secret agent, figuring the angles.".

"It's a tiny town," Georg said. "But the restaurant is renowned. Of course, with the war, not as many people are coming. I doubt you'll run into anyone you know."

"I'll only be in the kitchen, at the sink?"

"Are you sure you didn't commit a more important crime than snitching an apple?" Hubert asked.

Georg stood. "We've gathered a few things for you—a couple of shirts, a pair of pants, and some underwear. A toothbrush and a comb. A razor blade, if you want to bother."

"I don't have anything to put them in."

Hubert pointed to a weathered knapsack leaning against a chair.

He couldn't believe he was walking in broad daylight with two friendly men he'd known for a few hours. He shielded his eyes from the sun and gazed at the blanket of vineyards covering the hills. "Nice," he said.

"Gorgeous day," Hubert remarked. "Look at those clouds." The three men stopped and looked up. "They look like fluffy pillows."

"Dollops of cream," Stefan said.

"Hmm," Georg said. "You're a poet."

"And a romantic," Hubert guessed.

They turned onto a path through the edge of the vineyard toward a forest. Nestled next to the trees was a small barn with chipped yellow paint and a new door.

"What's in there?" Stefan asked.

"Gerti," Georg said. "Sebastien's cow."

"She produces milk for the children who live at the inn," Hubert said. "We're hiding her for my brother. During the day, she wanders as far as the grapes and eats the grass between the rows of vines."

Stefan's brain was swirling. "Sebastien is your brother?"

"Yes," Hubert said. "He's younger, and shorter. You'll like him, though. Everyone does. And his wife is divine."

They completed their walk through the forest, and back in the sunlight, Stefan gaped at the magnificent structure in front of him.

"We always go in the back, to our family kitchen," Hubert said. Stefan felt like he was in a dream, unable to pause the action. He stepped over the threshold.

Inside, an attractive young woman with large blue eyes, thick brows, and short, dark auburn hair stood holding a little girl. "Welcome to our *kochecke,*" she said. "You must be Emil."

"This is Hannah," Georg said.

"It's lovely to meet you. Georg never mentioned you."

"I hadn't seen Emil since he was a baby."

Sebastien bustled in from the hall. "Hello! Sorry I'm late. Pfortner arrived early with Viktor, of all people. I guess he needed relief from breakfast at *Der Reichshof.*"

Georg laughed. "Viktor finally came up with a new name for his unexceptional restaurant."

"Let's hope all the thugs move over there to eat." Hubert said.

"He can change the name, but even Pfortner knows he can't change the food," Hannah said. Her husband blew her a kiss. Sivan noticed her turn away.

Twenty minutes later "Emil," stationed at the sink, scrubbed his first round of dirty pots. He had gotten a short tutorial from Mathilde Marti, who informed him that for the first time in a while, the *biergarten* was full. Hubert directed the cooks. Sebastien ran in and out of the kitchen, yelling at him. Much more politely, Hannah recited her orders. There were two other servers, too flustered to give him notice, but the young woman chopping vegetables fluttered her eyelashes when he glanced at her.

Hannah brought all the used cooking utensils. "How are you doing?" she asked amiably. "You know, I met my husband over a sink full of dirty dishes."

"That sounds like a good story."

"A fairy tale, actually."

Stefan found himself watching for Hannah through the windows into the hallway. She moved confidently with an armload of plates or a hefty amount of beer steins in each hand, which eventually he would inherit.

"Sorry," she repeated with each visit.

"It's fine," he replied, wanting to say more, something that would make her stay, but then he remembered he was only a ghost of a man.

The kitchen emptied and he dried the last dish. He dawdled at the sink, folding and refolding his dishtowel, waiting to be told his bed was in the cellar.

It was Hannah who retrieved him, carrying the borrowed knapsack. She had accepted the story that he had a bad experience at another winery and couldn't stay there any longer. "You need a room," she said. He followed her up three flights of stairs and down a hall, where she opened a door. "It's small, but it's right next to the toilet."

"That's very thoughtful," he stammered. A bed in a heavy oak frame and an enticingly thick quilt was in the corner, a nightstand with a lamp sitting on a doily next to it. On top of the dresser was a pitcher, washbasin, and towel.

"In case you want to freshen up," Hannah explained. "You saw the shower room?"

"Yes, thank you. It's all very nice."

"Good. You have an hour for a nap. At three, please join Sebastien, Mathilde and I in the *kochecke* for coffee and something sweet."

"I wouldn't presume," he began, "I mean, I'm part of your staff."

"We're all staff," she laughed. "Anyway, you're Georg's cousin. We're grateful for your help."

"All right, I might do that."

"It should be a calm evening. I think Faber is busy tonight, ordering poor Georg and Hubert around."

"Faber?"

"Ratzener. The *Oberführer*. He grew up in Moosfeld, my home town. He's forgotten we knew him when he couldn't play *Fußbol* without his pants falling down."

Stefan's breath gained speed. "He's the one who's taken over *Winegut Maria Theresia?*"

"Georg and Hubert still have the winery to run. On top of that, Faber bullies them into being his own personal sommelier and chef." She put her hand over her mouth. "I shouldn't..."

"Believe me, I'm on your side. Where is Ratzener stationed the rest of the time?"

"Vienna. We love it when he's there and not here."

His stare turned icy. Hannah took a step back toward the door. "I have to go."

He fell across the bed and burrowed his face into the pillow. By evening, he would be on the run again. Or, he could stay, wearing his cloak of invisibility, biding his time. How he would love to kill the beast.

# 52

*St. Jakob, September, 1942*

Often, when Stefan wasn't working in the kitchen, he moved silently through the forest to the little yellow barn, where he talked to Gerti the cow and observed the winery from afar. Until the day came when he needed to move closer, to feel what he had once felt, being part of the back-breaking work, and the dizzy excitement of Crush. He stole glances at the men picking the grapes, their wide-brimmed hats bobbing up and down as they worked.

But here and there, when he got close, he sensed fear. Perhaps one or two of them were Jews, hiding in plain sight. How he wanted to talk to them, to actually be his mother's son.

Back in the kitchen, Stefan learned when Sebastien was away, it was Tobias Marti filling in at the bar and offering excuses for his absence to disgruntled regulars. That left Hannah to stop and make conversation with almost every guest. He wondered if Sebastien was aware of the strain he was putting on his faithful friends, and his wife, who was bone-tired by mid-afternoon.

Even though his back was to the kitchen and he was never in the restaurant, Stefan sensed when the Brandls were entertaining Nazis. Everyone was quiet and tense. Sebastien was more angry than usual. Hannah was clearly terrified.

So one afternoon, when Stefan arrived at the yellow barn to see Hannah having a chat with Gerti, he felt relieved for her, and for himself, foolishly happy.

"Hello Emil. Are you the one who's been tidying up this place?"

"If you mean getting rid of the cow dung, I guess that's me."

"It's odd we haven't run into each other, but I'm glad Gerti has another friend."

"Have you noticed she spits out the apple cores? I've never met a cow who's that particular."

Hannah laughed. They sat against the inside wall of the barn. Stefan learned Hannah had two sisters, only one of them was in her life: Siegi, who apparently had only two gears, animated, which was most of the time, and annoyed.

Stefan tried not to stare at the woman next to him. Hannah's curls were soft and springy; her skin as dark as his mother's. He fended off Hannah's questions about himself.

"You don't like to talk about your family."

"I'd rather not. But I enjoy hearing about yours."

To his surprise, Hannah suggested a time they could meet again. He ticked off the hours while he stood at the sink. Only two more sets of dishes, and he would be with her again.

She met him with an apron full of huckleberries, and gave him such an alluring smile, he yearned to open his soul to her. But he would keep the vow he had made to Moshe Fieg, the brother who used to be Michel Mayr.

"Who are you?" Hannah teased him.

As a child, I wanted to be a spy."

"Like in the movies?"

"I read every book about espionage I could find. I couldn't wait to discover one more secret agent with an exciting secret mission. Have you read *The Scarlet Pimpernel*?"

She rolled her eyes. "I don't remember that one."

"You should. You won't be able to put it down."

Hannah doubted that, but was pleased he had given her even a tiny glimpse of who he had been before he mysteriously appeared in St. Jakob. When they parted, she shook his hand and asked, "Don't spies have secret passwords?"

"It's usually a question. Like, 'Do you have the grapes?'"

"Good. When I come again, if the door is closed, I'll be sure to say it."

The morning of their next meeting, Sebastien had left at dawn. Stefan was very aware of his absences. "If I may ask, where does your husband go?"

"I don't know where he is right now. I'm just sure he's not away gathering ingredients for Nazi meals."

"So he has a story. What is he really doing?"

She hesitated. "It's a game we play. My role is to support him."

"So, you're trapped." In her eyes, Stefan saw he had voiced something she couldn't.

She changed the subject. "Thank God for Georg. When Faber isn't here, he brings us odd things Veronika, who is thankfully no longer his wife, left in his pantry. Mathilde can make a meal that satisfies the Germans out of soybeans and pickled herring."

A hummingbird, poised in flight outside the barn window, distracted them. The dainty little creature lifted up, swirled, and was gone. "Do you think it saw us?" Hannah wondered.

"It's hard to tell," Stefan sighed. "What could so tiny a being see in so short a glance?"

His eloquence surprised her, and, despite her guilt about spending time with this handsome young man, who was also wise and interesting, she craved connection with another human being who didn't know the fearful, constantly agitated creature she had become. The despair she felt with Sebastien's disappearances, and the conflict that consumed her when he was home, sent her running to the barn to have a few calm moments with a cow and her new friend.

One evening several weeks later, Stefan was the first one to arrive. "Do you have the grapes?" Hannah asked from outside the door.

"I have the grapes," Stefan said solemnly.

She came in and Gerti swished her tail like an annoyed cat. "She's upset." Hannah took an apple out of her pocket. "This is way overdue."

They talked about the unfamiliar SS officers who had overrun the inn for three straight days. Stefan had worked at the sink and retired to his room quickly in case some drunk German lost his way coming back from the toilet.

Hannah shivered, but Stefan had brought a blanket, in case he had occasion to spread it over both of them. Under the light of a single lantern, Hannah told stories. "Surely you've seen my sister, Siegi? She's outrageous." The convent. Her near miss. The day that, in a full dining room, Pfortner's suspenders had broken and his pants fell down, revealing an ugly white rear end.

Flat on his back in the hay, Stefan was still laughing when Hannah said goodnight and scooted out the door.

Humming to herself, Hannah realized halfway through the forest that someone was approaching. Veronika's voice cut into the suddenly chilly air. "What are you so happy about?"

"I took a little walk," Hannah said, as casually as she could. "Where are you going?"

"That's my business."

As she walked by Veronika, she felt cold black eyes focused on her back.

In the barn, Stefan snuggled under their blanket. He didn't hear her coming. "Who are you?" The woman demanded. "This is private property."

Stefan jumped up and reached for the lantern. "I wash dishes for Sebastien."

"I demand to know what you're doing here."

Think, Stefan told himself. "Resting. But I'm having a problem with the noise." He picked up the broom that lay against the wall and thumped it against the ceiling. Bats exploded out of the ceiling. The woman screamed as they collided with her face and snagged her hair.

"I'll find out who you are," she squealed as she lunged through the door.

Stefan was fairly certain the threat had come from Georg's ex-wife. From then on, he would watch for her.

# 53

Mathilde convinced Gabi to play a game with Benno so Hannah and Elke could have a moment alone.

Hannah's tears began. "Everything has changed." She was embarrassed, but who else could she share her misery with? "Even in bed."

"Oh, dear. But it will change back, Hannah. We all feel the sparks between the two of you. I'm ashamed to say I'm jealous. I never had that."

"I don't know anymore. Sometimes I think he's afraid to make love to me. He grabs my hand under the table and kneads my palm, and then twists my fingers into his, as if he's desperate for a moment of passion. Then he leaves, and when he returns, I wait for him to want me. Now, even when he's right next to me, I miss him. I worry that I've become barren, but even if I haven't, I wonder if I'll ever have another child."

Elke laughed mirthlessly. "I stopped allowing Gerhard in my bed, even before Daniel."

She studied Hannah. "You can't think there might be someone else."

"Until recently, I would have said that was impossible." She came close to telling Elke about Sebastien's date with someone named Helene. But she would also have to tell her about the leaflets and the locked room in the cellar. Defeat settled in her bones.

．　．　．　．　．

Two days before Christmas, Sebastien left. He returned early Christmas Eve morning, ebullient, with three boxes of food. Besides staples like bread, butter, flour and sugar, he proudly unpacked oil, vinegar, sardines, olives, jam, crackers, and two chocolate bars.

"Have you taken up thievery?" Mathilde squealed.

There were presents for everyone, and Hannah, too, wondered how he collected it all in such a short time, especially with his other activities. She didn't ask. They were back inside a bubble of ordinariness. The slightest prick would send Sebastien running.

"Isn't Emil coming to Christmas?" Sebastien asked her.

"I invited him, but he said he felt a little feverish and was going to bed."

"Maybe he's shy."

Hannah didn't think so. But she reveled in their joy-filled table. Georg and Hubert, Bernard and Sophie, Mathilde and Tobias, Siegi and Elke were passing platters and talking over each other. Next to them, the five children delighted in their own special table, complete with a Christmas tablecloth and little metal airplanes from Tobias next to each plate.

When they were relaxing after all the food and drink, Mathilde said, "I have an idea. Someone should write a history of *Grünen Baum.*"

"Brilliant," Georg said, indulging in more cherry *schnaps.*

"And I know just the person," Hubert said to his brother. "You should do it, for Gabi."

Sebastien shrugged and glanced around the table. "We know all the stories by heart. Papa made sure of that. I suppose I could try."

Hannah smiled. A reason to stay home. And for this project, he would have to think only good thoughts before he picked up a pen.

Everyone stood up, embracing and wishing each other a Happy Christmas. Hannah could guess what would happen next. This time Sebastien would whisk her away to bed, kissing her so passionately she couldn't talk, believing that as usual, he could love her doubt away. Her acquiescence was required, she felt, for a moment of physical connection, and the rare occasion of almost mindless joy.

For over two months, Sebastien stayed home, although they seldom made love. In bed, he kissed her, touched her sensually, but it ended with his arms around her, holding her while he slept. Wide awake, she wondered if he felt her agony.

He still urged her fingers to dance with his under the table.

One day she asked him if he had begun the history of the inn.

"I've only managed a few pages so far."

"Can I have a peek?"

"It's kind of rough. I need to do some editing."

The next morning, he wasn't in the *kochecke* when she brought Gabi down for breakfast. She went to the window, knowing his truck would be gone.

•     •     •     •     •

In the yellow barn, Stefan sat next to Gerti, brooding. After Christmas, Hannah was happy, but then Sebastien left without a word. He sensed her anger simmering near the surface. How could this man neglect the wife he was lucky to have? Besides that, Hannah was in jeopardy, and Sebastien was the cause.

She burst into the barn and threw herself down, her tears spilling onto the straw. He pulled her into his arms and kissed her hair. She didn't move away.

"I'm alone again."

Stefan tightened his arms around her and touched his lips to her forehead. He hoped she felt a measure of contentment, as he did, in the calm that followed.

"I've known for a while he's working for the resistance. At the very least, he's distributing anti-Nazi literature."

Stefan tensed. Had Sebastien known his father, or Michel?

"I'm tired of forgiving him." Hannah lifted her face to his. He's putting us all in danger so he can be a hero."

With the slightest of movements, Stefan lowered his head. "I wish I could help." Her eyes moved to his lips.

"I shouldn't be talking to you about my husband," she murmured.

Stefan released her.

"It's not your fault, Emil." She brushed the straw off her dress and vanished.

.  .  .  .  .

Stefan picked the lock on the door of what he assumed was Sebastien's hideaway. Anti-Reich leaflets were strewn across his desk. A notebook lay open on top of them, a pen hooked to its cover. Stefan flipped through a few pages and slowly lowered himself into the chair.

It was a litany of Sebastien's anger, in stages, at Adolf Hitler. He also condemned the Catholic church, for what they did to his friend, Niko. It was the language of frustration, but here and there, it was incendiary. He had drawn caricatures of Hitler and his followers, as loathsome as those the Reich circulated daily against the Jews, and page after page of ideas for perilous acts of resistance.

He studied the maps. Sebastien was doing more than throwing paper around.

He found nothing about the history of the inn, and was tempted to tell Hannah. But not yet. When Sebastien returned, Stefan would confront the bottomless rage he had read in his words, and accuse him of the slow destruction of his wife.

# 54

*St. Jakob, April, 1943*

Stefan didn't need to wait long. Sebastien returned, and the next morning he climbed down the cellar steps to the secret room, curiously unlocked.

Sebastien jerked around in his chair. "What are you doing here, Emil?"

"I came to see you."

"We can talk upstairs."

"It's too late, Sebastien. I've seen it all."

"Did you tell anyone?"

"That's all you can say, 'did I tell anyone?' I wanted to, but I thought I should give you at least a minute to explain. Your time starts now."

"The leaflets," Sebastien began.

Stefan grabbed a pile. "Why don't you call them what they are? Little bombs that will blow you and your family to oblivion as soon as Pfortner gets a brain and demands to know what's in here. And the maps. Very suspicious. And then, there's your journal. Fire on paper, wouldn't you say?"

"You had no right."

"I'm living here with you. I have a right to know vengeance makes you tick. As does your wife."

"You don't know what you're talking about. And you can't tell me you aren't angry at the Reich. I don't know what brought you to our home, but I doubt you're Georg's cousin."

"They murdered my family. Is that enough for you?"

"Why didn't you tell us?"

"It's my life. I can choose not to share it."

Sebastien narrowed his eyes. "You're running, but not from an unforgiving farmer. No wonder you hide behind a dish towel." Sebastien pointed to the extra chair. "Sit down. You're making me nervous. How did you get in here, anyway?"

"I picked the lock."

"You break into my office, read my private thoughts, and now you threaten to inflict my personal struggle on my wife. Unless you can assure me you'll keep your mouth shut, you can pack your things."

"Don't you get it? We both have secrets, but yours are grievous."

Sebastien rose, fists at his sides. "Is Emil even your real name?"

"It's good enough." Stefan pressed into Sebastien's face. "You don't realize what you're doing to your wife, do you?"

"Hannah is my business. She understands I need to resist."

"She's never happy, and always terrified."

"Did she tell you that?"

"I have eyes and ears, Sebastien. And she's not the only one who's worried your so-called private thoughts will spill all over the bar and alert the wrong people."

"I'll talk to her," Sebastien said, his face a mask of hard lines.

Someone had entered the cellar. "Sebastien, are you down here?"

"*Scheiß.* It's my brother."

"Don't worry. I know how to disappear."

"Georg and I want to talk to you," Hubert called.

"I'm coming! I'll meet you upstairs." Hubert's footsteps retreated. Sebastien gripped Stefan's arm. "Do you agree that silence is best for both of us?"

Stefan threw a bundle of leaflets across Sebastien's desk and pointed to the open journal. "Keep your dark side locked in this room."

Suppressing his anger, Sebastien turned away. When he looked back, Stefan was gone. He went upstairs and told Hannah he would no longer be tampering with the village quotas. She burst into tears. She never believed Pfortner was that stupid.

.   .   .   .   .

Hannah and Elke were the first ones to sit down in the *kochecke* later that evening.

"Veronika told me she is getting her marriage annulled," Elke said.

The Church didn't permit divorce. "How did she do that?" Hannah wondered. "An annulment is impossible."

"She talked Georg into testifying the marriage had never been consummated."

.   .   .   .   .

While Gabi and Benno ate breakfast, and, as Mathilde said, talked about life, Sebastien and Hannah stayed in bed, submerged in their own thoughts.

"I tell you, *liebchen*," Sebastien said. "I'd love to be worrying about menus instead of Faber Ratzener and his band of assassins prowling around my restaurant."

"You traded in your menus for those leaflets."

"The allies are dropping them from planes now."

That wasn't her concern. "Do you remember how it was, before?"

"Yes, of course. I suppose life was never meant to be that idyllic."

She, too, had given up on that.

"I want to tell you something important, You're right. My activities put you and Gabi in too much danger. I'm going to stop."

Hannah grabbed the back of his head and pulled him toward her, kissing him soundly. "You can still write the history of the inn." His face was sad, and she faltered. "You must believe that I'm proud of you."

"I'm proud of you, too."

Hannah remembered what he said Max told him. *Hide one child.* Her husband's acts of defiance meant he had opened his coat wide, while she had stuffed hers in a closet.

Sebastien stroked her hair. "I need to make one more trip."

The twinkling of relief she'd felt scattered like dust mites and floated dully in the soft sunlight coming through the window.

"I need to explain to my friends in Alkoven why I am retiring"

"Because of me."

"And I want to thank them all for their bravery, and allowing me to join them."

The woman, Helene.

"How long will you be gone?"

"Overnight."

He made love to her. But even though they lay entangled, she felt a wall, each brick solid and sure, rising between them.

Sebastien left after *mittagessen*. True to his word, he was back the next evening, just as Hannah had finished resetting the tables for the next day. Later, they sat alone in the *kochecke*. Elke was upstairs with Benno. Georg and Hubert were on their way. All week, spring had been teasing them with warm temperatures, so Mathilde and Tobias took a walk.

They were surprised to see Gerhard at the back door.

"Ratzener wants to know what you were doing in Alkoven," he said without preamble.

"How did he know I was in Alkoven?"

"Why wouldn't he know? You're being watched. They suspect you have been tampering with the donations to the Reich."

"Donating?" Sebastien sneered. "Are you pretending people can't wait to give their hard-earned crops to the Germans?"

"He's stopped," Hannah asserted forcefully.

Gerhard helped himself to Sebastien's beer. "I keep thinking you're going to get caught, but then I remember you're one of those people for whom everything always turns out all right. You leave the rest of us to clean up after you."

Hannah stood. "Did you hear me, Gerhard? Sebastien's not resisting anymore."

"It might be too late."

Sebastien scowled. "We're done here."

"If you don't mind, I'm going upstairs to see my son."

"Does Elke know you're coming?" Hannah asked testily.

"Do you think I care?"

•   •   •   •   •

From the shadows, Stefan watched Gerhard stalk down the hall toward the large room Sebastien had set aside for Elke and Benno. As he often did, Stefan had been listening from the stairwell. Back in his room, he lay on his bed and thought about his father, also warned, who had waited too long.

He sat up. What day was it? April 19. The night the Nazis celebrated while the Jews were in the walls beneath them. The night Ratzener cheerfully reminded his besotted guests that April 20 was the day the mighty *Führer* liked to get even. Like the Mayrs, the Brandls were underestimating Ratzener. He was coming for them. Stefan reached under his mattress to make sure the carving knife was still there.

•   •   •   •   •

"I think Georg and Hubert are hiding something," Sebastien said while he and Hannah finished the dishes.

"Like what?"

"I think they're part of the resistance. I'd never seen some of the men he hired for Crush last year. They looked down when I got too close, like they're scared."

Hannah twisted her towel. "They're Jews."

"Yes. Maybe there's more in his wine caves."

She tried to hide the shudder that invaded her every bone. "You envy Georg and your brother."

Sebastien dried a fork as fastidiously as Hannah had cleaned it. "I know I promised you, but I can't bury my desire to do more. The Allies aren't making any progress."

"Georg says they are."

"Don't you realize how long it will take for them to come here? And when they arrive, it won't be to rescue us. To them, we're as guilty as the Germans."

"But they know Hitler invaded us, like in Poland, and the other countries."

Sebastien put away the last of the silverware. "He's convinced the world Austria welcomed him 'not as a tyrant, but as a liberator.'"

Hannah took off her apron. "Why wouldn't Georg and Hubert tell us?"

"They wouldn't want to put us in danger."

"More danger than we're already in?"

Sebastien hung the dishtowel on the rack over the sink. "Let's go to bed."

They lay together, neither of them able to sleep. Hannah didn't want to talk about Georg and Hubert anymore. She burrowed into his shoulder. "How did you get all that marvelous food at Christmas? And the presents. You were barely gone a day."

"My friends in Alkoven. When I delivered leaflets, I visited a store here and there and went through my Christmas list. It made me look normal."

"What about the food?"

"They put those boxes together for me."

"So they paid you for risking your life with them."

"No! It wasn't like that at all. They appreciate me, and I appreciate them."

"Who's Helene?"

"What?"

"I saw your note. An appointment with someone named Helene."

He kissed her forehead. "How long have you been worried about that? She's a courier, like me. Once in a while we went to the same place and spread leaflets during the night. Two of us could be in and out in an hour."

"Yes."

Sebastien reached for her hand. "I've put you through so much."

She came up on her elbows and leaned over his face. "It's all over now." She kissed him hard, her tongue teasing his mouth open, her hands moving down his body.

Sebastien kissed her back, just as furiously. But then he stopped.

"We can't," he said.

It was as if a thousand bees were stinging every patch of her skin. "I don't understand."

"What if something happens to me? I can't leave you here, with no time for Gabi, and maybe, pregnant with another child."

"Why would you say that? You convinced me the danger has lessened because you stopped fooling Pfortner and going to Alkoven." She batted away a tear. "And besides, I haven't conceived a child in seven years."

Sebastien looked beaten. "Tomorrow morning, I'm going to burn every paper and make that room look deserted again."

Hannah pulled him over on top of her. "Please. Promise me you won't leave. I couldn't do this, the inn, Gabi, if I didn't believe you'd always be beside me."

He feasted on her mouth, and she clung to him. When his fingers worked their magic between her legs, her insides exploded. She rejoiced while he pulsated back and forth and dove deep into her. The moment of ecstasy passed through the walls of their room. She didn't care. Let them all hear.

Afterwards, her body felt like warm liquid. She was sliding away when Sebastien put his mouth to her ear. "I love you, Hannah Brandl. Never forget."

She yawned and snuggled under his arm. "Don't burn our Gabi's book."

# 55

*St. Jakob, April 20, 1943*

Hannah stood at the stone hearth in the *wintergarten.* absorbing its warmth and the scent of a recent fire. She stooped to open its metal door and push a poker around the lingering red glow.

Stefan ran in. "They're here!" he shouted. "Where's Sebastien?"

"Who's here?"

"Four carloads of Germans. We have to find him."

At the sound of violent rapping, she swiveled toward the patio door.

"It's over, Brandl," Viktor bellowed, crossing the restaurant, coming straight at Hannah. She opened her mouth but he pushed her, hard, and she toppled across a chair and onto the floor. He stood over her, regarding her with pity, as if she was a mouse cowering in a corner.

He stalked away, and Hannah crawled after him, eventually pulling herself up and following him down the hall. Both kitchens were empty. Furious voices shouted Sebastien's name and pounded on the front door. She arrived just as a stained-glass window splintered and glass shot across the room. A soldier propelled her across the porch, down the walk and onto the road, where she almost collided with Faber Ratzener. While blood dripped from her arm, she looked around wildly for Sebastien. SS officers and German soldiers had surrounded the inn.

"We will find him," Faber promised. "Look. Your friends have joined us." Elke stood huddled with Gabi and Benno on the porch, guns pointed at them from several directions. Siegi and the children were next to join them.

"But you and I will stay here and wait for your husband." He pulled a handkerchief from his pocket and gave it to Hannah. "Clean yourself. I hate the sight of blood." Several of the men behind Faber laughed.

He called one over. "Radio Pfortner. Is he with Wangermann?"

An armored car rumbled up the road. Pfortner and another officer pulled Georg and Hubert from the vehicle and pushed them to the porch. "Are you all right?" Hubert called to Hannah, but she was shaking so wildly, she couldn't answer.

"Silence!" Faber shouted. No one moved until Viktor came out with the group that had been searching the inn.

"He's not in there."

Faber rolled his eyes. "The cellar."

Viktor glared at him. "I tell you, he's not in there. His truck is here, but the horse is gone."

Faber took the radio and barked more orders. Gerhard came around the corner and glanced at his wife and son. "Take them inside," he directed one of the guards.

"I don't think so, Eigner," Faber said from the road. "You've known all along your friend was impeding the goals of the Reich."

"I did not," Gerhard said tightly.

"You've been confidantes since childhood," Faber chided him.

"The friendship is all but dead. We've been in serious disagreement for years."

"Arguments you did not win. Let your son watch what happens to traitors."

To the soldiers he barked, "Reinforcements are on their way from Krems. One car will join the hunt in the countryside. The rest of you, search every house. I want every man, woman and child in front of me in ten minutes."

Viktor walked toward the car that was preparing to leave. "I know where to look," he told his brother.

While they waited, Faber walked onto the porch and amused himself by bending down in front of each terrified child and brandishing his gun in their faces. Chopin ran up to Gabi, and he turned his gun on the cat. Gabi screamed, and he laughed as the animal skidded away. "No one moves," he reminded the guards, and disappeared into the inn.

Hannah wanted to shout at the top of her lungs for Sebastien to run. How much did Faber know? That he cheated the quotas? His leafletting, in God knows how many cities and towns? The maps. What else had he done? *The no vote*. Like Daniel, Sebastien would be dead in a day.

They stood for almost an hour. The children fussed and whimpered. Neither guard relaxed his murderous gaze or lowered his weapon. Machine guns herded frightened villagers down the narrow lanes. Trucks and wagons assembled on St Jakob's already crowded plaza, their passengers hauled out and forcibly packed together with the others, like sheep stuck on the road.

Mathilde came through the door, Faber prodding her with his gun. "Your maid was nice enough to make me breakfast," he said to Hannah. "Maybe I'll give her to my brother. He could get rid of that whore he keeps behind the bar."

Herr Haas pushed his way to the front and shot his arm into the air. "*Heil* Hitler! Adolf Haas, at your service."

"Do I know you?" Faber scoffed.

"Yes, *Herr Oberführer*. We've spoken several times. I'm in awe of the Reich's achievements."

"Oh, yes. You're the one who wanted to change the name of this rather laughable plaza. You're soon to be missing a mayor," he crowed to the crowd. "He looks about right."

"I'm honored, sir," Haas gushed.

"Right now, I suggest you shut up." Faber's radio crackled and he put it to his ear. "*Schieß*," he muttered after a few moments. "Tell them to get back here."

"What are the charges against my brother?" Hubert demanded.

"You dare to be impatient?"

Hubert did not drop his gaze.

"Listen carefully," Faber directed the crowd, "because I suspect many of you are complicit with Brandl's activities." He began a litany of Sebastien's crimes. "Stealing goods from the Reich."

The people crammed together in the grass oval did not move.

"Forcing treasonous literature on patriotic citizens. Aiding and abetting the defamation of *Der Führer*. Destruction of German property. In summary, Sebastien Brandl is charged with being a collaborator and a traitor, which carries the penalty of death."

The vehicles hunting the fugitive returned without Sebastien. Faber raised his gun and fired several rounds into the ground in front of Viktor and the SS officers, who leapt into a bizarre dance. "You stupid idiots," he seethed.

A scream came from down the street. Hannah squinted to see Veronika running toward them, a piece of paper in her hand. Daniel was dead all over again, and whatever Veronika held now was at least that lethal.

"Sebastien killed my brother," she shrieked, coming to a halt an inch from Faber's face. "He voted no!"

The *Oberführer* pushed her away and took the paper out of her hand. He read:

*Dear Veronika,*

*I was the one who voted no in the Referendum, and our dear Daniel was blamed. Hannah is innocent.*

*Sebastien*

"Well, well. I guess he felt the need to bare his soul before he deserted his family."

Hannah closed her eyes. Gerhard had been wrong. Everything did not turn out all right for Sebastien Brandl.

Faber turned on Gerhard. "Did you warn him we were coming?"

"Of course not."

'I don't believe you. You're under arrest for collusion." He pointed to a nearby soldier. "You, throw him in my car." Gerhard's entreaties went unheard.

"No one will leave here without being questioned," he told the crowd. "Except for you, Frau Brandl. You're coming with me."

•     •     •     •     •

Turning away from his bedroom window, Stefan banged his head against the wall and threw his useless weapon across the room, embedding it in one of the bed pillows. He had easily evaded the Germans searching the inn. But it soon became apparent that he and his knife would have been a joke to Ratzener and his convoy of SS and German soldiers.

Hannah. He didn't want to think about what they might do to her, but the image came anyway. A petite, bloodied body, lying in the filth and disease that lived on the floor of a prison cell.

Sebastien had destroyed almost all the evidence in his office. While he was throwing leaflets into the flames, did he wonder what happened to his journal? But he was out of time. He jumped on Apfel and rode to Veronika's house, and inexplicitly, felt the need to confess. Then he galloped up the mountain into the thick forest, almost impenetrable if you didn't know the hidden paths.

At least that's where Stefan would have gone.

Sebastien thought of no one but himself He must have known Ratzener was coming, so he made himself believe he was protecting her by divulging the no vote and disappearing. Instead, Ratzener would feed her to the Gestapo, and charge her as an accomplice to his crimes.

As for him? Again, Stefan had watched and done nothing.

# 56

Four days later, breathing in her own waste, Hannah sat shivering in the corner of her cell somewhere under the *Hotel Metropole,* and waited for them to come again. Relentlessly, they had questioned her about Sebastien, his crimes, her part in them, and where he was hiding. Ignorance was not the protective shield Sebastien thought it was.

The tremors worsened as a soldier approached. He pulled a key from his pocket and opened her door. She waited for the handcuffs that would set the open wounds on her wrists on fire. But he shoved her out of the cell and prodded her up two flights stairs into a long hallway. At the end, he unlocked a door. On the other side stood Georg.

Hannah knees buckled and Georg caught her. A guard motioned her to a desk, where he thrust a piece of paper at her. "Hannah Brandl," he said, sounding bored. "You are under house arrest. You may not leave your residence under any circumstances. Non-compliance means immediate deportation."

He tossed a pen at her and with a dirty fingernail, punched the line where she had to sign. Georg led her outside. She was shaking so fiercely he grabbed a blanket from the back of his truck and covered her before he lifted her onto the seat. "It's okay, Hannah," he said, leaning in to embrace her. "You're safe now."

"Did Sebastien come home?"

Georg stroked her hair. "No. Your parents came and took charge of Gabi, and like the rest of us, tormented themselves over what they could have done for you and Seb." He turned on the ignition and moved into the streets of Vienna. "Do you want to tell me?"

Hannah's voice was a thin rasp. "Two or three times a day, they brought me into a room, turned a chair around and made me squat while they tied me to the back. The rope, my wrists...." She swallowed. "I wished I could chop off my hands. I had to answer the same questions over and over. They asked me about the no vote so many times, I finally said I was only a woman and had no control over my husband's behavior."

"That was smart."

"The one in command brought a hot iron right next to my face and said they were going to brand me with a swastika. The next day they stripped me and hung me from a beam in the ceiling, like a crucifixion, and the questions started again. My arms felt wrenched from their sockets. I must have fainted, because I woke up in my cell."

Georg pulled off to the side of the road, put his arm around her shoulders, and pulled the blanket back. Her swollen, red wrists, cut and bruised, oozed blood and yellow-green pus and reeked of infection. "God damn them," he said. He reached over and felt the dense heat coming from her forehead. He tenderly touched Hannah's cheek. "Don't go away."

He sprinted past a few buildings to a Gasthaus, and was back in a few minutes with a cup of water, and warm, damp towels he carefully wrapped around her wrists.

"Let's get you home," he said, lurching back onto the road in a cloud of dust. "We were in luck. The owner had a phone. I called *Grünen Baum* to have them get the doctor."

She pulled the blanket closer. "Why did they let me go?"

"We didn't know what to do. Hubert suggested I call in a favor from Cardinal Innitzer in Vienna and ask him to intercede for you. He's in league with all the other bishops who've said very little about Nazi atrocities. But he loves my wine. As to why you were in jail, I told him very little and that it was all a mistake, hoping he would take your side."

"He decided to help?"

"He saw a way to assuage his conscience. When he commented he couldn't get his favorite Riesling anymore, I offered him six cases. Yesterday, I got a call from some Gestapo sub-commandant who believes he's a devout Catholic, and therefore vulnerable to the suggestions of a red cap. He compromised with house arrest."

"Faber must have been furious."

"I don't care and you shouldn't either."

Hannah returned her gaze to the farms and villages they passed. After a while, she stirred. "Where is he?"

"We don't know."

Hannah sniffled and wiped her nose with the blanket. "He lied to me. His plan was to leave."

"Here," Georg said, pulling a handkerchief out of his pocket.

"I'm forever in your debt."

Georg shook his head. "You're not alone, Hannah."

"I'll be alone forever."

•     •     •     •     •

Stefan watched for Georg's truck. The inn had been shuttered since Hannah's arrest. Tobias appointed himself the scout, anticipating a return visit from the SS. Stefan held his own vigil.

After Ratzener drove away with Hannah, the Germans pressed their way through the crowd, bullying them for information. They threw people to the ground, including two women, and beat them with clubs and whips.

Silently, he moved into the little room between the kitchens, leaving the door into the *kochecke* slightly ajar so he could peek through the crack. The same woman who had found him in the barn burst in, reminding everyone of Sebastien and Hannah's crimes.

Hubert threw up his hands. "For the love of God, Veronika, when are you going to get it? Evil murdered Daniel. Hitler and his demented followers murdered Daniel. If you want to blame someone, blame them, not Sebastien, who did what none of us had the courage to do, and not Hannah, who at least was there to say goodbye when Daniel jumped into the van for a ride to his death that you planned."

"They tricked me," she wailed.

"Maybe so. But you've known Sebastien your whole life. He would be the last person to give Daniel up for the sake of a personal stand."

"Listen to him, Veronika," Mathilde said. "The trail leads from Gerhard through Viktor, and then to Faber, who was happy to have a name to report."

Veronika was beyond reason. "Viktor told me he had nothing to do with Daniel's death."

Siegi jumped into the fray. "That makes no sense at all, you old bitch."

Before Veronika could attack, Georg planted himself between them. "You can't honestly say Viktor wasn't involved."

"He told Faber my brother was harmless!"

"Of course," Siegi said caustically. "He was harmless enough to be labeled a traitor to the Reich. I can't stand this anymore. I'm going to the toilet."

Stefan liked Siegi.

•　　•　　•　　•　　•

Georg's truck pulled up, and Hannah's loved ones rushed out. Hubert took one look at his sister-in-law and gathered her into his arms.

"Where's the doctor?" Georg demanded.

"I'm here," said an approaching voice. Dr. Kronberger examined Hannah and told Hubert to carry her upstairs.

A day went by. Infection plundered Hannah's body. Her fever spiked dangerously, and she vomited almost everything she managed to get down. She was rarely lucid. A large crowd filled Hannah's room while they waited for Kronberger's report.

"She needs penicillin," he told them.

"So, get it," Siegi demanded.

"There's a problem. Thousands of doses are out there, but they all belong to the army. I've reached out to every doctor in the area, but no one is having any luck. Several of their patients have died."

Siegi's eyes narrowed. "Someone watch my children." She kissed her sister's cheek. "I'll be back."

•　　•　　•　　•　　•

Halfway down the stairs into the *kochecke,* Stefan identified the voices of Mathilde, Georg, and Hubert. He felt safe to join them.

"How's Hannah?"

"Not well, Emil," Hubert said. "The doctor says she needs penicillin and the Germans have confiscated all of it for the war."

Stefan's mind spun with strategies that made no sense: He could return to Vienna and find their family doctor, who was one of the best in Austria. But he was also Jewish, and most likely in a camp, or dead. Would it be possible to steal penicillin from the army installation in Krems? Getting in, finding the infirmary, not being shot: It would be a futile, probably fatal, attempt.

"I'm sorry," he stammered, helpless to say anything more.

Two hours later, Siegi returned. She handed a package to Dr. Kronberger.

"My God, where did you get this?" He held up two syringes.

"Otto's friend. He works in the army infirmary in Krems."

Kronberger injected the penicillin into Hannah's thigh. Mathilde brought her rosary out of her pocket and fumbled with the beads. The others joined in.

Within two days, Hannah had improved to the point she could have visitors. Siegi brought Ernst, who climbed up next to Hannah and told a joke. "Two toothpicks were walking up the mountain. And a hedgehog came by. One of the toothpicks said to the other, 'Oh, I didn't realize there was a bus up here.'"

"That was very good," Hannah giggled.

Elke appeared at the door. "Gerhard's been sent to the front."

Should she say she's sorry? Hannah opened her arms to her friend, who joined her on the bed and allowed herself to be held. Ernst understood only he should put his arms around them, too.

One week later, Hannah, her hands, wrists and arms heavily bandaged, knocked on Stefan's door. "Would you come with me, Emil?"

He helped her down the cellar steps to Sebastien's office. The door hung precariously from a single hinge. Except for the broken furniture, it was empty.

"I guess he burned everything," Hannah sighed, "before they came."

"Not everything." From his coat, Stefan extracted the journal. Hannah threw her arms around him. "I don't know how you did it, but thank you."

"I'm not sure you're going to feel that way when you read it."

Hannah flipped through the pages, stopping to study it here and there. "He was never going to write the story for Gabi, was he?" She shoved the journal at Stefan. "He never left the resistance, either."

Another lie left for her to defend.

Stefan tried to take her arm, but she pulled away. "I'm done here."

The next day, Apfel returned without a rider.

# 57

*St. Jakob, January 1944*

Since Hannah was under house arrest, Stefan visited the old barn only long enough to give Gerti her apple. He slept restlessly and got up an hour before anyone else. He went into the kitchen, turned on Luigi, and made himself a cappuccino. Alone in the *wintergarten*, he started a fire in the pot-bellied stove.

One morning, Luigi was already warm when Stefan went to make his coffee. He walked across the restaurant and was met by the calming aroma of freshly cut burning logs.

"You found my new retreat," Stefan said at the door. "Shall I go get Gerti?"

Hannah smiled. "There goes the furniture."

Stefan walked to the bank of windows. A storm was brewing outside. "When I was young, I used to wait for the rain. The clouds got lower, and denser, until they squeezed the raindrops out all over the earth. I thought it was exciting."

"And now?"

"The darkening clouds are my nightmares, and the cold rain reminds me they are real."

"Emil," Hannah touched her hand to his. "I don't have your words, but you always manage to say what I feel."

He was pleased when she joined him several mornings a week. Hannah did most of the talking, more inclined to discuss Sebastien's desertion. He still did not share his past.

At first, Stefan agreed Sebastien was trying to protect her. Before long, however, he couldn't bring himself to soothe Hannah with a line from a fairy tale. He made two lists. Sebastien's noble deeds; after all, he cheated the Nazis, distributed anti-Nazi leaflets, and voted no. But Sebastien's sins were far greater: The danger he had brought to *Grünen Baum* when he slighted the Nazi allocations. His fiery journal. Lying about writing a book for his daughter. The bundled piles of damning evidence that lived in the cellar. His disappearances into the resistance without Hannah's blessing. His selfish abandonment.

The choice to vote no. Heroic, yes. But Sebastien couldn't stop himself from playing with fire. His crimes exposed, his wife and child could have ended up like Lily Mayr, or rather, Ester Fieg.

The months went on, and Stefan became Hannah's confidante, a role that thrilled him. His heart swelling with love, he accepted Hannah's changing moods. She was still confused, bitterly disillusioned, and lost in grief. In those moments, he wished only that they escape to their barn, where he would hold her, and she might not pull away.

·  ·  ·  ·  ·

Sebastien had been gone for almost a year when *Gasthaus Zum Grünen Baum* closed for overnight guests. The restaurant struggled. The public charges against Sebastien, and Veronika's lethal revelation, kept most townspeople away. They would not soon forget the abuse they suffered after Sebastien ran away. Elke and Siegi, who had to shop for the sequestered Hannah, found themselves pushed to end of the line when trying to buy even basic necessities, like cooking oil, flour and vegetables.

They combined their ration cards to feed the four adults and five children living at the inn. Obviously, Stefan couldn't help, but when he hinted he should leave, Hannah gave him a list of tasks Sebastien had abandoned and suggested he do them at night.

Every month, Faber, always accompanied by Viktor, came by to taunt Hannah.

"This place has gone downhill," Viktor remarked, and then extolled the success of *Der Reichhof.* "I'm always full. I have entertainment every night now," he said, giving Hannah a look of mock regret.

"If you know where he is, please tell me."

Faber locked his eyes on Hannah. "I saw him on a train, heading for hell." She didn't look away, and later congratulated herself for that minor act of defiance.

•　　•　　•　　•　　•

"I hear Viktor's serving German mishmash at *Der Wachauerhof,*" Mathilde reported one evening.

"Hotchpotch?" Siegi giggled. "He's such a good Nazi. He's resorted to army field recipes."

"There's even a hotchpotch cookbook," Hubert said. "Recipes for what to do with a pile of carrot tops and walnut shells."

"We're serving lots of stews and soups ourselves," Hannah reminded them.

"But they're edible," Georg chimed in.

"Hubert and I have been wondering how long the restaurant can hold on," Hannah said.

"We'll help you sort it out."

In March, Pfortner and Herr Haas came by asking for Mathilde and Tobias, who were setting tables with Hannah. When Sebastien eluded arrest, Pfortner's periodic show of friendliness disappeared, replaced with chronic nastiness. Because of Sebastien's creativity in the cellar, he was demoted to *Leutnant* Pfortner. He nodded at Haas, who unrolled a piece of paper with a wicked gleam in his eye.

"By order of the Third Reich, the property owned by Tobias Marti, a metal shop and an apartment, is hereby requisitioned for the local office of the SS."

"You have one day to vacate," Pfortner said, saluted, and left.

Hannah glared at him. "Herr Haas, " she said with as much revulsion as she could summon, "How could you?"

"It's *Bürgermeister* Haas. We need a new collection place, and I will join *Leutnant* Pfortner in keeping scrupulous records and enforce strict penalties on those Brandl helped to cheat the Reich. And of course, *Herr Leutnant* will move into the apartment."

Mathilde couldn't stand the thought of going home and packing up forty years of their lives together. Hannah called Georg. He and Hubert came immediately, with both their trucks, assuring Tobi they would help him dismantle his shop and carry out their belongings. Elke offered to pack Mathilde's precious possessions in boxes, promising to handle everything with care."

Hannah did not hesitate. "Tobias, set up your shop in our cellar. It will be empty soon." She put her arm around Mathilde. "Would you two be comfortable moving into Andreas' apartment?"

"Are you sure? That floor is for family."

"I think you qualify."

She looked at her husband, who nodded. "I don't know what to say."

Tobias joined the embrace. "Say thank you. And dry your eyes. We need to get busy."

The next day, the apartment where Andreas and Amalia Brandl had conceived their sons welcomed new tenants. "*Wunderbar*," Hannah said, when in a few hours, Mathilde had re-created their snug little home at *Gasthaus zum Grünen Baum.*

·   ·   ·   ·   ·

Georg, Hubert, and an exuberant Schnapsi burst into the *kochecke* where Hannah was playing a game with Gabi, Chopin purring on her lap.

"Where is everyone?" Georg shouted up the stairs. Siegi and Elke arrived a moment later, trailed by the children.

Mathilde and Tobias came in from the hall. "What's happened?" She asked anxiously.

"It's quite extraordinary," Georg said. He dropped a folded piece of paper onto the table, and they crowded around for a look. *Un Appel,* the title read.

"It's in French," Georg explained.

"Thank you, dear," Hubert teased.

"I got this from a friend who smuggled it in from Switzerland. But he said it's all over Austria, and even Germany. English and American newspapers reprinted it, where the title is *A Plea*," He smiled. "And here, it's *Eine Bitte.*"

"I want to see," Ernst said, climbing onto the table.

"I'll translate."


### Eine Bitte

*My fellow Austrians, consider who we have become.*

*Triumphantly, a demonic dictator rides into Vienna, our ancient, radiant city.*

*He comes unhindered, unconcerned about the welcome he will receive, and Austria eagerly becomes an accomplice in unspeakable evil.*

*We vanish into The Third Reich, the butcher of innocents:*

*Children, the elderly, the infirm, the disabled.*

*Homosexuals and Gypsies.*

*Anyone who raises an eyebrow in protest.*

*And our own Austrian Jews, who were never the enemy, slaughtered while we sleep.*

*Although only God can decide to forgive us,*

*We can still heed our once honorable Austrian Conscience.*

*Look again at your neighbors, whom you ate and drank with, built a barn with, sat next to on the train, celebrated and grieved with.*

*You will find others who long for a way out!*

*I beg you.*

*Hide one child in your coat, and you save yourself.*

*Hide two, and you alter the universe.*

Realization tightened around Hannah's throat, "Oh, my God," she gasped. The others were too wound up to notice.

"Who wrote this?" Tobias queried the table.

"No one knows," Georg said.

"Whoever it is will soon be the most hunted person in Europe." Hubert said soberly.

Hannah gulped down air. Should she take Gabi and run?

They continued to speculate the origin of this startling decree. Georg was aglow. "It's quite something, don't you think? It's become the anthem of the Resistance."

Inside Hannah, fear and disgust were doing battle. "How would you know that, Georg?" She huffed. "Are you part of the resistance?"

Georg eyed her. "I'm aware of them."

"I'm not as stupid as you may think, you know." Gabi started to cry.

"I'm sorry, Hannah," Georg said, "But I've given my word."

She handed her daughter to Mathilde, snatched the newspaper from Georg's hand, and walked to the door. "I know, to keep us safe. That may be the biggest lie of all. I'm going for a walk."

"You can't," Siegi began.

"Yes, I can." She left behind the prison of her home, and the shadow of their hero.

•    •    •    •    •

Stefan and Gerti were eating corn in the barn. She handed him *Eine Bitte*. "Can I trust you, Emil?" she asked. "Because if there's any chance I can't, I need to know now."

"Haven't you noticed I'm a master of secrets?" Stefan said. He read it while they sat on a pile of straw, arms touching.

"Sebastien wrote that. How could someone so bitter, so full of contempt, find these words?"

"The truth in this letter is formidable."

Hannah closed her eyes. "Did you confront him?"

"When he disappeared after Christmas, you were shattered. I was angry at him on your behalf, so I surprised him in the cellar."

"What did you say?"

"That his unexplained absences were making you miserable. That his secrets terrified you. I threatened to tell you about the vicious words and odious images I found in his journal."

"That's when he told me he was retiring from the resistance." She laid her head on Stefan's shoulder. "But I guess he wasn't finished."

Stefan took her hand.

"Do you think Gabi and I are safe?"

He hesitated. "I do. Connecting Sebastien to this statement—it's highly unlikely, Hannah. In any case," he added, "you've got me to help you."

She wiped her eyes. "You've done so much for me. I didn't think anyone understood how alone and afraid I felt all the time. When you offer to protect me, I can believe you. It's a different feeling. You're a different man." Her eyes traveled down his face, and she kissed him. "Thank you."

His thoughts tumbled incoherently. More than once, he had imagined what it would be like to make love to Hannah.

She took his face in her hands, angled their heads, and moved her mouth across his lips. Stefan did the same. The motion was tender, yet his body responded with an intensity that rocked him. His kiss pressed into her, and their tongues met, first tasting, then probing. Stefan lay her down on the straw. Not a second passed before they were clenched in passion.

Stefan was losing control, and afraid he was about to embarrass himself. But then, she stilled. He eased back, unbelieving, throbbing with desire.

"I'm sorry," she said. "I'm not sure what got into me. I'm not Gertraud."

"Who's Gertraud?" Stefan managed to ask.

"A loose woman who works for Viktor."

"Hannah, I can tell you for certain you're not Gertraud."

"But I am married."

"Are you? You've suffered more than anyone deserves."

"Because of him, you mean?"

Stefan faltered. "Because of the war."

"And now, he's written something so dangerous..."

"It was his mission. He did it for the homeland he lost."

Hannah struggled to stand up. "You're defending him. I thought it was me he loved. I never thought I'd come in second or third."

"I'm on your side, Hannah."

She stood up and fidgeted with her dress. "He might be back when the war ends."

He stared at the empty space where she had laid beneath him. Sebastien had used up his chances and disappeared, and Stefan Mayr wanted desperately to be her new savior.

·   ·   ·   ·   ·

Hannah walked toward home, her body still tingling pleasantly. She sat down and leaned against a tree. Never would she have imagined wanting another man. This thoughtful, considerate, open-hearted man. When she and Emil fell into each other, as naturally as can be, she felt a sweetness that was new. She needed, and felt she deserved, to be wanted.

Her eyes were drawn to the lights of the inn, shimmering through the trees, and her conscience rose with them. She had committed an act of betrayal to have someone else.

# 58

*October, 1944*

Hannah was standing in front of the bakery counter, talking to Elke while she swept the morning crumbs, when Willi Reiter limped through the door. Elke screamed, tossed the broom aside, and pulled his frail body into a ferocious hug. He exhaled sharply.

"Oh, Willi, *schatz,* you're hurt."

Without a word, he allowed his sister to help him up the stairs to his old bedroom. "Close the bakery," Elke called down. Hannah locked the front door and put the key under a flower pot.

She knew what to do next. It had begun before Otto died, when he was still in France. Not even a war could keep Siegi and Willi from enjoying each other's company. Hannah knew it was wrong. And yet, it was also right.

Her sister was in the *biergarten,* gathering dirty napkins and returning chairs back to their assigned places.

"Willi's back."

Siegi took off in a gallop up the garden steps and into the *wintergarten,* Hannah close behind. She went straight to his bedside and knelt down close to his face.

Willi smiled. "Siegi."

She brushed her fingers over the stained white bandage around his head. "Ich liebe Dich," she whispered, and crawled onto the bed next to him. Hannah and Elke backed out of the room and closed the door.

"She loves him," Elke said. "Did you know? I mean, they became very close friends. Sometimes I wondered if it was more."

Hannah nodded. "I questioned her about Willi several times. And then I stopped. I didn't want to be the sentry outside her door."

Dr. Kronberger's prognosis was that Willi had suffered a severe head injury, and he couldn't promise his speech and memory hadn't been affected. Veronika came to visit, fussed over him for a while, and told Elke to let her know when he was normal again.

Whenever Hannah dropped in, Siegi was there, talking to him softly and stroking his face. Hannah thought of her bossy, sometimes brusque, sister. Where had all this tenderness been hiding?

"I couldn't tell anyone how much I missed him," Siegi said, a tear rolling down her cheek.

"I understand," Hannah conceded. What else could she say?

On her second visit, Veronika was in and out of her brother's room in less than a minute.

"And she's off to Moosfeld," Elke told Hannah. "Does Viktor think she's rich?"

"You mean, did she get away with a lot of Georg's money?" Hannah smiled. "Sebastien said Veronika is completely ignorant of Georg's true worth."

Without a discussion, Siegi became his caregiver. After a month, conversations with Willi still required patience, but his mind became sharper. He spent an hour or two working in the bakery. Their shelves were hardly full, but Willi again wore lederhosen, and business picked up.

•   •   •   •   •

A week before Christmas, more than a year and a half after Sebastien left, Faber and Viktor walked into the *kochecke* without knocking. Hannah was having her nightly glass of wine with Georg, Hubert, and the Martis. They had been talking about the Allied invasion at Normandy four months earlier, when Georg had declared it was the beginning of the end for Hitler.

"Aren't you going to ask me to sit down?" Faber asked Hannah. Georg stood up and pushed his chair over with his foot. Hannah made room for Georg in the booth. Viktor tried to squeeze in next to Mathilde, but she wouldn't budge. He was left to stand awkwardly behind his brother, the *Oberführer*.

"They got him," Faber said casually

Hannah buried her face in Georg's shoulder.

"He's alive?" Hubert managed to ask.

"He's in prison in Linz, at Mauthausen. They say the survival rate there is about half. Every day, thousands of men walk up and down the rock quarry with slabs of rock roped to their backs. They call them *Die Totensteppen.*"

The death steps. Hannah gripped Georg's arm.

"There are so many prisoners, they've built three sub camps in Gusen. If he survives Mauthausen, you'd better hope he's not transferred there. Hell holes."

"You did what you came to do," Georg said. "Please leave."

"With pleasure." Faber pushed his chair back so abruptly Viktor stumbled backward into the pantry door. He gave Georg a sinister stare.

"I don't know why he looked at me like that," Georg said. "I wasn't the one who made him look like an idiot."

"I'm going to find him," Hannah said.

"We can't lose you, too. I'll go to Mauthausen and get some answers."

"Georg can be quite formidable," Hubert said, "when pushed to the brink."

"I wanted to punch them both," Mathilde said. "He's right though, Hannah. Who knows how many informers are lurking around town? You wouldn't make it out of St. Jakob."

They all stayed on alert. Georg was back in a day.

"At first, two guards told me Seb wasn't there. I insisted they search the records again, but they went back to their card game. I screamed at those two idiots to get somebody with more authority. A man with a lot of stripes and badges all over him pulled me into his office and said Sebastien was arrested near Alkoven, without a struggle."

Hubert frowned. "Why would he tell you that?"

"I think he was taunting me by suggesting Sebastien had no spine."

Hannah corralled her tears and smoothed her blouse. "Did you see him?"

"Apparently, he was transferred."

Her voice rose. "To a hell hole?"

"I'm not sure he was telling the truth. He might still be at Mauthausen, but it was clear from the beginning no one cared."

Hannah closed her eyes. Everything Sebastien had done. His unwavering determination. The danger, the risk to his family. Why would he give up?

There was no moon. Hannah held her lantern in front of her and walked through the forest, her emotions in turmoil. In the yellow barn, two blankets lay folded next to Gerti's pile of hay. She listened for footsteps and finally heard what she'd been waiting for.

Stefan sat down next to her and pulled the blankets around them. "I'm sorry, Hannah."

"They said he didn't resist."

Stefan thought this over. "He was trapped."

She picked up a handful of straw and sprinkled it across the blanket. "I can believe that. But another part of me wonders if he wanted to be found. Maybe *Eine Bitte* was the end of his crusade."

"He eluded them for a year and a half. I don't think he gave up."

Hannah was quiet for a while. "He lived recklessly," she said. "It was his nature to run, never believing he'd trip."

"He had a hard time connecting his passion with peril."

"One day he was stealing fruit to bring to me, and the next he was throwing himself into a battle he had no chance of winning."

Under the blanket, Stefan took her hand. "Perhaps it would be better to remember the good times. When he brought you love disguised as an apple."

"The memories are too heavy to carry around. Sometimes I can't even picture his face." Her hand moved in circles across his chest. "Thank God I have you."

He took a breath. "May I kiss you?"

Urgency engulfed them both. Under the blankets, they kissed until their lips were raw. A quick look up; silent agreement. She unbuttoned her blouse and pushed up her bra, took his hand and placed it on her breast. She guided his fingers to her nipple and moved them in a circle, and he breathed in her sighs of pleasure.

She removed his shirt and pulled him on top of her. He languished in the sensation of her heart beating beneath him. His lips trailed down her neck. He raised his eyes to hers, and she nodded. Tenderly, he sucked each breast.

After a while, Hannah stood up. "My skirt," she directed him.

He watched her the whole time. When it fell away, she undid his belt buckle, reached for him and pulled him back down on the straw. He pressed himself against her underclothes while they kissed with fervent abandon.

"I can't..." he panted.

She helped him push his pants down, surrounded him with her arms, and squeezed him to her. He entered her, penetrating deeper and deeper until she cried out. He shuddered noisily, and then sunk into sweet release.

They waited a long time to ease apart. He folded one of the blankets into a pillow, and they cuddled under the other. They gazed at the roof and listened to the soft squeaks between a male and female bat with their pups.

"It's a little family," Hannah whispered.

"Did you know that is the only bat sound a human can hear?"

"You astound me with your vast knowledge."

They were silent for a while. Stefan never imagined such contentment.

Finally, Hannah stirred. "Emil?"

"Yes?"

"No regrets."

# 59

Stefan turned his face to hers. "Regrets? Never."

She kissed him. "I have something to tell you."

"And I'm delighted to listen."

"For the first time in so long, I don't feel afraid."

He sobered. "Tell me about your fear."

"Only if you tell me about your past."

"You first."

She took his hand. "Sebastien took me to Vienna on our wedding trip."

"To the hotel that's now the Gestapo."

"Yes. A group of pro-Nazi thugs confronted us, and I thought he'd throw a fist. That was the moment I realized how angry he was. As time went on, I became more and more anxious. Almost everyone in St. Jakob knew where he stood. It's not like I didn't agree with Sebastien. He always included me in his little band of dissenters, but after a while, I didn't want to be in the room. I knew how fervent he was becoming, and I was fearful of knowing more."

"The man you loved was becoming a zealot."

Hannah closed her eyes. "I've never told anyone this before, because I'm ashamed. Do you know what scared me the most?"

"What was that?"

"The Jews."

Stefan swallowed. "What do you mean?"

"Sebastien, Georg, and Niko—you remember, I told you about Sebastien's friend, the priest sent to Dachau? They were always talking about what was happening to the Jews. Stories of horrible atrocities. I felt sorry for them. But I wanted them to stay far away from us."

Stefan propped himself up on an elbow. "You thought being near them would put you in danger?"

"I know how heartless that sounds. But Viktor said I looked Jewish. Faber made my father bring our bible to prove my lineage. Sometimes I felt people staring at me, the red in my hair, my skin a little darker than most Austrians, even my freckles."

"Go on."

"Sebastien's solution to my anxiety was to arrange a little holiday, so we returned to Vienna. We got caught in *Kristallnacht*, in a hotel in Leopoldstadt."

"The Jewish quarter."

"It was the worst night of my life. Children were on fire. The air smelled like death."

"You were a witness. Someday that might be important for the Jewish community."

She looked at him quizzically. "But after Vienna, I was even more terrified. I cut my hair, hoping it would make me look less Jewish. More normal."

Boulders were crushing his heart. He let go of her hand. "It's my turn now, Hannah."

"You know you can tell me anything."

"My mother was born in Poland. Her husband and family were brutally murdered in a pogrom. She escaped with my brother, who was a little baby, to Vienna. She met Papa, and they married, but she made him promise to keep her Jewish heritage and that of their children a secret. My brother and I knew nothing until just before the SS came."

"What are you saying?"

"I'm saying, Hannah, that I'm Jewish. On *Kristallnacht*, while you hid in your hotel, a young pro-Hitler mob murdered my mother and three Jewish children she was trying to protect. They burned to death."

Hannah covered her face with her hands.

"My father, brother and I joined the resistance. We weren't caught for over three years."

"And then?" she murmured.

"They killed my father and brother, and a family of Jews we were hiding." He stared at the ceiling. "The shots still rattle in my brain, like bullets fired in a tunnel, so loud I can't stand it. I couldn't help them." He paused. "I ran."

Hannah didn't move, less the onus of guilt strike her down.

Stefan swallowed the acrid taste filling his mouth. 'I assume your fear will keep you from telling anyone my story."

Tears inched down her cheeks." I don't know what to say," she said, aware she must have sounded pitiful.

Anger and disillusionment coursed through him. And yet, was he again losing everything and everyone?

The words came out unbidden. "We could try to wait this out."

She lowered her head. "Sebastien convinced me we won't be rescued because people will believe we helped the Reich."

"And they will be correct. Look at me, Hannah." She raised her red eyes to his. "Am I your secret enemy now?"

"No," she said.

He waited.

"I have a daughter, Emil. What if they come looking for you?"

"They won't find me."

"How do you know that?"

Practice.

How had it all changed so quickly? He had thought the wreckage of his life was behind him, and that he was free to love and be loved. But he was headed for darkness again, running and evading and risking everything, simply because he admitted to being the son of Ester Fieg.

"I meant only to love you. But I am who I am, and my people are being slaughtered. Hatred is evil. But so is apathy."

"Do you think I'm that cold? I care about you."

"You care about you, and Gabi, which you should." He stood, and she reached for him.

"Don't. This is good news, Hannah. With me out of your life, you have one less person to fear." He patted Gerti. "Don't forget her apple. She'll think you're indifferent."

•　　•　　•　　•　　•

It was late. Hannah veered off the forest path and waited until her tears had run out. When she finally walked into the *kochecke*, Georg, Hubert, and Mathilde sat at her table, with Veronika.

"I was telling my friends," she said pleasantly, "how I took a walk and ran into you coming from the yellow barn."

Hannah frowned. Where was this going? "You never told me what you were doing in the woods either," she said, scrambling.

"It's not important. But I ran into someone else that evening. A strange young man, lying on the straw. The buttons on his shirt were askew. I asked him who he was, and he became quite agitated. He banged the ceiling with a broom. I thought he might be possessed. A bat went after my head. They carry diseases, so I got out of there."

"I hate bats," Mathilde commented.

"I asked you, Georg, and you couldn't come up with a name. And now here you are, Hannah, back from somewhere you're not supposed to be, while we're all waiting for you. Were you with your lover again, in the barn?"

"Veronika!" Georg yelped.

She pointed a menacing finger at him. "I won't be silenced."

Hannah felt like an old tree felled in the forest, hollowed out inside. She could no longer block Veronika's blows, nor had she the slightest defense to offer the others, who would notice Emil's sudden absence.

"Well?" Veronika said, a malicious gleam in her eye.

Mathilde leaned forward until she was eye to eye with Veronika. "I've been wanting to say this for so long, and what you suggested took the plug out of my mouth. You are the most conniving, heartless person I've ever met."

"Why do you stand up for her?" Veronika sneered. "She's fooled this town for too long. But I will remember. Sebastien and Hannah Brandl sent my brother to his death. And now, she's cavorting with some outsider who looked like a German soldier to me." She glared at each of them. "I doubt that sets well with the likes of all of you. The truth will come out someday, and I'll be the only one left standing." She strode out.

The four of them sat in silence. Hannah knew they must be waiting for her to say something.

"Emil's gone."

"What?" Mathilde said. "Why?"

"He isn't the man he presented himself to be."

"He's German?" Hubert exclaimed.

"No. But the Germans are after him. I had to send him away," she said, tears pooling in her eyes. "Forget him. He was never here."

·  ·  ·  ·  ·

Stefan had listened to it all. He made his way to the front of the inn. He opened and closed the door so silently that a squirrel, sitting on the path to the road holding a walnut, didn't even look up.

He took with him his knapsack, and his names. He left his heart.

# 60

*St. Jakob, 1945*

For the next months, Hannah struggled to ban Emil from her mind. If the facts pushed their way in, shame threatened to bury her alive. She had used him to punish Sebastien, spurned his very identity, and most certainly sent him to his death. But the worst of it was, she had loved him in a way she thought Sebastien had taken with him when he abandoned her.

She saw confusion in the eyes of those who had known Emil. Yet they honored her request, something she did not deserve.

•    •    •    •    •

The war ended, but Austrians were too weary to celebrate. There were no signs of relief anywhere, only scarcity and disorganization. Hannah and Hubert closed the restaurant.

The prevailing thought was that Hitler victimized Austria in the same way other nations had been ingested into the belly of the Third Reich.

Mathilde found Hannah in her bedroom, furiously packing her satchel.

"You're going to look for him," she said.

"Could you ask my mother to help with Gabi?"

"Of course. But you can't go alone."

"Why not? I'm the one who...

"Who what?"

"Never mind."

She took the train to Linz, where haggard allied soldiers clogged the platform and did not return her smile. She decided against going to Mauthausen, and considered the schedule on the wall. Nineteen minutes later, she arrived at the town of St. Georgen, and asked a soldier to point her toward Gusen I.

"You don't want to go there," he replied, "unless you want to see rats feasting on a pile of corpses."

She steeled herself and walked down the crowded gravel road. Pebbles kicked up by covered military trucks pelted her legs. The people who poked their heads out the back stared at her with eyes that had taken over their shrunken faces. Here and there, someone would raise a shaky hand and wave.

Walking skeletons, still clad in striped pajamas, straggled toward her. Hannah studied each of them.

She passed fields where people tended the crops they had planted after the ground thawed. In front of a small farm, a woman worked in her vegetable garden while chickens and snot-nosed children milled around her. Smoke from a wood fire spiraled out of a chimney. A few kilometers down the road, where thousands of Jews and other prisoners died daily, farming families had continued to work the cycles of the seasons.

She passed by a wooden bridge over the River Gusen. Large chunks of concrete had fallen off their supports and were sticking out of the water like broken body parts. The bridge creaked ominously under the weight of a truck coming from the other side.

Ahead of her, a white van with a large red cross on the side had stopped, and she quickened her step. An American soldier stepped forward and smiled.

"Can I help you?" he asked in passable German. "Are you looking for someone?"

"My husband." She pulled a photo from her pocket. The soldier shook his head. Down a long path, large tents made of white canvas rippled vigorously.

"You might as well go have a look."

Hannah wiped the sweat off her face and approached a nurse standing in front of the tent. "Is this a hospital?"

"No. The field hospitals are full. "This is one of several tents of sick prisoners waiting to be treated. No one wants to have been liberated only to die here. Are you searching for a loved one?"

"My husband, Sebastien Brandl." The nurse studied the photo. "He would be much thinner now," she commented, taking a bandana from a basket and handing it to Hannah. "Cover your nose. For some people, it takes several tries to step inside."

Cruelly distinct odors accosted her. Disinfectants, but also blood, decay, and excrement. She wept as she walked down the first row, crushed by the heartbreaking scene. She stopped at every bed. If she found someone awake, she asked about Sebastien. Few patients had the strength to speak.

Here and there, a sheet covered the body on the cot. The nurse who she had spoken to at the opening of the tent came to her side. "I can do it, if you want me to." She folded down the sheet, and uncovered a man with one eye missing.

"No," Hannah cried. "It's not him."

She continued down the rows, making herself lift a sheet, and each time relief surged through her. In the middle of the fourth row, a man, his entire torso wrapped in bloody bandages, raised a shaky hand when she called out Sebastien's name.

"Down there," he said, gesturing toward the back. She skirted several cots and ran in the general direction he indicated until she reached the end. She expanded her search to the surrounding rows, despair weighting her down so heavily, she could barely retrace her steps.

His eyes were closed. She gave him a gentle poke, and he blinked awake.

"Are you sure you saw Sebastien Brandl in here?"

"Who?" he rasped.

"My husband, Sebastien Brandl."

"He must have died."

Two hours later, Hannah walked back to the entrance and the friendly nurse. "There's an extensive morgue at Gusen II," she said, her voice kind. "But search the other tents first."

Hannah shivered. "Do you know of a hotel nearby?"

"Try St. Georgen, but they all might be full." Back at the road, the same soldier offered to drive her into the town. Luckily, she found a vacancy, and rented the room for three nights.

The next morning, feeling steadier, she walked the aisles of the second tent, unaware of the passing hours. She reached the end of the last row and looked back on the cathedral of the dying.

"Sebastien?" she called one more time.

"Who?" came a voice.

Hannah looked around frantically. "Where are you?"

"Here." Several rows away, a man was sitting up.

"Sebastien Brandl," she said. "He's my husband."

His face fell. "Come sit," he said, patting the bed. "Are you Hannah? Would you like to sit with me for a moment?"

Her search was over.

She took his outstretched hand. "Tell me, please."

His voice was as gentle as her mother's had been, telling her little girl her beloved rabbit had run away. "I'm so sorry, Hannah. He was executed the day before the Americans arrived."

Hannah wrapped her arms around herself and held the trembling inside, something she had learned to do so well. "Why?"

"We were sabotaging airplanes."

"Oh, Sebastien." Of course. She unwound her arms and squeezed the man's hand. He squeezed back. All sound faded away. A benevolent calm came over her and time ticked away until she re-entered the scene. He was still holding her hand, waiting for her.

"Should you be sitting up?" She asked.

His eyes widened at her concern. "I'm being released tomorrow. Still pretty weak," he stretched out his other hand, "still bony and brittle. But stay as long as you want. There's a lot more."

"Only if you feel up to it."

"It's your story, too. The first day Sebastien arrived, we walked, yoked together, on the train tracks to the caves. The very next day, they started running a long line of boxcars. They squished us inside while they counted to 100. Then they went to the next one.

"He had come from Mauthausen, but he wasn't in terrible shape, compared to most of the others. We were all covered with fleas. I knew a man who named them."

The corners of Hannah's mouth twitched.

"We were in the same barrack, assigned to the *Bergkristall* tunnels to build airplanes. Have you heard of the *Messerschmitt*? "

"I think so."

"It was the pride of the German air force. Designed to be difficult to knock out from below."

"You became friends."

"To the extent friendship was possible. We worked fourteen-hour days or fourteen-hour nights. We weren't allowed to converse. We went home and slept. Then it started again."

"You knew my name was Hannah."

"Yes. And you have a daughter. You live in the Wachau Valley. He knew I was from Vienna and my family was murdered. That's about it."

"I'm sorry."

He waved a hand. "Sebastien had only been around for a week when he pulled me behind the barracks. He told me he was performing little acts of rebellion that might go unnoticed until it was too late. A loose bolt, here and there, a puncture wound to the radiator, things like that.

"I'll never forget what Sebastien said. 'The allies are winning. The Germans are frantic. Let's get some imperfect planes in the air.' I didn't hesitate. I have to believe at least one German pilot came down because we tinkered with the German pride and joy, the mighty *messerschmitt*.

"On May 3, someone informed on us. They took Sebastien first. I knew I was next. But no one came for me. Later, a prisoner who worked in the crematorium said after they shot Sebastien, the Kommandant roared away in a large black car."

Hannah let the tears come. Even though she already knew the answer, she asked, "Did he consider the risks?"

"It was as if he didn't believe them."

"I know this Sebastien you described. So sure of himself. Single-minded."

"You're saying he had purpose."

"Save Austria. He simply refused to fail."

"I heard the shots, Hannah. I felt him die. I wanted to let the guilt kill me, too."

"I understand, more than you know."

"It was strange. The day before, we stood on the parade ground for hours. If you fell, they shot you, in case you weren't already dead. Now we were milling around with no uniforms in sight.

"Prisoners took the weapons abandoned by the Germans. A group of *Kapos* barricaded themselves in Block 32. Some committed suicide after one of them was dragged outside and almost torn apart. The Allies arrived on May 5. Sick prisoners had been sealed in barracks without food or water. Unbelievably, a few of them survived."

"Why aren't you in the hospital?"

"I had a bad case of dysentery, and if I moved the wrong way, I could easily break a bone. But I didn't qualify."

Hannah blew her nose. "I have one more question."

"I'll try to have one more answer. Then we both rest until tomorrow, when I hope you'll come back."

"I'll come early."

"That's very good news. Your question?"

"The Nazi commander who terrorized our town and hunted Sebastien down told me he gave himself up without a struggle. It's hard to believe."

"You don't have to. This story I know. Sebastien was trapped in a 'friendly' farmer's barn. He had a wife and three sons. When the SS came, he walked out with his hands up because he was afraid a child would be struck by a bullet meant for him."

Just like Emil said.

Hannah embraced him. "I don't even know your name."

"An old habit. It's Moshe. Moshe Fieg. I'm a Viennese Jew."

# 61

When Hannah arrived at the tent the next morning, eyes swollen and weary, Moshe was already outside, standing with a man who was black as night.

"Hannah, this is Charles, one of the Americans who liberated us. He said he'd give us a ride to the train station."

"Good morning, ma'am," Charles said, extending his hand. In all her life, Hannah had only seen a few people who looked like Charles. Her father explained they were descendants of African people who over the centuries were kidnapped, enslaved, and made to work in countries that were predominantly white. His hand folded over hers.

"Could we stop at Gusen 1?" She asked him.

"If that's what you want to do," he replied. He helped Moshe into the front seat of his open car and gave Hannah a boost into the back. Five minutes later, they walked through the open gates of Gusen 1. Moshe led her toward a barrack. A few prisoners sat against its decomposing wall. Hannah went down the line, greeting them and shaking the hands reaching out to them.

"Your husband lived in here," Moshe said.

Hannah gaped: three beds, stacked on top of each other, in so many rows it was difficult to squeeze between them. Blankets, stained with blood and waste, brushed her clothes, and she stepped on a filthy mattress hanging off a cot.

Hannah touched the ripped canvas her husband might have slept on and then walked out quickly. "Show me where he died."

They walked to an office with a large sign on the door. Beneath the vulgarities scratched into it, she could still make out one word: *Kommandant.* Charles led them around the back to a dirt and gravel yard. "The firing squad lined up here."

Freedom, she noted, was just over a stone wall covered with dark stains. Hannah put her finger in one hole and looked at the ground, as if his blood might still be in the dirt. Charles went to her. "I'm sorry we didn't get here sooner," he said.

"One day," she choked. After a moment, she looked up at him. "The Crematorium?"

At a long, low-roofed building, American soldiers were going in and out, along with able-bodied men, women, and the occasional child.

"Curious neighbors," Charles said, shaking his head.

Straps and chains hung from the walls and ceiling of the first room.

"Torture," was all Moshe said. They moved through another door. "Where they were forced to undress." The next room contained shower heads on the ceilings and a line of drains on the floor.

Charles said, "We've heard until they outfitted this with gas, prisoners who were too weak were forced to stand under cold water until they died. The drains were blocked. Anyone left drowned."

An open door led outside. There were two ovens, each big enough for one body.

"Hannah," Moshe said. "Sebastien was the last one."

Hannah scooped up a handful of ashes and charred bits of bone. Charles offered her a clean handkerchief to put them in. She went to the other oven and added more.

"Let me help," Moshe said, lifting the four corners together and tying a tight knot.

"Thank you," she said to Charles, reaching out to him.

He returned her embrace. "I'm honored, Hannah."

They left the camp, Hannah cradling the little cloth coffin in her arms.

•     •     •     •     •

Charles left them to wait for the train back to Linz. Moshe had nothing except his shirt, pants and coat, donated by villagers, that hung from his gaunt frame. They sat together on a bench.

"Where will you go?" Hannah asked.

"I don't know. My body needs to heal. And my soul," he trailed off, tears filling his eyes. "I can't go back to Vienna, not yet."

"Could I persuade you to come with me to St. Jakob? I have an inn with a warm bed. It will be a while before the food is up to our standards, but you can rest and recuperate."

Moshe didn't respond.

"And have breakfast in bed," she added with a flourish. "Please, everyone will be more excited to meet Sebastien's last friend than see me again. Lately, I've not been at my best."

Moshe put one thin arm around Hannah's shoulders. "Thank you. But breakfast in bed is not necessary."

Hannah laughed. "You say that now."

He fell asleep on the train. Gripping her satchel, Hannah found the dining car and had coffee and a pastry. When she got back with the same for Moshe, he was sitting up, ready with another story.

"We heard that in April, the *Kommandant* ordered the murder of 40,000 prisoners at once by trapping us in the tunnels and destroying any trace of the airplanes. They set up an ammunition depot and walled off the five entrances to the tunnels. The only reason they aborted was Nazi authority in the Gusen camps was collapsing."

Hannah stared out the window. "So many people knew."

"Parents walked by with their children on their way to school. People going about their daily lives."

Hannah threaded a finger through her curls. "Sebastien and I were in Vienna, staying in the Jewish quarter, on *Kristallnacht*. I saw Jews coming out of an apartment house, their clothes on fire. When we were trying to get across the canal, we saw a woman who had been shot, along with her unborn baby."

Moshe closed his eyes.

"In St. Jakob, my husband and his friends talked constantly about what was happening to the Jews. It got to the point that I didn't want to hear about them anymore. But I couldn't pretend I hadn't seen it with my own eyes."

Moshe said nothing.

"It was as if fear lived inside me, consuming the scraps of compassion I had left." She pulled down the hem of her skirt. "I don't expect you to absolve me."

"Does telling me all of this help?"

"Because you're Jewish? I didn't consciously pick you to confess to. It's up to me to accept the part I played."

"But your witness is important."

Emil. She hadn't understood.

"Let's take a walk. The doctor told me to keep my legs moving." They headed for the dining car, Hannah again bringing her satchel.

Perhaps she could still be saved.

•    •    •    •    •

Everyone welcomed Moshe Fieg like a long-lost friend. They sat, hushed, wanting to hear about Sebastien's last days and the sabotage of the *messerchmitt* airplanes over and over again.

Georg raised a glass. "Brazen acts. Heroic."

Soon Moshe had his own place around the table in the *kochecke*, with Hannah, Georg, Hubert, Siegi and Elke, who continued to work the early shift at the bakery. Mathilde and Tobias, and Bernard and Sophie also had an open invitation to join their evenings.

Both Tomas the Fiddler and Finn Binder returned from the war, but it would be a while before they were the same men they were the day Reich sent them to truncated battle field training and taught them to be killers.

Willi Reiter often sat next to Siegi, saying little, but laughing more and more at the entertainment she provided. He still had moments of confusion, but Siegi had found her mate for life. They married in early July.

"You'll find someone, too," Siegi told Hannah during the reception at *Grünen Baum.*

"I don't think so," Hannah replied.

"You don't think you deserve happiness?"

Perhaps not. She had failed, twice, to love a man for who he was.

"Let's just enjoy your day."

# 62

*St. Jakob, November, 1945*

The restaurant was still closed and supplies scarce. German marks were gone and schillings were back, but prices inflated. Hannah found a box stuffed with schillings under their bed. Sebastien's doing. She felt she owed it to Georg, who used it to pay Hubert, who gave it back to Hannah.

She kept Sebastien's ashes in a jar in their bedroom. He had finally come back to her for good.

Moshe had been in St. Jakob for six months. Apologizing that he couldn't pay his room and board, he went about repairing everything that had stopped working or fallen apart during the war. No one wanted him to leave. He had become more than a testimony to Sebastien's persistent defiance. Their friend, and a hero in himself.

Moshe didn't talk about his life before Gusen, which Hannah explicitly understood.

"His pain is still raw," she told Hubert. "He may never want to bring the memories back."

By January, Moshe had gained twenty pounds and no longer required a three-hour nap. They knew he had been a winemaker, and Georg told him he could use his help. But for now, Moshe was content to stay near the inn.

Hannah couldn't help but notice the bond developing between Moshe and Elke. "Moshe's going to teach me how to drive," she announced one day. Gerhard's car was sitting idle at the side of their house. There had been no word from him, nor a knock on the door with news of his fate.

Hannah had been driving for most of her life, thanks to Bernard's tractor, so Elke insisted she sit in the back seat for moral support. During her first lesson, the car jerked down the road. When Elke finally found second gear, she stepped on the gas and flattened a chicken. Hannah looked back in horror at the cloud of feathers. That was the end of moral support.

One day, they disappeared without having said a word to Hannah or anyone else about watching Benno, which wasn't particularly unusual. They arrived home late that evening. Elke looked around the table. "We went to the missing persons bureau in Krems. Gerhard died in Russia last April, but by then, no one was around to inform the families."

Everyone mumbled their condolences.

"In the end, I hardly recognized him as the man I married, and I didn't want him alone with Benno. It's not that I thought he was going to make our son into a little Nazi. It's just that he spent a lot of time with the enemy."

With that, the subject of Gerhard Eisner was as dead as he was.

Veronika seemed to have relocated to Moosfeld, specifically, on a barstool at *Der Wachauerhof*, flirting with Viktor and doing whatever she could to dismiss Gertraud. But one evening she rapped on the back door.

"Since when does she knock?" Mathilde asked. But Veronika was obviously distraught. Hannah waved her to the table.

"Viktor has to go to Nuremberg to testify at the military tribunal prosecuting Nazi war criminals."

No one moved.

"I don't see why he has to go. His brothers were the guilty ones."

"My guess," Georg said, "is they will offer Viktor immunity in exchange for information about them. Faber was a ruthless SS officer, and Rudolf was the head doctor at Hartheim, where thousands of people were murdered, including Daniel."

"Viktor said Rudolf didn't know Daniel was there, or he would have saved him."

"He knew, Veronika," Hannah interrupted. "Rudolf Lonauer was in charge of the records they kept of every human being they gassed."

"How would you know that?"

"Sebastien went to Hartheim. He spoke to a man named Frank Sitter, who worked there until he asked to be transferred. He was sent to the front. If he isn't dead, perhaps you should contact him for the facts."

"You should go with Viktor," Hubert said, "and hold his hand through the ordeal."

Veronika missed the sarcasm. "Well, I can't have anyone think he was one of *them.*"

Viktor and Veronika were gone for two weeks, and no one knew the outcome of his testimony. Georg went down the road to Moosfeld to investigate.

When he returned, ten people were in the *kochecke* waiting for him. "I got some information, and you won't believe who I got it from."

"His mother," Hannah said.

"Gertraud."

"I don't believe it."

"She was quite forthcoming. When Viktor got to the courtroom, his lawyer informed him his brother Rudolf had committed suicide, after he poisoned his wife and two little daughters."

A collective gasp arose from the table.

"When Frau Lonauer found out, she ran around the restaurant hitting the customers and banging her head against the wall. Viktor had to drag her upstairs, but Gertraud said she screamed for hours, and all the diners left without paying."

"Did Viktor still have to testify?" Bernard asked.

"Wait. While Gertraud was telling me all this, a neighbor joined us. He said Viktor had to answer questions about both his brothers for several hours, although he claimed he didn't know Rudolf was murdering children at Hartheim."

"What about Faber?"

Faber Ratzener?" Moshe exclaimed. "He murdered my family."

They stared at him. Then they all started talking at once, united in their vehement condemnation. "He was trying to escape when the *Haupbahnhof* in Vienna was obliterated," Georg reminded them.

Moshe shook his head. "Pity he's dead. I would have run all the way to Nuremberg if they called me to testify,"

•   •   •   •   •

Hannah and Hubert needed to re-open the inn if the Brandl legacy was to survive. A few reservations trickled in. The restaurant served food that was as good as anywhere else, but still not quite the quality it had been.

In 1946, the Christmas holidays held little merriness. Ernst was thirteen, his sisters twelve, Gabi almost ten, and Benno, nine. Hannah, Elke and Siegi gave each child one gift, which they happily opened without complaint.

The adults, as usual, gathered after the children went to bed.

"Moshe and I went to Dürnstein," Elke informed them, "to see if the synagogue had survived the war."

"Moshe," Georg said. "I'm sorry. I don't think any of us gave a thought to the Jewish holidays."

"It's fine," Moshe said. "I've only known I'm Jewish for four years. Two of our closest family friends were a Rabbi and his wife, but that's the closest I got to Judaism. Anyway, the synagogue had been razed, but we found a man who told us about a Jewish diaspora in Dürnstein, twenty people perhaps, who keep to themselves."

"They're still afraid?" Hubert asked.

"Just because the war is over doesn't mean Austrian memory has been purged of prejudice."

Hannah flinched.

"If you don't mind my asking," Mathilde said, "what did you mean when you said you've only known you're Jewish for four years."

Moshe took a deep breath. "I haven't wanted to think about the past, much less speak of it." He glanced at Elke. "But in Dürnstein, I found the thread of connection I needed. My mother was born in Poland, and escaped a pogrom that killed her parents and husband when I was barely a year old. The horror of that moment never left her. Miraculously, she made her way to Vienna, and married the man I thought was my father. He had been raised a Catholic, so she hid our true identities behind his. That last moment, her family bloody and broken on the ground in front of her, never left her. The only people who knew their sons were Jewish, besides my grandmother, were our lifelong friends, Rabbi Elie Schett and his wife, Tovah."

Moshe's face creased with pain. "Your mother?" Georg finally asked.

"She was murdered the night of *Kristallnacht*. A mob set fire to her bookstore, and she died inside along with three children she was trying to protect."

"*Der Buchwald*, "Hannah murmured.

"Yes, how did you know?"

"Sebastien and I were in her store earlier that day." She pulled out Charles' handkerchief and dabbed her eyes. "When we trying to get out of Vienna, we saw it had burned down. I can't believe it, Moshe. That lovely woman, so gracious and welcoming, was your mother."

Moshe gave her a sad smile. "Ester Fieg, but known to everyone as Lili Mayr."

Georg went wide-eyed, and next to him, Hubert paled. It was their turn for tears.

"Was your father," Georg stammered, "Maximillian Mayr?"

"Yes. Ratzener and the SS shot him and my brother, Stefan, on April 20, 1942."

"They came for Sebastien on the same day, one year later," Hannah said.

"The night before, they made us throw a party for local party members with money. "Ratzener was delighted to inform us every year on his birthday, Hitler made his enemies pay."

Georg sat back and crossed his arms across his chest. "How did you survive?"

"I woke up in a hospital chained to a bed. Apparently, the SS discovered I was still alive when they went to pick up our bodies the next day. The bullets had gone through in me in two places, but missed anything important. Faber Ratzener and Klaus Kolbe, a Nazi who used to be a friend of our family, were waiting for me to wake up to interrogate me. The nurse, Maria, befriended me. She taught me how to pretend I was still in a coma and put them off for two weeks while I recovered."

"Unbelievable," Hubert murmured.

"The next time they came, I acted barely conscious, going in and out, and gave them short, groggy answers. That went on for a while until Ratzener lost patience. He stormed out, screaming at Maria she'd better have me alert and ready because the next morning would be my last chance to cooperate.

"That night, I died. Maria covered me with a sheet and wheeled me down the hall, telling anyone who asked she was taking me to the morgue. Down in the basement, I got dressed in the clothes she'd brought. She shoved me out a side door and I hobbled down the street."

"Tell me she disappeared, too," Hubert said.

"Oh, yes. She was smart. I know she survived."

Moshe smiled at their applause.

"Sebastien had to answer to Faber Ratzener," Georg said, "through his brother Viktor and their Nazi watcher, Dietrich Pfortner, who disappeared into the woods just before the end of the war."

"Max took Sebastien to Alkoven," Hannah said, "because he suspected Daniel had been gassed at Hartheim castle. That moment changed everything. Sebastien had voted no in the referendum, and Gerhard told Viktor, who told Faber, that it was Daniel. Guilt paralyzed Sebastien. He was never the same."

"Veronika still blames Hannah."

"I was the last one to see him, getting into a van with blackened windows. I tried to get him to wait, but the driver insisted they had to leave. Sebastien's last act before he ran was confess to Veronika that he had voted no. From then on, she blamed both Brandls."

"So that's how Sebastien ended up leafleting," Georg said. "He joined the resistance group in Alkoven."

Hannah knew that Sebastien had gone far beyond ineffective handbills. The missive he wrote in 1944 and was read by so many must have shaken Nazi resolve. But the credit due Sebastien Brandl was buried in some subterranean part of her being that had caved in long ago. She would not dig for it.

Around the table, they wrestled with the revelations entwining the Mayrs and the Brandls. Georg opened two more bottles of wine. Comfort came to Hannah. The evening that began with children delighting in very little ended with a new village of family, friends and survivors that would stand together, no matter the next blow.

# 63

*St. Jakob, April, 1947*

Georg took Hannah to Krems to buy a proper urn. She planned Sebastien's funeral for Saturday, May 3, two years to the day after his death. Her only concern was that Martin Vogl was still the parish priest, and would therefore say the funeral Mass.

Later, they would claim Sebastien had intervened. On May 1, a man hobbled into *Grünen Baum* and made his way into the kitchen where *mittagessen* was being prepared.

"*Pfarrer* Nikolas!" Hannah cried, and dropped a platter of dumplings and cream sauce on the floor.

"Hello, Hannah," he said, embracing her tightly. "And it's Niko."

Tomas came with towels and waved her away from the steaming mess. She looked her old friend over, frowning at the crutch he leaned on and the stump where his leg had been.

"Sit down," she commanded, guiding him to a chair. "What happened?"

He wiggled his half-leg. "Gangrene. Not a pretty sight."

"We didn't know where they sent you."

"Three priests pulled me out of my bed and told me to pack, that I'd been re-assigned. In Krems, they stopped the car in front of a church and told me to wait.

"That was your new parish?"

"Oh, no. A minute later a couple of SS thugs transferred me into their truck and the next thing I knew I was an inmate at Dachau."

"Thank God you survived."

"I kept busy. There were a number of priests and nuns in danger of execution. We made a list of their names, with their stories, and smuggled it out. It went public, which forced the Church to intervene. Most of them were still alive at the end of the war."

"You're a hero."

"Well," he sighed. "What I did was try to save falsely accused Catholic clergy. Nothing for the Jews at Dachau." Niko didn't notice Hannah's frown. "Since then, I've been in Munich, working with religious survivors, and once in a while, a stranded Rabbi. I heard about Sebastien's funeral before I knew he was dead. Did you want Vogl to say the Mass?"

"He's the priest."

"I took it upon myself to talk to him. He was a bit territorial, but then he seemed relieved to turn the funeral over to me."

"Thank you," Hannah said, brightening. That night, Niko joined them in the *kochecke* and was thrilled to meet Moshe. The conversation was lively, and Hannah was reluctant to leave them for her bed.

The morning of the funeral, Hannah opened the wooden box Tobias had made for Sebastien's remains. She took some ashes between her fingers and watched them float from her hand. "Time to leave me," she whispered. "but I'll know where you are."

The Church was half-full, but everyone who mattered to Hannah was there, even Moshe, who sat next to Elke in a place behind a post.

"He's present, and he's not." Hannah told Niko as he prepared for the Mass.

"Moshe's strong. He'll find his way home."

Neither Georg nor Hubert trusted themselves to give a coherent eulogy, so it was left to Niko to bring Sebastien back to life. Healing laughter washed over the congregation. Gabi read a poem. Hannah sat in the first pew with her parents, and Siegi and Willi, preoccupied with their infant son, Bernard, whom they called Bear.

They buried his ashes with his mother and father. Afterwards, a man stood away from the crowd, next to a woman who was weeping openly.

When Hannah offered her hand and introduced herself, he said his name was Johann Keppelmüller.

"I knew Sebastien through the resistance cell in Alkoven. I had the printing press."

"Ah. What else did you do for my husband?"

He held her gaze for several seconds. "Sebastien had a touch of recklessness in his soul. But he also had more courage than an entire army."

When Hannah didn't reply, Johann turned to the woman. "This is Helene Sitter, another friend of his."

Helene fingered a wet, wrinkled handkerchief. "Hello, Hannah," she said. "I'm sorry."

"Did your brother make it?"

"Yes, thank you for asking."

Hannah nodded and stepped away, surprised that the wound was still a bit raw.

The tables in the *biergarten* sat beneath a ceiling of blossoming trees, where Hannah and their loved ones listened to tales of Sebastien. Relief obscured any other emotion, something she didn't think would last, but clung to for the moment.

•     •     •     •     •

"It's time for me to go home." Moshe had been in St. Jakob for thirteen months.

"Benno and I are going with him," Elke said. "It's a visit," she clarified when she saw the look on Hannah's face.

"Yes," Moshe said. "I'm ready to see what's left of *Schloß Winzertal.* I assume the Nazis took it over, or burned it down."

They left the next morning and were back two days later. "It's good news," Elke whispered to Hannah as the group gathered.

"I was shocked," Moshe began. "The Chateau is still standing, a little worse for the wear. The vineyards are coming back after several years of neglect. Best of all, our friends from the resistance, Rafe and Sigrid, are living there, along with a charming Jewish woman, Rena Mendelssohn, who was one of the last people we hid beneath our winery."

"We went in the front door of the house," Elke said, placing a gentle hand on his arm, "and Moshe stood listening to three voices up in the kitchen he recognized right away."

"It was glorious," Moshe said. We cried and laughed. They wouldn't let go of me. I introduced Elke and Benno and they wouldn't let go of them, either."

Moshe looked into Elke's eyes and covered her hand with his. A memory prickled Hannah; she and Sebastien, alone in a crowded room.

"Until the end of 1944," Moshe continued, "Rafe and Rena lived in the Pump Room—that's what we called one of our hiding places, while the Germans drank our wine and ransacked our house. Then one day, the bastards disappeared for good."

"What about your grandmother?" Hannah asked.

"Sigrid shared a bunk with her in Ravensbrück, the death camp for women, but she became very weak with dysentery. The Germans came to remove her, but Sigrid said she had influenza and was contagious, so they didn't bother. "Sigrid held her all night, and she died just before dawn."

"I'd like to meet this Sigrid," Mathilde said, dabbing her eyes.

"Imagine their joy," Elke said, "when she surprised Rafe at *Schloß Winzertal* after the war. They're married now."

"It's a miracle," Moshe agreed. "My father's foreman and several of his long-time employees came back, wondering if they still had jobs. Rafe and Sigrid worked alongside them to repair the vines and get ready for the harvest, which was limited, but enough to fill one hundred bottles of several varietals only months after the war ended."

"Bravo," Hubert shouted.

"Rafe, Sigrid and Rena are my family now, and soon, Elke and Benno will be too."

"What?" Siegi shrieked.

Elke beamed. "We're getting married as soon as we can. I'm studying Judaism."

Moshe laughed. "We're learning together."

"Hannah, you and Gabi will visit all the time," Elke said quickly.

Hannah doubted it. Her work at the inn would never end.

Moshe and Elke married in August in the synagogue in Dürnstein. Hannah sat in the front row, trying to concentrate on the ceremony. First, Siegi, and now, Elke, found the love of her life, as she herself once had.

Another thought intruded, unbidden. Emil.

•    •    •    •    •

It took almost a year for Hannah and Gabi to board a train to Vienna. Moshe picked them up and took them to Kahlenbergerdorf. At *Schloß Winzertal*, Elke was waiting for them with Daniel, their new baby boy. When she placed him in Hannah's arms, the tears of joy she shed felt like warm rain, cleansing and comforting.

# 64

*Kahlenbergerdorf, 1948*

The next year, Hannah and Gabi made three more trips to *Schloß Winzertal*, and Elke begged them to return for the holidays. When they got home, Gabi told Hubert to work on her mother.

"Georg and I are going," Hubert announced. "And your daughter is already packed."

"Are you suggesting we close the inn for two weeks? What about the Christmas and New Year's parties? You said we could be out of debt by the first of the year."

"We need a holiday more than we need to balance the books. The rest of the money we owe is to people who like us."

"They like the discounts we give them."

Hubert laughed. "then it's settled."

Hannah, Gabi, Hubert, and Georg arrived in Kahlenbergerdorf on December 21, and Niko joined them the next day. The daily snowball fights got longer and noisier as teams formed and strategies were planned. Hannah had forgotten how to have fun.

On Christmas Eve, the household awoke to the sun shining on almost a meter of new snow. Later, the *Christkind* arrived right on time, and in the chateau's long living room, it took several hours to take down the mountain of gifts.

The women, including Sigrid and Rena Mendelssohn, who had become Dani's beloved nanny, filled the kitchen with cheerful conversation and the tantalizing smells of a traditional Christmas dinner. Under Hubert's supervision, Georg and Niko set the table. They gathered the children and had gotten seated when the front doorbell chimed.

Moshe went to open it. Five minutes went by. He returned with a somber-looking man in a rumpled black overcoat.

"Whatever you have to say to me, you can say to all of us," Moshe said.

"Who is that?" Hannah whispered to Elke.

"I don't know. He looks terrified."

The man cleared his throat. "Excuse me for interrupting your dinner."

"Hurry," Moshe growled. "We want to eat while it's still hot."

Elke stood. "Shall we set another place?"

Moshe's face hardened. "No."

"My name is Fritz Tollner. Maximillian and I were friends."

"When the Nazis executed my family," Moshe said, "you hadn't been friends for a long time. Why don't you tell them what you did during the war?"

"Like many others, I had to work for the Third Reich."

"No one forced you to become Himmler's personal secretary, I'm wondering why you aren't in prison or hanging from the gallows."

"Michel," Tollner pleaded. "I didn't have to come here. I heard you were alive, and I wanted to pay my respects."

"It's Moshe. All those phone calls with my father—you didn't realize he married a Jew and had two Jewish sons. Still want to claim you were friends?"

"I'm offering an apology," he stammered. "I could have done more for your father."

"You were on the side that killed him."

"I warned him over and over, to join The Party. That might have saved him."

Moshe gripped the top of a chair. "He had moral courage. You were a coward who went along. Get out of my house."

Tollner hesitated.

"Let us help," Georg said, as he and Hubert stood up and gripped Tollner by the arms. Niko cleared the way toward the door. "This way to the exit," he told Tollner as he stumbled by.

Moshe strode out behind them. A loud bang resounded, and Dani whimpered.

Moshe returned and took his son from Elke's arms. "I should explain..."

"Later, if you want to," Hubert said. "Why don't we start in on this grand meal."

Moshe sat down with Dani in his lap, who grabbed a spoon and enthusiastically banged his father's plate. "Another day," he said, glancing gratefully around the table.

Dani fell asleep during dinner and was tucked away in his crib while the kitchen returned to spotless order. Gabi and Benno got an hour's reprieve to play cards.

"They're tired," Elke said. "They won't mind putting themselves to bed." Everyone except Rena, who said the day was much too exciting for her to stay awake one more minute, moved back into the living room and sat around the fire.

"Niko, I wish you could return to St. Jakob," Georg said. "But Vogl seems to have an iron-fisted grip on his two little parishes."

"Are you interested in having your own church again?" Moshe asked.

Elke laughed. "Are you going to build him a chapel?"

"No need. When I delivered their altar wine, I found out the priest in Kahlenbergerdorf is retiring."

Niko threw up his hands. "Where do I sign up?"

"I know a monsignor in Vienna who worked at the Chancellery for years," Moshe said. "My father donated a lot of wine to that place. I could have a word."

"Tell him my answer is yes."

The conversation moved to Hanukkah, which they would begin to celebrate the next day.

Niko waved a hand at Moshe. "Perhaps you could give us a lesson."

"I'll try. Hanukkah means rededication. It commemorates the return of the Maccabees, Jews who revolted against the Greeks and liberated Jerusalem." He lifted the engraved Menorah from the hearth and lit the central candle. "According to the Talmud, only one jar of oil remained when they re-entered the desecrated temple, and yet, in what is known as the miracle of light, the oil burned for eight days. The celebration has ensued from those times until ours."

"The holidays go on and on," Elke murmured, her eyes aglow.

Georg brought out more wine. Elke and Hannah delivered pieces of *Sacher Torte*. The front door chimed once more.

"Now what?" Moshe groaned. He disappeared, and almost immediately, they heard shouts of delight. He came back with his arm around a white haired, slump-shouldered, wizened looking man wearing a yarmulke.

"Oh my God," Rafe said. "It's the Rabbi."

Joyful introductions made, Elie Schett settled in the chair closest to the fire. When he met Elke, he took her face in his hands and tenderly kissed her forehead.

"You are a bright light, my dear," he said. "I can't wait to hear about this, Michel."

"I'm Moshe now. Papa told me Mutti's story, and my name."

"That makes me very happy. When I returned to Vienna, I heard all of you were dead. Then, last month I heard that no, you had miraculously survived."

"And Tovah?" Moshe asked gently.

"Auschwitz. We arrived with several hundred other Viennese Jews." My wife was sent to the left, and I to the right, with most of the other men in our group."

"My dear God," Niko said.

"I didn't understand. I was assigned to a bunk with two other men. They explained Mengele's selection process and held me while I wept. Then they prayed the *Kaddish* with me."

By the light of the fire, tears shone on Elie's rosy cheeks. For the third time that night, the chimes sounded.

"Oh," Elie said, wiping his eyes. "That's for me. I've brought guests."

What happened next was something they would talk about for decades. Elie returned with two women, one carrying a little girl, the other a little boy.

Elie cleared his throat. "These are my old friends, Ruth and Nissa. We are part of the remnant that lives in a small neighborhood near where my synagogue once stood."

Elke and Hannah got up from the couch where they had been snuggling under a blanket. "Please sit down," Elke said. The children burrowed their heads into the women's shoulders rather than return the gaze of strangers.

"These little ones are orphans," Elie continued, "born in Ravensbrück. A few surviving women took care of them for a year. A Jewish group searching for displaced children took them to Switzerland, but soon there were so many, they called out for help. Ruth and Nissa brought twenty orphans to Vienna four months ago. They live in two houses we rebuilt from the rubble."

"This is Tamara," Ruth said, stroking her check. We know nothing about this beautiful little boy. He talks very little, and we suspect he never really had a name. We think they are both about three years old."

"May I?" Elke asked, and the women made room for her between them. She held out her hands to Tamara. "Would you like to sit with me?" The little girl hesitated for only a moment before she climbed onto Elke's lap.

"Moshe," Elie said, "You might think of them as two of the children your mother couldn't save."

Moshe's eyes widened. Elke pulled Tamara even closer. "Do we have room for two more?"

"It's a lot, I know," Elie said. "But I have other possibilities."

Hannah stifled a sob, and everyone turned to see her gazing at the little boy.

"I didn't expect this," she whispered. "I don't know. Gabi's so busy now..."

"Hannah," Elke exclaimed. "Are you offering...?"

She glanced at Elie. "I don't deserve him."

"And he didn't deserve to be left all alone," the Rabbi said.

Hannah choked out a laugh. "I can't believe it. What am I doing?"

"Coming alive again," Hubert said.

She squeezed onto the couch and touched his little hand. His head came up.

"He needs a name," Elie said.

Nissa held him out to Hannah. He stared at her for a moment before he allowed her to lift him into her lap.

"If you need a suggestion," Moshe said, "My grandfather's name was Jo'el. I thought it sounded strong."

"It's also sweet," Elke gushed.

The little boy nestled into Hannah, and she rocked him soothingly. "Do you like the name Jo'el?"

To their astonishment, he nodded.

Hubert got down on his knees and smiled at him. "You've got so many people to love you. Your new sister Gabi, Georg and I, and our dog, Schnapsi. Tilda and Tobi will fight over you and your new grandparents..."

"...Will think I've re-emerged as the impulsive girl who rejected God's plan at least twice," Hannah said.

"They'll be overjoyed," Niko said.

She frowned. " I'm not Jewish."

"Don't worry about that," Elie said. "Moshe and I will teach you both. Your first lesson, Hannah, is you're doing *Mitzvot*, a charitable deed that proclaims one's Jewishness during Christmas."

Hannah swallowed a sob. Was this what it was like to be saved?

The next day, Elie took Moshe, Elke and Tamara, and Hannah and Jo'el, into Vienna to sign the adoption papers. When it was her turn, Hannah's hand shook, and she struggled to sign the paper that would make Jo'el hers.

As they carried the children out, Hannah had no illusions about what she was doing. The mortal danger of the war had passed without her voice, and she would take certain elements of the story of Sebastien and Hannah Brandl to her grave.

It was too late to open her coat. But one lost little boy would have a name.

# EPILOGUE

*"I hear a voice telling me to stop mourning the past.*
*I too want to sing of love and of its magic.*
*I too want to celebrate the sun, and the dawn that heralds the sun."*
*–Elie Wiesel*

*St Jakob, Saturday, October 14, 1989*
Sivan Mayr awakens feeling hollow from sleep deprivation. His knee is sore from banging it during his frantic run up the stairs. But he's hungry, and feels brave. Wearing the hat that most conceals his face, he requisitions a cane someone left in the umbrella basket, and a discarded copy of yesterday's newspaper. He knows *Grünen Baum* opens early; laborers and a few locals treating themselves to an excellent breakfast.

He takes a corner booth in the *wintergarten*, and spreads the paper in front of his face. Gabriele Brandl Eigner approaches him, without a shred of recognition. "What would you like this morning?"

"Just black coffee and bread."

His order arrives quickly. Slathering butter on a piece of fresh rye, he peeks out from under his hat. Gabi is returning. An image flashes in front of him: Hannah's smile.

"Do you mind some company?" she says, taking the chair across from him. I enjoy greeting new visitors to *Grünen Baum*."

Sivan decides it's safe to fold up the paper. "Don't be offended, but I'm staying down the street."

"Not at all."

Sivan's composure is short-lived, because Benno Eigner, Gabi's husband, is balancing four cups of what appear to be cappuccinos, and presents one to Sivan. "Can I tempt you?"

Behind him is an older man with a cane that looks like it used to be a tree branch. He sits down next to Sivan. "Hello, he says cheerfully. "I'm Niko."

Sivan chooses this moment to take a careful sip through the foam. The others wait. After an awkward moment, he says, I'm Sivan."

"Unusual. Is that a French name?" Benno asks.

"Jewish."

"Ah, yes," Niko nods. Sivan doubts he knew that.

Gabi continues to chat about the inn, the family, and invites him to visit their kitchen.

Sivan takes another sip. The kitchen. No one would believe he knows it's every nook and cranny.

"Are you here for the Crush Festival? Gabi asks. "It's also my mother's birthday. You should stay. It's an extraordinary party. It's also my late father's birthday. My aunt Siegi, who is so much fun, will be there." Gabi prattles on. "When her husband died, she took over the bakery next door."

Sivan wonders how all of that happened, and waits for Gabi to keep talking.

"Until lately, everyone just said that my father died in the war. Not many people know he and a friend were sabotaging German *Messerschmidt* airplanes. He faced the firing squad just before the war ended."

*Messerschmidts*. Sivan can't help but be impressed. He's surprised Gabi doesn't mention Sebastien's letter to Austria, *Eine Bitte*.

"My mother is not happy about the commotion. She doesn't talk about the past.

However, our priest, Primo Baumgartner, has invited more than just our town. He told me yesterday that he has new information that my father might have been hiding Jews, but I think we would have noticed people roaming around our cellar." She stops, embarrassed. "I'm talking way too much."

"No," Sivan says. "Go on."

"Anyway, Primo seems to think that would make my father a Righteous Gentile."

"Well, I'm not sure…" Niko begins, but Sivan slams his cup on the table.

"It's not his job to elect someone to that honor!" he snaps. "You must know Austrians hated the Jews more than the Germans." He tosses money on the table, and as fast as his aching leg can carry him, heads for the door, feeling the shock wave that is following him.

•　　•　　•　　•　　•

Two hours later, at the bar at his hotel, Sivan salivates while his beer is being poured. He has failed to calm down. *Righteous Gentile.* The world turned upside down; the ovens are in the sky. He should end this foolhardy, pathetic excursion of his. The truth is dead, with no one left to revive it.

A slight, stooped man, more ancient than himself, Sivan decides, sits down next to him and scowls. "Are you staying for the fiasco later this afternoon? I hear Hannah Brandl's son is too busy to come. She adopted an orphan after the war, you know," He smirks. "Named the little Jew Jo'el. I'm Adolf Haas, by the way."

Sivan is stunned, but Haas isn't finished.

"I was there. I knew the real Brandl, and his wife, too. They may as well have poured gas over the entire town and invited the authorities to strike the match."

Sivan peers into pitiless eyes. "You were in favor of the Third Reich?"

"His plan to unite all Aryans under one great nation was inspirational. He would have made us all rich."

Sivan picks up his half-empty-glass, and for good measure, the one Haas has just set down. He throws the remaining beer from both glasses into the old man's face.

Haas yelps. The bartender grins.

"Put those on my bill."

•    •    •    •    •

At *Maria Theresa*, gaily decorated tables and chairs sit almost touching each other in the immense courtyard between the villa and the wine cellar. The celebration is already noisy. Gabi and Benno's children and their spouses, and Hannah's fourteen great grandchildren wave wildly as she walks in with Niko and Siegi. There are more people than usual, many of them strangers, including young people, chatting animatedly. At their table, Georg and Hubert saved places for them.

Conversation flows as easily as the wine, and glasses are often atop heads.

Hannah has almost finished a bottle all by herself. Georg is smiling, holding Hubert's hand, and she nods at them. "A couple in love should hold hands all the time," she declares. "Then they know what the other one is thinking."

Everyone at the table is getting a glimpse of the carefree, innocent girl who fell in love with an irresistible innkeeper. She turns to Niko, "You know I was headed to the convent, so when Sebastian and I were first married," she pauses for an indelicate burp. "Every time we made love, I asked God's forgiveness for my reckless abandonment."

Still laughing, Georg steps onto the platform where the musicians are waiting. It's the first year he's had a microphone. "Is this working?" he asks, and his voice booms across the courtyard.

"Yes, dear," Hubert tells the table.

"Welcome to the Crush Festival. And this year, to the birthday party for my lifelong friend, Hannah Brandl." Hannah blushes and glares at Georg, who grins. "It's okay to have your own day. Let everyone love you."

After over an hour of eating and drinking, the dance floor comes alive. Moshe and Elke, who had chosen one of the furthest tables, explaining that their grandchildren might be rowdy, are among the first. Rafe and Sigrid are just behind them. Hubert pulls Hannah in, and they move flawlessly into a familiar Austrian folk dance. She remembers the feeling of twirling in

Sebastien's arms. The life they shared, however conflicted, had moments of brilliance.

The musicians take a break, and *Pfarrer* Primo Baumgartner bounces onto the stage. He taps the microphone. Hannah knows what is coming.

"As you know," he begins with great flair, "we celebrate not one birthday today, but two. Sebastien Brandl was born seventy-nine years ago today. Sebastien and Hannah were faithful Catholics. Even when he felt abandoned by the Church, he stayed on the path of righteousness, and was martyred for his fidelity."

Nausea rises in Hannah's throat. She wants nothing more than for him to stop fictionalizing their story. Niko is shaking his head. Georg's perpetually friendly face falls. Hubert holds his head down, seemingly absorbed in his twirling thumbs. Siegi is somehow containing herself.

Primo stretches out his arms. "Who would have thought a saint lived among us? Let us pray for his blessing." He bows his head, and the crowd automatically obliges him.

A voice disturbs the silence. "He was no saint." A man with a green feathered hat and sunglasses comes into the sunlight and walks toward Hannah. "But he was fearless. In the end, he found his voice, and performed heroic deeds for his country."

From the platform, Primo says into the microphone, "We all know about the airplanes." He wags a finger, "and you are interrupting."

Gabi nudges Benno. "The man at breakfast the other day,"

Sivan removes the hat and sunglasses. For Hannah, recognition is instantaneous.

"Emil," she whispers.

"I suspect, Hannah," Sivan says, peering down at her, "that you persisted in keeping the whole story to yourself." She can't return his gaze. "For your husband, all this talk of Righteousness is a fairy tale. You're familiar with those. My question is, why would you deny Sebastien Brandl his most powerful act of resistance?"

Georg leans forward and takes her hand. "What's he talking about, Hannah?"

"Sebastien wrote *Eine Bitte*," she says under her breath.

Georg moves closer. "I didn't hear you."

It's way past time, Sebastien. I'm sorry.

"My husband wrote *Eine Bitte*," she says, straining to elevate her voice. "Emil is right. I should have told you long ago."

"No, Hannah," Sivan says. "Emil was the boy who died in my place. In addition, I once was Stefan, but my true identity, as you are well aware, is that of a Jewish son and brother. My name, in case you care, is Sivan Mayr."

Someone at the next table calls out, "Sebastien wrote the letter to Austria!" The applause begins. Several young voices shout, "Bravo!" Soon almost everyone is standing.

Primo seizes the moment. "A toast to our hero, Sebastien Brandl!" But the attention is on Hannah, who is watching Moshe walking toward them. Sivan's eyes widen, and he stumbles forward. They meet in an embrace that drops them both to their knees. Eventually their sobbing lessens and tentatively, they start to laugh.

Elke arrives at Hannah's side. "That man. Sivan. He's Moshe's brother."

The voices of the crowd, which have gone silent, as if giving them privacy for their reunion, rise again.

After almost ten minutes, Moshe leads Sivan, Elke, their son Daniel, and his wife and four children to the platform. Moshe relieves the flabbergasted priest of the microphone and directs the crowd to be seated. He beams.

"This is my brother, Sivan," he announces. Neither of us knew the other was still alive!" Sivan smiles and tightens his grip on his new family. "Together, we have a request. We ask you to raise your glasses to the memory of our mother, Ester Fieg Mayr, who died saving Jewish children, and Maximillian Mayr, a resistance hero, and our father."

Every hand comes together in thunderous ovation.

"And my brother has asked me to invite Georg Wangermann and Hubert Brandl to stand up and be counted."

The couple rises awkwardly to their feet.

"These two men saved the lives of our fellow Jews. When Sivan arrived here, grieving for what he thought was the loss of his entire family, he hid in their wine caves. Like our father, he discovered they, too, had Jewish guests, being kept alive by the courage of a rare breed of altruists."

The floodgates of appreciation burst open. People move through the tables to surround Georg and Hubert, and Siegi is first in line. "Tell us everything!" she demands.

Elke returns to sit with Hannah. "We didn't know," Hannah says desperately. "Sebastien suspected, but they never told us what they were doing." She pulls Elke closer. "Emil, uh, Sivan, wanted me very much. But I sent him away."

"Why?"

"Because he was a Jew, and the Nazis might come to our town, looking for him." Tears glisten on her cheeks. "And because I wanted him, too."

Admirers press Georg and Hubert toward the winery doors, while questions are shouted out from all around them.

"At night," Georg explains, "We had to wait for Faber Ratzener to pass out from my wine and Hubert's stupor-evoking food before we could move people in and out, or bring them supplies."

"How many people did you hide?" Someone shouts.

Georg looks at Hubert, who replies, "Maybe 100, in the end." Astonishment bubbles up from the crowd.

Primo has pushed people aside to stand between Georg and Hubert. "We have our Righteous Gentiles!"

"They did a good deed, Primo," Moshe says into the microphone. "They remained human. But their acts don't redeem an entire nation. Why don't you simply thank them for being rare souls in Nazi Austria?" He leads Sivan away and they disappear into the forest.

The crowd wants to see the hiding places, so Georg and Hubert invite them inside. Elke pulls Hannah close. "He's staying at that other hotel," she whispers.

• • • • •

"Sivan Mayr's room?" It took her what feels like a lifetime to decide to come. Hannah waits for the receptionist to shuffle some papers. Perhaps Moshe is there, which would make her an intruder.

In front of his door, she wants to run, but the list of her cowardly acts is already long.

She knocks. "Do you have the grapes?"

After a long moment, the door opens. Sivan stands back, and she walks in. He closes the door, sits down on the bed, and folds his arms. "You're still short," he remarks.

Hannah drags over a chair and sits down in front of him. Her body stirs, and she jerks back. Sivan regards her with steely eyes.

"I care about your name, Sivan," she manages.

"When you knew me," he replies bitterly, "I didn't know who I was. Stefan was the boy who played among the grapes and practiced disappearing. For the young man Georg and Hubert discovered, I chose Emil, after the Jewish boy who, thanks to Hitler, would never fulfill his dream of being a famous *fußbal* player. When I met my wife, Rachel, I decided to be Sivan Mayr, the son of both my mother and my father. The name keeps them both alive."

"What happened to you after...."

"You sent me away?'

"I'm sorry."

"After a year of terror I don't like to remember, I came to a winery owned by a man named Marcel Bisset and let myself be found in his cellar. This time I was lucky. I worked for him until 1948. But I felt I hadn't run far enough. Marcel got me a new passport, and sent me to his brother, Beau, in California. I worked in the fields, and then the tasting room. I lived quite comfortably with my wife, Rachel, and our two sons in a cottage on the grounds of Chateau Bisset. I became head sommelier, and Beau lent me to other wineries."

"Is Rachel waiting for you at home?"

"She died three years ago."

"I'm sorry."

Sivan walks to the window. "Stop saying you're sorry."

Her shoulders fall. "Why did you come to St. Jakob?"

"I shouldn't have. But as it turns out, it was the best decision I ever made."

"Moshe."

"When I met my wife, I felt resurrected, if you'll excuse the use of the word. I feel that way again. After all the anger and regret," his voice catches.

Bile rises to her throat. Is this what it feels like to drown in guilt?

"Why did you find me?" Sivan asks,

"To face you, " she begins, trying to steady her voice. "For a long time, I was angry at Sebastien for leaving, for choosing his convictions over his family. You came, and I could imagine myself to be blameless. But then, you were a Jew, and I was back to being the coward I'd been all along."

"Was Jo'el your penance?"

She searches for a coherent thought. "I never wanted to admit my son was anything but an abandoned child who needed me."

"He was Jewish, Hannah. You must have understood your own motives."

"It wasn't unfeeling. I loved him from the beginning. But we were never close, like Gabi. I tried hard to deepen our connection, but I was too wrapped up in my own misery."

"Sadly, you missed out."

"Yes," Hannah admits, not bothering to wipe away her tears. "When I adopted him, I felt it possible to be a worthy human being again, after I'd fallen short. That was selfish of me."

Sivan hands her his handkerchief.

"People don't carry these the way they used to," she sniffs, folding it.

"Keep it.' For the first time, Sivan's expression softens. He picks up an apple from the night table and rolls it across the comforter. "I was in France, working the Crush, living in a house with a busload of Polish men. They were always celebrating. I didn't understand what they had to be happy about, day after day."

Nervously, Hannah picks up the apple and hopes he'll continue.

"They would drink and march around the house singing Polish folk songs, waving little Polish flags. They always invited me to join them."

"Did you?"

"Once. I enjoyed it for a few moments, but then it felt like a betrayal."

"You betrayed no one," Hannah says. "You deserve every moment of happiness that comes your way."

"And you don't?"

Hannah doesn't dare respond. "What will you do next?"

"I'll go to Vienna to find my life, for the third or fourth time."

She can feel his eyes boar into her soul. "My advice to you is to tell your children and grandchildren everything. It's your only way out."

"Please believe me, Sivan. I thank God that you are who you are."

"It's inescapable."

She walks to the door, but he makes no move to follow. They are separating, again. She is well acquainted with the pain.

The door closes softly behind her. Sivan moves closer, listens for her retreating footsteps, and wonders at the silence.

·　·　·　·　·

It is dusk. Gabi sits with Niko and Hubert on the veranda of *Winegut Maria Theresia,* awaiting her mother's arrival. Georg has gone to the cellar to pick a fine vintage for their little party. After spending precious time with Sivan, sharing their stories of grief and survival, Moshe and Elke decided to stay and play with their grandchildren in the famous sunroom.

The shadows of the lingering day dissipate into the darkness of a moonless night. The group is becoming impatient. "I hope Hannah is all right," Hubert says. "Today was difficult."

Georg opens the wine and pours it. "She's going to be sorry when there's no more of this."

Gabi goes to the balcony and peers into the dark. "She said she might take a walk. That was over an hour ago." She turns back to them. "Georg, your grapes are lighting up."

"It's people," Hubert says in wonderment. "With candles." They join Gabi at the railing.

"They're saluting you, Georg, and you, Hubert," Niko says. The lights are moving now, up and down the rows, and they are singing an Austrian hymn. Whenever they come to the front, they raise their candles to the balcony.

"Austrians," Gabi whispers, "acknowledging what only a few were brave enough to do."

Eventually, mist settles on the vineyard. The candles begin to move toward the path and into the trees, and the lights evaporate.

"Everyone's gone," Gabi sighs.

"Not quite," Georg points to a pair of bright beams, bobbing along one of the rows. They all lean forward.

Gabi squints. "Mutti?"

The beams come together, separate, and come back together again, as if in conversation.

Gabi smiles.

Not one, but two.

Two.

# About the Author

Molly Fumia is the author of *Honor Thy Children*, the highly-praised story of AIDS, Homophobia, and one family's surprising survival. She also wrote three other books on the transformative power of grief: *Safe Passage: Words to Help the Grieving*, *A Piece of My Heart*, and *A Child at Dawn*, a personal story told with the help of her friend, Elie Wiesel. Fumia holds degrees from Santa Clara University and the Graduate Theological Union at Berkeley. She and her husband Chuck live in California and have six children. *The Crush of Wine and War*, her first novel, is the result of 30 years of Holocaust study and her close friendship with the family of a celebrated Austrian war resister, executed in 1943.

# Note from Molly Fumia

Word-of-mouth is crucial for any author to succeed. If you enjoyed *The Crush of Wine and War*, please leave a review online—anywhere you are able. Even if it's just a sentence or two. It would make all the difference and would be very much appreciated.

Thanks!
Molly Fumia

# Acknowledgments

My thankfulness might fill another book:

To the late Leon Zelman, Sam Oliner and Lizzi Lauber, survivors of the Holocaust.

To Claudia and the late Heinz von Opel, for your warm welcome at Schloß Westerhaus, a gorgeous model for my wine estates.

To Siegi Witzany and Elizabeth Jungmeier for showing me Gusen and the railroad tracks. Also, along with Christian Marti, Andreas Maislinger, Gerhard Macek, and Elke Augustino, for lending me your names.

To the late Sigrid Dale, intrepid translator, for the story of her father, a victim of T4.

To Florian Schwanniger at Hartheim, and to my amazing guides at the wineries at Klosterneuberg and Nikolaihof, for providing me answers.

To Kathy Imwalle, Judy Peckler and Tonie Malone, for accompanying me in my research.

To my "driver" in Vienna and many other places, Annemarie Schnaitl, for the sisterhood I cherish.

To David Ferst, for his wood expertise and Hubert Sigl, for his metal artistry.

To my guru and editor, Mary Jane Ryan, for your love and powerful suggestions.

To my oldest friend, the artist Nancy Holleran, for putting my dream on paper.

To Marlene Decker, my wise and talented copy editor.

To Mark Malatesta, your help was invaluable.

To my husband, Chuck, for being the best first reader. And to my children, Melissa and David, Mark and Jamie, Nicholas and Katherine, Gino and Brittney, Kristen and Brian, and Joel, for your unconditional belief in me.

To my grandchildren, Logan, Mateo, Evie, Will, Luca, Fiona, Vincenzo, Roman, Carlo, Charlie, Emmy and Josie, when it comes to taking sides, I will always choose you.

To my late friend, Elie Wiesel, for your witness.

To the late Robert McAfee Brown and Sydney Thomson Brown, for your mentorship, and lovely friendship.

And finally, my love and tribute to my "family" in Austria. You have no idea what you mean to me.

We hope you enjoyed reading this title from:

www.blackrosewriting.com

Subscribe to our mailing list – *The Rosevine* – and receive **FREE** books, daily deals, and stay current with news about upcoming releases and our hottest authors.
Scan the QR code below to sign up.

Already a subscriber? Please accept a sincere thank you for being a fan of Black Rose Writing authors.

View other Black Rose Writing titles at www.blackrosewriting.com/books and use promo code **PRINT** to receive a **20% discount** when purchasing.